CHAPTER ONE
THE THING

From: trishhhhbequiet@mymail.net
To: acciopancakes@mymail.net
Subject: DON'T LEAVE ME!!!

kat,
are you packed yet? fyi, i'm working on a plan to keep you in Chelsea. so far, it involves setting a box of frogs loose in the airport to create a diversion while i steal your luggage. mark says my plan lacks finesse. it's a work in progress.
<3 trish

MY first real memory was hearing my grandma scream bloody murder while being attacked by zombie hamsters. That scream won her Best Actress at the Dark Cheese B-Movie Awards in 1979. It was also her standard reaction for birthday presents, hide-and-seek, touchdowns, and any other scream-worthy occasion.

So when I heard her award-winning shriek come from downstairs while I was duct-taping a box of books, I didn't even flinch. Picking up a Sharpie, I scrawled *Mysteries & Harry Potter* on the side, then tossed the marker down and left my room.

"Was it that diaper commercial again?" I asked when I

entered the living room. "With the creepy dancing babies?"

"Hang on, KitKat." Grandma's eyes were glued to the television. "This is the Glasgow episode, that old inn with the haunted garden. The grate scene is coming up."

I glanced at the screen and rolled my eyes. "Again? You've probably seen this a—"

But Grandma flapped a perfectly manicured hand at me, so I zipped it and sat on the armrest of her chair.

Passport to Paranormal claimed to be "the most haunted show on television." Translation: "The most low-budget ghost-hunting show ever, which blames equipment malfunctions on paranormal activity." During the pilot episode last year, the show had blacked out for almost two minutes near the end. The network, Fright TV, couldn't explain the dead air. So naturally, the crew claimed ghosts were responsible.

Ratings weren't off the charts, but *Passport to Paranormal*'s small group of fans were pretty intense. They had a website and forums with heated debates over each episode, plus lots of gossip about the cast of *P2P*. They sold merchandise, too. Grandma was currently wearing a *P2P* baseball cap that said I BELIEVE.

You never saw anything legitimately supernatural, but the show was still pretty entertaining. Besides, ghosts had nothing to do with why most fans—like Grandma— were so obsessed.

On the screen, a guy with a flashlight edged around a stone wall. He was pretty good-looking, I had to admit . . . I mean, if too-long-to-be-real eyelashes and cheekbones sharper than a knife are your idea of good-looking.

"I heard something," a female voice behind the camera whispered—Jess Capote, I knew right away. I'd never met her in person, but she and my dad went to college together. They'd both worked on the university's morning news show. "Right down there. Sam?"

Sam Sumners closed his eyes. "I feel his presence."

I snorted. Grandma swatted my arm.

"I think it's coming from the grate," whispered Jess, and Sam bent over to examine it. The camera zoomed in on the grate—and paused, just for a second, on Sam's butt.

Grandma sighed happily. "There it is."

"*Grandma!*"

"What?" She finally tore her eyes off the screen to hit pause on the remote. "That's some serious eye candy."

I groaned. "Oh my God."

"Oh my God is right," Grandma agreed, her gaze straying back to the screen.

"I don't get why everyone freaks out over him," I said, wrinkling my nose. "He looks like a Ken doll. Plastic."

Grandma pressed her hand to her heart. "You will not speak ill of Sam Sumners in my presence. And twenty bucks says you change your mind when you meet him in person."

"Doubt it." But a flash of nerves hit me anyway. Not about meeting Sam, the show's psychic medium and resident pretty boy. About being a part of *Passport to Paranormal* in general. After losing their third and most recent host, they would resume filming the second season at the end of this week with the newest host: Jack Sinclair, former anchor for

Rise and Shine, Ohio! He was also my dad.

In less than two days, Dad and I would be somewhere in the Netherlands. Instead of sleeping in my horror movie–postered bedroom, I'd be living in hotel rooms and buses. Instead of coasting through eighth grade on a steady stream of Bs at Riverview Middle School, I'd be homeschooled (or, I guess, roadschooled). Instead of hanging out with my best friends, Trish and Mark, I'd be spending most of the next year with a bunch of people who chased ghosts for a living.

Dad had given me the option to stay in Ohio with Mom. Which, to be honest, wasn't an option at all. Because of the Thing.

"How's the packing coming?" asked Grandma. I realized too late that she'd been squinting at me from under her baseball cap with her I-can-read-your-mind expression.

"I'm pretty much done," I replied. "Dad's got to weigh the bags, though—they can't be over fifty pounds."

Grandma leaned over and pulled something out from behind her armchair. "Well, I hope you have room for a little going-away present."

She held out a stuffed, wrinkled gift bag with snowmen all over it, and I laughed. We'd been recycling that bag for all gift-giving occasions since the Christmas when I was nine. It looked really festive until you realized the snowmen were zombies and the snow was spattered with blood.

My smile faded when I peered inside and spotted the DVD. "*Invasion of the Flesh-Eating Rodents*? You know I've got this already!"

"It's the latest special edition!" Grandma said defensively.

"Not officially released yet. And there's three minutes of never-before-seen footage. A guinea pig attacks me in the shower."

Flesh-Eating Rodents was "Scream Queen" Edie Mills's (aka: Grandma's) seventeenth and final movie. At age six, I watched her play a butt-kicking veterinarian who saved the day when a rabies vaccine went horrifically wrong. I kept examining her fingers while the credits rolled, marveling that I couldn't see all the chunks the hamsters had gnawed off.

She'd shown me her movies in reverse order over the next few years—as I got older, film-star Grandma got younger. My least favorite was *Vampires of New Jersey* (her hair looked freaking ridiculous). The best one was *Cannibal Clown Circus* (she played a trapeze artist whose safety net was gnawed to pieces by zombies halfway through her act). I saw her first movie, *Mutant Cheerleaders Attack*, on Thanksgiving when I was eight. Watching your teenage grandmother in a cheerleading uniform with oozing scabs all over her legs is best done after eating your cranberry-sauced turkey, not before.

"Anyway, that's not so much a gift for *you*," Grandma admitted, tapping the DVD. "I thought you might want to show it to Sam."

I tried to glare at her and failed. "Grandma. No."

"You never know, he might like what he sees." She winked coyly, smoothing back her silver-streaked hair, and I laughed. "Now look back in that bag. I think you missed something."

Eagerly, I reached in the bag again and pulled out something wrapped in tissue paper. I tore it off, and the smile froze on my face.

It was a camera. Specifically, it was the Elapse E-250 with a pancake lens, silver with a cool purple strap, the smallest and most compact digital SLR camera ever—and the exact one I'd spent most of seventh grade begging for. But that was last year, when I was still tagging along with Mom to every wedding or party she shot, drooling over all her cool professional camera equipment.

Then she moved to Cincinnati, and I stopped caring about photography.

Still . . . My hands gripped the Elapse, finger tapping the shutter button. Without really meaning to, I flipped it on and held it up to my eye. Grandma's beaming face filled the viewfinder, and I lowered the camera hastily.

"This is way too expensive," I blurted out. "I mean, thank you, but I know it's—I mean, I don't . . ."

Grandma waved a hand dismissively. "Don't start with all that. Consider this a going-away-birthday-Christmas present, all right?"

I swallowed hard. "Yes, but . . ."

But I'm not into this anymore. I don't want to be a photographer. That's what I kept trying to say, but I couldn't.

"Listen to me," Grandma said, and once again, I was pretty sure she'd read my thoughts. "You're about to go traveling the world. Not only that, you're going to hunt *ghosts*. You and your father keep calling this your big *adventure*, and I demand pictures."

"I could send you postcards," I said, flipping the mo~ dial with my thumb.

Grandma rolled her eyes. "What is this, the fifties? I'm not waiting by the mailbox. E-mail me. Hit me up with a text."

"Grandma," I groaned. "Stop talking like that."

"Of course, you won't be able to text from out of the country," she went on, as if I hadn't spoken. "Still, you can put them on Facebook. Or . . ." Grandma's eyes widened, and she clapped her hands. "I've got it."

I held the camera up again, touching my finger lightly to the shutter button. "What?"

"You should start a blog!"

Click!

Lowering the camera, I made a face. "I don't think so."

"Why not?" Grandma demanded.

I shrugged, examining the Elapse more closely. "I don't like writing. And a blog sounds like too much work."

"I'll tell you what's going to be too much work," she said. "Repeating the same stories over and over again when you talk to me and your friends and your mother and everyone else who'll want to know what the glamorous ghost-hunting life is like. This way you can just tell us all at once."

"Eh, I'll think about it." I chewed my lip, flipping the mode dial back and forth again. "Hey, Grandma?"

"Yes?" She was reaching for the remote when the question I'd been dying to ask for weeks now finally came tumbling out.

"Is Mom back in Chelsea?"

Grandma's hand froze over the remote, and her mouth pursed slightly. "What makes you think that?"

ıach plummeted. I'd been hoping for *No, of*

"Trish," I said, trying to sound casual. "Her

she was at the Starbucks by his school a few

weeks ago. And she thought she saw her at the mall last weekend, too," I added. Actually, Trish had been positive. *"No one besides you and your mom has that crazy-long hair, Kat."*

Grandma rewound the grate scene, chewing her lip a little. She seemed to be waiting for me to say something else. Or maybe she was just stalling, trying to think of a lie. Not that Grandma would ever lie to me. Neither would Dad. They both knew better.

"Anyway, I thought maybe she came back to . . . say good-bye to us, or something," I finished lamely. Sighing, Grandma settled back in her chair and looked at me.

"If you want to know what your mother's up to, maybe it's time you start taking her calls."

She didn't say it meanly, but I reeled a little bit. Grandma reached out to pat my hand, and I jerked it away.

"Never mind," I said shortly. "It doesn't matter, anyway. I've got to finish packing."

Without looking at Grandma, I hurried back upstairs and closed my bedroom door. My oversize, must-weigh-less-than-fifty-pounds megabackpack was propped up against my wardrobe, stuffed with T-shirts, jeans, and hoodies. Most of my other stuff was in boxes for storage, although my furniture was staying put. That was the nice thing about having Grandma as a landlady—she would just rent this place to new tenants until Dad and I came home, so I didn't have to say good-bye to the house I grew up in.

Although to be honest, a small part of me didn't care if I ever saw it again.

I knelt down next to one of the storage boxes. This one was filled with sundresses I hated. The Thing crouched next to me, radiating disapproval as I taped the box closed. I ignored it.

I'd almost told Grandma about the Thing probably a hundred times, but I knew she'd never believe it existed. In *The Monster in Her Closet*, Grandma played a girl whose childhood imaginary friend Edgar was terrorizing her neighborhood, and no one believed her.

The Thing was kind of like Edgar. I couldn't prove it existed. But that didn't mean it wasn't real.

For a few minutes, I tried to distract myself by taping and labeling boxes. It didn't work, though. There was no way Trish had mistaken someone else for my mom—we'd grown up in each other's houses; she knew what my mother looked like as well as I did. And her hair—our hair, I guess—*was* pretty hard to miss. The superlong thick braid suddenly felt heavy against my back.

It was the only feature Mom and I shared. She was pale in winter and fake-tanned in summer, with Grandma's dark blue eyes and tiny nose. My skin and eyes were the same shades of brown as Dad's, and our noses were both a little on the longish side. But Mom and I had the same slightly coarse, brown-black hair that fell in waves down to our waists. Two summers ago at the beach, I'd begged her to let me chop it off, but she'd said I'd regret it. What I really regretted were the hours I spent trying to get out all the saltwater knots and tangles.

Grabbing the scissors, I cut a strip of tape a little more viciously than necessary and slapped it on a box of dressy shoes. Then I marched over to my dresser and set the tape and scissors down next to the Elapse.

It really was an awesome camera. But I didn't want to be a photographer anymore.

My fingers tightened around the scissors.

Maybe I didn't want long hair anymore, either.

Suddenly, my heart was pounding loud and fast in my ears. With one hand, I pulled my braid over my shoulder. With the other, I held the scissors to it at about shoulder level. Then I slid them an inch higher. And then another . . . and another.

Then I started cutting.

It took longer than I expected, probably half a minute of hacking away. When I finished, I set my braid down on my dresser and stared at it. It was weird, kind of like looking at my own severed arm (but obviously not as gross). Then I looked in the mirror.

My hair was *short*. And slanted, since I'd cut it over one shoulder. I used a comb to part it down the center. Then I trimmed the left side until it was as short as the right and examined my reflection.

It was about chin-length, and really choppy. My head felt a lot lighter. I liked it.

I went back to packing, whistling the *Passport to Paranormal* theme song as I worked.

CHAPTER TWO

THE CURSE OF THE STALE MUFFINS

From: acciopancakes@mymail.net
To: trishhhhbequiet@mymail.net
Subject: Re: DON'T LEAVE ME!!!

Trish,
Am at airport. Guessing Plan Frogpocalypse was a fail. Also a fail: waking up at 4 a.m. Our cab came at 4:30, and me and Dad were both still asleep. Oops.
Kat

"I'M sorry, Mr. Sinclair. This is more than a pound over the limit."

"No problem."

Dad's talk-show host smile was going strong this morning. The airport check-in lady smiled back and watched, along with me and the approximately four zillion people behind us in line, as he unzipped my bulging megabackpack and started rummaging inside.

"Dad—"

"I got it, Kat," he said. "It's all just a matter of weight distribution."

I glanced at the line. A couple of blond girls, both

younger than me, clutched the handles of their bright pink suitcases. Their parents were right behind them, the mom balancing a little boy on her hip.

"Mickey!" the kid shrieked, and his mom smiled.

"Mickey!" she agreed, stifling a yawn. "We're going to meet Mickey tomorrow!"

"Assuming we actually make this flight," her husband grumbled, shooting Dad a dirty look.

Family of five kicking off fall break with a trip to Disney World. How lovely for them.

I turned back around to face Dad, who was holding up my puffy blue parka in one hand and a giant baggie stuffed with underwear and socks in the other. A green plaid bra was pressed up at the front like a kid's face smooshed in a candy-store window.

"Dad!" I hissed, and he tossed me the parka.

"Don't know what I was thinking!" Kneeling, he unzipped the already-stuffed duffel bag at his feet and crammed the baggie inside. "Jackets don't count as carry-ons; we can just take them on board with us."

Dad pulled his own black parka out of my backpack (he'd run out of room in his), and we watched the scale drop from 51.2 to 50.5.

"Almost there," the check-in lady said encouragingly. Behind us, Blond Dad groaned.

"Sorry, folks." Dad beamed at the line of bleary-eyed travelers, and a few smiled back feebly. "Just another second."

He started groping around the backpack again, and the

check-in lady cautiously peered inside.

"What about that jar?"

Dad turned to me, and I swallowed hard.

"A jar of sand is pretty heavy," the check-in lady added, her face suddenly uncertain as she glanced from Dad to me.

Dad lifted the jar out of my backpack. The three of us had been bringing it to the lake every summer since I could remember, adding a little more sand every time. It had been Mom's idea. I was in charge of packing it for every vacation—I hadn't thought twice about bringing the jar. Dad cleared his throat. "What do you think, Kat?"

"It's just sand," I said with a shrug. "Leave it."

Dad nodded slowly. "Okay. If you're sure."

"Perfect!" the check-in lady chirped, and I saw that the weight had dropped to 49.6. "Now you're ready to fly."

She set the jar under her console as we picked up our stuff, and I wondered what she'd do with it. Throw it away, I figured. She probably thought we were weirdos, trying to bring a jar of dirt to Europe.

Once we'd made it through the crazy-long security line and the crazier-long Starbucks line, Dad and I flopped gratefully into a pair of black plastic chairs. I devoured two day-old blueberry muffins in about a minute. Dad burned his tongue chugging his latte and said it was worth it.

"This hair's freaking me out," he said, making little circles in the air as he pointed at my head. "I could've taken you to a barber, you know."

I was trying to pick the blueberries out of my teeth. "It was a last-minute decision."

"Mmm." Dad stirred his coffee, eyeing me. "You didn't leave all that hair in your room, did you? It'll scare the new tenants."

"Grandma took it," I told him. "She said she'd donate it to some organization that makes wigs for cancer patients."

Dad smiled. "That's nice, Kat."

"Hey, want to see something cool?" I asked.

"Of course."

"I need your laptop."

After a few minutes of trying to get his clunky old laptop to connect to the airport's Wi-Fi, I opened the browser, typed in a URL, then turned the screen to face Dad. His eyebrows shot up.

"*The Kat Sinclair Files*?"

"It's a blog!" I said. "It was Grandma's idea. This way I can post stories about the haunted places we visit for her and Trish and Mark and . . . anyone else. Plus pictures and stuff like that, too."

Dad laughed. "Very Nancy Drew."

"And Hardy Boys," I agreed, thinking sadly of all the boxes of books I'd left in storage.

"*Ladies and gentlemen, we'll begin boarding flight 221 to New York in just a few minutes.*"

A rush of nervous excitement flooded through me. Now that we were actually at the airport, this whole thing felt more *real*. When Mom took off last spring, I was convinced she'd come back. After all, she'd done this twice before—once when I was five, and again a few years later. Both times, she returned in less than two weeks, full of apologies and new promises.

Not this time, though. Two weeks passed, then three. A month later, she was still in Cincinnati.

That's when things got weird. By the time school let out, I'd realized Mom probably wasn't coming back. But I was still in a constant state of anticipation, waiting for something I knew logically wasn't going to happen. And Dad started acting . . . restless. Like he needed a distraction, but nothing worked—not our traditional summer-slasher movie marathons, not a nighttime visit to Chelsea's one and only supposedly haunted house, not even a visit to the paranormal museum on the other side of town. When I started school in August, Dad decided he was bored at *Rise and Shine, Ohio!* and started looking for anchor jobs at other networks, in other cities. After a few weeks, he posted something about job-hunting on his college's alumni Facebook page, and Jess Capote left a comment:

P2P *needs a new host! Want to chase ghosts with me? ;)*

I still wasn't sure if Jess had been kidding around. For all I knew, she was just as shocked as I was when Dad replied: *Yes!*

"An adventure, Kat!" he'd said in a hyperenthusiastic sort of way, already looking up plane-ticket prices. "Traveling all over the world . . . It'll be an experience, visiting all these new places. *Haunted* places," he added, beaming. "That's where the best stories are, right? The haunted places."

He went on and on like that. But I understood what he really meant. Yesterday at the going-away party my art teacher had given me, everyone kept asking about all the places I was *going*. And all I could think about was that I was finally *leaving*.

I mean, I loved my house, school was easy enough. And I'd definitely miss Trish and Mark, and Grandma, of course. But I still wanted to go. It felt like an escape. I knew Dad must feel the same way.

And secretly, I was hoping maybe the Thing would stay in Chelsea.

"If the plane has Wi-Fi, I might work on my blog," I told Dad when the other passengers started boarding. "I bet I can find a cooler layout."

"Sure." Dad took a final swig of his coffee and tossed the paper cup into the trash can next to his chair. "I'm sleeping the whole flight. And the one after that." He groaned, stretching his arms over his head. "And the one after that. Two layovers, bleargh."

I bounced up and down, watching the line of first-class people form at the gate. "I don't know how you can even think about sleeping," I told him. But ten minutes after the seat-belt light went off, I was crashed out, facedown on the laptop before the drink cart even rolled by.

CHAPTER THREE
THE BOY WITH NO EYES

Post: Travel Is a Beating
Seriously, all I want is a shower and a bed.

THAT was my first blog post. No pictures, nothing else. I wrote it in Munich during our second layover. I didn't think anyone needed to hear the details of the almost eighteen hours of boarding and unboarding I'd endured— squinting at airport maps, dragging luggage from gate to gate, chewing insanely dry turkey sandwiches, and kneeing the backs of inconsiderate people who insisted on reclining their seats into my lap before the plane even took off.

When Dad and I finally checked in to our motel in Rotterdam, I passed out face-first on one of the twin beds and slept so hard not even Dad's chainsaw-snores woke me.

RING-RING. RING-RING.

I groped around without opening my eyes, wondering why my alarm sounded so weird. Then I heard Dad's groggy voice.

"'Lo? This is Jack . . ." He cleared his voice, suddenly

sounding much more awake. "Lidia, hello! Yes, we're up. Half an hour? Sounds good, see you soon!"

"Why'd they call in the middle of the night?" I mumbled. Dad pulled open the curtains and I yelped, ducking under the blanket to shield my eyes from the evil sunshine.

"It's almost eleven," Dad said. "That was the producer—I'm going to check out the entrance to Crimptown, where we're filming." He yanked the blanket from my face. "Haunted tunnels, pirate ghosts . . . you coming?"

My response was a grunt. I flipped over, piling two pillows on top of my head.

But I couldn't go back to sleep, despite my grainy, tired eyes. By the time Dad got out of the shower, I'd dug some clean jeans and a *Tales from the Crypt* T-shirt from my megabackpack.

"Two minutes," I promised, ducking around him and into the bathroom.

Fifteen minutes later, we were out the door, the tangy smell of saltwater slapping me in the face. A man in a suit whizzed past us on a bicycle, jacket slung over his shoulder. I watched him head off the boardwalk toward the skyscrapers to our left. Farther down the harbor, I saw a massive bridge arched over the river, dozens of cables sweeping up from one end and connecting to a white, geometric sort of tower. It was oddly graceful-looking.

"The Erasmus Bridge," Dad told me. "Beautiful, isn't it? They call it the Swan."

I nodded without responding. My head felt like someone had stuffed it with cotton balls, but through the fuzz, realization was starting to dawn.

I was in another country.

I followed Dad mutely down the wide boardwalk, eavesdropping on conversations and not recognizing a single word. Dad and I had listened to a Learn Conversational Dutch app he'd downloaded on one of our flights. Apparently nothing had sunk in through my jet-lagged stupor.

Suddenly, I was very aware of how far from Chelsea I was, like someone had just swooped me from Ohio to this spot in two seconds flat. It was exciting and terrifying, like one of those elevator-drop rides at an amusement park. The breeze ruffled my newly cropped hair, and I felt a rush of giddiness. Maybe I really had escaped the Thing.

"Do you see Jess?" I asked.

"Lidia's meeting us, actually," Dad replied, his eyes scanning the crowd. "Jess is with the rest of the crew."

My stomach rumbled loudly. "Are we going to have breakfast with them? Do you think they have pancakes in the Netherl—"

"Jack?"

Dad and I both turned to face a woman barely taller than me. The frames of her glasses were huge and bright blue, the lenses magnifying her amber eyes. Strands of frizzy dark hair that had come loose from her ponytail whipped around her face in the wind. She looked kind of frazzled, but her smile was warm and friendly.

"Lidia!" Dad turned on the talk-show charm full force. "Great to finally meet you."

They shook hands, and then Lidia held her hand out to

me. "You must be Kat. Lidia Bettencourt."

"Nice to meet you, Ms. Bettencourt," I said, taking her hand gingerly. It felt frail, like I might snap a bone if I squeezed a little too hard.

"Oh, just Lidia, please!" Rummaging in her purse, Lidia frowned. "Now, let's see, I thought I . . . here!" She pulled out an odd-looking gadget I recognized from watching the show—an EMF meter, which was supposed to . . . well, I wasn't entirely sure how they worked. Grandma called them *spook sensors*. "Nope, that's not it . . ." After another few seconds of groping around her bag, Lidia pulled out a few granola bars with a triumphant "Aha!" and held one out to me.

"Thanks!" I said eagerly, ripping the wrapper off and devouring half in one bite.

Dad took the other bar, watching me in amusement. "We haven't had a chance to eat breakfast yet," he told Lidia.

"I figured," Lidia said. "Jet lag is brutal, but don't worry—you'll get used to it. So, the theater's just a few blocks . . . You don't mind walking?"

"Not a bit!" Dad replied cheerfully. I trailed behind them most of the way along the waterfront, staring out at the boats and wishing I had about eight more granola bars.

Ten minutes later, we were looking up at a ramshackle theater. The bulbs around the marquee had all been removed, and only three letters were still hanging on—an *I*, an *O*, and a crooked *U*. The box office was boarded up and covered in faded graffiti.

"Very creepy." Dad said it like a compliment.

"What's with the 'IOU'?" I asked, pointing at the marquee.

Lidia tilted her head.

"Ooh, I hadn't noticed that," she replied. "Good eye! Remind me to point it out to Jess—we should get a shot of it for the opening sequence."

I stared at the marquee again and found myself mentally framing it, adjusting the focus . . . Then I shook my head. I'd left the Elapse in my suitcase intentionally.

"Do you believe in ghosts, Kat?"

Startled, I looked at Lidia. She was smiling at me. "Oh, um . . . I don't know."

"Good answer," Lidia said with a grin. "I'll ask you again in a week or so. Maybe your answer will be different."

"Maybe." I couldn't keep the doubt out of my voice.

"We'll fill you in on the Crimptown story during the meeting," Lidia said to Dad. "I've got a few people lined up tomorrow for you to interview. There are a couple of entrances to Crimptown, but the theater's got the entrance where the official tour starts, so that's where we've set up camp for now." She turned to me again. "Kat, I hope you don't mind hanging out for an hour or two while we get your dad settled in. My nephew's here, so he can keep you company. We're *so* glad this homeschool thing worked out with the two of you."

I blinked a few times. "Um . . . what?"

"I actually haven't filled Kat in on that yet," Dad cut in, shooting me an apologetic look.

"Filled me in on what?"

"Oh, it's my fault—this was all so last minute," Lidia said quickly. "My nephew, Oscar—he's your age—he's been asking if I could take custody of him since last winter. He's been with my sister in Oregon, but he . . . well, he had some problems at his school. But I'm always on the road—I couldn't just pull him out of school altogether . . ." She paused for breath, beaming at Dad. "Then Jess found us a new host with a thirteen-year-old daughter! And Jack said—"

"He's homeschooling me," I interrupted. "Right?"

"That was the initial plan," Dad said quickly. "But Lidia came up with a better idea."

"We have an intern," Lidia rushed on. "Her name's Mi Jin, she graduated last May—college, not high school!—and we asked her if she'd be willing to tutor you *and* Oscar since she'll be less involved with the show than your dad and I, and she'd have more time. Plus, you know, a little extra cash in her pocket."

My mouth opened and closed soundlessly. Lidia talked so fast it was hard to keep up. "Hang on," I sputtered. "So this guy's mom let him come with you just because he doesn't like his school?"

"No, no, his mother died years ago," Lidia said. "He's my brother's son, and . . ." She paused, then waved her hand dismissively. "It's a long story. Anyway, let's get in there so you can meet everyone! Kat, I hope you can tag along tomorrow for your dad's interviews; there's a pretty cool story behind Crimptown . . ."

I tuned her out as she led the way into the theater. So I had a new teacher *and* a new classmate. That could be interesting.

The inside of the theater didn't look too bad. It was chilly and dim and pretty run-down, but it wasn't falling apart or covered in mold or anything like that. But this was just the entrance to Crimptown, the focus for this episode. All I knew was that it was a tunnel system beneath the Rotterdam waterfront that was supposedly haunted by the ghost of a pirate. And tomorrow we would spend the night down there.

Not that I was scared or worried or anything—growing up watching horror movies starring my grandmother helped me develop an immunity to creepy stuff. (Like the kissing scenes. Oh God, the kissing scenes were the *worst*. You haven't experienced real horror until you've watched your grandmother make out with a vampire.)

As we passed the small bar in the lobby, I heard the low murmur of people talking. Lidia opened the door to the box office and gestured for me to enter. The chatter stopped, and several heads turned in my direction.

"Hi!" I said brightly, doing my best Anchor Dad impression. "I'm Kat Sinclair, your new host." In my mind, I could hear Trish and Mark snickering. Of course they weren't actually here, so my stupid nonjoke was greeted with silence and raised eyebrows. Sighing, I stepped aside to let Dad in.

Soon everyone was shaking hands, and all sorts of names were flying around. I hung back, trying to figure out who was who.

Of course Sam Sumners was easy to spot. Somehow, he looked even more plastic in real life than on TV—shiny black hair, crayon-blue eyes, and eyelashes straight out of a mascara commercial. He smiled at me, and I imagined Grandma swooning and tried not to snicker.

Next to Sam was a scruffy-faced guy with thick eyebrows permanently arched in a way that suggested he was about to say something sarcastic—Roland Yeske, the parapsychologist. (Seriously, a psychologist specializing in the paranormal. Grandma swears it's a real profession. I have my doubts.)

I also recognized Jess Capote—bleached-blond hair and a gazillion freckles—just before she threw her arms around Dad in a bear hug. Behind them, a girl with an eyebrow ring sat with her combat boots propped up on the table, toying with one of about a dozen cord bracelets. I'd only seen her in a few of the more recent episodes.

Lidia spoke up over all the chatter. "Hey, where'd my nephew get off to?"

"He said he was going up to the projection room," Roland said, tilting his chair back. He looked at me pointedly. "Did we get picked up by Nickelodeon or something? What's with all the kids?"

Jess swatted him on the back of the head. "You knew Jack was bringing his daughter," she said airily before turning to me with a broad smile. "Great to have you here, Kat! We're about to talk your dad's ear off and it's probably going to get real boring real fast, so . . ."

"She'll be fine on her own for a bit, right, Kat?" Dad smiled encouragingly at me, and I nodded.

"The theater's not all that big," Lidia added. "You probably saw the entrance to the tunnels by the bar—they still do organized tours, so stay up here. Oh, we've got a laptop set up by the projection room upstairs. The connection is slow, but you should be able to get online if you want. That's probably where Oscar is."

Roland let out a groan that sounded half-amused. "Oh God, we've got two thirteen-year-olds. This place is gonna be hormone central."

"Don't worry," I said dryly before anyone else could respond. "I'm pretty sure I can control myself."

Everyone laughed, and even Roland grinned a little. "Good to know. Nice shirt, by the way."

"*Great* shirt," the girl with the eyebrow ring said fervently. "Do you like the comics, too?"

I glanced down at my shirt, where the Crypt Keeper leered up at me. Mom hated this shirt. Well, she hated all my horror shirts. But this one especially. "No, I've only seen the show. Are the comics good?"

She swung her legs off the table, combat boots clunking on the floor. "Good? They're *classic*. They—"

"Hang on, Mi Jin," Jess interrupted. "Meeting, remember? We need to get started."

"Sorry," Mi Jin said cheerfully. "We'll talk *Crypt* later, Kat." "Okay!"

I closed the door quietly. Everyone seemed nice enough, and not nearly as weird as I'd worried they might be. Well, Roland was kind of annoying. *Hormone central.* Right. Now, if Grandma had been there in the same room as Sam Sumners, *that* would've been hormone central.

All the same, I couldn't deny that I was curious about Oscar.

When I got to the top of the stairs and saw the laptop Lidia mentioned, my thoughts turned to something far more important than Oscar—the Internet. I sat down eagerly, but paused with my hand over the mouse.

The PRINT window was open, and the arrow hovered over "Yes," as if someone had left in the middle of a printing job. I stared at the screen, thinking. The crew probably used this laptop for work, and I didn't want to accidentally mess something up.

Still . . . I hadn't been online in, like, twelve hours.

I grabbed the mouse. Whoever had left this open clearly wanted to print it. I'd just do it for them.

A green light flashed on the little portable printer next to the laptop, and the first sheet began sliding through. On the screen, the print window vanished. The word processor was still open, but to a blank page.

"Weird." Shrugging, I closed it, then opened a browser and logged into my e-mail account.

From: trishhhhbequiet@mymail.net
To: acciopancakes@mymail.net
Subject: COME BAAAAAACK!!!!

seriously, it's only been a day, and life is intolerable without you. what's rotterdam like? is the cast nice? is sam really ditzy? mark wants to know if they'll let you be on the show. (would they?? it'd be so crazy to see you on TV!) your blog looks awesome—can't wait for the first ghost story!
can we video chat soon? it's weird not having you here. :(
<3 trish

Reading Trish's e-mail was strange—it made me smile, but my throat got kind of tight. I pulled up my blog and scrolled down to find three comments on my first post. But before I could read the first one, a muffled *click* made me jump.

I looked around. The door to the projection room was closed, and I was fairly sure it had been open when I got upstairs. I'd almost forgotten about Oscar. Standing, I'd taken only a step when the paper sticking out of the printer caught my eye.

It wasn't blank.

Glancing at the door to the projection room again, I grabbed the page.

KEEP HER AWAY FROM THE MEDIUM

"Oookay." I glanced around but didn't see a trash can. Folding the page a few times, I stuck it in my jeans pocket and opened the door to the projection room.

Boxes and old pieces of equipment cluttered the floor. Straight ahead, I saw the small window overlooking the auditorium, and in front of it, the projector. And next to the projector . . . a boy.

His back was to me, head bowed, shoulders hunched.

"Oscar?"

He didn't move. Slowly, I took a step forward, then another. Was he crying?

"Hello?" I tried again, louder this time. Nothing. When I was within arm's reach, I touched his shoulder lightly. "Are you okay?"

At last, he turned around. And I found myself staring into black, empty sockets.

CHAPTER FOUR

IT CAME FROM THE LASER PRINTER

Post: Travel Is a Beating
Comments: (3)
trishhhh: miss u! seen anything spooky yet?
MARK: ghost pics?
EdieM: Sam pics?

HE had massive yellow fangs, too. And blood smeared around his mouth.

"You've got something on your chin," I informed him, keeping my voice as flat as possible. Reaching up, he pulled the mask off—brown eyes, black hair, normal teeth, blood-free mouth—and glared at me.

"Geez, you didn't even scream."

I shrugged. "Why would I scream at something so obviously fake?"

"It worked on Mi Jin," he said defensively. "She screamed so loud, Jess said you could hear her out on the street."

"Well, either she was faking it or she scares insanely easy," I retorted. "I'm Kat, by the way."

"I figured. Nice to meet you." His voice indicated it wasn't nice at all. "I'm Oscar."

"I figured."

We didn't shake hands.

"Okay, then," I said after a few seconds. "I'm going to use the laptop for a while. Unless you need it?"

"Nope."

"Okay." I left the projection room without another word.

Sitting back down behind the laptop, I pulled up the comments on my blog post, smiling as I read. If Grandma thought I'd be taking stealth photos of Sam's butt, she was dead wrong. Just before I clicked REPLY to tell her so, Oscar appeared at my side. He leaned against the table, setting the gruesome mask next to the mouse.

"So how long do you think your dad'll last?"

I stared at him. "Excuse me?"

"You know, hosting," Oscar said. "He's the fourth host. The job's cursed."

I snorted. "Right, I forgot about that."

The most haunted show on television was, of course, "cursed." The curse was that they couldn't keep a host. Because it couldn't just be that the low budget and lower ratings drove people to quit. Nope, must be evil spirits.

"You should check out the *P2P* forums," Oscar told me. "They're all taking bets. Most of them think he'll be gone after two episodes."

"Whatever." I turned back to the screen, taking care to sound as indifferent as possible. But his words nagged at me. It was weird to think that a bunch of fans online were gossiping about my dad.

Oscar leaned forward, squinting. *"The Kat Sinclair Files?"*

"My blog," I said, resisting the urge to close the laptop so he couldn't see. "Mostly just to keep in touch with my grandma and my friends Trish and Mark." Oscar's hand twitched, and his expression went from surprised to oddly closed in a heartbeat. I stared at him curiously. "Something wrong?"

"No," he said flatly. "I had a friend named Mark, too, that's all."

"Oh." I clicked REPLY, wishing he'd go away. "Had? What, is he dead or something?" After a few seconds of typing, I looked up to find Oscar staring at me.

"Oh God, your friend didn't actually die, did he?" I said nervously. "I was just kidding, I didn't—"

Oscar rolled his eyes. "Quit freaking out. He's not dead."

"Oh." I waited, because it looked like he was going to say something else. But he just stood there. I turned back to my screen just as the door swung open.

"Hey, guys!" Mi Jin stepped inside. "Meeting's almost over—Jess is still going over some stuff with your dad, though."

"Okay," I said. "So you got stuck teaching us, huh?"

Mi Jin laughed. "I guess. It'll be fun, though. Your dad and Lidia told me you guys both have pretty good grades."

"I tried this out on Kat," Oscar informed her, twirling the mask around his finger. "Your reaction was way better."

"Yeah, I'll be starring in a slasher movie one day, just you wait," Mi Jin said with a grin. "My mom used to say my scream could shatter glass." She nodded at the door. "We just ordered some lunch if you guys are hungry."

30

My stomach rumbled again. "Starving," I said, closing my window on the laptop. Then I remembered the page I'd printed. "Should I leave this on? I think someone was using it before I came in."

Mi Jin shook her head. "Nah, we've all been downstairs all morning. You and Oscar are the only ones who've been up here."

"But there was a . . ." I trailed off, glancing at Oscar. He stared back, his expression blank. "Never mind."

I followed them out of the room, watching Oscar twirl that stupid mask around his finger and thinking of the message folded up in my pocket. *KEEP HER AWAY FROM THE MEDIUM.* Another prank, no doubt. He'd probably typed it up right before I got upstairs, then hid to watch my reaction. Apparently he was into playing jokes on people. Very unfunny ones, too.

And I was stuck with him as a classmate. Awesome.

After lunch (sandwiches with cold cuts and probably the best cheese I'd ever tasted), I slammed into a wall of exhaustion. Oscar had spent the whole meal having an intense debate with Mi Jin about some video game. Jess was going over the Crimptown story in detail with Dad and Lidia. It actually sounded really interesting, but my eyelids drooped like my lashes were weights. When my head slipped off my hand and I jerked awake, Oscar snickered.

"I need some air," I announced in the most dignified voice I could muster, righting the jar of pickles I'd knocked over before heading for the door.

Roland was outside of the theater, sitting on a backpack

31

with a sucker sticking out of his mouth. I sped up, hoping he wouldn't want to talk.

"So, Kat," Roland said. Groaning inwardly, I stopped and turned to face him. Time for some awkward conversation. Dislike. "Parents just split up, huh?"

I blinked, startled. "Uh . . . yeah. My dad told you?"

Roland lifted a shoulder. "He mentioned it. But it wouldn't have been hard to guess."

Before I could respond—and I had no idea what to say to that, anyway—Sam Sumners wandered around the corner of the theater. His eyes looked glazed over, like he was half-asleep. I could empathize.

"It was her brother," he said to no one in particular. Roland pulled the sucker out of his mouth and shot Sam a purplish grin.

"Her brother? Really? You usually say it's a boyfriend or husband. These things are always about jealousy."

Sam nodded vaguely. "Usually, yes . . . but not this time."

I cleared my throat. "What are you guys talking about?"

Turning, Sam squinted at me with a strange expression, as if he wasn't quite sure whether I was real. I had the sudden crazy idea that he could see ghosts better than living people. "Sonja Hillebrandt," Sam said. "Her presence is quieter than the pirate's, but more rooted to this place. The pirate wants to roam."

"Um . . ." I glanced at Roland for help.

"Sonja's one of the Crimptown ghosts," he explained, crunching down on the purple sucker with a sharp *crack*. "Sam's trying to figure out why she's still hanging around.

Apparently, it has something to do with her brother."

Sam frowned, his eyes glazing over once more. "Protective . . . she's very protective . . ."

I stared as he wandered off around the corner of the theater without another word. "He looks like he needs some sleep."

"He's fine," Roland replied. "That's just how he acts when we're on-site. It's an occupational hazard when you're a medium. Hard to communicate with the dead and not walk around looking like a zombie."

Crossing my arms, I studied Roland. He sounded mocking, although I wasn't sure if it was me or Sam he was making fun of. "You're a parapsychologist, right? Like a *paranormal* psychologist?"

"Parapsychologist, like a scientist who looks for evidence of any sort of paranormal activity, such as clairvoyance, precognition, and telepathy." Roland yawned widely. "Or, you know. A spook shrink, if you prefer."

Was he making fun of himself now? This guy was so weird.

"Okay, I have to ask," I said. "Do you really believe in all this?"

"All what?"

"You know, *this*." I gestured to the theater. "Ghosts, haunted tunnels, a walking Ken doll who thinks he can talk to dead people."

Roland let out a snort of laughter. "Walking Ken doll. Nice."

I winced. "Sorry, it's a joke I have with my grandmother.

She's got the hots for him pretty bad."

What? Seriously, brain. Time to start controlling the words coming out of my mouth.

Roland was still chuckling. "Oh no, your grandma's a Sumner Stalker?"

"A *what*?"

"That's what Sam's 'fans' call themselves." He made little air quotation marks with his fingers on the word *fans*. "They get pretty intense."

I made a face. "She's not that bad, I promise."

"Glad to hear it," Roland said around his sucker. "You should see some of his fan mail—it gets pretty creepy. And he never realizes when they cross the line. He's way more tuned in with the dead than with the living. Pretty sure that's why he gets those kinds of fans, actually."

"What do you mean?" I asked curiously. "He's got fans because he's . . . well, good-looking."

Roland shrugged. "True, but he's also haunted. You don't make a career out of contacting the dead without a reason. And people are drawn to that."

I frowned. He had a point. I knew Sam's story from all the interviews Grandma showed me—how he'd fallen into the deep end of a pool when he was little and it was a few minutes before someone found him and gave him CPR. He'd nearly drowned, and ever since then, he claimed to have a connection with the spirit world.

But Sam wasn't the only one who was haunted by something. Everyone on *Passport to Paranormal* had, for one reason or another, decided to chase ghosts for a living. Maybe everyone had a Thing that haunted them, that they wanted to escape.

"Our first host was a Sumner Stalker," Roland was saying, his expression sour. "Emily Rosinski. Total nutjob. Wasn't sorry to see her go."

"What about the other two?" I asked, thinking of the so-called curse. "The hosts?"

"Carlos was fired. Bernice just got freaked out and quit."

"So you don't believe in the host curse, then?" I asked. "Or any of this 'most haunted show' stuff?"

Roland shrugged. "It doesn't matter what I believe. That's not what the show is about."

"Really? I kind of thought that was the whole point of your job," I said. "Finding proof of paranormal activity."

His eyebrows shot up. "Proof? Like what—video of a ghost? A photo? You seem like a smart kid. What do you think would happen if we put that on the air?"

I thought about it. "I guess people would say you faked it."

"Exactly." Roland tossed the sucker stick into a trash can. "It's a no-win situation." He pulled another sucker out of his pocket.

"What's with all the suckers?" I asked, watching as he ripped off the wrapper. This one was red.

"We just had lunch," Roland said matter-of-factly. "Normally I'd be having a cigarette right now, but I quit. Therefore . . ." He waved the sucker at me before sticking it in his mouth. "I've got more. Want one?"

"No, thanks," I said. "So what did you mean, it's a no-win situation?"

Roland leaned back against the wall and closed his eyes. "If we prove ghosts exist—people think it's fake. If we find nothing—people think it's boring."

"Well, you find *some* creepy stuff sometimes," I said thoughtfully. "I mean, I don't think everyone who watches the show believes in ghosts, or wants proof or whatever. I think most of them just like being scared. They want something to talk about."

"Dead on," Roland agreed. "That's why we do our best to make things . . . entertaining."

"What do you mean?"

The door opened again, and Lidia stuck her head out. "We need you guys in about five minutes," she said, then looked around. "Isn't Sam out here?"

"Wandered off," Roland said. "I'll find him." Once Lidia was gone, he stood up, shouldering his backpack. "So what about you?"

"Huh?"

Roland looked at me expectantly. "Do you believe in ghosts?"

"Nope," I replied firmly.

The corners of his mouth twitched up a little. "Good. You'll have more fun that way."

I stared after him as he sauntered around the corner where Sam had vanished. Slipping my fingers in my pocket, I pulled out the piece of paper again. *KEEP HER AWAY FROM THE MEDIUM.* I frowned. I'd clicked print, but the document had been blank on the screen. Even if this was just another one of Oscar's pranks, how could he have managed that? It was more like a computer glitch . . . but then again, *someone* had typed this message. This warning about a medium.

Was it about Sam? And who was supposed to stay away from him?

After a second, I rolled my eyes. It hadn't even been a day and I was already getting creeped out over nothing.

Shoving the paper in my pocket, I headed back into the theater.

INVASION OF THE NUTJOBS FROM PLANET FANDOM

Post: The Pirate Ghost of Crimptown

I don't believe in ghosts. (Sorry, Grandma.)

I just figured that since this is my first real, not-jet-lagged blog post, I should make that clear before I say anything else about *P2P*. I don't believe in ghosts—but I do love scary stories.

For the first episode, we're spending the night in Crimptown, which is this supposedly haunted system of tunnels under Rotterdam. This morning, I watched Dad interview a guy who owns a restaurant on the waterfront that's been around since the 1800s. He told Dad all about the legend of Crimptown and why people think it's haunted.

A bunch of the bars and hotels and restaurants in downtown Rotterdam have cellars connected by the tunnels. The tunnels all lead to the waterfront, because the point was to easily get food and supplies from the boats to the businesses. There were pulley systems to get the supplies up to street level, and chutes to drop stuff down into the cellars for storage.

Sometime in the mid-1800s, a bunch of men in Rotterdam started going missing. And they were always last seen at a bar. After a while, people noticed another connection—all the bars they disappeared from were connected to the Crimptown tunnel system.

It turned out a pirate named Falk Von Leer had this horrible scheme going on. He'd get someone at the bar to drug the guy's drink. After the guy passed out, they'd throw him down one of the chutes into the cellar. From there, Red Leer would have his crew members drag the guy through the tunnels to the waterfront, and then he would sell his prisoner into slavery on cargo ships. (His nickname in Dutch is Rood Leer—*rood* means *red* in English. The restaurant owner said they called him that because of all the blood he spilled.)

Everyone knew what Red Leer was doing, but they were all too afraid to do something about it. But when a teenage boy named Bastian Hillebrandt went missing, his older sister Sonja decided to organize a rescue. She gathered a group of women whose husbands or sons or brothers had all been kidnapped by Red Leer. One night, the women disguised themselves as men, secretly armed themselves with all kinds of weapons, and visited all the bars connected to the tunnels. They ordered drinks but didn't actually drink them, and pretended to pass out like they'd been drugged. Once they got thrown down the trapdoors into the cellars, they attacked Red Leer's men and freed all the prisoners who hadn't been sold to ships yet. Sonja came face-to-face with Red Leer and demanded he return her brother. Red Leer refused and then he killed her. But the freed prisoners and all the women who had joined Sonja attacked and killed Red Leer. Eventually, all the men Red Leer had kidnapped and sold were found and set free.

But both Red Leer's and Sonja's ghosts are said to haunt Crimptown, forever at war with each other.

The guy Dad interviewed said people who tour Crimptown report all sorts of strange stuff, like flickering lights or chilly breezes. Sam says he can "feel the tension between Sonja and Red Leer in my gut." Roland says Sam just ate some bad oysters. (Honestly, I can't even tell if Roland believes in any of this stuff. He's weird like that.)

As for me, I'm still feeling pretty skeptical. Wouldn't ALL old tunnel systems have bad lighting and chilly breezes? I mean, it would take a lot more than that for me to consider a place haunted. But I guess I'll find out tonight, since we'll be camping out down there. Either way, it's a really cool story. And I found these portraits of Sonja and Red Leer online. Isn't Red Leer creepy-looking?

WHEN Grandma had first suggested the blog, I'd thought it sounded like too much work. But it turns out when you don't have to worry about outlines and a thesis statement and grades and all that stuff, writing is pretty fun. After watching Dad's interview, I'd wandered along the waterfront until I found an Internet café where I could write up Sonja and Red Leer's story and add their portraits. Red Leer had a thick, curled mustache and a ghoulish grin. Sonja looked so . . . innocent. And normal. Just a kind-faced woman with dark hair wearing a simple dress and a delicate smile. It was hard to imagine her leading an attack on a band of pirates.

Once I published my post, I found the *Passport to Paranormal* forums. I couldn't help it—I had to see what people were saying about my dad. The top thread had his name in the title. I scanned the first page quickly.

P2P FAN FORUMS
Meet Jack Sinclair, Victim #4

Maytrix [admin]
Okay, guys, we've got ourselves another host! But for how long?
evil laugh
So, Jack Sinclair hosted a morning show in Chelsea, Ohio, for several years. You can watch clips of him <u>here</u> . . . seems like a fun guy. Let's recap our former *P2P* hosts:
Victim #1: Emily Rosinski, sixteen episodes
Victim #2: Carlos Ortiz, eight episodes
Victim #3: Bernice Boyd, four episodes
On to Victim #4! Thoughts?

spicychai [member]
two episodes. do the math.

YourCohortInCrime [member]
IDK, this "host curse" thing they're doing can't really last, right? It's obviously just for publicity—the ratings shoot up for a few episodes every time. Remember when Carlos published that exposé? He said they fake all kinds of stuff on the show. That's why he got fired. And the first episode with Bernice as host after Carlos left had the highest ratings they'd ever seen.

beautifulgollum [moderator]
Firing hosts isn't good publicity, YCIC. And Carlos denied writing that exposé—he said he was set up. The curse is because the show is haunted—some restless spirit has been with them since the first episode in the lighthouse. I think that spirit is responsible for getting rid of the other hosts. Hopefully it will approve of Jack.

AntiSimon [member]
I miss Bernice. (Anyone's better than Emily, though.) Anyway, I think spicychai's right—the length of time is cut in half from one host to the next, so Jack's got two episodes. My prediction: Jack does a couple of episodes and then they go hostless. Let Samland take over the whole thing. (Or the show gets canceled . . . and let's face it, that's a pretty big possibility.)
    BTW, the fact that the timing works like that PROVES the curse is real. It can't be a coincidence.

YourCohortInCrime [member]
Uh, wrong. It proves the producer firing the hosts for publicity can do basic math like the rest of us.

beautifulgollum [moderator]
Come on, YCIC—the point of the show is to find ghosts. They don't WANT to lose hosts.

YourCohortInCrime [member]
Funny, I could've sworn the point of the show was ratings.

Thomas Cooper's gonna can it if it doesn't do better this season.

skEllen [member]
#TEAMSAMLAND

I got to the bottom of the page and clicked over to the next . . . and then the next. It was kind of unnerving, watching all these fans make bets on my dad and bicker about whether his job was cursed.

Did they really believe a *ghost* was getting rid of the hosts? I mean, weren't these people supposed to be adults? Even more interesting was that some of them seemed to think Lidia was actually firing hosts just to make viewers *think* there was a curse, like a publicity stunt.

The weirdest thing was that no one knew where the old hosts all went. Not like any of them were all that famous, but Emily Rosinski and Carlos Ortiz were reporters before joining the show, and Bernice Boyd had worked for the History channel. And apparently they were all way low-profile now, refusing to give interviews or talk to anyone about why they left. That was a big part of why the ratings always went up—all the mystery and drama surrounding their sudden departures.

Fans loved gossiping about Emily, in particular—and they didn't say very nice things. I remembered the face Roland made when he called her a "Sumner Stalker." A lot of fans thought she'd quit because Sam didn't return her feelings, but some speculated they secretly dated and had a huge breakup. Personally, I couldn't imagine Sam dating anyone. (Well, anyone *living*. He'd probably date a ghost if he could.)

There were tons of other interesting threads, too. The forums were organized by season and episode, but also by topic. The most popular thread was about Sam and Roland—or "Samland," which made me snort my soda. I wondered if Roland knew about that particular nickname.

As much as I wanted to just sit in that cushy chair and bask in an Internet glow all day, I didn't think Dad would appreciate me blowing twenty euros here when he had a laptop (no matter how clunky and slow it was). So when my hour was up, I logged off and headed back to the hotel. I found Dad in our room, studying his laptop screen.

"Hi, Dad."

"Hey, sweetie," he said distractedly.

I flopped back on my bed. "What's that?"

"Just reading up on the local history." He smiled, eyes still on the screen. "Crimptown is fascinating, isn't it?"

"Yeah." I yawned widely. "Hey, Dad?"

"Mmhmm?"

I paused, trying to think of how to ask the question. *Why'd you choose this job?* But that would only lead to more questions I wasn't sure I wanted answered. *Why do you want to chase ghosts? What if Mom decides to come back?*

Did she leave because of the Thing?

"Kat?"

I glanced over to find him staring at me in concern.

"Um . . . can I use the laptop when you're done?"

"Of course."

He turned back to the screen and started pecking away at the keyboard. Within a minute, I was sound asleep.

CHAPTER SIX
WHAT LURKS IN THE CYBERSHADOWS

From: acciopancakes@mymail.net
To: EdieM@mymail.net
Subject: This whole curse thing

Hi, Grandma,
I found the *P2P* forums (those people are kind of insane btw).
What did you think of the other hosts? Roland said Emily Rosinski
was a nutjob because she had a huge crush on Sam. Do you think
maybe they've been firing the hosts just so fans will think the
show is cursed? I don't want that to happen to Dad. Pretty sure
he's not ready to go home yet.
Love, Kat

"YOU know what?"

Mi Jin and I both glanced up. Oscar was sprawled
out on an old sofa, lazily kicking the door to the theater's
projection room in a steady rhythm. *Thud. Thud. Thud.*

"What?" Mi Jin swiveled away from the laptop, one hand
still on the keyboard.

Oscar tapped his math sheet with his pencil. "There are
fifty-three questions on this."

"And?"

"And I think that's *irrational.*"

Mi Jin laughed. I rolled my eyes, focusing on my own sheet. I'd slept a record-setting eleven hours straight last night, but it still didn't feel like enough. When I'd woken up at seven this morning—with *no* alarm, which was pretty freaky—I felt great. But the closer we got to lunchtime, the more I wanted to crawl back into bed.

A few minutes passed, during which I tried to ignore the fact that my eyelids were beginning to droop. Suddenly, Oscar dropped his pencil on the floor next to me.

"Done." He leaned over, and I shifted in my spot so he couldn't see my work and stared resolutely at the page.

1.92 – 5.6
A) integer
B) rational
C) irrational

"You're not done yet?"

I pressed my lips together. "No."

Oscar sighed wearily. "Are you at least close?"

I ignored him, and after a few seconds, he leaned back on the sofa.

Thud. Thud. Thud.

"Could you maybe quit that?" I asked through gritted teeth.

"Quit what?"

Thud. Thud. Thud.

"*That*," I said sharply, flipping my page over. "And by the way, fifty-three is a rational number."

45

Oscar groaned. "I know. It was a *joke*. Man, you have no sense of humor."

"I do, actually." I punched a few keys on my calculator. "I laugh when something's funny."

Thud. Thud. Thud.

"Oscar, I swear to—"

"*Okay*," Mi Jin cut in loudly. "It's almost time for lunch—Oscar, will you go see if Lidia's ordered anything yet?"

"Sure." Swinging his legs off the sofa, Oscar stood and stretched. "Let me know if you need help with that," he said, then sauntered out of the room before I could think of a response.

I stared after him in disbelief, then realized Mi Jin was giggling. "Sorry," she said quickly. "You two really push each other's buttons, huh?"

"He's just. So. *Obnoxious*." I set my pencil on the floor next to me and rubbed my eyes. "I mean, seriously. I've never met anyone so annoying, it's like he—"

"Kat," Mi Jin interrupted. I lowered my hands to find Lidia in the doorway, and my face went hot.

"Oh . . . hi."

Smiling, Lidia walked over to the desk and started rifling through a folder. "Talking about my nephew?"

"Well . . ." I hesitated. "Yeah. Sorry."

She laughed. "It's okay. Although I promise he's usually a nice kid. He's just had a rough time this year."

"He said he got expelled for fighting?" Mi Jin asked, and I glanced up.

Lidia nodded. "Yeah. Poor thing . . . lots of bullying at his school."

I snorted quietly, hiding my face behind my worksheet. It was pretty much impossible to imagine someone as arrogant as Oscar getting bullied. He seemed more likely to be a bully himself.

"Kat, do you need any help with that?" Mi Jin asked, pulling her hair back into a ponytail and pointing at my worksheet with her boot.

"Nah, thanks. I've only got four problems left."

"Just leave it in the folder when you're done, okay?"

"Okay."

I stared at the same problem, the numbers swimming in front of my eyes. I was so taking a nap after lunch. My head felt like it was stuffed with tissue, and a muffled beeping sound filled my ears. It was a few seconds before I realized it was coming from Lidia.

"Sorry," she said, pulling her phone out of her pocket and silencing the alarm. "Just a reminder to take my pills." Setting the folder down, she unzipped a small purple bag next to the laptop and took out a bottle.

"Are you sick?" I asked, watching as she shook a few pills into her hand.

Taking a swig of water, Lidia popped the pills and swallowed. "A minor heart problem. Nothing serious."

My eyes widened in surprise. "*Heart* problems? Aren't you a little young for that?" I winced as soon as the words were out of my mouth, but Lidia just smiled.

"It's a condition I was born with," she explained, setting her water bottle down. "Seizures, fainting, the works. I had a pacemaker put in when I was eight."

"Oh." I watched Lidia toy with the locket on her necklace. "I'm sorry."

"Oh, it's fine," Lidia said. "Kind of a bummer when I was younger, though. Strobe lights can trigger my seizures, so that meant no concerts or haunted houses. Not that that stopped me," she added with a wink. I grinned as she tucked the pill bottle back inside the purple bag. "Are you coming down for lunch?"

"Um . . ." My eyes strayed to the laptop, where the Internet beckoned. Lidia laughed, heading to the door.

"I'll make sure to save you some food. Take your time."

"Thanks."

Flopping down onto the desk chair, I logged into my e-mail account. As much as I was trying not to let it bother me, I couldn't help thinking about the host curse. To my relief, Grandma had already responded to the e-mail I'd sent her before breakfast.

From: EdieM@mymail.net
To: acciopancakes@mymail.net
Re: This whole curse thing

Hi, KitKat,
So now you're lurking in the *P2P* forums, hmm? I suppose I'll
have to watch what I say in there from now on.

I groaned. So Grandma was one of the fans in the forum. What a surprise. I wondered what her screen name was, then immediately decided I didn't want to know. Ever. *Ever.*

I agree, it's pretty weird to watch them all argue about my son-in-law. Try not to take what you read on the boards too seriously. Lidia isn't just firing hosts for publicity. This is a show that struggles with low ratings—people are going to come and go, that's just how it is. And it's true that ratings go up when a host leaves, but that lasts only an episode or two. Not exactly a smart long-term publicity plan, right?

The other hosts . . . Bernice was really knowledgeable about the local history and folklore, but she was skittish—afraid of her own shadow. Why she ever took the job is beyond me. Carlos did indeed publish a piece accusing the crew of faking things, and he was promptly canned—although he always said he didn't actually write it. And Emily couldn't have cared less about ghosts. She spent every episode doing nothing but fawning all over Sam. I guess after a while he must have rejected her, and she flounced. (And good riddance! She was a poor representative of us Sumner Stalkers.) Funny that you talked to Roland about that. It was always obvious that the way Emily acted around Sam bothered him. Between you and me, I think he was a bit jealous.

I smiled, but something nagged at me. *Sumner Stalkers.* I knew Grandma probably thought that name was funny, but I couldn't help remembering what Roland had said. *Our first host was a Sumner Stalker. Total nutjob.*

Would he consider Grandma a nutjob, too? She really wasn't. No one knew the difference between a fan and a real stalker better than Grandma. She got threatening letters for almost two years after *Mutant Cheerleaders Attack* came out, before the police finally caught the guy. That was way before I was born, but she'd told me all about it. It sounded really scary.

I wondered, too, if Grandma was right about Roland

being jealous. He definitely looked irritated when he talked about Emily. If he'd been in love with her and had to watch her flirt with Sam all the time, well, I guess that would be pretty annoying.

Yawning, I opened a chat window and checked for Trish and Mark—both gray, both off-line. Which made sense, seeing as it was, like, six in the morning there. A wave of homesickness hit, and I had the sudden urge to call one of them, or Grandma, or . . .

One of my contacts abruptly flipped from gray to green, and my heart leaped. Then I saw the name.

MonicaMills [Mom]

I froze, my hand on the mouse. And sure enough, after a few seconds:

Kat? Are you there?

A lump rose in my throat. Numbly, I clicked the chat window closed and logged out. Then I shoved my unfinished math worksheet in Mi Jin's folder and went to go get some lunch.

CHAPTER SEVEN
IF LOOKS COULD KILL

MonicaMills [Mom]
This contact has been blocked. To unblock, go to your privacy settings.

MY after-lunch nap turned out to be a total bust. I lay on my bed staring at the ugly hotel curtains for almost forty-five minutes before giving up and heading to the waterfront to join the crew.

After stopping to buy a soda, I peered up and down the boardwalk until I spotted them huddled together. A cool breeze ruffled my hair as I walked, and I shivered—I still hadn't gotten used to my short cut. The back of my neck felt weirdly exposed.

Still, the crisp air woke me up from my post-almost-nap trance. And I wasn't the only one out enjoying the perfect fall weather. I squinted down at the crew, wondering if the crowds of families and couples strolling along the boardwalk were making it difficult to get the shots they needed.

Ring, ring! Glancing over my shoulder, I jumped out of the way just as a cyclist went zipping past. When I turned back around, I slammed into someone and dropped my soda bottle.

"Oh, *great.*" Kneeling down, the dark-haired woman scooped her binoculars and camera up and away from a trickle of soda. I winced, picking up the bottle.

"Sorry, I didn't . . ." Pausing, I tried frantically to remember how to say sorry in Dutch. Then I realized she'd spoken English. It was hard to tell thanks to her oversize sunglasses, but I was pretty sure she was looking at me like I'd just kicked a kitten.

"Just look where you're going, kid," she snapped in a high, nasal voice, tucking a strand of hair behind her ear. She was young, and her face was really angular—she looked almost gaunt.

"Sorry," I said again, not bothering to hide my irritation as she made a show of inspecting her camera. "Is it broken?"

Rather than answering, she just turned and headed in the opposite direction, muttering under her breath. Rolling my eyes, I tossed my empty soda bottle in the trash and headed toward the crew.

I couldn't help picturing the Elapse E-250 still stuffed in my suitcase. With so many interesting sights around—the boats, the vendors, little kids playing jump rope—the urge to take photographs was strong. Unfortunately, that urge always came with my mom's voice giving instructions.

Look, that girl over there near the railing; such a textured background with the boats behind her . . . The light is dim this time of day, so use a slower shutter speed . . .

Keeping my eyes firmly fixed on the crew, I walked fast and avoided looking for any more frame-worthy moments. Dad and Lidia were side by side going over Dad's notes, while Jess adjusted the large video camera on her shoulder. Sam was watching a group of teenagers take photos near the water. Roland simply looked bored. I noticed Oscar hovering around Mi Jin and stifled a groan—I'd been hoping he stayed back at the hotel.

"Almost ready, guys," Jess said. "Mi Jin, Jack's going to need the windscreen."

"Got it!" Mi Jin rummaged through the massive camera bag hanging off her shoulder. A second later, she let out a bloodcurdling scream and flung something long and wriggly straight at me.

I jumped back as a snake went sailing past my head. It hit the boardwalk with a *smack* and . . . laid there. I took a hesitant step forward, then nudged it with my toe.

"Fake," I said, giving Oscar a pointed look. "Totally fake."

"Oscar, come on," Lidia groaned, but the others started laughing. No one laughed harder than Mi Jin, though. Which was kind of disappointing. It would've been fun to watch her chew him out.

But she seemed to find the whole thing hilarious. "Nice one," she told Oscar, still snickering as she handed Dad a cover for his mic. "That's two to one, then?"

"Yours didn't count," Oscar said with a grin. "I'm not afraid of spiders."

"You jumped a little." Mi Jin zipped the camera bag closed. "But yeah, your reaction was nowhere near as epic as mine."

"You scared off some of this crowd." Roland sounded mildly appreciative as he glanced around the boardwalk.

"That was a pretty legit scream."

Mi Jin beamed. "Horror movie–worthy, right?"

"I'll say."

I smiled at Dad and he winked. Grandma would love Mi Jin.

"All right, we need to get this wrapped up in the next hour," Jess announced, shifting under the weight of the camera. "Jack, we'll shoot the first thirty seconds in place, then get the three of you walking toward the theater. Let's get a couple of takes of the intro first, all right?"

Dad nodded, handing Lidia his notes. "Sounds good."

I took several steps back as everyone else got into their places, and something squished under my foot. Stooping down, I picked up the rubber snake just as Oscar reached my side.

"Not afraid of snakes either, huh?" he asked.

"Not fake ones."

"Real ones, though?"

"Not really," I said, watching as Dad launched into a description of life in Rotterdam in the eighteen hundreds. "Trish has a pet snake. His name's Fang, but he's harmless." I glanced at Oscar. "I mean, if you'd hidden a live cobra in there or something, I might have screamed."

To my surprise, he cracked a smile. "*Might* have?"

I shrugged. "Yeah. And I *might* have jumped over that railing and swum to England."

Oscar actually laughed a little. Before either of us could say anything else, Jess let out a frustrated cry.

"*Cut.* Sorry, Jack . . . what is *wrong* with this thing?"

Mi Jin joined Jess and Lidia in inspecting the camera. "What *is* this? An error code?" Jess asked Mi Jin, who frowned.

"I've never seen that come up before . . ." After a second, Mi Jin whirled around to face Oscar, her eyes wide. "Is this another prank? Did you do this?" she asked. Confusion flickered across Oscar's face.

"Do what?"

Jess was shaking her head. "No way, he couldn't have."

She turned slightly so we could see the viewfinder. The screen was black, but a row of letters scrolled rapidly at the bottom.

XXXXXXXXXXXX . . . XXXXXXXXXXXX . . . XXXXXXXXXXXX . . .

Dad frowned, leaning closer. "Maybe try turning it off?"

Jess obliged, pressing the button. But the scrolling continued.

"Thirteen *X*s," Mi Jin said excitedly. "Ah, what am I doing—we need to get a picture of this! Anyone have a camera? Wait, there's a handheld in here somewhere . . ."

My fingers twitched at my side as Mi Jin dug the small camera out of her bag, my thoughts once again drifting to the Elapse. I watched Mi Jin begin filming the scrolling letters on the viewfinder. Sam drifted over to stand next to Jess.

"Thirteen *X*s," he mused. "A message from the beyond."

Roland looked highly amused. "Must be."

"Wait . . . I feel something." Sam's expression was so intense I had to bite the inside of my cheek to keep from laughing. "There is a presence with us."

Mi Jin stepped back, grinning, as Roland joined Sam in the shot. "Is it Red Leer?" he asked Sam in a low, serious voice. "Tell him we're not scheduled to be drugged and kidnapped until tomorrow night."

Oscar and I started to snicker as Sam squinted and looked around like he was trying to locate a ghost pirate standing among the rest of us. His gaze rested on me, and my laughter faded. "I'm not sure it's Red Leer," he mused, apparently oblivious to Roland's sarcasm. "I'm not sensing a lot of anger."

"Ah. Should I antagonize him, then?" Roland cleared his throat loudly, but Jess cut him off.

"Look, it's stopped." She turned slightly so we could see the viewfinder, which was back to normal. Jess swung around, aiming the camera at Dad. "Ready to give the intro another shot?"

Dad gave her the thumbs-up. Sam glanced at me again before turning away, and I felt slightly unsettled.

As they started filming, Mi Jin hung back and zipped the camera up in her bag. She glanced over at Oscar and me. "How'd you do it, though, seriously?" she asked in a low, eager voice.

Oscar's brow furrowed. "Do what?"

"Thirteen *X*s!" Mi Jin said. "You did it, right? Like what you did to Lidia's EMF meter yesterday? But how—"

"What did you do to her EMF?" I interrupted, picturing the gadget Lidia had pulled out of her purse yesterday when she was searching for granola bars.

Oscar shrugged. "Messed with the calibration a little so that it went nuts when we first got to the theater."

"But how'd you get those *X*s on the camera?" Mi Jin pressed, and Oscar grinned.

"It's a secret."

Mi Jin laughed. "Well, good one," she said with a wink, then hurried back over to the others.

I stared at Oscar. If he knew enough about electronics to sabotage Lidia's EMF, maybe he really had somehow gotten that message to print out. "Did you type up that thing about the medium?" I blurted out.

Oscar blinked. "The *what*?"

"The message," I said impatiently. "The one that printed out yesterday when you were hiding in the projection room with that stupid mask. *Keep her away from the medium.* You did it, right?"

"Hang on there, crazy," Oscar retorted. "I have no clue what you're talking about."

I scowled. "So you messed with Lidia's EMF and Jess's camera, but *not* with the laptop up in the projection room?"

He opened his mouth but hesitated, glancing back at the camera. I crossed my arms impatiently. He really didn't seem to know anything about the medium message. And I was positive he looked confused when Mi Jin first suggested he'd tampered with the camera. Maybe he really had nothing to do with either. Maybe they were both just glitches.

Or maybe Oscar was an amazingly good liar.

Oscar was still staring at the camera. Jess handed it over to Mi Jin, then joined Lidia and the others to go over the next take. Mi Jin turned away from them, studying the viewfinder closely. Then she glanced over at Oscar and me.

"Just tell me how you did it!" she called. "Please?"

Oscar looked pleased. "Didn't you say you majored in electrical engineering? You figure it out!"

Laughing, Mi Jin turned her attention back to the viewfinder. "Touché."

I stared at Oscar for a second, then grinned. "*Oh*. I get it."

"Get what?"

"Why you lied about the camera," I said lightly. "You didn't do it, but you want Mi Jin to *think* you did. I know she's impressed and all, but she's a little old for you, don't you think?"

I waited for a defensive comeback, a blush, anything. For a few seconds, Oscar just gazed at me. Then he started cracking up.

"You're right," he said. "You're totally right. I don't have a chance." He let out an exaggerated sigh. "Thank you for helping me see the light."

His sarcasm was infuriating. Not to mention his complete lack of shame. "Seriously, she's like ... twenty-two."

Oscar nodded solemnly. "Yeah. You're right. I'm completely delusional."

"Apparently." I turned away, watching as Dad, Roland, and Sam began strolling down the boardwalk toward the theater. Jess kept pace at their side, camera steady on her shoulder. Mi Jin and Lidia trailed not far behind her. I set off after them without another word to Oscar.

His stupid crush on Mi Jin aside, it was pretty strange

that both the crew's camera *and* laptop had briefly malfunctioned. The laptop glitch came with a message. Mi Jin had said the camera glitch wasn't an error code—maybe it was a message, too. Sam said he sensed a presence, but not Red Leer . . . was it the show's ghost? The one so many fans seemed to think was behind the host curse and all the equipment glitches? I remembered the way Sam had stared at me a few minutes ago when the camera freaked out, and had a mental image of a ghost floating at my side.

Suddenly, I felt ridiculous. One day with a bunch of ghost hunters and I was already buying into the whole paranormal activity thing. Still . . .

When Jess called "Cut!" and started talking to Dad and the other guys, I hurried over to Mi Jin.

"Do you have a pen or anything?"

"Sure!" She dug a pencil out of the camera bag and handed it to me.

"Thanks." I turned away, quickly jotting down the second message under the first.

KEEP HER AWAY FROM THE MEDIUM
13 Xs

"What's that?" Mi Jin asked curiously, and I folded the paper and shoved it back into my pocket.

"Nothing important."

CHAPTER EIGHT
TEA PARTY OF THE DAMNED

P2P WIKI
Entry: "Dead Air"
[Last edited by Maytrix]

"Dead air" refers to the approximately ninety seconds of dead air during the pilot episode of *Passport to Paranormal*, which took place at the Limerick Bed & Breakfast on the northern coast of Oregon. The disturbance occurred during the last ten minutes of airtime. Viewers suddenly lost audio and video during a scene showing the crew walking from the B&B to the nearby lighthouse. No one, including Fright TV, could explain the dead air. The episode resumed to show the crew back at the B&B, leading many fans to believe the missing footage took place in the lighthouse.

To date, the crew refuses to discuss what happened in the lighthouse, nor will they share the footage. When asked for a possible explanation of the dead air, *P2P* creator and producer Lidia Bettencourt commented: "I guess it's just part of being the most haunted show on television." The phrase immediately became the show's unofficial slogan, an idea supported by the crew's frequent tech glitches and apparent inability to keep a host (for more, see: <u>The Host Curse</u>).

MY post-dinner nap attempt was a success—a solid hour of blissful unconsciousness. I rolled over and stared at the clock: 8:31 p.m. Yeah, there was no way I was going to sleep normally tonight.

Both Dad and his laptop were gone, but he'd left one of his key cards behind. I vaguely remembered Jess saying something at dinner about a meeting that night in the hotel's conference room. Slipping on a pair of shoes, I grabbed Dad's key to the room the crew was using to store equipment. Maybe there was an extra laptop in there I could use.

A minute later, I swiped the key to room 301, then pushed the door open a crack. "Hello?" I stuck my head inside. The room was deserted.

Both beds and the floor were covered in camera bags and cables, mics and tripods, thermal scanners and EMF detectors. Propping the door open behind me, I scanned the room quickly and spotted a closed laptop next to the TV. "Hallelujah," I whispered, hurrying over and pulling up a chair. I opened the laptop, powered it on, and waited impatiently for it to load.

And waited. And waited.

I frowned, tapping my fingers on the table. This show seriously needed some better equipment. Finally, the desktop appeared. But before I could click on anything, a video popped up and began to play.

"Are you ready?"

I recognized Sam's voice immediately. The camera sat perfectly still at eye level—on a tripod, I figured—in front of a tiny table in a cramped, circular room. Sam sat between Lidia and a blond, round-faced woman wearing a ton of makeup—Emily Rosinski, the first host. All three were holding hands. The only light came from a single, dim bulb over their heads.

Lidia nodded. *"Yes,"* she whispered.

I tapped the escape key several times, then held down the power button. Nothing. The video just kept playing.

Sam tilted his head back, his expression serene. *"Close your eyes,"* he instructed. Lidia obeyed immediately, but Emily continued to stare at him, her expression rapt. Sam started to speak so softly, I couldn't catch all the words.

"We invite you to join ... present, let us know you're ... our energies, if you wish ..."

Lidia drew a slow, steady breath, her hands visibly trembling. Emily leaned closer to Sam. *"Are you sensing a presence?"* she said in a loud, exaggerated whisper.

Sam didn't respond. *"If you're willing ... communicate, we ask that you ... let Lidia know you're present ..."*

I'd seen every episode of *Passport to Paranormal*, but this scene didn't look familiar. The bulb hanging overhead flickered once, very briefly. Emily gasped.

"Did you see that, Sam?" she cried shrilly. *"I think you've made contact!"*

I snorted. No wonder they'd never used this footage. Uber-cheesy.

Sam didn't even open his eyes. *"Focus, Emily,"* he said dreamily.

He continued murmuring, his voice barely audible. Lidia's breathing grew heavier and heavier, while Emily just gazed adoringly at Sam. The lightbulb flickered again, and she squirmed in her chair.

"*Sam, I think—*"

Suddenly, Lidia's eyes flew open. She sucked in a sharp breath just as the lightbulb exploded. Emily's shriek cut off abruptly.

I blinked in the sudden darkness, goose bumps breaking out all over my arms. The laptop had powered off, and the hotel room was pitch-black.

Heart thudding in my ears, I got to my feet. I hadn't turned on the lights when I came in, but I'd definitely left the door wide open.

Now it was closed.

"Hello?" I whispered. Feeling for the desk lamp, I flipped the switch. Nothing.

I felt a flicker of fear, quickly replaced by irritation. "Oscar," I said firmly, turning in a full circle. "Knock it off, this isn't funny."

No response.

I made my way slowly across the room, carefully navigating around the bags and coils of cables on the floor. Twice I paused and listened, but the room remained silent. When I reached the door, I yanked it open. Light from the hallway flooded the room. I spotted a light switch next to the bathroom door and flipped it on.

"Where are you hiding?" I muttered, poking my head inside the bathroom before checking the closet. "Oscar, come on . . ."

But he wasn't there. Hands on my hips, I stared at the laptop. Oscar must have been walking down the hall, seen me using the laptop, and shut the door. And the lamp . . .

Crossing the room, I flipped the lamp switch a few times. Then I saw the cord lying across the table. Someone's phone charger was plugged into the socket instead. Well, that explained that.

I shook my head, my relief mixed with annoyance. Apparently Oscar was determined to scare me. He could have set it up so that the video automatically started playing when someone turned the laptop on. Although . . .

How could he have fixed it so that the laptop turned off right when the bulb exploded in the video?

I shivered, remembering the creepy way Lidia's eyes had flown open. Before I could talk myself out of it, I powered the laptop back on and held my breath. The desktop looked normal—no videos, nothing unusual. I waited a few seconds, but nothing happened.

So that made three weird glitches: the printer, the camera, and the laptop. I sat down and opened the web browser. I wasn't ready to believe the glitches were all thanks to a restless spirit haunting the show, but at least now I had something to write about for my second blog post.

At a quarter to ten the next morning, I stumbled off the elevator and into the lobby. Mi Jin waved at me from where she sat curled up in an armchair with her laptop. "Morning!"

"Mmmph," I mumbled, eyeing the bagel in her hand. "Where'd you get that?"

She pointed to a door by the front desk. "Breakfast room."

"Thanks."

A few minutes later, I returned carrying a bagel smeared with grape jelly and a paper cup filled with chocolate milk. I started to take a sip as I sat in the chair next to Mi Jin, then yawned widely.

"You look dead," Mi Jin observed. "Bad night's sleep?"

"I don't think it qualified as sleep." I balanced my cup on the armrest and took a bite of bagel. "Where's everyone else?"

"Your dad and Jess went to check out Crimptown for tonight," she replied. "Roland might've gone with them, I'm not sure. Lidia's on the phone setting up stuff for Brussels next week. And Sam's having a tea party with Sonja Hillebrandt and the pirate who killed her."

I choked on my bagel, giggling. "He's *what*?"

Mi Jin grinned. "Sorry, that was mean. He's . . . you know, doing his medium thing. Trying to contact Sonja and Red Leer by sitting at a table in a dark room." She shrugged. "Whenever I watch someone conduct a séance, it reminds me of when I was little and I'd host tea parties for my imaginary friends."

I took another sip of chocolate milk. "So you don't believe in ghosts?"

Her eyes widened. "Oh, I totally believe. I just take a more technical approach than Sam."

"What do you mean?"

Mi Jin sat up a little straighter. "It takes a really high amount of energy for a ghost to do something big, like move a solid object or possess a person," she said seriously. "But they can affect electrical currents pretty easily. Like with white noise. If a ghost is speaking, your ears won't pick it up. But if you get an audio recording, you can isolate the voice in the white noise. It's called EVP—electronic voice phenomena. Same thing with photos—even if we can't see a ghost, a camera can capture its image because it detects a broader spectrum of energy than the human eye."

She paused, popping the last bite of bagel into her mouth. "So I try to use technology to communicate. It's not that I think Sam's way doesn't work, I just think my way has a higher possibility of success. You should see my electronic Ouija board."

"Seriously? Where'd you get that?"

"I made it," Mi Jin said proudly. "It's a regular Ouija board with some modifications."

I took a sip of chocolate milk. "So the camera yesterday . . . You're saying that could've been a ghost? Not that I think it was," I added hastily. "But I know a lot of fans think the show's haunted."

Mi Jin nodded. "Yeah, totally. That's why I recorded it happening."

"So you don't really think Oscar did it?"

"Nah. He's good with electronics, but I don't think he could've managed that."

"Me either." Propping my feet up on the coffee table, I tried to sound nonchalant. "Speaking of haunted equipment, I tried to use that laptop in room 301 last night, and it kind of freaked out."

Mi Jin tilted her head. "How so?"

"Started playing old footage of the show," I said. "And then it just weirdly shut off."

"Huh. What was the footage?"

I smiled. "A tea party. Just Sam, Lidia, and Emily."

"Which episode?"

"Dunno," I said with a shrug. "I've seen every episode, but I didn't recognize it. I figured it was footage they never used."

Mi Jin paused, lips pressed together like she was weighing her words. "Could you tell where they were?" she asked at last.

"Um . . . a really small room." I squinted, picturing the scene. "There were windows, but it was dark outside. They were sitting at a little table. It looked like the room was filled with junk, like maybe an attic. But the light was too dim to make anything out."

Actually, the image would have made a beautifully creepy photo, I thought. The bulb casting a yellowish light on three people huddled around a table holding hands, surrounded by shadowed boxes and objects, the night sky visible through the windows behind them . . . *Never use flash in low-light shots, Kat; you'll flatten the background . . . Use a higher ISO—it'll give you more contrast and depth . . .*

It was a few seconds before I realized Mi Jin was talking. "What?"

"Do you think maybe it was the missing lighthouse footage?" Mi Jin said, studying me over her coffee cup. "You know, the dead air from the first episode?"

I blinked. "Actually . . . maybe, yeah. It could've been a

lighthouse. Have you ever seen that footage?"

"Nope," Mi Jin replied. "But I do know that Sam had a tea party in the lighthouse. Originally, he was going to do one for every episode, but Jess made him stop after that one." She glanced around, lowering her voice. "I overheard Jess and Lidia arguing about it once. Lidia's *way* into tea parties. You know, because of her brother."

I frowned. "You mean Oscar's dad?"

"No, Lidia's twin," Mi Jin replied. "He died when they were teenagers."

My eyes widened. "How?"

"Heart condition," she said simply. "They were both born with it, but his was much worse than hers, apparently."

I remembered Lidia taking her pills yesterday and explaining about her pacemaker. "Oh."

"They grew up in Oregon," Mi Jin went on. "On the coast, really close to that lighthouse—that's why Lidia chose it for the first episode of *P2P*. She and her brother were totally obsessed with it when they were little, because it was abandoned, but sometimes the light would just start flashing, like it was trying to signal a ship. They were convinced it was haunted." Mi Jin shrugged. "Apparently Lidia got pretty worked up during the séance. It's not good for her health. So Jess convinced her to stop doing them on the show."

We sat in silence for a minute. I pictured Lidia seated at the table, so intent, so focused . . . the way her eyes had flown open just as the bulb exploded . . .

"Morning!" Mi Jin called. I glanced over as Oscar stepped off the elevator, eyes bloodshot, black hair sticking up in all directions. Mi Jin snickered. "Wow. Kat, looks like you're runner-up in the most beautiful zombie competition."

Oscar shuffled across the lobby to the breakfast room without a word. I shook my head. "Cheerful, isn't he?"

She smiled. "You two just got off on the wrong foot. He's a nice guy."

"If you say so."

Hearing about Lidia's childhood made me wonder yet again about Oscar's father. Why wasn't he living with him? I opened my mouth to ask Mi Jin, but closed it when Oscar returned, carrying a bowl of cereal and a plate stacked with what looked like a loaf's worth of toast. He flopped down on the sofa and crammed a piece of toast in his mouth, eyeing me.

"*Psycho*?"

I was offended for a split second before I realized he meant my Bates Motel T-shirt. "Oh. Yeah."

"All you wear is horror stuff," Oscar said dryly, and I gave him an icy stare.

"One of the perks of my mom leaving. I can wear what I want without getting harassed."

As soon as the words left my mouth, I felt a pang of guilt. After all, Oscar's mom had died. He'd been really young, according to Lidia, but it had still been an insensitive thing to say. And I had no idea what the deal was with his dad.

But Oscar didn't flinch. He just held my gaze, his expression inscrutable. After a few seconds of awkward silence, Mi Jin cleared her throat.

"The first time I saw *Psycho* was at a friend's sleepover

in seventh grade," she said, and Oscar finally looked away. "I hid my eyes through most of it. Same thing with *House on Haunted Hill.*"

"That's one of my favorites," I told her. "Apparently when I was in kindergarten, I went around telling everyone I was going to marry Vincent Price."

"You watched that movie in *kindergarten*?" Mi Jin said incredulously.

"My dad and grandma love horror movies. I grew up watching them."

"And you weren't scared?"

"Well, yeah, but in the fun way," I said. "There's the kind of scared you get from movies and stories, and then there's the real kind of scared. Two different things. Horror movies are the fun kind of scary."

"I guess that makes sense." Shaking her head, Mi Jin took a sip of coffee. "I can't believe you had a crush on Vincent Price. That's amazing. And a little frightening. Although now that I think about it," she mused, "I went through a serious obsession with Cruella De Vil when I was seven. I wore fake furs and tried to convince my mom to let me bleach my hair on the left side so it'd be black and white. Somehow the fact that Cruella wanted to kill puppies didn't register till later."

Oscar was staring at Mi Jin, wide-eyed. She grinned at him. "Problem?" Shaking his head silently, Oscar shoved the last piece of toast into his mouth. "No horror villain crushes for you?" Mi Jin added teasingly, causing Oscar to choke a little. I tried to hide my laughter behind my cup.

Clearing his throat, Oscar tossed his napkin on the table. "Thomas Cooper's coming," he said curtly.

Way to change the subject, I thought, wiping my eyes. "Who?"

"Fright TV executive vice president," Mi Jin explained. "He's meeting us in Brussels."

"Nope. He's getting in this afternoon," Oscar told her. "I heard Lidia on the phone with him this morning."

"Really? Oh boy." Mi Jin leaned back in her chair, chewing her lip.

"Is that a bad thing?" I asked.

"Yup." Oscar picked up his bowl of cereal. "My guess is that he's gonna cancel the show if the next episode's ratings aren't better."

"No way." Mi Jin shook her head vehemently. "We *just* got a new host—he's not going to cancel that fast."

Oscar shrugged. "That's not what it sounded like on the phone. Lidia said something about the Halloween episode being our last shot."

He sounded supremely unconcerned, but his mouth tightened a bit. I drummed my fingers on my armrest, trying not to look as worried as I felt.

"But that's the next episode we're shooting," Mi Jin said, forehead crinkled. "In Brussels. That one will air on Halloween."

Two episodes. Do the math. I grimaced, remembering the thread about the host curse on the *P2P* forums. It didn't matter if the curse was a publicity stunt or paranormal activity—all that mattered was that if it was real, then

Brussels would be Dad's last episode.

Mi Jin must have noticed my expression, because she nudged my leg with her boot. "Cheer up!" she said. "We'll find out what's going on when Thomas gets here. And hey, bonus—he usually brings his kids! They're probably on fall break right now. Jamie's around your age, and Hailey's in sixth grade."

I smiled, but I couldn't muster any enthusiasm. This wasn't fair—they weren't giving Dad a chance. If Thomas canceled the show after Brussels, we'd be back in Chelsea by the end of the month.

And the Thing would be waiting for me. So I had no intention of going back.

CHAPTER NINE

ATTACK OF THE KILLER RATINGS

From: timelord2002@mymail.net
To: acciopancakes@mymail.net
Subject: hey

Kat—I'm not supposed to be online (grounded again, like it's my fault Trish brought Fang over and he decided to hide in our dryer while Mom was doing laundry) but I had to tell you—yesterday Trish's parents took us all out to dinner and we saw your grandma. She was with your mom. I figured you'd want to know about another sighting. Do you think she's moved back?

I'm ungrounded this weekend. Maybe we can video chat or something.—Mark

AFTER breakfast, I endured an entire hour of Oscar's dumb jokes during a geography lesson with Mi Jin. Then we read a creepy poem by Edgar Allan Poe, which would've been awesome if it wasn't for Oscar adding his own stupid commentary every other line. I was relieved when Mi Jin gave us a few worksheets to do on our own so she could meet up with the crew. Grabbing the sheets, I hurried back to my hotel room for some quiet time.

"Hey, Dad—oh, sorry," I whispered when he glanced up, phone pressed against his ear.

"Yeah, I understand," Dad said, rubbing his forehead. "Well . . . that's up to you."

I flopped back on my bed, staring at Dad's reflection in the vanity mirror. He looked nervous. He *sounded* nervous. Which was weird, because Dad was a total pro when it came to stressful job stuff. If he was stressed, it had to be because of Thomas Cooper.

"Okay. Well . . . now's not a good time, honestly. I don't . . . Look, I'll let you know, okay? I've got to go." Dad hung up and sighed.

"Everything okay?" I asked tentatively.

"Hmm?" Dad blinked a few times, then smiled at me. "Yeah, fine. Lessons going all right?"

"Pretty good," I said. "Mi Jin's really cool. Oscar's obnoxious."

Dad laughed. "You'll be friends before you know it."

"No, we won't," I said flatly. "Why does everyone keep saying that?"

"You're right, sorry." Dad stood, slipping on his jacket. "You're clearly mortal enemies born to destroy one another. Neither can live while the other survives."

"Exactly." I watched as he slipped his room key into his pocket. "So . . . Thomas Cooper's coming today, huh?"

"Yup." Dad's expression didn't change as he headed for the door. "Around four, I think—you should come down to the lobby, I hear he's bringing his kids. See you in a bit!"

"Bye." The second the door clicked shut, I tossed my worksheets aside and grabbed Dad's laptop. I had to see what the *P2P* fans were saying now.

But when I opened the forum, the title of the newest thread

pushed all thoughts of the host curse out of my head.

The Kat Sinclair Files???

Maytrix [admin]
Someone sent me a link to <u>this blog</u> . . . Looks like Jack's got a 13-yo daughter who's traveling with the show! Could be interesting. She's got a post up about the next episode in Rotterdam, which is pretty cool. But it's the second post you guys should check out—apparently the show's ghost is restless. Printer spitting out random messages, cameras going wonky, laptops turning off and on . . . great stuff! I kind of love that this girl's giving us a behind-the-scenes look.

skEllen [member]
OMG I <3 THIS!!!1!!

presidentskroob [member]
do you think fright tv knows about this blog? like, is she getting paid or something? could just be another stunt.

AntiSimon [member]
It's not a stunt. The show's haunted, that's why the equipment keeps freaking out.

YourCohortInCrime [member]
Yeah, that must be it. Couldn't have anything to do with the fact that electronics glitch out sometimes.

AntiSimon [member]
YCIC, sometimes I wonder why you even watch this show. You're not a believer.

YourCohortInCrime [member]
I watch because I want them to show me proof. THEN I'll believe.

And some kid whining about a broken laptop's not gonna do it.

beautifulgollum [moderator]
I wouldn't call it whining, YCIC. She seems like a smart girl to me. And it's great to have someone with the show blogging about this stuff!

spicychai [member]
too bad she'll be gone after the second episode. along with her dad.

I scrolled down the thread, then hopped over to my blog. Maytrix and AntiSimon had left comments on my last post: *"wow, thanks for sharing!"* and *"great posts, keep 'em coming!"* Grandma commented, too—*"Love it! Have you asked Sam about the messages? (And where are my pics??)"*

I clicked back over to the forums, relieved I hadn't described the video in detail in my post. I just said it was extra footage they never used. It wasn't my fault the video had started playing, but I kind of didn't want the rest of the crew to know I'd seen the lighthouse séance. After my chat with Mi Jin, I couldn't help wondering what the fans would think if I posted about what really happened during the dead air.

Watching the fans talk about me was bizarre, too. Most of them were nice, but the "some kid whining about a broken laptop" comment was pretty irritating. I didn't say it was *broken*, I said it started playing a random video before turning itself off. And I so did not *whine* about it. But that wasn't the comment that bothered me the most.

Too bad she'll be gone after the second episode. I pictured how stressed Dad had been on the phone just now. Roland said they did their best to make things *entertaining*—were they going to fire my dad as part of a publicity stunt?

At four o'clock, I leaned back and rubbed my eyes. I'd been poring over the *P2P* forums, looking for anything I could find about the curse and the former hosts. There was a lot. These fans were seriously chatty. I'd just clicked on yet another thread about Sam and Emily when I remembered Thomas Cooper had probably arrived.

A minute later, I stepped off the elevator and froze when someone shouted my name.

"Kat!" A round-faced girl ran toward me, her curly brown ponytail bouncing. "I'm Hailey Cooper and oh my God I think it's so *cool* that you started that blog about the show and is it really true that a ghost printed out a message for you and what did it *say*?"

Without waiting for a response, she threw her arms around me in a giant hug. Bewildered, I stared over her shoulder. Everyone in the lobby was watching.

"Everyone" included Dad, the entire crew, Oscar, a stern-looking man in a rumpled suit, and a boy my age with curly brown hair just like the girl currently wrapped around me like a spider monkey.

I cleared my throat. "Um . . . hi."

"Mr. Cooper, this is my daughter, Kat." Dad stepped forward, motioning me over. "Kat, apparently Hailey here is a fan of your blog."

"No kidding," I said dryly. Hailey giggled, pulling away so I could shake Mr. Cooper's hand.

"She's been blogging about the show for friends and family back home," Dad told Mr. Cooper, who nodded with this expression like he couldn't care less.

"That's nice," he said without giving me so much as a second glance. "Lidia, can we—"

"A bunch of fans found it, though!" Hailey interrupted, beaming at her father. "They *love* it!"

"It's true," her brother chimed in. "They linked it on the *P2P* boards."

Roland groaned. "Did they really?" I saw him and Jess exchange a look.

"They did, and a couple of them commented on her post!" Hailey informed him before turning back to me. "Seriously, though, what was the message? The first one, with the printer?"

"Um . . ." I could feel Oscar's eyes on me. I still wasn't entirely positive the printer hadn't been another one of his pranks. "Nothing, really. Just . . . gibberish."

"Oh." Hailey's face fell. "Still, though, it sounded so creepy, plus the camera thing—Mi Jin, did it really have thirteen *X*s?"

Mi Jin grinned. "It totally did."

"Awesome! Are you bringing the Ouija board to Crimptown tonight?" Hailey plowed on without pausing for breath. "Can we try it before you guys start filming? Did you tell Kat and Oscar about that time Jamie contacted that dead lady in the hotel in London? Jamie is *so* good at Ouija,

Kat. You've got to see it. It's *amazing*."

Stifling a laugh, I glanced at her brother. "It's true," he agreed, his expression as serious as Hailey's. "I'm the Ouija master." Then he smiled at me.

It was one of those happy smiles that makes you smile back like a reflex. And not that I'd thought he was bad-looking before or anything, but his whole face kind of lit up, and . . .

. . . it was a nice smile, that's all I'm saying.

"So, tonight maybe we can contact Sonja Hillebrandt!" Hailey exclaimed. "And Red Leer! See, I know the names and all about the history of Crimptown because—"

"Hailey," Mr. Cooper said with a sigh.

"Hold that thought, sweetie." Smiling, Jess ruffled Hailey's hair. "Tom, we've got the conference room all ready—should we meet you there in ten minutes?"

"Sounds good. I'll get our room key." As Mr. Cooper headed over to the desk, the rest of the crew filed slowly across the lobby. I snuck a glance at Dad, but his inner anchor had taken over—he didn't seem nervous at all. Everyone else looked a bit on edge, though. (Well, except for Sam, who wore his usual glazed "my mind is in the realm of the spirits" expression. He started wandering into the breakfast room until Roland grabbed his sleeve and led him down the hall.)

As soon as the adults were out of earshot, Oscar turned to me. "Why'd you lie?"

"Excuse me?"

"The message, the one that printed—you said it was a

bunch of gibberish. It wasn't."

"So you *did* type it up, then," I said triumphantly.

Oscar smirked. "Uh, no? You told me yesterday, right after the camera freaked out."

"Oh, right." *Dang.* I pressed my lips together, aware of Hailey and Jamie looking back and forth between us like this was a ping-pong match. "It's nothing. I just didn't want to bother Lidia and everyone else with it."

"So there really was a message? What did it say?" Hailey asked, her eyes round. Glancing over to make sure their father was still preoccupied, I pulled the paper from my pocket and unfolded it. Hailey, Jamie, and Oscar huddled in to read.

"*Keep her away from the medium,*" Hailey whispered slowly, tucking a stray curl behind her ear. "Whoa. So it's about Sam; he's the medium . . . who's the *her*?"

I shrugged. "No idea."

"And it wasn't on the screen? It just printed out?"

"Yeah."

"What's with thirteen *Xs*?" Jamie asked, and I gave Oscar a sidelong look. But either he was innocent or he had a killer poker face.

"Camera malfunction," I said carefully. "It showed up on the viewfinder for a minute or two."

"This is *excellent!*" Hailey clapped her hands in delight. "You should add this to your blog post, Kat. Like, take a picture of it or something. Oh, oh, oh, you should take a camera down to Crimptown tonight, too!" she cried, and I felt a pang of longing at the thought of all the potential eerie pictures. "I bet the fans would love to see photos before the episode comes on."

I laughed. "Fans? Like, two people from the forums left comments, that's it."

"Yeah, but . . ." Hailey's eyes darted over to her father.

Jamie cleared his throat. "We found your blog yesterday when they started talking about it in the forums, so we started hyping it up to Dad a little."

"A *lot*," Hailey corrected him. "Not that he listened. He never . . ." Jamie shot her a look and she fell silent, glowering.

"Why were you telling him about it in the first place?" I asked curiously.

"Well, because it could bring more fans in, and that couldn't hurt . . ." Jamie trailed off, looking uncomfortable.

Oscar shoved his hands in his pockets. "You think your dad's going to cancel the show, don't you."

Jamie winced. "Well . . . maybe. Fright TV is talking about making the Halloween episode the last one. They've got some new series about vampires they want to put in *P2P*'s time slot."

"But that's the next episode," I said, struggling to keep my voice low. "In Brussels."

"It's not definite yet," Jamie assured me. "That's what they're meeting about. When Dad called to tell Lidia, she swore they'd figure out a way to improve the ratings. And he said they'd have to try something new, because what they've been doing isn't working. So Hailey and I thought maybe your blog might be the 'something new' that saves the show."

I laughed dryly. "Thanks, but doubtful. That blog's really just for my grandma and a few friends."

"Let's go, kids!" Mr. Cooper was heading toward the elevator, pulling his suitcase behind him. "I promised your mom we'd call when we got in."

Jamie picked up his suitcase. "See you tonight?" he asked, looking from me to Oscar.

"Definitely," I said, and Oscar nodded. Jamie smiled, I smiled back—seriously, reflex—then he and Hailey followed their dad onto the elevator.

The doors slid closed, leaving Oscar and me alone in the lobby.

"It's over," he said, pulling an iPod out of his pocket. "Two episodes, then we're going home."

"Positive thinker, huh?"

"Just realistic." Oscar plopped down on one of the armchairs. "Can't run away from your mom forever."

It was a few seconds before his words sank in.

"*Excuse* me?" I stared at him until he looked up. "What do you know about my mother?"

Oscar shrugged. "Yesterday you said your mom left, and you seemed pretty bitter about it. If you go home, you'll have to deal with her getting . . ."

I crossed my arms. "Getting *what*?"

For a second, I could have sworn I saw a flicker of guilt in his expression. Then he rolled his eyes. "I don't know. Getting on your case about wearing all those stupid T-shirts?"

My mouth opened and closed a few times before I managed to speak. "How did you convince Lidia the reason you got expelled for fighting was because you were bullied?" I snapped. "Obviously it was the other way around."

Without giving him a chance to respond, I crossed the lobby and jabbed the elevator buttons, fuming all the way back to my room.

CHAPTER TEN
FROM BEYOND THE OUIJA BOARD

From: acciopancakes@mymail.net
To: trishhhhbequiet@mymail.net, timelord2002@mymail.net
Subject: stuff

I'm spending the night in the "haunted" tunnels tonight, so I figured I should send you guys one last e-mail before Red Leer gets me.

Mark—sorry you got grounded. And I'm pretty sure there's no way they'd let me actually be on the show. Trish—I haven't gotten to see much of Rotterdam yet, but the waterfront is really pretty. The cast and crew are cool—especially Mi Jin. You'd both love her. (Mark, she brought a huge backpack filled with nothing but comic books; she's totally obsessed. Maybe even more than you, if that's possible.) Lidia's nephew Oscar is with us, too. He's our age, but he's really annoying. Too bad.

The executive VP of Fright TV is here and he brought his kids—I just met them. Jamie's thirteen and Hailey's eleven, and they're really nice. They're both WAY into the show, and they found my blog. They think just because a few *P2P* fans from the forums like it, maybe the ratings will get better. Aaaand they said the network's probably going to cancel the show after the Halloween episode. So. That's not good.

So, you guys saw my mom out with Grandma the other night? That's the third sighting since August. I bet she thadfewfwidskefaszaaaaaaaaaaaaaaaaaaaaaaaaaaaaaaa

I woke up with my cheek pressed against Dad's laptop. Blinking, I stared blearily at the screen. Apparently I'd ended up face-planting on the keyboard. Through my sleep haze, I noticed the sticky notes with the hotel's logo printed along the bottom. On the top was a message in Dad's neat script.

Heading down to Crimptown early. Everyone's meeting in the theater lobby next door at nine—if you'd rather stay in tonight, call Lidia's cell to let me know. The front desk can connect you. If you do come, bring your camera! Grandma would love to see some pics. :)

Stay in my room while everyone else spends the night in a haunted tunnel system beneath Rotterdam? Sorry, Dad, that's not why I signed up for this adventure. I shot to my feet, staring at the clock—five to nine. Dad had placed the Elapse out on the dresser where I couldn't miss it.

Mirror check: My hair was smashed flat on the right side, sticking up on the left side. My eyes were pink and glazed over. Sweet. Nothing in the tunnels could possibly look any scarier than me.

There was no time to shower, so I swiped on some deodorant and swapped Bates Motel for the least wrinkled T-shirt in my suitcase (Zombies Are People, Too!). Four minutes later, I burst through the theater's front doors, still trying to smooth down my hair. Normally I'd just braid it, but that wasn't exactly an option now that it didn't even reach my shoulders. At some point I'd have to figure out another way to keep it out of my face.

Dad and the rest of the crew were deep in discussion

with a guy I didn't recognize, surrounded by tons of equipment. Not far from them, Oscar stood talking to Jamie and Hailey. He said something that made them laugh, and I felt a sudden flash of irritation. Did Oscar get along with *everyone* except me?

"What's with the roar face?" Mi Jin appeared at my side, looping a cable around her arm into a neat coil.

I tore my eyes off Oscar and the Coopers. "What?"

"You look pretty ticked off."

"Oh." I shrugged. "It's nothing."

"Okay," Mi Jin said easily. "So, are you excited about tonight? I brought the Ouija board!"

"Cool! Do you use it on the show?"

"Oh, no way," she replied. "It's just for you guys. You've got to stay off camera, you know. Figured I'd bring some entertainment in case you get bored."

"Ah." I glanced over at the Coopers again, and this time, Hailey spotted me.

"Over here, Kat!" she yelled, waving wildly. Jamie waved, too, and I found myself wishing I'd spent that extra minute putting a comb to good use.

"Well, go over there," Mi Jin said, nudging my arm. "Don't be shy."

I snorted. "I'm not shy. I just figure I'm about to spend the whole night around Oscar—no reason to start any earlier than necessary." Mi Jin pursed her lips together like she was trying not to smile, and I sighed. "What?"

"Well . . ." She finished looping the cable and carefully pulled the coil off her arm. "That's pretty much what he said about you right before you got here."

"*What?*" Turning, I glared at Oscar, but he was too busy blabbing away with Jamie and Hailey to notice. "See? I *told* you he was a jerk. I can't—"

"Hang on there, Miss Hypocrite," Mi Jin teased, zipping her camera bag closed. "You said the same thing, after all."

"Who's a hypocrite?" Roland appeared at Mi Jin's side, sucker sticking out of his mouth. "This one?" He gave me a pointed look, and I scowled.

"Kat and Oscar got off to a bad start," Mi Jin informed him. "They think they don't like each other." I opened my mouth, but Roland beat me to it.

"Wrong," he said, taking the camera bag from Mi Jin. "They really *don't* like each other."

I blinked in surprise. "Yeah, we don't."

Mi Jin sighed. "But why not? You're so much alike!"

"That's exactly why." Crunching his sucker, Roland grinned at me. "Something wrong?"

"Um . . . Oscar and I are *not* alike," I said, vaguely aware that my voice had risen in both volume and pitch. "At *all*."

Roland studied me for a moment. "I bet your last report card was all Bs."

Taken aback, I glanced at Mi Jin. "Did you tell him that?" I asked, and she shook her head. Roland pulled the sucker out of his mouth and smiled.

"You're smart but you don't study," he told me. "You figure why bother when you know you can at least pass, right? You usually take charge when you're in a group— teachers like you because they think you're a leader, but the real reason you do it is you'd rather delegate the work than actually do it yourself. You get along fine with almost everyone, but you have very few friends you really trust. And if someone betrays that trust, you're done—no second chances."

He smiled smugly before popping the sucker back in his mouth. Mi Jin let out a low whistle.

"How'd you know all that?" she asked Roland, clearly impressed. He shrugged.

"Back when I was a therapist, I could diagnose new patients before they finished introducing themselves," he replied. "And everything I just said about her? Oscar's exactly the same."

Mi Jin's eyes widened. "Seriously? Whoa."

"Wait, just . . . hang on," I sputtered, my face hot. "That doesn't make sense."

"Sure it does," Roland replied. "It's obvious you both have trust issues. You're classic cases."

"Not the trust thing. You said Oscar and I don't like each other because we're *alike*," I said loudly. "And let's just—let's just pretend you got it all right, everything you said. Why wouldn't I like someone who was just like me?"

Roland flashed his purple-toothed grin. "Aha. *Now* you're thinking like a psychologist."

"All right, guys, we're moving!" Jess called. Roland winked at me before heading over to the rest of the crew, and once again I had no idea if he was mocking me.

Mi Jin thumped me on the back, laughing. "Look at you, all shell-shocked. Was that stuff really true?" I shoved my hands in my jacket pockets without responding, and her eyebrow ring shot up. "Well, I guess that answers that."

I hung back as the crew gathered around the guy I now realized was wearing a Crimptown tour guide T-shirt. Jess had her camera on as the guide chatted with Dad, but I barely heard a word.

The truth was, Roland nailed it. It was weird—beyond weird—to hear someone just sum me up like that. Especially when I hadn't even thought about most of it. I mean, yeah, when teachers split the class into groups, I usually took charge of mine. But I wasn't pushy or anything. Actually, the way Roland said it made me sound kind of lazy. *Student achieves below apparent ability.* I got that comment on report cards a lot. But whatever—my grades were good enough. What difference would a few points higher really make?

And as much as I hated to admit it, Roland was dead-on about the trust thing. I'd always had lots of friends, but there were only a handful of people I really, truly trusted. Right now it was down to Dad, Grandma, Trish, and Mark.

If someone betrays that trust, you're done. No second chances.

That part was 110 percent accurate, too. I mean, if someone you trust betrays you, why would they deserve another chance? You can forgive them, but you can't force yourself to trust them again.

"Hi, Kat!" Hailey said in a stage whisper. I looked up, startled to find her at my side.

"Hi," I whispered back, struggling not to try flattening my hair again when I noticed Jamie right next to her. Oscar had followed them over, and while his gaze was fixed on the crew, I could tell he was listening. "So, you guys have done this before?" I asked. "Spent the night in a haunted place while they film?"

Hailey nodded enthusiastically. "Four times! The haunted hotel in London was my favorite."

"What about your dad?" I asked, glancing around. Hailey rolled her eyes.

"He's back in our room, of course," she muttered. "We always ask him to come, but . . ." She shrugged.

"We usually find a place to camp out," Jamie added softly. "Jess doesn't like us too close to the cameras."

"Mi Jin brought the Ouija board," I said, nudging his elbow. "After all the big talk earlier, you'd better introduce me to some ghosts."

"Just you wait."

And there was that smile again. Jamie didn't just smile with his mouth—he smiled with his whole face. His nose crinkled, his eyes brightened like he was about to laugh, even his ears seemed to stick out a little more. (And they already stuck out quite a bit. Which was fairly adorable.)

The guide started moving toward the theater's bar, and the crew followed, Jess's camera still rolling. Dad stood next to her, listening intently to the guide. I caught his eye and gave him a thumbs-up, and he grinned. Well, he *looked* confident. Maybe the meeting with Thomas Cooper had been okay after all.

Of course, Dad was a pro at pretending nothing was wrong, even when everything was falling apart.

Crimptown was a labyrinth of tunnels made of crumbling gray brick and moldy wooden planks. Rusting pipes hung low overhead, occasionally dripping what I chose to pretend was water, despite its yellowish color, on the hard-packed dirt floor. Each tunnel had a few small storage rooms with rusty barred doors, which Red Leer had used as cells to lock up the men he kidnapped until he could smuggle them to his ship.

According to the guide, Crimptown only spanned about a dozen city blocks, but the complex system of winding narrow tunnels was several kilometers long, connecting all the theaters, hotels, restaurants, and anyplace else with a bar on the waterfront. Dim bulbs hung from the ceiling, and long, wooden slides marked the spots directly below the bars. The crew all shined their flashlights up the first one we'd seen, illuminating the trapdoor overhead. It was pretty horrifying to imagine all those poor guys getting thrown down the slides, waking up a prisoner in one of these dark, depressing cells.

Two hours, five rat sightings, and countless stubbed toes later, Jess lowered the camera and stretched her arms.

"Time to set up camp," she announced. "Mi Jin, Sam, Roland, we need more footage of the trapdoors—seems like the best place for Sam to start trying to make contact. Jack, Lidia, we'll take the EMFs and start checking out the cells."

Dad glanced at me. "And the kids . . . stay in a cell?"

"Jamie and Hailey know the drill," Lidia assured him.

"No splitting up, no exploring unless it's with an adult, and everyone gets one of these." Rummaging through her backpack, Lidia pulled out a few walkie-talkies. "No goofing around with them," she added, giving Oscar a pointed look.

"Goofing around how?" Oscar asked innocently.

Lidia smiled as she handed me a walkie-talkie. "Oh, I don't know . . . adding your own sound effects while we're filming, maybe?"

Oscar stuffed his walkie-talkie in his pocket. "Amateur stuff. I can do better than that," he told her.

I rolled my eyes as we followed Mi Jin into one of the cells. "Because masks and rubber snakes aren't amateur?" I muttered. Oscar ignored me.

"All right, gather round," Mi Jin said cheerfully, plopping down on the dirt and unzipping her backpack. Jamie and Hailey immediately sat on either side of her, and I knelt down next to Jamie, doing my best to avoid a damp spot from the leaky pipes. Oscar sat cross-legged between Hailey and me just as Mi Jin pulled something out of her bag and set it in the center of our circle with a flourish. "Ta-da!"

"Wow." I leaned forward, staring at the Ouija board.

YES   NO

ABCDEFGHIJKLM
NOPQRSTUVWXYZ
1234567890
GOOD BY E

Mi Jin had attached a small, square circuit board along the top between *YES* and *NO*. A thin cord connected the circuit board to a mouse, which was embedded in the center of a wooden teardrop-shaped planchette. At the tip of the planchette was a small, circular lens.

"Why's it all . . ." Oscar waved his hand at the board. "Computerized?"

"Moving solid objects takes a lot of energy for ghosts— electricity's easier to manipulate," Mi Jin explained, flipping a switch on the circuit board. It hummed to life, the tiny lightbulb flashing green. "You use it just like a regular Ouija board."

"The electrical current helps them move the planchette," Jamie added. "Much better chance of communication."

Oscar looked about as skeptical as I felt. Our eyes met for a second, and his lips quirked up. I ducked my head to hide my grin.

Mi Jin looked amused. "We've got a couple of nonbelievers here," she informed Jamie and Hailey. "I'm counting on you two to change their minds."

"You don't believe in ghosts?" Hailey asked me, wide-eyed.

"Um . . ." I sat back on my heels, thinking carefully. I didn't want to offend her or Jamie. "I guess I just need to see proof before I believe something's real."

Hailey nodded, turning to Oscar. "You too?"

Oscar shrugged. "Something like that."

Laughing, Mi Jin stood and brushed the dirt off her jeans. "Try *exactly* like that. Just one of the many things Kat and Oscar have in common. Right, Kat?" She winked at me on her way out of the cell.

"So who are we contacting?" I said quickly, before Oscar could ask what Mi Jin was talking about.

"Sonja Hillebrandt," Hailey replied immediately, her cheeks flushed with excitement. "She's the nice one. Red Leer was evil."

"Good call," I said. "No evil pirates invited to this party."

"Oh no, I totally want to contact him, too!" Hailey pulled a small notepad and a red pen from her pocket and set them next to the board. "Angry ghosts have more energy, so it's a little easier. But Sonja's the hero, right? She sacrificed her life to save her brother and all those prisoners. It's only polite to invite her first."

I couldn't help smiling at her enthusiasm. "You're not scared at all, huh?"

Jamie shook his head. "Nothing scares her."

"True," Hailey agreed, flipping the notepad open. "Oh, Kat! Do you still have that piece of paper you've got with the other messages? Can I use that instead?"

"Sure." I pulled the square of paper out of my back pocket and handed it over. Hailey unfolded it, smoothing it out on the dirt. Jamie adjusted the Ouija board, then took the planchette and set it in the center.

"Ready?"

"Why not."

He and Hailey placed the tips of their fingers along the edge of the planchette. Oscar and I followed suit.

"So, I'll try to contact Sonja," Jamie explained. "Hailey'll write down any responses we get. We all have to focus on Sonja. Maybe try picturing her, like that portrait from your blog post," he added to me. "Okay?"

"Sure," I said, and Oscar shrugged again. The four of us stared at the board. When the planchette immediately started to move, I looked up at Jamie. "You're doing that," I blurted out, then cringed at how accusatory I sounded.

Jamie smiled without taking his eyes off the planchette. "This is how we get started—like a warm-up. We'll move the planchette around until Sonja takes over." He cleared his throat. "Sonja Hillebrandt . . . please join us. We'd like to ask you a few questions. We invite you to talk with us."

As he spoke, we continued moving the planchette in slow circles across the board. I pressed my lips together, trying not to giggle at Hailey's dead-serious expression. Jamie cleared his throat.

"Remember, everyone needs to focus on *Sonja*," he said quietly. I chanced a peek at him. His gaze was still fixed on the planchette, but the corners of his mouth twitched. The urge to laugh increased, and I bit hard on the inside of my cheek.

Nearly a full minute passed with the four of us sitting in the dingy cell in silence, scraping a computer mouse stuck in a wooden plank across a board. The whole thing seemed more and more absurd with every second.

"Oookay," Oscar said at last. "No offense, but this is—"

"It's not working because you aren't focusing on Sonja," Hailey interrupted. Her tone was terribly patient, as if she were talking to a toddler. I started snickering—I couldn't help it—and she turned to me. "You too, Kat! You have to *focus*."

Her schoolteacher voice and stern expression just made me laugh harder. "Sorry," I said, ducking my head. "It's just . . . Has this really *worked* for you guys before?"

Hailey nodded. "Yeah! We contacted our grandfather right after his funeral."

The laughter died in my throat. "Oh, I didn't realize," I said, flustered.

"It's okay," Jamie said quickly. "It was a couple of years ago. And it was just a regular Ouija board. But we definitely talked to him."

"Why are you so sure it worked?" Oscar asked.

"We asked him a few yes-or-no questions first," Hailey replied, tapping on the board. "Stuff only he would know. And then we asked where his pocket watch was."

"His watch?"

"It belonged to his father," Jamie explained. "Kind of a family heirloom. And after the funeral, we couldn't find it anywhere. Our mom was going nuts looking—she kept blaming herself for losing it."

"So we used the board to ask Grandpa," Hailey said in a low, conspiratorial voice. "And the planchette spelled out *J-A-R*."

"And you found the watch in a jar?" Oscar said. To his credit, he seemed to be making an attempt at not sounding too disbelieving.

"Nope." Hailey's eyes sparkled. "We looked in all the jars we could find, but no watch. And then we realized Grandpa just hadn't finished the word."

"Our mom interrupted us," Jamie added. "She got really freaked out when she saw us using the Ouija board—she hates these things. She made us get rid of that one, actually. Anyway, she walked in right after we got to the *R*."

"So what word did you think your grandpa was trying to spell?" I asked.

"Jared," Hailey said. "Our uncle—Mom's brother. Turns out he was going to *sell* the watch."

Oscar looked dubious. "He actually had it?"

Jamie nodded. "Yeah. We told Mom, and . . . Well, like I said, she hates Ouija boards, so at first she didn't want to listen to us. But Jared was at the funeral, obviously, and that was the last time we saw the watch, because Mom had laid it out on a table with some family photos and other stuff of Grandpa's, and . . ."

"It wasn't the first time Uncle Jared did something like that," Hailey said sadly. "Mom always calls him the black sheep of the family."

"He and Mom don't exactly get along," Jamie finished. "So she went and confronted him about the watch. She got it back, but they haven't spoken since then."

"You see?" Hailey said, sitting up straighter. "Proof. Grandpa told us where to find the watch."

I exchanged a glance with Oscar. I had to admit, it was a good story. But I wouldn't call it *proof*.

"I don't think they're convinced just yet," Jamie told Hailey with a sigh.

"Not quite." Leaning forward, I placed my fingers back on the planchette. "But I'm getting there. Convince me."

Grinning, Jamie reached for the planchette. Hailey and Oscar did, too, and we fell silent.

This time, I focused on Sonja.

I pictured her dark hair, her pale face, her delicate smile. I imagined her swapping her dress for her brother's clothes, tucking her hair up into a cap and hiding a knife under her coat. Sitting on a bar stool, fake-sipping a drugged drink, pretending to pass out, getting thrown through a trapdoor, sliding down, down, down until she hit the dirt floor, then whipping out her knife and running through the tunnels, sprinting toward this very cell—

The planchette twitched.

I barely managed to stop myself from pulling my fingers away. No one said anything, but I could tell they all felt it, too. Hailey leaned forward, staring intently at the board. Jamie closed his eyes. I glanced at Oscar, wondering if this was another prank. If so, it was a pretty mean one, considering how seriously Jamie and Hailey took this.

The planchette twitched again, then slid over until the lens magnified the letter *H*. I squinted at Oscar's fingers—it didn't *look* like he was moving the planchette, but I couldn't tell for sure. An *E* followed, then *L* . . . It slid away briefly before heading back to *L*. Then, slowly, the planchette scraped across the board to the left side, stopping on *O*.

"Hello." Jamie's voice, though soft, made me jump. "Is this Sonja?"

As the planchette crept across the board to *YES*, I glanced over at Oscar. His brow was furrowed, no trace of a smile on his face. Leaving two fingers on the planchette, Hailey reached over and picked up her pen.

"Hi, Sonja," Jamie said calmly. "Thank you for joining us. How many spirits are present right now, including you?"

The planchette moved down to the line of numbers, where the lens settled over *3*.

Jamie nodded. "Three. Thank you. Can you tell us who they—"

The planchette jerked violently, and Jamie fell silent. Our hands all moved quickly across the board as the lens magnified letters: *G–A–T–H–E* . . .

"Are you doing this?" I whispered to Oscar. He just shook his head without looking up.

Hailey carefully wrote down letter after letter, whispering each one under her breath. The planchette fell still at last, and she held the paper up for us to read:

G A T H E R T H E W O M E N

"Gather the women . . ." I chewed my lip. "That's what Sonja did, right? She gathered a bunch of women to—"

Before I could finish, the planchette jerked beneath my fingers again. The four of us stared as it scraped across the board. *F–R–E–E–T–H–E–M—NO*.

Jamie cleared his throat. "Sonja, are you still there?" The planchette twitched, then slid back over *NO*. "Who are we speaking to?"

The little green light on the circuit board started to flicker. I held my breath as the planchette began to move again.

L–E–E–R

"Wait, hold on," Hailey breathed, her handwriting getting messier as she scribbled down the new letters. "Ask about the third ghost. Sonja said there's three here."

Jamie nodded. "Is there another—"

The planchette jerked up to *YES*, then immediately zoomed over to *NO* before heading back to the letters. F–R–E–E–T–H . . . It paused, twitching.

"What's the deal?" Hailey asked, pen still poised over the paper.

"I think they're both trying to answer," Jamie said quietly. "Red Leer and whoever the third ghost is, they're both trying to control it."

Oscar and I shared a look. He wasn't buying this any more than me, I could tell. Not that I thought the Coopers were moving the planchette on purpose to trick us. They clearly *believed* they were communicating with ghosts . . . but that didn't make it true. If Jamie and Hailey knew their uncle was the kind of guy who'd steal his dead father's pocket watch, maybe spelling out their suspicions on a Ouija board had been easier than admitting it out loud.

I glanced down when the planchette lurched again. K–E–E–P–H–E–R–A–W–A . . .

"*Keep her away*," Hailey said excitedly, still scribbling. "*From* . . . Kat, this is the same message that printed the other day! *Keep her away from the medium*!" She waved the paper at me, and I let go of the planchette to take it.

The green light flickered faster . . . then stopped. The planchette fell still, and Hailey groaned.

"Did the batteries die?"

100

Before anyone could respond, a distant crash caused us all to jump. A split second later, a scream echoed through the tunnels.

Hailey leaped to her feet first. She was halfway to the cell door when Jamie grabbed her wrist.

"What are you doing?" Hailey yelled, trying to tug her arm away. "Someone might've gotten hurt, we should—"

"You know the rules." Jamie's voice cracked a little. "We can't just go running around looking for them. Dad would flip out. We don't even know where they are. We'd get lost."

Hailey opened her mouth to retort, but Oscar waved his walkie-talkie at her. "That's why we've got these, right?" Without waiting for a response, he held it up to his mouth. "Aunt Lidia? Is everyone okay?"

My heart pounded in my ears as we waited for a response. Ghosts aside, there were plenty of ways someone could get hurt in the tunnels. The last thing Dad needed was a broken leg or something. After a few seconds of silence, I pulled out my own walkie-talkie, cramming the paper back in my pocket. "Dad?" I said, trying to sound calm. "Mi Jin? Is anyone there?"

For a moment, there was nothing but a soft crackle. Then someone spoke, but it didn't sound like Dad or anyone else on the crew. The voice was distant and echoey, like a soft whisper in a large hall. But the words were very clear.

"Help her."

The four of us stood frozen, staring at the walkie-talkie. Then Hailey wrenched her arm out of Jamie's grasp and sprinted into the tunnels.

CHAPTER ELEVEN
DEAD WOMAN WALKING

I raced after Jamie, Oscar right behind me. I could just make out Hailey's curly brown ponytail as she whipped around a corner. Seconds later, Jamie stopped so abruptly, I slammed into him.

"Which way?" he said frantically. Rubbing my shoulder, I squinted in the dim light and realized we were at a fork in the tunnel. "Which way did she go?"

"I don't know." I took a deep breath. "Um, try your walkie-talkie again."

Jamie fumbled with his walkie-talkie. "Hello? Jess, Mi Jin . . . anyone there?"

I swallowed hard, willing my pulse to slow down. Maybe I didn't believe in ghosts, but between the Ouija board, the dark tunnels, and that creepy voice . . . Well, being a *little* freaked out was understandable.

After a few seconds of static-filled silence, Jamie let out a frustrated groan. "Nothing. Should we—"

THUD.

A cry of pain ripped through the air, and goose bumps broke out all over my arms. Without a word, the three of us raced down the path on the left, toward the noise. I heard shuffling sounds around the corner, and voices—one familiar voice in particular . . .

"Dad!"

"Look out!"

Jamie went flying through the air in front of me, landing hard on the dirt. I managed to skid to a halt right in front of the thing that had tripped him. When I realized it was Jess lying on the ground, a scream rose up in my throat. I leaped backward into Oscar just as Jess sat up with a sigh. *"Cut!"*

Relief flooded through me as my eyes adjusted. Roland lowered the camera and hurried over to help Jamie while Dad pulled a very irritated-looking Jess to her feet. Behind them, a huge sack lay on the ground in front of one of the trapdoor slides.

"What happened?" I asked. "We heard screaming—"

"Flour," Roland interrupted, kicking the sack. "Or sugar, I'm not sure. Came shooting down the slide and knocked Jess over."

I watched Jess angrily swipe dirt off her jeans. "Are you okay?"

"Yeah, fine," she muttered. "That was *great* footage, and now we can't even use it."

"Why not?"

"Because you three can't be in the show," Dad said with a sigh, and I winced. "You got in the shot when you came barreling in here. Are you okay?"

"Yeah. Sorry."

Roland stared up at the trapdoor. "How long have you guys been wandering around, anyway? Did you do this?"

"We haven't . . ." I hesitated, confused. "Do what?"

Nudging the sack with his toe, Roland glanced at Oscar. "This. As a joke. Because Jess could've been seriously hurt."

Oscar's eyes widened. "What? I didn't—"

"We've been with Oscar the whole time," I interrupted, glaring at Roland. "We were in the cell and there was a crash and someone screamed. Hailey ran off, and we all went after her, but we lost her, and—"

"You *lost* her?" Without waiting for a response, Jess whipped out her walkie-talkie. "Lidia? Sam? You there?"

Roland groaned, rubbing his forehead. "We lost the network VP's daughter. Perfect."

"Hello?" Mi Jin's voice crackled through the walkie-talkie, and we fell silent.

"Mi Jin, do you have Hailey?" Jess said immediately.

"Um . . . yeah, she's right here with me." Everyone let out a collective breath, and Jamie's shoulders slumped in relief. *"But I can't . . . I . . ."*

Mi Jin's voice was breathy and strange. "Are you okay?" Jess asked, brow crinkled. "Is Lidia with you? Mi Jin?" No response, just a long, crackly silence.

Jess lowered the walkie-talkie. "Okay, let's find them. And we need to keep filming." She held her hand out, and

Roland handed her the camera. "Jack, can you take these guys back to the cell, please? Roland, come with me."

Jamie shook his head. "But Hailey—"

"I'll get her, and then the four of you are going back to the hotel," Jess said shortly. "We can't afford to throw away any more footage." With that, she set off down the tunnel with Roland, speaking in hushed tones.

Dad turned to Jamie, who was rubbing his elbow. "Do you need the first-aid kit?"

Jamie shook his head. "I'm fine."

Guilt burned in my chest as we followed Dad through the narrow tunnel. What if we'd ruined his first episode? Then again, no one could possibly expect us to just sit in the cell when people were screaming bloody murder and the walkie-talkies weren't working . . .

"Help her!"

I stopped cold, staring at my walkie-talkie. Dad glanced at me over his shoulder. "Something wrong?"

"Didn't you hear . . ." I paused, looking from Oscar to Jamie. They both stared at me blankly. "Um . . . never mind."

We continued down the tunnel. Had I imagined the voice? Probably, I told myself. Crimptown was creepy, it was the middle of the night, we'd been playing Ouija . . .

There had to be a logical explanation. Just like there had to be an explanation for the sack of flour that had knocked Jess over, and Mi Jin's strange, breathy voice. An explanation that did *not* involve the show's so-called ghost.

I frowned as another thought occurred to me. Jess was pretty irritated that we'd messed up her footage of the flour sack. And Roland had been quick to accuse Oscar of setting it up. But maybe that was just a cover. Maybe this was all just part of them "making things entertaining."

Or maybe I was trying too hard to pretend something genuinely supernatural wasn't happening here.

"Jack?"

The four of us spun around. Mi Jin peered out from behind the bars of one of the cells, her eyes glassy. And behind her . . .

"Hailey!" Jamie hurried forward and pulled on the bars, then the latch. "It's locked," he said in disbelief, standing back to let Dad try. "Why is it locked?"

Dad frowned, squinting at the latch. "It's not locked, just stuck," he said, tugging on it. "Mi Jin, what's going on? Why aren't you with Lidia and Sam?"

Hailey stepped up to the bars, too, rubbing her eyes. "What happened?" Jamie said urgently, grabbing her hand through the bars. "How'd you end up in here?"

Mi Jin tilted her head, watching as Dad continued yanking at the rusty latch. "I'm not sure. Sam was trying to contact Sonja, I had the camera, Lidia went to get . . . something . . ." She blinked, shaking her head. "It's weird, I can't remember anything after Lidia left."

Dad asked question after question, the screechy sounds from his war with the latch drowning out every other word. Jamie stood pressed up against the bars, still gripping Hailey's hand. It was eerie how dazed both girls were. Neither could remember how they'd ended up in the cell. I still wasn't sure what to think about the voice on the walkie-talkie or the flour sack, but Mi Jin definitely wasn't faking this. Her handheld camera hung forgotten at her side.

Quietly, I pulled the paper from my pocket and unfolded it. The bright red letters in Hailey's increasingly messy print stood out beneath my handwriting.

KEEP HER AWAY FROM THE MEDIUM
13 Xs
H E L L O
Is this Sonja?—YES
How many spirits?—3
G A T H E R T H E W O M E N
F R E E T H E M—NO
Is Sonja here?—NO
Who is this?—L E E R
Third ghost here?—YES/NO
F R E E T H—(Leer & ghost #3 fighting?)
K E E P H E R A W A Y F R O M T H E M E D I U M

I frowned. *Gather the women.* Jess had been knocked over by a sack of flour. Mi Jin and Hailey were locked in a cell. And Lidia had apparently disappeared. So far, Crimptown didn't seem to like us girls very much.

My neck tingled, and I spun around, staring down the tunnel. No one was there. Except . . .

Wiping my palms on my jeans, I took a step down the path, then another. Dad didn't notice—he was too busy trying to get the latch to open. But Oscar grabbed my arm.

"What are you doing?" he whispered, and I pointed.

"Do you see that?"

Oscar glanced down the tunnel. "See what?"

"A light," I said. "Well, not a light . . . it's kind of a glow."
Ignoring the weird look he gave me, I took a few more steps. I
opened my mouth to call out for Lidia, then closed it. Because
this light wasn't from a flashlight. It was soft blue, and it rippled
like water.

"Kat," Dad said, and the light vanished. I whirled around.
"Where do you think you're going?"

"No, I—I thought I saw a light down there," I replied, feeling
foolish. "It could be Lidia or Sam."

"We'll find them as soon as I get this latch open." Dad turned
back to the cell door. "Stay here." The screeching resumed, and
I waited a few seconds before I took a tentative step forward.
Oscar shot me a questioning look, but I just shook my head.
And when I took off, he didn't say a word.

Well, score one for Oscar. At least he knew when to keep his
mouth shut.

I crept down the path as fast as I could, hardly daring to
breathe. Dad would kill me for sneaking off—*if* I was sneaking
off. But I was just going to the end of this tunnel. I'd seen some
sort of light, I was sure of it. Keeping my hand on the wall, I
peered around the corner. The breath flew from my lungs.

A woman stood several yards down the path, surrounded
by that bluish light—definitely not the same light coming
from the dingy yellow bulbs that hung from the ceiling. Her
hair floated in wisps around her head, and she was smiling a
tiny smile. I recognized her from the portrait in my blog post.

Sonja Hillebrandt.

CHAPTER TWELVE
CLOSE ENCOUNTERS OF THE FAKE KIND

Post: The Pirate Ghost of Crimptown
Comments: (6)
Anonymous: You poor, stupid girl. You have no idea what you're getting into.

PROOF. I'd said I needed proof to make me believe in ghosts, and here she was. But I still couldn't believe my eyes.

I stood, paralyzed, as Sonja drew closer. Weren't ghosts supposed to be transparent? Because she wasn't—she looked as solid as me. And her clothes were . . . wrong. No old-fashioned dress like in the photo. She wore a sweater, and . . . were those *jeans*?

Sonja stopped a few feet from me and held out her hand.

It was like being enveloped in a cloud of static electricity. All the hairs on my arms and neck stood straight up, and my skin tingled. I blinked furiously, my vision suddenly blurry. When something moved in my pocket, I nearly screamed before remembering the Elapse.

Tearing my eyes off Sonja, I pulled out the compact camera. It was turning off and on, off and on, the lens protruding and retracting. My hands shook as I flipped it on. *Proof.* A photo. I needed to get a photo of Sonja.

109

Her face swam before my eyes. My head felt fuzzy, like my brain had turned to cotton. I held the viewfinder up to my eye and took a deep breath.

It's dark, so you'll need a wide aperture. Hold it steady, Kat, steady—if the camera shakes even a little bit, the picture will blur . . . Kat? Are you listening to me? Kat!

"Leave me *alone*," I hissed. My mother's voice faded, and dimly, I realized another voice was yelling in the distance.

My eyes slid in and out of focus, but I could just make out movement behind Sonja. Someone was running straight toward us from the other end of the tunnel—yelling, panicked. Sonja reached for me again, her hand just inches away. Gripping the camera, I fumbled with the dials, trying to get her into focus. I zoomed in too far, and the locket around her neck filled the screen. *Locket? Locket. I've seen that locket before . . .*

"Stop moving," I whispered, dizziness causing me to sway. I had to get this photo. Actual proof.

Sonja's fingers closed gently around my wrist, and I gasped at the static spark. Her hand was warm, solid, real. When I pressed the button, the flash filled the tunnel like lightning.

Sonja stumbled—*ghosts stumble?*—and yanked my arm hard, pulling me into a cell. I tripped, too, and my head slammed into the wall just as the cell door clanked shut behind me.

Spots of light danced in my vision. I fumbled for my camera—Sonja was right there on the other side of the bars, I could still get the shot. I squinted at the screen, confused.

"What?" I mumbled, flipping the camera off and on. The message vanished, and I lifted the viewfinder to my eye. Through it, I saw Sonja on the other side of the bars. And next to her . . . a shape, an outline.

A boy.

Flash.

Sonja crumpled like a paper doll. Outline-boy made a motion as if to catch her, but his arms passed right through hers . . . except they didn't.

I lowered my camera just as Sonja's body hit the ground. But another outline—*her* outline—was still standing, gripping outline-boy's arms. Like her spirit had just stepped out of her body. Pain throbbed where I'd hit my head, and I squeezed my eyes closed for a second. When I opened them, the ghosts were gone.

But Sonja's body was still curled up on the ground.

Sam appeared and knelt next to her. "No, no, no . . . Are you okay? Can you hear me?" I realized he was the one who'd been yelling. I'd never heard Sam sound so panicked before.

"She fell," I mumbled, but Sam was patting Sonja's cheek and didn't notice me. A low buzzing filled my ears, and when I blinked, everything doubled before slowly sliding back together. I stayed there, slumped against the wall of the cell, as a distant herd of footsteps grew louder and louder.

Roland arrived next. Kneeling down, he felt Sonja's neck for a pulse, then checked her eyes. "She's breathing." Whipping the first-aid kit from his bag, Roland cast Sam an odd look. "Passed out. Did she get dizzy again?" he asked in a weirdly forced tone.

Sam nodded mutely. Roland's mouth was a thin line as he rummaged through the kit.

I almost giggled at the absurdity of the whole scene. *Ghosts don't get dizzy,* I told them, only I couldn't say it out loud. My mouth was too dry.

Jess nearly dropped her camera when she saw Sonja, her face ashen beneath her freckles. "Oh God, not again!" Turning, she shoved the camera at Mi Jin before dropping down on her knees next to Sonja. Dad appeared behind Mi Jin, out of breath. "Is that . . .?"

Sonja, I told him. *Look, Dad. A real ghost! She fell down.*

Behind him, Jamie and Hailey came to a halt, staring as Roland held a small bottle under Sonja's nose. But Oscar shoved past everyone and crouched down next to her, his eyes wide with fear.

She fell, I told them. *Sonja fell.* But no one heard. I still couldn't seem to find my voice.

Sucking in a huge gasp, Sonja sat upright. But her face looked different; that wasn't Sonja's face . . .

"No . . ." I croaked, and Dad's head jerked up.

"Kat!"

He yanked open the cell door and knelt at my side, feeling my forehead. I brushed his hand away, hotly aware of everyone staring at me. "I'm fine," I said, although I felt anything but fine. "What about Sonja?"

Dad gazed at me, eyes filled with concern. "What, sweetie?"

"Sonja Hillebrandt." I struggled to stand, the fog

still clearing from my brain. "She fell. Is she . . . ?" I stopped, openmouthed.

Lidia stared up at me from where she sat on the floor, Roland's hand on her shoulder. Her eyes were glassy, her hair even frizzier than usual . . . but it was her. Lidia in her jeans and sweater, the locket around her neck. Next to her, Sam watched me intently.

"I thought . . ." I paused, closing my eyes. I'd seen Sonja, I was sure of it. But considering everyone was looking at me as if they feared for my sanity, I'd apparently been the only one. Except—

"Mi Jin," I said loudly, stepping out of the cell. "Hailey, what happened before you ended up in the cell? Did you see her?"

"See who?" Roland said, and Mi Jin frowned.

"I don't know what happened," she said. "I was filming Sam, and then I started feeling dizzy so I stepped away, and . . . and then I was in that cell with Hailey."

Hailey nodded. "I heard Sam and Lidia talking, and I was trying to find them to see who screamed, but the same thing happened. I felt woozy, and . . ." She rubbed her arms. "Crackly."

"Crackly?" Jamie repeated. But before Hailey could respond, the lightbulb overhead flickered.

For a few seconds, everyone stared at it apprehensively. Dad and Jess held their flashlights up, and Mi Jin lifted the camera. Then the flickering stopped, and the bulb stayed on.

Lidia slumped over, and Roland and Sam both reached for her. "It's fine, I'm fine . . ."

"Get her upstairs and get the front desk to call a doctor to check her out," Jess ordered Roland, who nodded as he helped Lidia to her feet. Jess turned to Dad. "Can you take Kat and Oscar to their rooms? I'll bring these two up and tell Thomas what's going on. Jack, Roland, Sam, Mi Jin—meet back down here in an hour."

"No, please let us stay!" Hailey cried. "We won't leave the cell, I swear!"

Jess shook her head, her face tense. "Sorry, kiddo. We don't want any of you to get hurt. I'm sure your dad will agree."

Hailey opened her mouth angrily, but Jamie put his hand on her arm and shook his head.

"I want the doctor to check Kat and Hailey out, too," Dad said tersely. "Mi Jin, as well. They were all pretty . . . out of it there for a minute."

"I just got dizzy, it's not a big deal," Hailey muttered, and my cheeks started to feel warm. At least she and Mi Jin hadn't thought they'd seen Sonja. Maybe I had a concussion or something.

Jess nodded in agreement. "I'll be in to check on Lidia as soon as I talk to Thomas," she added to Roland. Her face softened when she turned to Lidia. "Sure you're okay?"

Lidia smiled weakly, her eyes downcast. "Same old, same old. I'm fine."

Same old, same old? What, did she regularly turn into centuries-old dead women? But I kept my mouth shut. I was still light-headed, and the whole experience already seemed so distant and dreamlike . . . *Had* I really seen Sonja?

I tuned out the chatter as we all headed back up to the

theater. In the hotel lobby, I waved good-bye to Jamie and Hailey before Jess herded them off to their room, promising to bring the doctor around to each of us. As the elevator doors slid shut, I watched Roland ring the front desk bell impatiently while Sam guided Lidia to the sofa. "I'm fine, stop making a fuss," she said lightly. "You know how this goes, Sam . . ."

The elevator lurched, then started to rise. Dad stared straight ahead, a tiny muscle twitching in his cheek. I knew what that meant. Grandma called it his "patience timer." When that twitch started, it meant his patience had just about run out.

I swallowed. "Is Lidia really okay?" I asked Oscar, just to break the silence. He nodded, though he looked a bit shaken.

"Yeah. This happens sometimes."

"What is *this*, exactly?" I asked carefully. "I mean, what happened to her back there?"

He glanced at me. "Seizure. Wasn't it? You were there, not me. You saw her."

"Um . . . I guess, yeah."

The doors opened, and we followed Dad off the elevator. "I'm sure they'll be sending Lidia up soon," Dad said as Oscar swiped his key card. Oscar glanced at me, opened his mouth, closed it, and shut the door in my face.

"Well, good night to you, too," I muttered. Dad stayed silent until we reached our room. The door clicked closed behind him, and he turned to face me.

"Kat . . ."

"I'm sorry," I said immediately. "I know you said to stay there, but I—"

"Snuck off anyway," Dad interrupted. "Want to give me the short version of what happened?"

I swallowed hard. "I saw a light and . . . I guess I thought it might be Lidia or Sam. I wasn't going to go any farther than the end of the tunnel, I swear. But then I, um . . ." I couldn't say it. I just couldn't tell Dad I'd seen Sonja Hillebrandt. "I tripped and hit my head and fell into that cell," I finished lamely.

"Okay." Dad eyed me in a way that suggested he wasn't buying my story. "We're filming until five. You've got my cell number?"

"Yeah."

"We'll talk about this more tomorrow," Dad said. "And we'll come up with a set of new and improved ground rules that, if you're lucky, won't involve me hiring a bodyguard to shadow your every move."

I sighed. "Sure."

"Kat, look at me."

Steeling myself, I lifted my eyes to meet his.

"If this adventure of ours is going to work," Dad said, "I need to know I can trust you."

My throat suddenly felt hot, so I just nodded.

"Good night, Kat."

"'Night."

As soon as the door closed, I flopped back on my bed and stared at the ceiling. My eyes ached with exhaustion, but no way was I sleeping tonight. Not after I'd seen a ghost.

Or hallucinated that I'd seen a ghost. I wasn't sure which thought was more alarming.

Now that the fuzziness in my head had faded, I went over every detail in my mind. Lidia's sweater and jeans. Sonja's soft smile. Sonja's features were smaller, delicate. Lidia's were more angular, more defined. They didn't look alike. I'd seen Sonja clearly, zoomed in on her face, the locket around her neck—

Gasping, I shot up off the bed and jammed my hand in my pocket. The camera!

My fingers trembled as I flipped the Elapse on and started to scroll. There was Lidia's locket with the engraved *L*, and after that, the image of Sonja standing on the other side of the bars . . .

I held the camera close to my eyes in disbelief. The clarity wasn't great, but it was enough for me to see that the woman was definitely, absolutely, without a doubt Lidia.

Had I really somehow hallucinated Sonja? Was this all part of the "entertainment"? I had no idea how Lidia could have done all that, with the light and her floating hair and the static electricity . . . It was hard to imagine the crew pulling off that kind of hoax.

I stared at the photo for nearly a minute before I noticed what was next to Lidia. A sort of shape in the air next to her, a strange blur . . .

My heart pounded in my ears. It was faint, but unmistakable—and on a computer screen, it would be even more obvious.

The outline of a boy. I had a photo of a real, actual ghost.

Wasting no time, I grabbed Dad's laptop and plugged my camera in. Jess would bring the doctor up soon, but first I had a post to write.

Maybe Jamie and Hailey were right—with this photo, my blog could be the "something new" *P2P* needed to stay on the air.

CHAPTER THIRTEEN
THE THING 2: BACK FOR BLOOD

From: EdieM@mymail.net
To: acciopancakes@mymail.net
Subject: Phone call?

Hi, KitKat,
I miss your voice! How's everything? Want to chat tomorrow?
Don't worry about the time zone, you know I'm a night owl.
Love, Grandma

SUNLIGHT streamed through the window, heating my face until I sat up and threw the covers off. In the bed next to me, Dad was chainsaw-snoring away. I glanced at the clock—almost eleven. I wondered what time the crew had finally finished.

Twenty minutes and one hot shower later, I stood in front of Oscar and Lidia's door. Lifting my hand, I hesitated before knocking twice, very, very lightly.

"What are you doing?"

Startled, I swiveled around to see Oscar stepping off the elevator holding an armful of chip bags from the vending machines. "I, uh . . ." I felt flustered. Then I felt irritated for feeling flustered. "I wanted to see if Lidia was okay."

119

"She's sleeping right now." Oscar stopped in front of the door, but made no move to take out his key. "She has this heart condition."

I nodded. "Yeah, she told me."

"Every once in a while she has these . . . seizures. She has pills for it, but it still happens."

"Right." I pressed my lips together, thinking. After a few seconds, Oscar sat cross-legged on the floor and gave me an expectant look. Sighing, I slid down the wall next to him and stretched my legs out. My stomach growled loudly. Oscar held out a bag of chips.

"Thanks." I took it, eyeing him suspiciously. "Why are you being nice all of a sudden?"

"Because you look like you've seen a ghost," Oscar deadpanned, and I smiled despite myself.

"You have no idea."

"Sure I do." Oscar crammed several chips in his mouth. "Sonja."

I gaped at him. "Wait—you saw her, too?"

Swallowing, Oscar shook his head. "You said *Sonja*. Last night, when you were on the floor in the cell. Everyone heard you." He cleared his throat. "And I don't think *you* think Aunt Lidia had a seizure. So what happened?"

I ripped open my bag, debating how much to tell him. Really, I shouldn't have been confiding in him at all—we hadn't gotten along from the moment we met. But as much as I hated to admit it, Roland was right about us being alike. Oscar didn't believe in ghosts any more than I did. I had to tell someone what had really happened, and I wanted to tell someone who thought the same way I did.

I took a deep breath. "I saw her."

"Sonja?"

"Yeah." I stared at my chips. "She tried to put me in a cell, like she did with Mi Jin and Hailey. But when I took a picture of her, she, um . . . Look, I know this sounds insane, but one second she was Sonja and then she was Lidia."

"Does she look like Sonja in the picture?"

"Nope, she looks like Lidia," I admitted. "Right after I took the picture, Sonja sort of . . . um, stepped out of Lidia's body, and disappeared."

"Like she was possessed or something?"

"Yeah."

"Okay."

I glanced at him. "You don't believe me, right?"

Oscar chewed slowly. "I believe you think you saw Sonja," he said at last, and I almost laughed. That was exactly what I'd thought about Jamie and Hailey with the Ouija board. Pretty soon I'd be on my way to Planet Nutjob with half the fans in the forum.

"There's something else." I flicked a crumb off my shirt. "There was another ghost—the shape of a person next to her. A boy. You can see him in the photo."

"A *shape*?" Oscar repeated. "What do you mean?"

Standing, I brushed off my legs. "Come on, I'll show you."

Half a minute later, we stepped off the elevator and walked down the hall to room 301. Oscar had already pulled Lidia's key card from his pocket when I pointed ahead.

"Door's open. Someone's already in there."

121

"Can't you just get your dad's laptop?" Oscar asked.

"And risk waking him up?" I made a face. "I'm trying to put the lecture off for as long as possible, thanks. Maybe whoever's in there isn't using the laptop."

I pushed the door open a little, then all the way. The room was empty. Oscar and I glanced at each other, shrugged, and walked inside.

"Carlos? It's Roland."

At the sound of Roland's voice, my heart leaped into my throat. I shoved Oscar into the bathroom just as Roland stepped into view over by the closet, cell phone pressed against his ear.

"What's wrong with you?" Oscar hissed, and I flapped my hand at him to be quiet. I pushed the bathroom door closed, leaving it cracked so we could still hear Roland's conversation as he paced the room.

"Look, I know it's been a while, but I'm trying to get in touch with Emily and I was wondering if you . . ." There was a long pause, and Roland sighed. "I know, and I don't blame you. I tried to . . . No, I really did, and . . . Carlos, would you just stop for a second and . . . That wasn't how it . . . Okay, *listen.*"

Oscar and I glanced at each other. Roland was just outside the bathroom door.

"It's going to happen again, Carlos." His voice was low and dangerous. "The *curse*, or whatever you want to call it . . . No, I'll take care of that, believe me. I just need to find Emily. Look, I know you're angry with me, but frankly, I don't care. I need you to—" He stopped abruptly, then muttered an impressive string of swear words. A few seconds later I saw him through the crack, slipping his phone into his pocket on his way past the bathroom. I waited until I heard the door click closed before exhaling.

"You," Oscar announced. "Are. Insane."

"Possibly," I agreed, stepping out of the bathroom. "Who cares, it was worth it. Now we know the truth about the stupid host curse."

"We do?"

I stared at Oscar in disbelief. "Weren't you listening? Roland told Carlos the curse was going to happen again! He said *I'll take care of that.* It really is just a publicity stunt." I shook my head. "And it sounded like he was trying to get Carlos to help him, even though he got him fired. No wonder Carlos hung up on—*ah!*"

The hotel door slammed into my arm. Rubbing my elbow, I spun around and found myself staring into Jamie's wide blue eyes.

"Sorry!" he said quickly. "Are you okay?"

"I'm fine," I replied in what was probably an overly casual voice. Jamie smiled and my anger dissipated. (Well, mostly. Oscar was still snickering at me.)

"What are you guys doing in here?" Jamie asked.

Oscar didn't miss a beat. "Spying on Roland because Ms. Conspiracy thinks he cursed the show."

"You think so, too," I shot back, irritated. "You heard what Roland said." Oscar shrugged and I checked the hallway before closing the door. "Where's Hailey?"

"No way she'll be up before noon," Jamie said. "She was

awake till almost five talking about your post."

It was a moment before I realized what he was talking about. "You read my post about Sonja already?" I asked, trying not to sound too flattered.

Jamie nodded. "Well, we figured you'd blog about it. Hailey kept refreshing the page until you posted. That picture is amazing."

"Yeah, that's what I wanted to show Oscar." I sat down behind the laptop, ignoring Oscar's loud, weary sigh. When I saw what was already on the screen, my mouth fell open.

P2P FAN FORUMS
Do you believe? Think again.

Anonymous
All you're watching is a bunch of morons hanging out in the dark faking sound effects. You've got a better chance of talking politics with a Chihuahua than Sam Sumners does of actually contacting a spirit.

Want proof? I've got it. Stay tuned to this thread to find out why this entire show is a sham.

skEllen [member]
OMG DO NOT TALK ABOUT SAM LIKE THAT HE IS PERFECT I MET HIM ONCE AND HE TOLD ME DOCTOR MEW DIDN'T BLAME ME FOR GETTING HIT BY THAT CAR SO HOW DO U EXPLAIN THAT????!!!!1!!!!11!!!!!!!!

Maytrix [admin]
Boys and girls, we've got ourselves a troll!

AntiSimon [member]
Who's Doctor Mew?

skEllen [member]
MY CAT. HE DIED LAST YEAR AND SAM CONTACTED HIM FOR ME.

YourCohortInCrime [member]
I'm listening, Anon. Enlighten me.

AntiSimon [member]
Don't feed the troll, YCIC. Sorry about your cat, Ellen.

"It's Roland," I whispered. "Anonymous is Roland. Look at the time—it was just posted an hour ago. He must've done it before we came in. And then he called Carlos."

"Carlos Ortiz?" Jamie asked, and Oscar filled him in on Roland's phone call.

I drummed my fingers on the desk. "The first time I met Roland, he admitted they fake stuff sometimes. He said, 'We do our best to make things entertaining.' Like the host curse."

Jamie frowned. "So you really think Roland actually fired all the other hosts?"

"I think he set them up, yeah," I said, relieved he was taking me seriously. "It started with Emily. She was in love with Sam, but Roland was in love with her. He was jealous— that's what my grandma says, anyway, and I think she's right. So he got her fired, and the ratings went up because everyone was wondering what happened to her. Then Carlos . . ." I paused, thinking. "Carlos was fired for writing that exposé about the show, but he denied writing it. And

125

he didn't—because *Roland* wrote it. He knew ratings would shoot up again if they lost another host."

"What about Bernice?" Jamie wondered. "They never explained why she left."

"Grandma said she was afraid of her own shadow," I said slowly. "That's why she only lasted four episodes. I asked Roland about her, too—he just said she got freaked out and left. He must have scared her off somehow. And now he's stirring things up in the forums because the show's probably going to get canceled after Halloween."

"But Roland asked Carlos if he knew where Emily was, remember?" Oscar said. "After he said he'd take care of the curse, he said, 'I just need to find Emily.' That doesn't make sense."

I gazed at the screen, dread settling like a rock in the pit of my stomach.

"Yes it does."

"It does?" Jamie glanced at the screen, too. "How?"

"The host curse," I said quietly. "My dad's next—two episodes, right? Then he's gone. But Fright TV wants to cancel the whole show after Halloween—two episodes from now. Unless something big happens." I swallowed. "Roland knows he can't keep doing the host curse. That's why he's looking for Emily. He wants to bring her back."

Oscar squinted at me. "What, to be the host again?" When I nodded, he laughed. "Why would that work? Most fans hate her!"

"Exactly!" I said. "They hate her, but they love gossiping about her. Haven't you seen those old threads in the forum?

She loved Sam, Sam was clueless, Roland was jealous . . . The fans love all the drama, you know?"

"That's true," Jamie admitted. "Although . . . if Roland's in love with Emily, why would he want to bring her back when Sam's still on the show?"

I frowned. "Maybe he thinks she's over Sam?"

"Maybe." Looking doubtful, Jamie grabbed the mouse and opened a new tab. "Oscar needs to see that photo of Lidia," he reminded me, and I leaned back as he typed in my blog's URL.

Lost in Crimptown
Comments: (27)

"Whoa, twenty-seven?" I made a move to click the comments open, but Oscar swatted my hand away.

"Hang on, I want to see the photo first."

"Fine." I scrolled down until the photo of Lidia filled the screen, and the three of us huddled close to the screen to study it. Maybe she didn't look like Sonja, but the image was still creepy—strands of hair floating around her head like she'd just pulled on a sweater straight out of the dryer, eyes wide and unfocused . . . and the outline of a boy at her side, reaching for her, just barely visible against the crumbling gray brick wall.

I glanced at Oscar. His mouth was open, but he closed it when he realized I was looking. "Okay," he said slowly. "That's . . . weird. What *is* it?"

"It's a ghost," Jamie said matter-of-factly. "Not Sonja, and not Red Leer—too small. The third ghost we contacted with the Ouija board, remember?"

"Mi Jin said something about cameras picking up ghosts even when we can't see them," I added, tracing the outline with my finger. "Something about a broader spectrum of energy."

Jamie beamed at me. "So you really do believe now?"

Flushed, I pulled my hand away from the screen. "I'm not sure," I admitted. "I mean, I don't know how else to explain this picture. And . . . she was Sonja. Lidia *was* Sonja. She grabbed my arm, and it felt like . . . like electricity."

"So you think Sonja possessed her?" Jamie asked.

"I don't know what I think." I turned to Oscar. "Have you ever seen Lidia have a seizure?"

He shook his head, glancing back at the image of his aunt, glassy-eyed and wild. "No. But I never spent a whole lot of time with her before now—she was always traveling. And she and my dad aren't really close."

As soon as Oscar finished speaking, his face tightened. I stared at him, Sonja and Roland and the curse momentarily forgotten. This was the first time Oscar had even mentioned his father. Why wasn't he living with him?

Something about his expression told me not to ask.

Jamie cleared his throat. "It doesn't *look* like a seizure," he said, pointing to the screen. "I mean, don't people fall over when they have seizures? But you said she was walking down the tunnel, right, Kat?"

"Yeah."

"She *did* fall," Oscar said. "She was lying on the ground when we got there."

"Only after I took her picture," I pointed out. "But she was walking before that. And she . . ." Sighing, I turned to face Oscar. "Look, her face was Sonja's face. I know you think I'm crazy, and I know it doesn't make sense, but that's what I saw."

Oscar gazed at the picture. "I don't think you're crazy."

"Kat?"

Startled, the three of us whirled around. Dad stood in the doorway, yawning.

"Hi," I said, suddenly nervous even though I wasn't doing anything wrong. "Everything okay?"

"Yup," Dad replied lightly. "Just need to talk to you about something for a few minutes."

He headed back into the hall without waiting for a response. Sighing, I stood up. "Time to get chewed out for running off last night."

Jamie made a face. "Good luck."

"Thanks." I glanced at Oscar, but his eyes were back on the picture of Lidia.

Dad was waiting for me by the elevator, hands stuffed in his pockets. I watched him press the up button. Worry lines creased around his bloodshot eyes. My stomach clenched uncomfortably. I waited until we were on the elevator, then blurted out:

"I'm really sorry again about last night. I didn't mean to—"

Blinking a few times, Dad waved his hand at me. "No, it's . . . not that. I mean, we still need to have that talk. But that's not why I came to get you."

The elevator doors slid open. Dad ruffled his hair absentmindedly as he stepped into the hallway. I followed him to our room, the knot in my stomach cinching tighter and tighter with each step. Something was up. Something really not good. Outside our door, Dad turned to face me.

"Your mother's on the phone."

The knot snapped.

A sort of floating numbness spread through my chest. I stood there silently, waiting. After a few seconds, Dad sighed. "Look, sweetie . . . I've really been trying not to push you. But it's been six months, and—"

"I don't want to talk to her."

"I know." Dad sounded so weary, I felt another stab of guilt. "And like I said, I've been trying to respect that. But this is different. She has . . . news."

News. A thousand possibilities jammed my brain all at once. *She got into a major art gallery. She finally opened a studio in Cincinnati. She scored a cover shoot for a magazine. She's moving to New York. She's moving to Paris.*

She wants to come back.

Not that I wanted her to. Not at all. But I wanted *her* to want to.

Dad swiped his key card and held the door open. I stepped inside, and he squeezed my shoulder.

"I'll be down in the breakfast room," he said before closing the door softly behind me. I listened to his footsteps fade as he walked down the hall, eyeing the phone on the desk. The light flashed red.

Steeling myself, I sat on the edge of my bed and picked up the receiver. "Hi."

A pause. Then: "Kat? Is that you?"

"Yeah." After half a year, I figured hearing my mother's voice again would be . . . I don't know. I thought it would make me *feel* something. But it didn't.

I heard her take a deep breath. "H-how are you?" she said.

"Okay."

"Good. That's good." Another pause. I stared at the wallpaper. Yellow with a swirly beige pattern. Fairly nauseating.

"Is it . . ." She paused, then there was the muffled sound of talking. I frowned. Did she have her hand over the mouthpiece? Who was she talking to? "Sorry, sorry," she said quickly. "So, Kat, what's it like in the Netherlands?"

"Fine."

"I'm so jealous of the traveling you're getting to do. Where are you headed next?"

"Belgium."

"Wow. And your grandma said something about a haunted prison next—sounds creepy!"

"Yeah." I twisted the phone cord around my finger and listened to her take a deep breath. *That's right, I'm not making this easy, huh? Poor you.*

"Well, um . . ." Mom cleared her throat. "So, I have some news."

News, news, news. I waited, tightening the cord until the tip of my finger went numb.

"I'm . . . engaged."

I watched the clock change from 12:06 to 12:07.

"Kat?"

"What?"

"I said I'm engaged."

My fingertip was starting to turn a sort of mottled dark purple. "What do you mean?"

"I . . ." She trailed off for a moment. "I mean, I'm getting married."

"That doesn't make sense," I heard myself say. My voice sounded calm. Detached. "You can't get married when you're already married."

Mom was quiet. In the background, I heard the theme music to some cartoon I'd forgotten the name of. "Well," she said at last. "Your dad and I are . . . taking care of that."

The cartoon sound effects got louder. Slowly, I began to realize what she meant. Married. Again. Second marriage. First marriage? Taking care of that. So:

Divorce.

Even though a small part of me had known this was probably going to happen, it was still sort of a shock. Not because I didn't think they'd ever really go through with it. But because I'd always figured when they did, Dad would be the one who told me. But he knew, about Mom's engagement— and Grandma, she probably knew, too—and neither of them had said anything. The list of people I trusted was shrinking even more.

"Kat? Are you still there?"

Releasing the cord, I flexed my numb finger until it started tingling. "Yeah, I'm here."

Mom sighed. Not in a sad way. In an irritated way. I'd heard that sigh a million times: when I wore my *Bride of*

Frankenstein T-shirt for school photos, when I polished off a pint of ice cream in one sitting, when I begged her to let me cut my hair short again and again and again . . .

"So. Congratulations." I gave each and every syllable equal, deliberate weight.

"Thank you," Mom replied. "We're thinking May for the wedding. I know it's sudden, but . . . well, that's how it happens sometimes. Anthony can't wait to meet you. I think you'll really like him, Kat. And I'd really love for you to be a bridesm—"

"You're staying in Cincinnati permanently, then?" I cut in. My face and neck suddenly felt hot, like I'd been sunburned by the hideous yellow wallpaper. It was peeling a little near the edge of the desk.

Mom cleared her throat. "No, Cincinnati . . . It didn't work out. I'm back in Chelsea."

I knew it. I *knew* it. "When did you get back?"

"June."

I froze in the act of picking at the frayed patch of wallpaper. "*June?*"

"Kat . . ."

"*June.*" I sat up, my pulse suddenly racing. "You left in *April.*"

"Kat—"

"You said you needed to move to the city for your *career,*" I said loudly. "You said you weren't happy in Chelsea. You said you wanted to be in galleries or open your own studio. *The next step.* That's what you said."

"Kat, I—"

133

"And you were only there for two months?" I laughed, a weird, high laugh that didn't sound like me. "And you—you didn't even bother telling us when you moved back. Are you seriously telling me you were in Chelsea all summer, and when I started school?"

"*Kat.*"

"What?" I yelled, squeezing the phone. "Why didn't you tell us?"

"You weren't taking my calls," Mom snapped. I felt a grim satisfaction at hearing her lose her patience. Not that it ever took much. "I told your grandmother, I told your father. They both thought I should be the one to tell you. But you didn't want to talk to me."

"I'm sorry, you're right," I said, interjecting as much sarcasm as possible into every syllable. "This is totally my fault."

"I didn't say that." Mom took a deep breath. "Look, I just . . . I wasn't happy in Cincinnati. I thought it's what I wanted, but it wasn't."

"So what *did* you want?"

Silence. I squeezed the cord again, listening to the cartoon in the background. Suddenly, I heard a child shriek in delight.

Wait, what was a kid doing with . . .

Oh.

I closed my eyes. "Who's that?"

Mom waited a beat too long to answer. "I'm sorry?"

"Who *is* that?" I repeated. "There's a kid there. Does your, um . . ." *Fiancé.* The word caught in my throat. "Whatever his name is, does he have a . . ."

"His name is Anthony." Mom paused. "And yes, he has a daughter."

For a split second, the room went blurry. It was like a physical shock—like seeing Sonja Hillebrandt gliding toward me down a dark tunnel. Then everything came into sharp, dizzying focus.

"She's five," Mom went on, her voice higher, nervous. "Elena. She's a sweetheart, you'd really like—"

"I've got to go," I said shortly. "Congratulations again."

And without waiting for a response, I slammed the phone down.

Forget ghosts. Now I had proof that the Thing was real.

From: acciopancakes@mymail.net
To: EdieM@mymail.net
Subject: Re: Phone call?

Hi, Grandma,
Everything's great. Really busy, though. Maybe we can talk
next week.
Kat

I slept for five solid hours.

It was one of those dead-to-the-world sleeps, too. Facedown,
arms tucked under the pillows, left leg hanging off the side
of the bed. When I woke up, the comforter's stitch pattern
was imprinted on my cheek.

I felt about as awesome as I looked.

After a scalding hot shower, I pulled on jeans and the
Attack of the Killer Tomatoes T-shirt Grandma had given me
for my last birthday. I rummaged through my bathroom-
supplies travel bag and found a pack of rubber bands
before giving my reflection a critical once-over. My hair was
settling into the new cut, but it was still a little uneven—
slightly shorter in the back than in the front. I gathered

what I could up into a supershort ponytail that stuck out like a bristly makeup brush, then used a few barrettes to keep the stray pieces in place.

"Nice," I told my reflection. The Thing hovered in my peripheral vision, shaking its head disapprovingly. I turned my back on it and walked out of the bathroom.

When I stepped off the elevator and into the lobby, Hailey waved from the doorway as if she'd been waiting for hours.

"Kat!" she hollered. "We've been looking for you all day! Want to come get some dinner?"

"Sounds great!" My spirits lifted when I stepped outside and found Jamie standing near the entrance, studying his cell phone. He looked up and his face broke into a smile.

"Hey! I was wondering what happened to you," he said. "Everything okay with your dad?"

"Yup!" I said, maybe a little too cheerfully. "I ended up taking a nap."

"Your dad and Jess went to do a follow-up interview with the tour guide, and everyone else is editing and stuff. We were going to walk down the boardwalk and look for a pizza place Hailey swears she saw yesterday." Jamie glanced at my bare arms. "Do you want to get a jacket?"

"Nah, I'm good."

We set off down the boardwalk, the cold, salty wind whipping my face and arms. The ponytail and barrettes were a good call, I decided.

"Are you sure you're not cold?" Jamie asked again. I shook my head vigorously, spreading my arms out wide.

My T-shirt billowed around me like ship sails, and Hailey giggled. We talked about Crimptown for the rest of the walk, and by the time Hailey spotted the pizza place, I'd gone over the entire story about Lidia and Sonja in excruciating detail.

While we worked our way through an enormous pizza with ham and extra cheese, I outlined my theory about Roland for Hailey—that he'd fired Emily just because he was jealous that she was in love with Sam, but when the ratings spiked, he realized it was a great way to get publicity. So he set Carlos up by publishing that fake exposé in his name, then found some way to scare off Bernice.

"And now he's going to try to get rid of my dad and bring Emily back," I finished, dragging my crust across my plate to soak up the cheese grease. "He's delusional."

"Should we tell someone?" Hailey asked. "Our dad?"

"No," I said quickly. "Not yet, anyway. If your dad finds out what Roland's been doing, it might just make him want to cancel the show even more."

"What about Lidia?" Jamie suggested, and I frowned.

"Maybe . . ." I popped the last piece of crust into my mouth. "Let's ask Oscar first. Where is he, anyway?"

Jamie shrugged. "We played video games for a little while after you left, but he said he wasn't feeling good, so he went back to his room. Hopefully he didn't catch Lidia's cold."

"Oh." I chewed slowly, thinking. Lidia had definitely been looking ill since Crimptown. I pictured her crumpling to the ground, the ghost of Sonja stepping out of her body, helped by another ghost . . . a boy . . .

"Who do you guys think the third ghost was?" I blurted out. "The boy ghost in the photo?"

Hailey's eyes brightened and she sat up a little straighter. "I have a theory," she said seriously. "Sonja and Red Leer weren't the only ones who died during the fight, right? Other women died, and some of the prisoners, and some of Red Leer's men. I was thinking maybe . . ." Casting a glance around the near-empty pizza place, she lowered her voice. "I was thinking maybe it was her brother."

"Whose brother?"

"Sonja's!" she said eagerly. "Bastian Hillebrandt. Red Leer kidnapped him, right? He was one of the prisoners, and he was really young!"

"But I don't think he died in the tunnels," Jamie pointed out.

"Yeah, I'm pretty sure when Dad interviewed the tour guide he said Bastian survived thanks to his sister," I added.

"Aw." Hailey's face fell, and Jamie and I snickered. "Well, I mean I'm glad he wasn't killed," she added hastily. "I just really thought he was the ghost."

"The ghost reached out to catch her when she stumbled," I mused. "I don't think he was one of Red Leer's men. Maybe he was just one of the other prisoners who died."

"Hang on!" Hailey exclaimed. "Do you still have the paper I wrote all the Ouija messages on?"

"Yeah, I think so." I dug the paper out of my pocket, pushed the empty pizza tray to the side, and spread it out in the center of the table.

KEEP HER AWAY FROM THE MEDIUM

13 Xs

H E L L O

Is this Sonja?—YES

How many spirits?—3

G A T H E R T H E W O M E N

F R E E T H E M—NO

Is Sonja here?—NO

Who is this?—L E E R

Third ghost here?—YES/NO

F R E E T H—(Leer & ghost #3 fighting?)

K E E P H E R A W A Y F R O M T H E M E D I U M

"Look," Hailey breathed, tapping the bottom of the page. "After Sonja left and Red Leer was moving the planchette, the third ghost tried to take over. *Keep her away from the medium*." She stared at me. "Whoever the third ghost is, he was with you in the theater. He gave you the same message there, too."

"So . . ." I chewed my lip. "You think maybe he's not a Crimptown ghost?"

Jamie shrugged. "He could be—the theater's got one of the entrances to Crimptown. Or he could be the show's ghost." He grinned at me. "Or maybe he's haunting *you*."

"What?" I said, startled. The Thing leaned closer, and I shifted uncomfortably.

Hailey bounced a little in her seat. "Aw, maybe he's *your* ghost." She sighed dreamily. "Lucky you."

I stared at her, then burst out laughing. "You

guys are both totally insane."

"Wait a minute," Jamie said. "The camera—remember? You were with the crew when the camera started acting weird. *Thirteen Xs.* And that was on the boardwalk, far from the theater and way above Crimptown."

"He followed you!" Hailey placed her hand on her heart. "How romantic."

"Yeah, a ghost stalker," I said, trying and failing to keep a straight face. "That'd be very romantic and not at all creepy. So what do you think his thirteen *X*s meant?"

Jamie opened his mouth, but Hailey cut him off, flapping her hands wildly. "Ohmigod, thirteen kisses! *Thirteen kisses!*"

I half-laughed, half-groaned. Jamie shook his head, his expression solemn. "It's the kiss of death, Kat."

"Thirteen of them." Hailey gave me a wicked grin, ducking when I threw my napkin at her.

"We should head back soon," Jamie said, glancing at the clock on the wall. "I told Dad we'd check in at eight."

Hailey snorted. "Yeah, like he'd notice if we didn't." I glanced at her in surprise as she slid out of the booth. "I'm gonna use the restroom first, okay?"

"Sure." Jamie watched her go, his brow slightly furrowed.

"What was that about?" I asked.

He blinked a few times. "What?"

"Hailey seems kind of . . ." I paused, unsure of how to say it. "Well, upset with your dad."

"Oh, yeah." Jamie wrinkled his nose. "It's no big deal. Our parents don't spend a lot of time with us, that's all. They're really busy at work," he added hastily. "I'm used to it, but

Hailey gets mad sometimes."

"Oh," I said. "What does your mom do?"

"Have you heard of *Head Turner*?"

Immediately, I pictured the stack of magazines that used to sit on our coffee table, each one featuring an impeccably dressed, flawlessly beautiful model on the cover. They disappeared sometime in July, although I'd never asked Dad what he did with them.

"Fashion magazine, right?" I asked lightly, and Jamie nodded.

"My mom's the editor in chief."

"Wow, that's really cool." I winced at how perky my voice suddenly sounded.

"She and Dad both travel a lot for their jobs," Jamie went on. "So, you know . . . We don't see them a lot. And even when they take us, like this trip, they just . . . They're always busy, so we still don't really see them much."

I made a face. "That sucks, I'm sorry."

"It's fine," Jamie said, a little too quickly. "Hailey's still upset that they missed open house at our school last month. They usually take turns with school stuff, but they got it mixed up this time. Dad thought Mom was going, Mom thought Dad was going . . ." He trailed off, shrugging. "Stuff like that's been happening more lately, that's all. Hailey can't stand it."

"It doesn't make you mad, too?" I couldn't help asking. "They're your parents. They're supposed to *be* there."

It came out louder than I intended. Pressing my lips together, I stared down at the table.

"Yeah, they are," Jamie agreed. "But . . . I don't know. Being angry about it isn't going to change things, is it?"

I didn't know how to respond to that. He was right, of course. But like Hailey, I had a hard time just letting go when something made me mad. The best I could do was pretend the problem didn't exist in the first place.

Hanging out with Jamie and Hailey turned out to be the perfect distraction from my phone call with She Who Must Not Be Named. We checked in with their dad when we got back to the hotel and found him on a call. He handed Jamie a handful of bills for the vending machines and waved us out of the room without lowering the phone from his ear. Hailey rolled her eyes but said nothing as we headed to see how the crew was doing.

Room 301 had been transformed into a makeshift production control room. Jess paced between the beds, barking questions and commands left and right. Lidia and Mi Jin kept scribbling, erasing, and scribbling again on this giant dry-erase board they'd propped up by the TV. Roland sat hunched over the laptop, reviewing footage and editing, a pile of sucker wrappers on the floor surrounding his chair. Next to him, Sam lounged in an armchair, occasionally interrupting Jess with comments like, "Sonja would prefer the first shot; it's more atmospheric."

"That was just lens flare," Jess said impatiently, and Roland snorted, choking a little on his sucker. I watched him closely, wondering if even now he was plotting his next anonymous post on the forums. Or if he'd managed to get in touch with Emily yet.

On Roland's screen, Sam and Lidia walked slowly through the tunnels. Lidia was rubbing her arms, like she had a chill. Roland rewound a few seconds and hit play again.

Sam tilted his head, watching the footage of himself. "That cold spot right there, that was where I felt Red Leer's presence most strongly," he mused. "Hopefully I can find it again when I go back down."

Jess sighed loudly. "Sam, we're not going back. We don't have time."

"Not to shoot," Sam said, his expression suddenly frustrated. "Sonja moved on, I'm sure of it—but Red Leer is still here. I might be able to help him."

Jess's lips were a thin line as she turned away from Sam. "Jack, did you find a few minutes we can trim out of the interview with the restaurant owner?"

"Yeah, I've marked a couple of places here . . ." Dad glanced up from a binder he was studying and noticed me hovering near the doorway with Jamie and Hailey. "Kat!" He hurried over, jumping aside as Lidia stepped back from the dry-erase board. I felt a sudden surge of panic at the concerned expression on his face. Was he was going to ask about the phone call in front of everyone?

"Hi, Dad!" I said in a pointedly cheerful voice. "How's the episode coming?"

Dad studied my face closely. I stared back without blinking. "All right," he said at last. "Good. Lots of material to work with."

"Even with you three getting in my shots," Jess added, wagging her finger at us. Her voice was light, but I heard a tinge of irritation in her tone and felt another rush of guilt.

Next to me, Hailey fidgeted. "Why *couldn't* you use those shots, though?" she blurted out. "I mean, if all of our parents gave permission, couldn't we be on the—"

"This isn't Nickelodeon," Roland yelled without taking his eyes off the screen.

"Hey, having kids on the show would probably help us bring in a younger audience," Jess joked, causing Roland to groan loudly.

Sam was watching me with a thoughtful expression. "That's not such a bad idea, actually. Children are often more receptive to messages from the spirit world," he said, and I shifted uncomfortably.

Shaking her head, Lidia stepped back from the dry-erase board. Her oversize lenses magnified the shadows under her eyes, and I couldn't help wondering if she should be working this hard after . . . whatever it was that happened to her last night. "Would you guys mind checking on Oscar?" she asked. "I think he's up in our room—I haven't heard from him in a while."

"Sure." As I turned to go, Dad put a hand on my shoulder, his raised eyebrows asking the question he didn't want to say out loud. I shrugged his hand off.

"You'd better get back to work," I said, smiling at him before turning and following Hailey and Jamie into the hall.

"They really *should* use the footage with us in it," Hailey muttered once the door was closed. "Especially you, Kat—

do you think Jess got there in time to film Sonja shoving you into the cell? I mean, can you *imagine* how much the fans would freak out if they saw that?"

"My blog post," I said suddenly. "There were a bunch of comments this morning, but I forgot to read them! Were they all people from the forums?"

"Mostly," Jamie replied, punching the button for the fourth floor. "They started a thread about it, too. They're pretty obsessed with the photo—you should check it out."

Oscar looked mildly surprised when he opened his door and found the three of us standing there. "Um, hi?"

"Lidia said to check on you." Hailey brushed past him without waiting for an invitation, and I struggled not to laugh.

"Can we come in?" Jamie asked loudly and pointedly, but Hailey was already sitting down at the desk and didn't seem to hear him.

Oscar shrugged and stepped aside. "Sure."

"Are you okay?" I squinted at him. His eyes were shiny and pinkish. "You look kind of . . ." I trailed off, reluctant to say it out loud. *Kind of like you've been crying.* "Tired."

"So do you," Oscar said, arching an eyebrow. "Are *you* okay?"

We stared at each other and for a moment, I felt like my mask had slipped. Oscar knew. Somehow, he knew about my mom's "news."

Then I shook it off. Just my imagination. It *had* to be. There was no way he could know.

The four of us spent almost an hour combing through

the comments on my Crimptown post, then the forum thread AntiSimon had started about the photo of Lidia. It was just like Roland predicted—a lot of them thought the outline of the boy ghost was faked (as if I knew how to edit photos like that). Some of them believed it was the show's ghost . . . or *wanted* to believe. But I could tell most of them were still just a little bit skeptical, even the really hard-core fans.

Not that I could blame them. I would be, too, if I hadn't seen it with my own eyes. And even so, a small part of me regretted being so honest. I'd published a post claiming to have seen the ghost of a woman killed hundreds of years ago, possessing Lidia until some random boy ghost helped her move on. Trish and Mark left comments that made it clear they thought I was joking—or at least, that they hoped so. (Grandma completely believed it, though. Shocking.)

While Oscar and Jamie raided the vending machines, Hailey and I flipped through the limited TV channels. Hardly anything was in English, so I hurried down the hall to my room to grab the *Invasion of the Flesh-Eating Rodents* DVD Grandma had given me. We'd just gotten to the extended shower scene (*not* nude—the shower curtain and careful camera work hid everything important, thank you) when Mi Jin stuck her head in.

"Just checking in on you guys . . ." Glancing at the screen, she squealed and let the door close behind her. "Edie Mills, oh my God! I love her!" Mi Jin sat on the edge of the bed where Hailey had sprawled out with a pile of candy bars. "*Flesh-Eating Rodents*—classic. *Vampires of New Jersey* is my favorite Edie movie, though. I was Maribel Mauls for Halloween a few years ago. Used a whole can of hairspray."

I wrinkled my nose. "*Vampires* is your favorite? Seriously? It's so cheesy!"

"That's why I love it!" Mi Jin leaned forward, squinting at the TV. "Hang on . . . I don't remember this scene! Are those guinea pigs?"

"Yeah, this is a special edition," I told her, holding up the case with *Never-Before-Seen Footage!* blazoned in red across the top, right above Grandma's wide, horror-filled eyes.

"Whoa, when did this come out?" Mi Jin grabbed the case and flipped it over to read the back. "I have *all* of her movies. She's the best."

"I don't think it's been officially released yet."

"Then how'd you get a copy?"

"My, um . . ." I closed my eyes briefly. *Good job, Kat.* "My grandma gave it to me."

Jamie shot me a curious look. "How'd she get it before it came out?"

"She's, uh . . . she's Edie Mills."

Four heads swiveled in my direction. "*What?*" Mi Jin yelped.

Oscar reached up from his spot on the floor and pressed a button on the laptop we'd connected to the television. On the screen, Grandma froze midscream, a rabid guinea pig gnawing at her neck. Everyone stared at me expectantly, and I sighed.

"Yeah, so, Edie Mills is my grandma."

"Um." Jamie squinted at me, then at the screen. "You and

your grandma kind of don't . . . look alike?"

"She's white," Hailey added bluntly, and I bit back a laugh.

"She's my mom's mom. I look more like my dad. Er, obviously."

"Oh, *wait*!" Hailey lunged for Oscar's laptop and sent the candy wrappers flying. "The comments on your blog— there's an Edie, right? There *is*!" She turned the laptop so we could see the screen, a triumphant smile on her face. "Edie M! She comments on every post! She's the one always asking for pictures of Sam!"

At that, Oscar burst out laughing. Mi Jin clapped both hands to her mouth, her eyes round with shock.

"Oh my *God*, Edie Mills is seriously your *grandmother*? Why didn't you tell us sooner?"

"Well, it's not like she's *that* famous," I said. "Most people have never seen her movies. I didn't know you had."

"Are you kidding? She's, like, my *idol*!" Mi Jin exclaimed. "No, for real—when I was in middle school, I only auditioned for the cheerleading squad because I wanted to be like Kimmy Kickwell in *Mutant Cheerleaders Attack*. They got mad when I brought fake blood to the first game to use during a routine, so I quit. And when I was sixteen, I was a cannibal clown for Halloween, and my friend Laura dressed up as Tina Soares—she even made this trapeze swing as part of her costume. And this one!" Mi Jin flapped her hand excitedly at the TV, where Grandma's battle with the guinea pigs was still paused. "*Vampires* was my favorite movie, but Katya Payne's definitely the best character Edie ever . . ."

Mi Jin trailed off. The room fell silent as realization dawned, and I sighed, bracing myself. Oscar was the first to say it.

"*Katya?*"

Giving him an innocent look, I ripped open another bag of Skittles and popped a few into my mouth. "Mmhmm?"

"Oh. My. God." Mi Ji gazed at me, shaking her head in disbelief. "You were named after Doctor Katya Payne, weren't you. Katya Sinclair."

Chewing slowly, I pretended to consider it. Then I shrugged. "Hey, it's better than Kimmy Kickwell."

"It's *awesome!*" yelled Hailey, while Oscar and Jamie cracked up. "No, shut up, you guys—she's named after a character her grandmother played in a horror movie. That is, like, the coolest thing *ever!*"

"Not just any character," Mi Jin added, her eyes still wide with awe. "Katya Payne—"

"Gets attacked by guinea pigs in the shower," Oscar cut in, and Jamie fell on his side, laughing. "Hiding any scars, Kat?"

Mi Jin swatted him on the head. "Stop, you don't understand—Doctor Payne is one of the best horror-movie heroines of all time. Edie won—"

"Doctor Pain?" Hailey interrupted, giggling. "Like, *ow* pain?"

"Oh man, I'm *so* calling you Doctor Pain from now on," Oscar said, grinning at me. I flicked a yellow Skittle at his forehead, sending Hailey into hysterics.

Jamie grabbed the laptop. "I'm changing the name of

your blog to *The Doctor Pain Files*," he announced, and a moment later a red Skittle bounced off his nose. Within seconds, the room was a tornado of flying candy, chips, and wrappers.

"I should get back downstairs," Mi Jin called, hurriedly backing up to the door. "You guys have a good night. Watch out for guinea pigs in the shower, Doctor Pain."

A half-empty bag of Cheetos smacked against the door the instant it closed behind her.

CHAPTER FIFTEEN
RETURN OF THE JERK

P2P WIKI
Entry: "Automatism"
[Last edited by Maytrix]

Automatism refers to a spontaneous, involuntary movement caused by spirits. In most cases, the individuals are unconscious of their actions, which are influenced by the presence of the spirit. Automatism may also be a sign of possession.

RING-*RING. RING-RING. RING-RING.*

"Make it stop," I moaned, blindly groping for a pillow and cramming it over my face. A moment later, I heard Dad flip the alarm clock off.

"Sorry about that." His voice was muffled, thanks to my pillow. "I must've hit snooze when I turned it off earlier."

"Mmmph."

"I'm heading downstairs to get some work done," Dad went on. "It's already after nine—try not to sleep in too much, okay?"

"Mmmph."

"Kat."

Heaving a sigh, I pulled the pillow off my face. "I'm on fall break, you know. We're not doing lessons this week."

"Yes, but you'll never adjust to the time-zone change this way," Dad said matter-of-factly. "Naps in the middle of the day, staying up late, sleeping in."

"Why bother getting used to it?" I mumbled. "We're leaving for Brussels in a few days, anyway."

"Brussels is in the same time zone as Rotterdam."

I wrinkled my nose. "Oh."

Dad headed to the door, then stopped and turned around. "Kat, about your phone call with . . ."

Rolling over to face the window, I yanked the blankets up and over my head. I heard Dad sigh, and a moment later the door clicked closed.

I slept for another two hours.

By the time I stepped off the elevator and into the lobby, it was almost eleven thirty. The breakfast room was empty except for Lidia and Oscar, who sat at a table in the corner talking quietly. I studied the remains of the free continental breakfast: a few cantaloupe slices, some sugar-free, taste-free bran cereal, and two muffins I was pretty sure were from yesterday.

Okay, maybe Dad was right. I needed to start waking up earlier.

Grabbing both muffins and a couple of grapes I found hiding beneath the cantaloupe, I headed over to Oscar and Lidia. "I'd kill for some bacon pancakes," I announced, pulling out a chair. They jumped, startled, and I set my plate down. "Sorry, I thought you saw me come in."

"No, we were just . . ." Blinking, Lidia smiled a little too cheerfully. "Just chatting. How'd you sleep?"

I shrugged. "Okay. How's the episode coming?"

"Great!" Lidia chirped. "Jess didn't want to use the footage of my seizure, but I convinced her." She paused, toying with the locket around her neck. "So . . . we all read your blog post last night."

"You did?" I glanced at Oscar, but he was staring blankly at his uneaten toast. "Wait, who's *we*?"

"Everyone," Lidia said. "Jess, Roland, Sam, Mi Jin. Thomas Cooper. And your dad, of course. That, um . . ." She squeezed her eyes closed for a second, as if she had a headache. "That photo of me was certainly interesting."

I choked a little on a grape. "I should've asked," I said, suddenly mortified. "I shouldn't have just posted that without asking you first. I'm really sorry."

Lidia waved dismissively. "No apologies necessary. But . . ." She coughed, and I flinched at how raspy it sounded. "But now that your blog is getting attention from fans of the show, we're going to have to monitor it. Make sure you don't publish anything . . . er, inappropriate."

"Inappropriate? Like what?"

"Anything that could violate someone's privacy, for example," Lidia said. "I'll be honest, Kat—I think it's great that you're blogging about the show. The fans seem to love it. But not everyone feels the same."

"Who was upset about it?" I asked, then answered my own question. "Roland."

Nodding, Lidia took a sip of coffee. "He's pretty against having any sort of behind-the-scenes blog, especially one written by a kid. Jess felt the same. But I convinced them that the most important thing is how much the fans love it. In the end, they agreed with me . . . so long as you allow us to check your posts before you publish them, and make any changes we ask. We'll need to monitor the comments, too—you've had some odd ones pop up."

I sat back in my chair, chewing my lip. I hadn't been planning to post about Roland and the host curse—not yet, not without proof. Still, the idea that I couldn't post *anything* without his approval was irritating. I glanced at Oscar again, but he refused to look up, which just increased my annoyance. What was his deal this morning?

"Kat, it's your blog," Lidia said. "If you want to keep writing whatever you like without us monitoring, you can set your blog to private and just give your friends and family access. But if your blog is going to be part of the show, then we have to treat it that way. We don't air any footage without approval from everyone on the crew. Same applies to a behind-the-scenes blog."

I swallowed. As much as I hated to admit it, that was fair. "Okay," I said. "I'll show you my posts before I publish them."

"Thank you." She was still twirling the necklace around her fingers. "So . . . you really thought I was Sonja, huh?"

I nodded, my mouth full of stale blueberry muffin.

"I've been trying so hard to remember what happened, but . . ." Trailing off, Lidia sighed. Then she smiled at me. "Starting to believe, are you?"

"Er . . . I guess I'm keeping an open mind." I hesitated,

watching as Lidia twisted the necklace tighter and tighter around her trembling fingers. Her face was flushed, her eyes shiny. "Lidia, are you feeling okay?"

"Hmm?" Lidia blinked a few times, her hand falling still. "Oh, I'm still just trying to kick this cold. Nothing to worry about." Yawning, she pushed her chair back and stretched. "All right, back to work. I think the others are in the conference room."

She touched Oscar's arm lightly, but he didn't look up. For a brief second, a strangely familiar expression flickered across Lidia's face. She'd left the breakfast room before I realized where I'd seen that look before.

It was exactly how Dad looked at me this morning when he'd tried to ask about my phone call with Mom and I ignored him.

I crammed the last of the muffin into my mouth, eyeing Oscar. "We saw an arcade on the boardwalk yesterday," I said at last. Oscar lifted a shoulder, still staring at his toast. "Want to go check it out?" Another shrug. I hesitated, then pressed forward. "I was thinking we could find Jamie and Hailey and—"

"No, thanks," Oscar said shortly. Tossing his napkin on the table, he got to his feet. "See you later." And with that, he walked back out into the lobby.

I stared after him, mouth open. I hated to admit it, but him blowing me off kind of hurt my feelings. Although on second thought what did I expect? Oscar had been a jerk since we'd first met. Just because he'd acted like a seminormal human being last night when we were all watching movies didn't make him a nice guy all of a sudden.

Beep! Beep! Beep!

Frowning, I pushed aside the pile of napkins in the middle of the table. A smartphone's screen was lit up with a message. Alarm: TAKE YOUR MEDS!

Lidia's reminder about her heart medicine. I stood quickly, swiping the alarm off.

I was halfway to the conference room before I realized that the phone was still lit up. The alarm message had disappeared, leaving the screen open to whatever Lidia had been reading earlier. I was about to close it when Oscar's name caught my eye.

> Dear Ms. Bettencourt,
>
> In regard to your brother, Oscar Bettencourt Sr., and his request for parole: After careful review during yesterday's hearing, we regret to inform you parole has been denied. We will notify you when the date for his next annual hearing has been set.
>
> Sincerely,
> Grace Fletcher
> Lafferty Federal Correctional Institution

For a few seconds, I just stared at the screen. Then guilt flooded through me as I realized I was reading what was obviously a very private e-mail. I pressed the button on the smartphone, and the screen went black. But I could still see the words in my mind, and with a slow, dawning horror, I realized what they meant.

Oscar's father was in prison. And he apparently wasn't getting out anytime soon.

Still staring at the screen, I walked around the corner and ran straight into Sam.

"Oh, sorry!" My voice was all high and weird. But Sam seemed preoccupied, as usual.

"Have you seen Lidia?" he asked, glancing around the lobby.

I tried to sound casual. "Conference room. She left her phone at breakfast. I was just bringing it to her."

Sam faced me, his blue gaze suddenly intense. "You thought she was Sonja."

My mouth went dry. "Oh . . . You saw my blog post?"

"Post?" Sam frowned. "Oh, yes—Lidia showed us. But when we were in the tunnels, you called her *Sonja*."

"Yeah, but—"

"You weren't hallucinating."

I stared at Sam silently for a moment. "How do you know?" I whispered.

"People always doubt their first paranormal experience . . . and second, and third," he said. "You think if you tell someone, they'll think you're crazy, so you convince yourself it was a trick of the light, or a concussion, or some other excuse. When you start to doubt—that's the real trick. You convince yourself of some other explanation. You trick yourself out of believing. But your eyes didn't lie."

I just stood there, unable to look away. For the first time, I really, truly understood why people loved Sam Sumners, and it had nothing to do with his looks. His expression

158

was open and earnest, and his airy, flaky demeanor had vanished—he spoke with such conviction, I found myself nodding along.

"I believe you, Kat," Sam said simply. "You saw Sonja. You saw her leave Lidia's body."

Swallowing hard, I nodded again. "That other ghost helped her," I said. "The one in the photo. A boy, I think."

Sam's lips curved up in a small smile. "Yes, him. He likes you, I think."

"What?" I felt my face heat up. "Who is he?"

"A friend of the show." Sam laughed when I rolled my eyes. "No, really. He's always with us. But I've never been able to communicate with him—he doesn't like me." He paused, looking thoughtful. "Ghost children always prefer other children to adults, though. They trust other children. That's why he's been reaching out to you."

"He tried on my first day in Rotterdam." I couldn't believe I was saying this out loud. But something about Sam made me want to talk about it. "When I used the laptop, there was a blank document open, but it printed out with a message: *Keep her away from the medium.*"

Sam sighed deeply, his eyes glazing over. "Ah."

"Do you know what it means?" I asked hesitantly.

After a moment, Sam nodded. "Yes. I think I might."

I waited, then cleared my throat. "Well? Who does he want you to stay away from?"

Down the hall, the doors to the conference room opened. Dad and Jess exited first, laughing and chatting. Roland, Lidia, and Mi Jin followed, all carrying armfuls of folders and binders. They headed down the hall toward the back exit. Glancing over his shoulder, Roland saw Sam and me.

"We're going back to that café Jess found," he called to Sam. "Coming?" His eyes flickered to me, and I stared back defiantly.

"I'll be right there," Sam replied. I waited until Roland had turned back around before touching Sam's arm.

"Who does he want you to stay away from?" I repeated. Sam blinked, his gaze sliding back over to the rest of the crew.

"It doesn't matter," he said quietly. "I'm already trying to keep my distance."

He gave me a small smile before wandering down the hall after the others. It was only after the exit doors closed behind them that I remembered Lidia's phone was still in my hand.

CHAPTER SIXTEEN

THE SECRET OF
THE DEAD AIR

Post: The Eternal Prison

The day after tomorrow, we're heading to Brussels to visit Daems Penitentiary, which is a few miles (er, kilometers) outside the city. Out in the middle of nowhere, according to Dad. He's been doing lots of research to prepare for his interviews, and the prison has a history pretty much as creepy as Crimptown. In 1912, there was a massive escape attempt that ended really gruesomely.

It started with one prisoner, who managed to steal a key from a guard during lunch. That night, he unlocked his door and quietly crept from cell to cell. He told each prisoner to wait until midnight, then all break out of their cells at the same time. That way, the guards would be overwhelmed and more of them would be able to escape. He promised he'd hide in the tower and deactivate the electric fence that surrounded the courtyard. The prisoners all agreed to his plan. So the first prisoner unlocked all the cells, but left their doors closed. Then he crept up to the tower, and everyone waited.

At midnight, chaos erupted. The prisoners all burst out of their cells and started running out into the courtyard for the fence. The first prisoner threw the switch and turned the fence off, then hurried downstairs to make his escape.

A few prisoners were killed, but some guards were, too. There weren't enough guards left to stop most of the prisoners from escaping. All around the courtyard, men were climbing the fence.

They were almost free.

But one guard had noticed the first prisoner fleeing the tower, and realized he'd deactivated the fence. So the guard ran up the tower and flipped the switch back on.

Ninety-four men were electrocuted. They fell from the fence, dead before they hit the ground.

The prison was abandoned after that. Dad said people are so superstitious about it that after the bodies were taken away, the city could never get anyone to buy the property, or even set foot on it to clean it up. The local legend is that every night at midnight, the ghosts of those ninety-four men roam the courtyard and try to escape. But they never make it past the fence. Locals call it *la Prison Éternelle*—the Eternal Prison.

JAMIE finished reading my post out loud and sat back in his chair.

"Wicked," Hailey announced, and I grinned.

"Yeah?"

She nodded, still studying the pictures on the screen. "Yeah."

"It's great," Jamie agreed. "These photos are really cool, too."

"Jess found those for me," I told him. Jess and Dad had read my post last night before I'd published it. After what Lidia had told me, I'd kind of expected Jess to be annoyed by the whole thing. But she'd actually seemed impressed. She'd even said my blog reminded her of an article Dad had written for their college newspaper about local urban legends.

Hailey sighed. "This episode is going to be so creepy. I wish we could come."

"Me too," I said, and I meant it. I'd barely known the Coopers for a week, but I was really going to miss them. Especially with Oscar being so . . .

Well, antisocial would be the nicest way to put it. Not that I blamed him one bit.

I hadn't told Oscar what I'd learned about his father. I felt awful about invading his and Lidia's privacy, even though it was by accident. And every time someone said *prison* or *prisoner*—which was, like, a hundred times a day, since they were all preparing for the next episode—I cringed.

Oscar never flinched. But then, he'd been spending a pretty decent amount of time holed up in his hotel room. Except for yesterday, when, after a lengthy video chat with Trish and Mark, I'd found Oscar in Mi Jin's room, where they'd been paired up against Jamie and Hailey in what was apparently a pretty epic *Mario Kart* battle. Oscar had been laughing and everything, but his eyes had still looked funny. Pink and a little too dry, like he'd been holding back tears for so long, he didn't even have to try anymore.

"Hello*ooo*?"

Blinking, I realized Hailey was waving her phone in front of my face. "Sorry, what?"

"Laser tag!" she said excitedly. "That giant arcade we saw the other day on the waterfront has it. Dad just texted—he said he'll be ready to leave in fifteen minutes. You're still coming, right?"

I smiled. "Yeah. Is, um . . . is Oscar coming, too?"

"We told him about it yesterday," Jamie replied, standing up and stretching his arms. "I think he's in his room—I'll see if he still wants to go."

After Jamie left, I clicked over to the *P2P* forums to see if there were any more comments about the picture of Lidia. But the most recent thread update pushed all thoughts of the photo from my mind.

P2P FAN FORUMS
Do you believe? Think again.

Anonymous
I said I'd prove this show is a fraud, so here we go. *P2P* claims to be the most haunted show on television, starting back with the dead air during its first episode. What really happened in the lighthouse? As it turns out, it was just a botched attempt at tricking hapless viewers. Don't believe me? Watch this little clip and see for yourself . . .

"It's the same one," I breathed, clicking the link to the video. "I bet it's the same one . . ."

"The same one as what?" Hailey asked eagerly, but the video was already playing.

And sure enough, there were Sam, Lidia, and Emily seated around the same small table, holding hands, the single dim bulb dangling over their heads. Lidia shivered with anticipation, while Sam looked perfectly peaceful. Emily gazed at Sam in a worshipful way that hovered between laughable and creepy.

Hailey let out a low hiss. "This is the one you were talking about. The video that randomly started playing, then all the lights went out, right?"

"Yeah." I glanced around my room. It was hard to feel creeped out with all the sunshine streaming in through the windows, but my arms and neck still prickled. "This is the scene . . . but it's not the same video. Look."

I pointed at the screen. A camera set up on a tripod in front of the table was just barely in the shot, capturing the video I'd seen. This camera sat at an odd, high angle, almost like it was hidden. And the quality wasn't nearly as good for the video or audio. In fact, I was pretty sure it had been taken with a phone.

"Close your eyes," Sam said softly.

"Are you sensing a presence?" Emily whispered loudly, her gaze still locked on Sam.

Hailey snorted. "I can't stand her. Bernice was the best host. I mean," she added quickly, "besides your dad."

I smiled without taking my eyes off the screen. "His first episode hasn't even aired yet."

"Well, that's true."

The lightbulb flickered and I leaned forward. "Here we go. Watch this . . ."

Emily wiggled in her chair. *"Sam, I think—"*

Lidia's eyes flew open . . . and she stared right into the hidden camera. Right at us.

Goose bumps broke out on my arms. Hailey gasped, recoiling a little. The lightbulb exploded, plunging the scene into darkness, and Emily shrieked. Shadows moved across the screen as Sam and Emily bumped into one another, knocking over chairs. Behind them, the door flew open. Light from the hallway filled the small room, and Roland stood framed in the doorway.

"Oh no, poor Lidia," Hailey murmured, and I shook my head in disbelief. Lidia was sprawled facedown on the table, completely unconscious. Sam reached for her, but Roland beat him to it.

"*Jess, hurry!*" he yelled over his shoulder. "*Lidia? Lidia, can you hear me?*" Gently, Roland rolled her back into her chair, her glasses hanging askew. He took them off and placed them on the table, checking Lidia's pulse with his other hand. Her eyelids fluttered open, and she sucked in a deep breath.

"*Wha? 'Mokay,*" she murmured. Roland's shoulders slumped in relief, and Sam sank back down in his chair, looking shell-shocked. Emily stared at Lidia with a mixture of fear and irritation.

"*What's wrong with her?*" she snapped. "*And what was that? Did you use one of those trick lightbulbs Jess bought?*"

Roland didn't look up. "*She fainted,*" he said, jaw clenched. "*Turn the camera off.*"

Glancing around the room, Emily headed over to the camera on the tripod and flipped it off. A few seconds later, the video clip ended abruptly.

Hailey exhaled loudly. "Oh boy," she said, clasping her hands over her head. "Trick lightbulbs?"

I grimaced, clicking back over to Anonymous's post.

Whoops! Looks like they let a little secret slip there. Fake bulbs. For shame. Lidia puts on quite a performance, too. No wonder they ditched this footage and went for the dead air scam instead.

It's all just a hoax, folks . . . more soon . . .

YourCohortInCrime [member]
Well, there you go. Thanks for the proof, Anon. Disappointing, but not surprising.

spicychai [member]
i am devastated

AntiSimon [member]
Hang on—Anon, how'd you get this video?

YourCohortInCrime [member]
Does it matter? The show's a fake.

skEllen [member]
OMGOMGOMGOMGADFIOAWENG NOOOOOOOOO!!!! ROLAND WOULD NEVER SCREW UP SAM'S SEANCE LIKE THAT!!!!! EMILY IS EVILLLLLLLLLL!!!!!!!!111!!!!!!!11!!!!!!!1

Anonymous
Emily Rosinski was the best thing about this sorry show. She can do a lot better than Sam, believe me.

AntiSimon [member]
EMILY was the best thing about this show? Uh . . . do you even WATCH this show, Anon?

Maytrix [admin]
Okay, everybody calm down. All that video proves is that the exploding bulb *might* be fake. (Yes, MIGHT. Roland doesn't confirm it.) And even if they've used fake bulbs, that doesn't mean *everything* is faked. Also, I'm not convinced Lidia was acting. Remember Kat Sinclair's <u>recent blog post?</u> Lidia passed out in Crimptown, and Kat's right about her heart problems. Lidia's

mentioned that on the show before. She looked like she had some sort of seizure in this video, too.

   Simon's question is a good one. Anon, we welcome everyone on this forum, skeptics and believers alike, so long as the conversation stays respectful. Please register to be a member— you don't have to publicly reveal any information about yourself. You and I can chat privately about your sources.

beautifulgollum [moderator]
Maytrix has a great point. The lightbulb thing is a bummer, but it doesn't mean the whole show's a fake.

YourCohortInCrime [member]
Your problem is you want to believe.

AntiSimon [member]
Your problem is you don't.

skEllen [member]
THIS IS THE WORST DAY OF MY LIFE

   "It's Roland," I said grimly. "I *knew* it was Roland."

   Hailey chewed her lip. "Yeah, it has to be someone from the show. Nobody else would have that video. It looked like that camera was hidden."

   "And Roland was on the forums the other day, right when Anonymous first posted," I added, pointing to the screen. "And look at what he said here. *Emily Rosinski was the best thing about this sorry show. She can do a lot better than Sam.*" I snorted. "Grandma was right—Roland's jealous. And delusional. I bet he thinks if he gets her back on the show, she'll fall in love with him instead."

"So what do we do?" Hailey asked. "Tell Lidia? Or my dad?"

I was already heading for the door. "We can't tell anyone yet. Not without proof."

I put all my anger and frustration about Roland into three solid hours of laser tag, scoring ten hits in the first fifteen minutes. I'd never played before, but it was pretty similar to paintball, which I loved. Despite my mother's protests, my thirteenth birthday party had been at this huge outdoor paintball field just outside of Chelsea. I came home with a medal, but all she cared about was my new tennis shoes, all spattered with mud and paint.

Oscar's mood seemed slightly improved, so I filled him in on Roland's latest anonymous post in the forums as we crouched behind a short wall to catch our breath.

"So you want to spy on Roland again?" Oscar said.

"Not *spy*," I said impatiently, leaning around the side of the wall and aiming my laser gun at a teenage girl with dark blond hair. "Just . . . keep an eye on him. Find some way to prove he's going to do something to get rid of my dad so he can bring back Emily." I took my shot, and a second later the top right shoulder of her vest glowed red.

"And that's not spying?"

I rolled my eyes. "Look, you don't have to help. It's my dad who's about to get fired, not . . ." I trailed off, mortified at what I'd almost said. *Not yours.*

I was saved from having to think of something else to say when Oscar's vest lit up blue.

We glanced up just as Jamie threw himself behind a glowing green column. We took off after him, weaving between columns and around other players. Finally, Jamie spun around to face us, his back pressed against the side of a fluorescent-pink staircase—but before any of us could fire, the center of Oscar's vest lit up red.

"What the . . . Who did that?"

"Gotcha."

The three of us looked up to see Hailey, lying on her stomach on the top step with her laser gun aimed right at Oscar, smiling smugly. With an exaggerated wail, Oscar staggered around in circles, clutching his chest. He fell to the floor, limbs twitching. Between his melodramatic howls of pain and Hailey's contagious laughter, for a few minutes I managed to forget the Thing had been breathing down my neck all afternoon.

CHAPTER SEVENTEEN

TALK IT TO DEATH

Post: The Eternal Prison
Comments: (1)
Anonymous: Nice post. Enjoy your last episode.

SAYING good-bye to the Coopers was painful.

"We'll e-mail lots," Hailey promised. "And we can video chat!"

"Promise?" I asked, and she nodded vigorously.

We were sitting on the couch in the lobby, waiting while their dad checked out of their room. Jamie pulled his laptop out of his backpack and flipped it open. "Almost forgot to show you this!" A second later, he turned so the rest of us could see the screen, and Oscar started laughing.

THE DOCTOR PAIN FILES

A behind-the-scenes look at the most haunted show on television.

"How did you do that?" I cried in amazement. It was my blog, but way cooler-looking. Jamie hadn't just changed the title—the whole look was different. The background was a world map, the countries a shade of gray barely lighter than the charcoal water. The header stretched across the top looked like a blurred image of a tunnel filled with a bluish light surrounding the warped black outline of a person in the center. A wispy, animated fog drifted around the title.

"It's only a template," Jamie said quickly. "And I just used Doctor Pain as a joke—I made another version with your real name. You'd have to log into your blog to upload it. If you want it, I mean."

"Um, yes, please." I leaned closer, watching the fog twist around each letter. "This is amazing. You're really talented."

Jamie's cheeks reddened. "Thanks. You have to keep posting, okay? See if you can get more photos, especially."

My fingers twitched at the thought of the Elapse. "I will, but I doubt it'll do any good," I said. "Roland's going to do something to get my dad fired, I know it. I showed you that anonymous comment he left on my last post. *Enjoy your last episode.*" I tried to sound dismissive, although in truth that comment had creeped me out a little. I'd deleted it before Dad or anyone else on the crew could see.

"That's why you have to keep posting." Jamie lowered his voice, glancing at his dad. "The fans love the curse. But they love your blog, too. And if your dad leaves, then you leave, and the blog's finished. Don't you think they'd rather have all this cool behind-the-scenes stuff than just seeing another host get canned?"

He had a point. My post about Crimptown had gotten almost seven hundred hits, mostly thanks to that photo of Lidia. Maybe my blog actually could be the "something new"

Fright TV thought the show needed to bring in more fans.

Hailey groaned, pointing at the doors. Through the glass, I saw a taxi pull up to the curb.

"Ready, kids?" Mr. Cooper called. Jamie closed his laptop and zipped his bag closed.

"Coming!" We all stood, Hailey and Jamie gathering up their bags. Hailey hugged me, then Oscar.

"Promise to tell us all about the prison!" she insisted as we walked to the doors. "Oh, and try the Ouija board again there! Oh, oh, and tell us if your stalker ghost gives you any more messages!"

"I will," I said, smiling. But a heavy sadness filled me as I watched her and Jamie pile into the taxi. It had been nice having friends here while everyone else was working. They waved through the back window, and I waved back until the car disappeared around the corner.

For a few seconds, Oscar and I just stood there in silence. That was the other thing about the Coopers—Oscar and I almost got along with them here as buffers. We hadn't technically had an argument in a few days. But things between us were still . . . prickly. It didn't help that I felt a rush of guilt when I remembered the e-mail about his father. I had to tell him I knew.

Oscar shoved his hands in his pockets. "What time did Jess say we're leaving?"

"Five, I think," I replied. "Hey, Oscar?"

"Yeah?"

"Are you, um . . .?" I paused, wishing I'd thought this through better. "I was—"

"Oscar!"

We turned to see Lidia in the entrance, her frizzy hair pulled back into a bun. She gave Oscar a bemused sort of smile.

"I thought you were going to pack this morning, but apparently you decided to fling your belongings all over our room instead." Her voice was even more hoarse than it had been yesterday.

Oscar rolled his eyes. "It's not *that* messy."

"Come on, you know it's going to take you forever to get packed." Shrugging, Oscar headed inside. Lidia gave me a pointed look. "Are *you* packed?"

"No," I admitted, following Oscar.

Lidia sighed. "Two peas in a pod, I swear."

Oscar and I glanced at each other briefly before looking away. I followed them to the elevator, saying a silent prayer of thanks that Mi Jin hadn't been around to hear that.

At six thirty that evening, I was curled up in the back of an old prison van. Jess had bought it that morning, saying she could sell it once we were finished in Brussels, so it was cheaper than renting a regular van. The seats weren't exactly comfortable, but at least it was roomy. A sliding door separated the front half from the back. Jess insisted on timing our drive so that we would drive into Brussels at sunset, which was right now. So while the rest of the crew was crammed into the front getting footage of the drive into the city and talking about the haunted prison, Oscar and I lounged in the back reading Mi Jin's comic books. Dad's voice was just audible through the door as he summarized the tragic Daems Penitentiary story. "Nearly one hundred men died during the escape attempt, most of them on the electric fence . . ."

Finally, I tossed my *Avengers* comic down. "Oscar, I should tell you that I know about your dad."

His head jerked up, his eyes wide. "You what?"

"I know about your dad," I repeated. "That he's . . . you know, in prison. Lidia left her phone on the table the other day and her alarm went off to remind her to take her heart medicine. When I turned it off, I saw an e-mail about his parole getting denied. It was an accident, and I'm sorry. But I saw it."

Slowly, Oscar lowered *X-Men*, blinking a few times. "Oh."

"I'm really sorry," I said again. "Not just that I saw it, but because . . . well. That really sucks."

He shrugged. "It's okay."

"Do you, um . . . ?" I hesitated, and Oscar watched me warily. "Do you want to . . . to talk about it, or anything?"

After a second, the corner of his mouth lifted. "Talk about it? Why?"

I sighed in frustration. "I don't know, I'm just trying to help."

"How will talking about it help?"

"You know what? Never mind." Grabbing the comic, I opened it up and furiously flipped through the pages to find my spot. "I was just trying to be nice."

We were silent for nearly a minute, listening to Jess and Roland argue about the directions. Then Oscar said: "Do you want to talk about your mom getting married again?"

The van hit a bump, and I gasped as *Avengers* went flying out of my hands. *"What?"*

Oscar rubbed the back of his head where it had bumped into the side of the van. "If talking about stuff is so helpful, why don't you talk about your mom getting engaged?"

"How do you know about that?" I demanded, sitting up straight.

Sighing, Oscar tossed his comic down. "When I first got here, I kept waking up really early," he began. "I could never go back to sleep, so I'd go to the breakfast room to make some waffles, and—"

"They had *waffles*?" I interrupted, outraged.

Oscar looked like he was trying not to laugh. "Yeah, but they were always out of batter by the time you woke up," he said, and I made a face. "Anyway, once I was full, I could usually go back to sleep. I think it was maybe the second day you were here—I went down right before six, and your dad was in the breakfast room video-chatting with someone. I guess he didn't want to wake you up. And . . . well, I figured out it was your mom he was talking to, and she told him that she was engaged."

I pictured Dad alone in the breakfast room, laptop open, Mom on the screen. *I have some news.* A rush of anger flooded through me.

"Sorry," Oscar added, and I glanced at him. "I mean, it was an accident, just like you with Aunt Lidia's phone. But still. I'm sorry."

I nodded stiffly. "It's fine."

"Do you want your parents to get back together?"

I blinked, surprised at the bluntness of the question. "No."

"Really?"

"Really," I said honestly. "Neither of them was happy." I pressed my lips together. There was more to it than that, of course.

"Do you want to talk about it?" Oscar asked, his tone slightly mocking.

For a moment, I just gaped at him. Because he was smirking. Like this was funny.

Then I realized . . . it *was* kind of funny.

"You know, I really, really don't," I said, shaking my head. "At *all*. Why do people always think talking about something that makes you miserable is going to help?"

"Exactly!" Oscar exclaimed. "Maybe it'll just make you feel worse."

"Let's see." I cleared my throat. "Last April, my mom suddenly decided she wanted to go be a famous photographer, and she had to do it *alone*. So she ditched us and moved to Cincinnati. She's taken off twice before, by the way, but she always came home after a few weeks. This time she came back to town in June without even telling me, and now all of a sudden she's marrying some guy *who has a daughter*. Gee, saying that out loud helped a ton. I feel *so* much better now."

Oscar leaned forward in his seat, his expression earnest. "My dad used to own a chain of cafés. When I was nine, he got audited and they found out he had some sort of embezzlement thing going on. He basically stole a ton of money from his own employees. During the trial, his name was all over the headlines of the local newspapers every day, and they made him sound like a supervillain with all these stupid nicknames. And we have *the same name*. He was sentenced to ten years in prison, and I got called 'Bettencrook' for most of fifth grade." Oscar threw his hands up in the air, eyes wide in mock surprise. "Magic! Talking about it fixed everything."

We both started laughing. It was that uncontrollable kind of laughter, where your chest starts to really ache but you can't stop. A minute later, the door slid open.

"Everything okay back here?" Mi Jin asked.

I nodded, wiping my eyes. "Great."

"We just solved all our problems," Oscar added.

Mi Jin looked amused. "Glad to hear it, but could you guys keep it down a little? We're going to start filming again—we're just a few minutes from the city. And be careful with the preciouses," she added sternly, gesturing to the comics strewn on the floor before sliding the door shut again.

I reached down to pick up *Avengers*. "Do you at least get to visit your dad?"

"Yeah." Oscar grabbed his comic, too. "But I haven't since I got expelled. Don't really want to have that conversation."

"I don't blame you," I said, flipping back to my spot. "All of that happened when you were nine, and kids at your school were still giving you a hard time about it in eighth grade? Lame."

"What?"

"That's why you got expelled, right?" I glanced at him.

"Lidia said you were bullied—wasn't it because of what happened with your dad?"

Oscar's smile vanished. "No, it wasn't about that. I, um . . . got in a fight with Mark."

Frowning, I remembered my first conversation with Oscar.

I had a friend named Mark, too.

Had? What, is he dead or something?

"Oh. What, um . . ." I trailed off as Oscar buried his head in his comic. Whatever had happened, obviously he didn't want to talk about it. So I closed my mouth and went back to reading. I was curious, but we'd already talked enough. And after all, I hadn't told him about the Thing.

Some stuff just hurt too much to say out loud.

Talking about *not* talking about our problems actually did help in one way—all the tension between Oscar and me had pretty much disappeared. It was like we'd bonded over our mutual agreement to shove our feelings down and not talk about them, ever. Roland would probably have a lot to say about how unhealthy that was, but I didn't care. Telling someone about the Thing wouldn't make any difference at this point. The Thing was officially indestructible.

"Why do we have to completely unload?" Mi Jin grumbled, crawling back into the van. "Can't we leave some of this stuff in here?"

"Can't lock it," Jess said, grabbing a stack of tripods. "It's a prison van—two lock systems. The exterior lock keeps people in, the interior lock keeps people out. The guy I bought it from said the interior lock has been broken for a few years, so we can't stop anyone from getting in. That's why it was so cheap."

She headed back inside, followed by Sam, who was loaded down with several equipment bags. The drive through Brussels had been amazing—I'd never seen such opulent buildings, with arches and turrets and intricate carvings all lit up and golden against the purplish-blue sky. We'd passed some of the fanciest, most castle-like hotels I'd ever seen.

Our hotel was not one of them.

"Looks like my college dorm," Mi Jin joked when she noticed my expression. "Only with smaller rooms."

I grinned, taking the bag she was holding out. When I stepped away from the van, Oscar pulled me aside.

"What?" I asked, but he just shook his head. I watched as he checked to make sure Mi Jin was all the way inside the van. Then he grabbed the handle to the sliding door and pulled hard. The door slammed shut, and through the barred window, we saw Mi Jin spin around.

"Hey!" She tugged on the door, her expression confused. "What are you doing?"

"Exterior locks!" Oscar said. "Just wanted to test them out."

Mi Jin grabbed the bars, and made a face like she was screaming. Laughing, I pulled the Elapse out of my pocket. "Do that again!"

A minute later, Dad came out of the hotel and found

us in the middle of a photo shoot, with Mi Jin smashing her face between the bars, and Oscar pretending to pick the lock.

"That's enough," Dad said mildly, pulling the door open. Mi Jin hopped out, looking pleased.

"Send me those, okay?"

"Sure!" I flipped through the photos on my viewfinder. Several of them were pretty funny-looking. Hopefully the *P2P* fans would think so, too. I turned off the Elapse, and it promptly turned on again. "What the . . ."

WARNING! High Voltage

I frowned, holding the camera closer to my eyes. I'd almost forgotten the other time I'd seen this message—in Crimptown, right before I'd tried to take the photo of Sonja. But it didn't make sense. It wasn't like a camera could *shock* you.

"There's an Internet café over there," Oscar said.

"Huh?"

Oscar pointed across the street. "You could post those on your blog."

"Oh," I said. "How'd you know I was thinking about posting these?"

"Why do you think I locked her in there in the first place?" he replied, and I smiled.

"Dad, we're going to the, um . . ." I paused, squinting at the name of the café. *Ciel Numérique.* "Uh . . . whatever that says."

"Ciel Numérique," Oscar said. "It's French, I think . . . Which is weird. I thought Aunt Lidia said they speak Dutch in Belgium."

"Dutch, French, and German are all official languages here," Dad replied promptly, heaving a speaker out of the van. "Be back at the hotel by nine, okay? Not a minute later, and no detours."

"Okay."

Oscar and I headed to the intersection and waited for the light. "You speak French?" I asked him.

"Portuguese," he replied. "Sort of. My grandparents speak it—the only time I really use it is around them. Some of the words are similar to French and Spanish, though."

"That's really cool," I said, reaching for the door. "I—ow!" A thin, pale woman with dark hair and a haughty expression pushed past us.

"Excuse you," Oscar said loudly. Scowling, she glanced from Oscar to me, and her eyes widened a little. Shoving on a pair of oversize sunglasses, she hurried down the street toward the bus stop without so much as an apology.

"Rude," Oscar muttered.

I stared at her retreating back, hit with a feeling of déjà vu. "I've seen her before, I think. Did she look familiar to you?"

"Nope." Oscar pulled the door open, and I followed him inside. We found two free computers side by side and sat down. I powered on my computer and waited for it to load, thinking about the sunglasses woman. It wasn't until I saw the coastal wallpaper on the desktop that I remembered.

"The waterfront!"

"What about it?"

"That's where I've seen her," I told Oscar excitedly. "The

day on the waterfront in Rotterdam. I bumped into her and she dropped her camera. It was her, I'm positive."

Oscar opened his browser. "So?"

"So don't you think that's kind of weird that she's here now, the same time as us?"

He shrugged. "Just a coincidence. She's a tourist. Brussels isn't that long of a bus ride from Rotterdam."

"I guess." But something nagged at me. Closing my eyes, I pictured her: pale, pointed face, sunken cheeks, sharp nose, long, straight dark hair . . .

"Kat."

"What?"

"Look at this."

Leaning over, I stared at Oscar's screen, and all thoughts of the snotty waterfront woman vanished.

P2P FAN FORUMS
Do you believe? Think again.

Anonymous
"The most fraudulent show on television" is heading to Brussels to visit Daems Penitentiary. Fake lightbulbs are nothing compared to what they've got planned for this episode—after all, they know it'll be their last one. Desperate times call for desperate measures . . .

Maytrix [admin]
Anon, please set up an account.

presidentskroob [member]
what makes you so sure it'll be the last episode?

YourCohortInCrime [member]
Rumor is if ratings aren't up by Halloween, the show's getting replaced with that new vampire series. The Brussels episode will air on Halloween, so it'll probably be the last one.

randomsandwich [member]
don't forget the curse. even if the show makes it, this is Jack's last episode.

Anonymous
It's everyone's last episode.

AntiSimon [member]
You don't know that for sure. The preview of the Crimptown episode they released yesterday is already getting a lot of buzz. I think ratings are going to be good for that one.

skEllen [member]
SAM LOOKED AMAZING IN THAT PREVIEW!!! I CAN'T WAIT!!!

Anonymous
[comment deleted by administrator]

skEllen [member]
WHAT????!!!!!!!11!!!!!!!!!!!1!! D:

YourCohortInCrime [member]
Whoa. Anon, I was on your side. But death threats aren't cool.

Maytrix [admin]
Post deleted. Sorry, all. Please keep an eye out for this troll and let me know if he pops up in another thread. I'm closing this one permanently.

"*Death* threat?"

Oscar frowned. "Why would he threaten anyone?"

"To cause trouble," I said in disgust. "Look—that post says it's my dad's last episode, and then Roland said it's *everyone's* last episode. And then he followed that with a death threat. The fans will definitely talk about *that*."

Oscar watched as I opened the forums on my computer and clicked CREATE NEW ACCOUNT. "Um, what are you doing?"

"Making a forum account."

"Why?"

Logging into my e-mail, I opened the new message that had popped up asking for me to confirm my *P2P* forum membership. "Because I want to post. I can't write about this on my blog since I promised Lidia I'd get approval first. But they can't stop me from joining the forums."

Oscar stared at me. "You're not going to say anything about Roland, are you?"

I ignored him, already typing furiously.

"Don't." Oscar shook his head, and I smacked his hand away from the mouse. "No, seriously, Kat. Don't post that."

"Too late." I clicked SUBMIT, then sat back in my chair. My heart was pounding like I'd just sprinted a mile. Oscar let out a long, slow breath.

"Roland's going to be mad."

"So?" I tried to sound indifferent. "I'm not going to let him get my dad fired."

Oscar grimaced. "I'm starting to think firing your dad isn't the worst thing he could do."

"Don't be so dramatic," I snapped, clicking back over to

my e-mail. "Roland's not actually going to hurt anyone. It's just stupid publicity stuff."

But I couldn't shake off a tingle of fear. And as I wrote a long e-mail explaining everything to Jamie and Hailey, I kept glancing over my shoulder, half-expecting to see a furious Roland barge through the doors at any second.

CHAPTER EIGHTEEN
STALKER IN THE CITY

P2P FAN FORUMS
A Message for "Anonymous"

Doctor Pain [new member]
My name is Kat Sinclair, and my dad is the new host of *P2P*. Some of you have already seen my blog. I actually only started it for my grandma and my friends to read. But I'm glad you guys like the posts.

I'm a skeptic when it comes to ghosts, but since I joined *P2P*, I've honestly seen some stuff I can't explain. (I didn't fake that picture of the outline next to Lidia. I still haven't figured out what that was.) I'm going to keep posting behind-the-scenes stuff about Brussels and the Daems prison episode, and hopefully more episodes after that. I hope you'll share them with your friends and convince them to watch and decide for themselves what's real and what isn't.

And Anonymous, if you're reading this: The only fraud here is you.

BETWEEN traveling to Brussels and the creepy situation with Roland, I'd pretty much forgotten about school. Oscar and I spent most of the next few days in Mi Jin's room going over history lessons and math problems. With our minds full of death threats and impending visits to haunted

187

prisons, focusing on something as mind-numbing as linear equations was next to impossible.

The Crimptown episode aired our second night in Brussels. Jess streamed it on her laptop, and I watched it in her room with the rest of the crew (minus Lidia, whose cold was getting really nasty). I had to admit, the episode was pretty freaky. The fans on the forum seemed to agree. So did Grandma, who'd e-mailed me an in-depth review a few hours later. But the best news came the following morning, right in the middle of a lesson on the Battle of Antietam.

"Ratings are up 20 percent from the last episode." I barely got a glimpse of Jess's freckled face before she hurried down the hall to the next room. Oscar and I stared at the door, then at Mi Jin. She blinked a few times.

"Good," she said at last. "Yeah, that's good."

Oscar and I shared a cautious smile. The response to my forum post had been insane—as of this morning, the thread was already six pages long. Most of them seemed to think I was either really brave or really stupid. But more important, there were lots of new members. More fans were joining the forums, which I figured had to be a good sign. And my blog post with the funny prison-van photos had gotten almost one hundred comments, most of them from people I didn't know (in real life *or* from the forums). "Anonymous" had been silent so far.

I was on my way to the vending machines for some celebratory candy bars when I heard Roland's voice coming from Sam's room. I paused outside the door, listening closely.

"How many e-mails has she sent you?" Roland sounded

angry—none of his usual sarcasm. "You promised you'd tell me if you heard from Emily again."

Sam's response was inaudible. I pressed my ear to the door, heart pounding.

"...how these things work, trust me," Roland was saying. "I'm telling you, Sam—she's coming back."

There was a muffled sound that I realized a second too late was footsteps. I leaped back as Roland yanked the door open. He froze, staring at me. I stared back defiantly, my face and neck suddenly scorching hot.

"What are you doing?"

"Snacks." I pointed unnecessarily to the vending machine at the end of the hall.

Roland stepped out of Sam's room and closed the door, still eyeing me. "Doesn't that require walking?"

I glared at him, then continued down the hall. When I got to the vending machines, I glanced back as he stepped onto the elevator. The doors slid closed, and I breathed a sigh of relief. *Well, that could have been worse.* Although my fingers still shook pretty badly as I dropped a few coins into the slot.

So I was right—Roland was bringing Emily back. All he had to do now was find a way to get rid of my dad. Slowly, anger began to overtake my fear. I gathered up the candy bars and turned around just as Sam stepped out of his room.

"Hi, Sam."

Blinking, he turned and saw me. "Oh, hello."

"Everything okay?" I asked.

"Yes, why?"

"I heard Roland yelling," I said brazenly. "He sounded mad about something."

"Oh, that." Sam's expression cleared. "It's nothing. Kat, has our ghost tried to communicate with you again?"

"Huh? Oh, the boy ghost." I shook my head. "No, why?"

"Just wondering." Sam gave me a vague sort of smile as he fished a few coins out of his pocket. "Let me know if he does, okay?"

"Sure."

I watched Sam head to the vending machines, whistling softly.

The next afternoon while Dad and the rest of the crew packed up to head to the prison, Oscar and I had a video chat with Jamie and Hailey. I couldn't wait to tell them what I'd overheard between Roland and Sam.

"We've only got fifteen minutes before we leave for school," Jamie told us. Next to him, Hailey yawned widely. "But we had to talk to you guys, because—"

"We found Bernice!" Hailey interrupted, beaming. My mouth fell open.

"What? How?"

"I was going through some of the older forum threads," Jamie explained. "Someone mentioned seeing her at the natural history museum when they visited New York. The museum's just a few blocks from where we live, so yesterday Hailey and I went after school. It turns out Bernice works there now."

"And she was there!" Hailey added.

Oscar's eyes widened. "Did you talk to her?"

"Yup. We asked her why she left the show, and . . ." Jamie paused, glancing over his shoulder and lowering his voice. "Sorry, thought I heard Mom. Anyway, Bernice didn't really want to talk about it, but we told her we were afraid your dad was going to get fired, too. So she told us what happened."

"Someone *threatened* her," Hailey said in a loud whisper.

My pulse quickened. "Did she say who?"

"She didn't know," Jamie said. "She said she got unsigned letters telling her to quit by a certain date, or . . ." He paused, glancing at Hailey. "Well, she didn't tell us exactly what the threat was. But obviously it was pretty bad."

"So Roland's sent death threats before." I shook my head in disbelief. "Did you see his latest 'anonymous' post on the forums?"

"Yeah, that's why we wanted to talk to you about Bernice." Jamie leaned closer to the screen. "You guys should tell someone. Your dad, Kat—and Lidia, too. I'm sure Roland wouldn't actually *hurt* someone, but still . . ."

"We can't prove it, though," I pointed out. "It's our word against his. If we tell them, I bet Roland will have a whole story worked out."

Jamie looked troubled. "Yeah . . . well, be careful. Especially at the prison tonight."

Oscar and I shared a glum look. "We're not going," I said, and Hailey let out a yelp.

"Why not?"

I shrugged. "Dad and Lidia said we'd be bored sitting in a cell all night—like this hotel is so much more exciting than a haunted prison. Really, it's because this episode is a big deal and they don't want us screwing it up."

Hailey sighed. "That's—"

"Jamie? Hailey?"

"Gotta go," Jamie said quickly, glancing over his shoulder. "E-mail us, okay?"

"Okay!" I got the briefest glimpse of his smile before the call ended. Feeling deflated, I turned to Oscar. "What do you think? Should we tell someone about Roland?"

He shook his head slowly. "You're right about the proof. Maybe . . ." He stopped, mouth open, gazing at the chat window still open on the screen. I turned to look, too, and my breath caught in my throat.

XXXXXXXXXXXX XXXXXXXXXXXX XXXXXXXXXXXX

They filled the window, as if an invisible hand was tapping the *X* key thirteen times, space, again, space, again . . . I jabbed at the keyboard and the typing stopped.

I turned to Oscar, who held his hands up. "Not me," he said. "I swear, I . . . I have no idea what that was."

It's the boy ghost, I wanted to say, but it sounded too melodramatic. Still, I couldn't help glancing around the otherwise empty hotel room.

"We're heading out in about fifteen minutes." Startled, we turned to see Lidia in the doorway, looking more haggard than ever. "Kat, your dad wants to see you before we leave—I think he's in your room."

"Okay. Be right back," I told Oscar, then slipped past Lidia and headed to the elevators.

I tried to tell myself it was just a glitch, but the reappearance of the thirteen *X*s was too weird. I wondered if I would have time to tell Sam about it before they left.

I found Dad in our room zipping up his backpack, and decided a little last-minute begging couldn't hurt. "Please, please, *please* let us come. I swear I won't wander off."

"Kat, we already discussed this."

I crossed my arms. "Have you considered the fact that this means I'll be staying in a hotel all night with a boy, unsupervised?"

Eyebrows raised, Dad shouldered his bag. "Is that something I should be worried about?"

Instantly, I wished I'd never brought it up. "Ew, no."

"Glad to hear it." Dad started searching the desk, moving his laptop and shuffling stacks of paper. "Of course, I've already set up a curfew for both you and Oscar with Margot—she's the receptionist tonight. She's going to make sure you're both in your rooms by ten. Your *own* rooms."

"What?" I cried. "Dad, what am I supposed to do all night?"

"There's this thing some people do," Dad replied, grabbing his key card from under his binder. "They lie down and close their eyes and lose consciousness for a while. I hear it's called *sleep*."

"Hilarious," I muttered. "Come on, can't I at least—"

"Kat, stop." Dad turned to face me in the doorway. For

the first time, I noticed how exhausted he looked. "I'm not making you stay here because I'm worried you'll interfere with the show. It's because I'm worried about *you*. It'd be one thing if you could stick with the crew, but—"

"Let us!" I interrupted. "We won't get in the way, I swear—"

"It won't work." Dad paused, closing his eyes. "In fact, I'm starting to think maybe this job won't work at all."

My stomach plummeted. "What do you mean?"

"I mean . . ." Dad shook his head. "We'll talk about it tomorrow, okay?"

"Wait." I stepped forward, heart pounding in my ears. "Did someone threaten you?"

"Did . . . what?"

"Is someone trying to make you leave the show?" I said urgently. "You know all the fans are wondering if this will be your last episode—that stupid host curse. Are you getting death threats?"

Dad set his backpack on the floor, eyebrows knit with worry. "Kat, why would you think that?"

And everything came pouring out. I told him about Roland, the messages on the forums, the deleted death threat. "He's bringing Emily back," I finished. "He told Sam so, I heard him. Roland was behind the host curse the whole time, and now he's trying to make you leave, too."

Pinching the bridge of his nose, Dad took a deep breath. "Kat . . ."

"You don't believe me?"

"No, I . . . I believe you think you're right," he said, and

I snorted. Perfect. "Listen, tomorrow you and I are going to have a talk. Because while I appreciate you're trying to help, I do *not* appreciate you eavesdropping on people."

I couldn't believe my ears. "But—"

"We'll talk about it tomorrow," Dad said firmly, picking up his bag. I could see his cheek muscle starting to twitch, but I didn't care.

"And Roland?" I yelled. "Maybe it was wrong of me to eavesdrop, but isn't it kind of worse to send *death threats* to people?"

Dad grimaced, glancing down the hall. "Roland's not sending anyone death threats," he said quietly. "He found some recently in Sam's fan mail, and he's trying to figure out how to handle it. No, *stop*." He held his hand out when I started to protest. "Kat, you're just going to have to trust me here—I've talked to Roland and Jess about this, and I know more about it than you do. Get some sleep tonight, okay? We'll figure this out in the morning."

He kissed the top of my head, and then he was gone. Fuming, I marched over to the window and yanked open the curtains. I glared down at the parking lot, waiting. Soon the crew appeared, loaded down with bags and equipment. I watched as they packed up the van and drove off.

Checking to make sure I had my key card, I stormed out of my room and headed for the elevators. So Roland had a story worked out, just like I'd figured he would. I remembered him talking about Sam's obsessive fans when we first met, too. He probably wasn't even lying about the creepy mail. But what about Bernice's death threats? And

Carlos's forged exposé? That was all Roland. And I had no doubt he was going to try to make this Dad's last episode, too.

I was so caught up in my anger, it was a few seconds before I noticed the 6 button was lit up instead of the 3. Frowning, I jabbed at the 3 button, but it stayed dark. The elevator arrived on the sixth floor, and the doors slid open.

"Come on," I muttered, pressing CLOSE DOORS repeatedly. Finally, they slid shut. I tried the 3 button, then the 2. Nothing. The elevator didn't move. Just as I was starting to get freaked out, the 6 button lit up on its own.

Ding.

The doors slid open again.

Okay, then. Looked like I was taking the stairs back down to Oscar's floor.

I walked fast, feeling unsettled. Up ahead, a maid grumbled as she rummaged through her cart of cleaning supplies. A moment later, the round-faced receptionist walked out of the room next to the stairs entrance—Margot, I remembered. She said something in Dutch to the maid, who immediately launched into a long, angry rant. When Margot saw me approaching, she waved for the maid to stop talking.

"Hello," Margot said, switching to thickly accented English. "Did your father tell you I'd be checking in on you tonight?"

I nodded. "Yes, ma'am. We'll be in our rooms by ten." I glanced at the maid, and my eyes widened. "Oh my God, what happened?" Her hands and wrists were stained a dark reddish-brown, along with about a dozen rags piled on top of her cart.

"It's only hair dye," Margot explained quickly. "The woman staying in this room decided to leave us with quite a mess to clean up." She said something in Dutch to the maid, who nodded curtly, grabbed a few bottles, and headed back in the room. Then Margot smiled at me. "Lidia requested that I order you and Oscar a pizza for dinner. Just call the front desk when you're ready, okay?"

"Okay, thanks."

Margot headed to the elevators. The maid had propped the door open, and I glanced inside the room on my way to the stairs entrance. Then I did a double take and, checking to make sure Margot wasn't looking, stepped inside.

The room was a *wreck*. Inside the bathroom, the maid knelt with her back to me, scrubbing the tub and muttering what I assumed was every possible curse word in Dutch. The white tiled floor, the sink, the mirror—everything was spattered in what looked horribly like blood (although I spotted the box of hair dye on the counter).

But that wasn't the worst part.

The bedding was slashed. Pillows ripped open, tufts of cottony stuff torn out and flung all over the room. The comforter and the sheets were shredded to pieces, as were the curtains. Even the wallpaper had a few gouges. I shuddered. It looked as if someone had gone berserk, grabbed a knife, and tried to tear the room apart.

I'd taken only a few steps back when I spotted the binoculars on the desk.

A feeling of dread crept up my spine and for a few seconds, I wasn't sure why. Then I noticed the pair of oversize sunglasses, and I remembered.

The woman at the waterfront in Rotterdam. The woman at the Internet café here in Brussels. I'd bumped into her both times. She'd followed us here—she was even staying in the same hotel. And judging by the state of her room, she was pretty ticked off.

But something else was nagging me. I squeezed my eyes closed, picturing her pale, sharp face. Young but kind of gaunt, shadowed eyes, dark hair . . . that nasal voice . . .

I thought of the box of hair dye and suddenly, everything slammed into place.

Sprinting down three flights of stairs, I raced down the hall and burst into Oscar's room, breathing heavily. He looked up from his laptop, startled.

"What's wrong?"

"Pull up photos from the first season."

"Huh?"

Without bothering to explain, I grabbed the laptop and typed in the URL for the official *P2P* site. I clicked PHOTOS, then SEASON ONE, and scrolled down till I saw her—young, blond, lots of makeup. She'd lost a little weight since then and her face had hollowed out, but there was no question.

"It's her," I said softly.

Oscar looked thoroughly confused. "Emily? What about her?"

I took a deep breath.

"She's here."

198

CHAPTER NINETEEN
THE ROAD TO THiRTEEN KiSSES

P2P Fan Forums
A Message for "Anonymous"
Doctor Pain [new member]

Anonymous
[comment deleted by administrator]

Maytrix [admin]
Enough is enough. If anyone knows how I can get in touch with
the Brussels police, let me know. This creep has gone too far.

Iphysically couldn't stay still. Jiggling my leg, I leaned
against the receptionist's desk, clenched and unclenched
my hand, drummed my fingers on the counter. Margot
frowned deeply, cradling the phone between her shoulder
and her ear. I watched her hang up, then immediately
dial again. With every second that passed, the knot in my
stomach doubled. Finally, she sighed and set down the
receiver.

"No response from Jack or Lidia," she told us. "But I will
keep trying."

I turned to Oscar. "We have to go to the prison."

"How?" he said immediately. "Lidia said it's a half-hour

drive—that'd be a pretty expensive taxi ride. How much money do you have?"

"Not enough, probably." I thought fast. We'd already asked Margot about the woman who'd wrecked her room. Margot refused to give us her name, but as Oscar pointed out, Emily was probably smart enough to use a fake name, anyway. And while her hotel-room rampage was probably enough to convince police she was unbalanced, we had no way to prove she was going to Daems. Or that Roland was involved in any way.

But he was. Emily was dangerous. And if Roland was in love with her, well, maybe that made him dangerous, too. All I could think about was getting to my dad before one of them could hurt him.

"Can you add it to our room charge?" Oscar asked, and I glanced up. Margot gave him a quizzical look.

"Sorry?"

"Can you call a taxi and pay for it, and add it to our bill?"

"Please?" I added, jumping in before Margot could protest. "They won't mind—this is an emergency."

Margot's eyes narrowed. "Your father was very clear that you were to stay here."

"But it's an *emergency*," I repeated. "A real one. If we can't get them on the phone, we have to go to Daems."

"Then I will call again."

I suppressed a groan of frustration as Margot calmly picked up the phone. Oscar and I exchanged irritated looks as she dialed, listened, hung up, dialed another number, and on and on. Finally, she set down the receiver with a loud sigh.

"It's an emergency," I said again, firmly. "Look, if they want us to come back to the hotel, we'll just ask the taxi driver to bring us back. No harm done."

"We'd be back way before ten, too," Oscar added, pointing to the clock behind her. "It's not even eight yet."

Margot eyed him, then me. Then, to my relief, she relented and picked up the phone.

"Very well. I will call for a taxi."

I exhaled slowly. "Thank you."

We stepped away from the desk, and Oscar lowered his voice. "Do you have your camera?"

I blinked visions of Emily sneaking up behind Dad with a knife from my mind. "What? Oh . . . no. Should I bring it?"

"Don't you think your post about the psycho former host crashing the prison episode would look good with a few photos?"

I made a face. "You know, sometimes you can just say *yes* without getting all sarcastic."

When I returned to the lobby, the Elapse safely in my pocket, I saw a taxi parked along the curb. I hurried outside and waited next to Oscar while Margot spoke to the driver in rapid French. Judging by his expression, he wasn't too thrilled about whatever she was saying.

Finally, Margot handed him a note. He took it, giving Oscar and me a contemptuous look. "*Treize baisers,*" he mumbled, settling into the driver's seat with a scowl. "*Mon dieu.*"

He slammed the door. Margot smiled at us wearily.

"Cyril is your driver. He has promised not to let you out of his sight until you are with the adults. But he is not happy about going to *la Prison Éternelle*," she added. "Everyone knows about the haunting. He is . . ." She glanced at the driver's window and lowered her voice. "Chicken."

I snickered, but Oscar was still staring at the driver. "Did he say *treize baisers*?"

Margot nodded, pulling the passenger door open. "Yes. It's what some locals call the road to Daems. You know what it means?" she added with a wink. But Oscar didn't smile back.

"Yeah, I think so."

I waited until we were pulling out of the parking lot, then sighed loudly. "Well?"

"Well what?"

"What does it mean?" I said impatiently. "Tres . . . whatever you said."

"Oh." Glancing at the driver, Oscar lowered his voice. "*Treize baisers.* I'm pretty sure it means *thirteen kisses.*"

"You've *got* to be kidding me," I said loudly, and Cyril shot me a dirty look in the rearview mirror.

We didn't talk much on the drive after that. Before long, the city was just a cluster of tiny bright lights behind us. The sky was that purplish-blue shade it gets right before turning completely black; a few stars twinkled around the sparse clouds that still hung low from yesterday's thunderstorm.

"Do you think Emily's there already?" Oscar asked at last.

I pictured her room, all slashed and ripped apart, and tried to sound calm. "Maybe. But even if she is, she and Roland are outnumbered. And—"

Suddenly, Cyril slammed on the brakes. Oscar and I lurched forward against our seat belts. "What's wrong?" I gasped, massaging my rib cage. Cyril muttered nervously and smacked the side of his GPS console, which had gone dark. The screen flickered back to life, a blue dot marking us on the map with instructions in French down the side.

Continuez tout droit sur la 13e Av

Tournez à droite sur la Rue de la Paix

Still eyeing the console, Cyril stepped on the gas again. When we started to turn right, Oscar grabbed my arm.

"*Look*," he hissed, pointing out his window. I leaned over and caught a glimpse of the two battered street signs at the intersection, which were sprayed over with graffiti:

A chill raced up my spine, but I tried to keep my voice light. "Thirteen *X*. Well, I guess that explains the nickname."

Cyril tensed up as we edged down the road, shoulders hunching, fingers clutching the wheel. Privately, I thought he was overreacting a little. Then Daems Penitentiary came into view, and my palms went clammy.

The massive compound loomed in front of us, made up of at least five buildings that I could see. The brick was so grimy and stained, it was impossible to tell what color it had been originally. Instead of windows, slits barely wide enough to stick your arm through marked the floors. A tower rose twice as high as the prison, overlooking the courtyard. And the entire thing was surrounded by an imposing wire fence—probably three times my height, with giant barbed coils along the top.

"Pretty," said Oscar.

"Looks like my old Barbie Dreamhouse," I agreed. We smiled briefly at each other, and I was relieved to see he looked as nervous as I felt.

Because the truth was, Daems was the most horrific-looking place I'd ever seen.

When Cyril let out a piercing shriek and slammed on the brakes again, I nearly jumped out of my skin. The cab jerked to a halt, and Oscar and I stared at the GPS console. The map was gone, and two symbols flashed repeatedly on the otherwise black screen:

X <3 X <3 X <3 X <3 X <3 X <3 X <3 X <3 X <3 X <3

Letting out a stream of curses in who knew how many languages, Cyril threw the car into reverse.

"Wait, *stop!*" I yelled.

He shouted a reply in stilted English, his voice shaking. "I will not drive closer!"

"You don't have to," Oscar said urgently, leaning past the

front seat and pointing. "Look."

I squinted and realized with a wave of relief that the crew's van was parked not far ahead. Even better, the doors were open—maybe they were still unloading equipment.

Cyril hesitated, hands gripping the wheel. The hearts and Xs were still flashing on the screen. Finally, with a strangled grunt, he threw open his door. "We walk. Hurry."

I scrambled out of the taxi, and Oscar and I hurried after the driver as he set off down the path toward the van. I couldn't keep myself from staring up at the prison, taking in every detail—the faded graffiti and large patches of dark mold spreading over the walls, the slits revealing the inky blackness of each cell, the tiny points protruding from the coils at the top of the electric fence, waiting to gouge and slash anyone who somehow managed to get that close to freedom . . .

It was horrifying, the kind of place that should have made me want to jump back in the taxi and get as far away as possible. But my fingers still itched to pull out my camera and take a few shots.

"Hello?" Cyril approached the van, casting anxious glances at the prison entrance every other second. There was a muffled response from inside, and my heart lifted. The feeling didn't last long.

"What are you two doing here?" Roland emerged from the van, staring from me to Oscar in disbelief, and my throat went dry. I glanced around him, but the van was empty. Cyril stepped forward and thrust something at Roland—the note Margot had given him. Oscar and I exchanged anxious looks as Roland skimmed the letter. When he finished, he gave us a calculating look.

"So what's the emergency?"

"Uh . . ." I glanced helplessly at Oscar. "I need to talk to my dad."

Before Roland could respond, Cyril cleared his throat loudly. "You stay?" he asked me pointedly, already taking a step back.

"Just wait one minute." Turning, I squinted at the prison entrance, but there was no sign of Dad or anyone else.

"They're setting up in the mess hall." Roland leaned against the van, eyeing me. "Something wrong?"

"I need to talk to my dad," I repeated. My palms were starting to sweat. "I'm not—"

"Hey!" Oscar yelled. I spun around to see Cyril sprinting toward his cab. We stared as he threw himself inside and slammed the door. The tires spun on the gravel as the cab turned in a sharp circle, leaving a cloud of dust in its wake as it sped back toward the main road.

Shaken, I exchanged a panicked look with Oscar. Roland waited to speak until the sound of the taxi's engine had faded.

"You two really shouldn't have come here. It's too dangerous."

I shivered, but managed to keep my voice steady. "I want to talk to my dad."

Roland nodded slowly. "All right, hang on. I just need to grab the extra flashlights." Casting a quick glance around, he hopped back into the van. "Stay right there."

My breath grew shallow. Reaching out, I touched Oscar's

arm and nodded at the door. He stared blankly for a few seconds, then his eyes widened in understanding.

Quietly, we edged closer to the van. Oscar pressed his hands to the sliding door, I grabbed the handle, and we yanked hard. Roland spun around just as the door slammed shut.

"Hey!"

I stumbled back as he tugged at the door, but the exterior locks worked just as well as they had on Mi Jin. Turning, Oscar and I left Roland yelling and pounding on the windows and ran flat out to the prison entrance.

CHAPTER TWENTY

THE THING 3: ESCAPE INTO THE ABYSS

Alarm: TAKE YOUR MEDS!

"**OKAY.**" Oscar leaned against the metal double doors, breathing heavily. "That was dumb. That was really, really dumb. Aunt Lidia's going to freak out."

Smiling shakily, I rubbed a stitch in my side. "Yeah. We're so dead." Oscar half-laughed, half-groaned. Neither of us spoke for a full minute. I imagined I could still hear Roland, yelling and pounding on the windows of the van. Oscar was right—Dad was going to flip when he found out what we'd done.

Well, whatever. Saving him from a psychopath—possibly two—would be worth the punishment. Hopefully.

"Okay," I said at last. "He said they're in the mess hall. Let's go."

Oscar nodded. "Which way?"

For the first time, we took a good look around. Directly opposite the entrance, another pair of double doors was bolted shut with a rusted chain. The corridor extended to our left and right, both paths equally dark. Tiny patches of dim, gray light along the floor marked where the moonlight seeped in from the slit windows in the cells. Silence hung in the air like a heavy curtain.

Oscar and I edged closer to each other.

"Should we just yell? Maybe they'll hear us," Oscar suggested.

"What if Emily hears us first?"

He made a face. "Good point."

"So which way looks less creepy?" I asked.

"Let's see." Oscar squinted down the hall. "To our left, we have Serial Killer Avenue, and to our right is Rue de la Zombie. Coin toss?"

"Nah, easy choice. We can outrun zombies." We started down the hall on the right, arms bumping together as we walked. "Unless they're those really fast zombies," I added. "You know, the ones with superhuman strength that can run up walls and stuff. Of course, the good thing about them is they move so fast, we'd barely have time to feel scared before they were eating our brains."

"Thanks, Miss Sunshine."

"No problem."

Each time we passed a cell, I felt a chill—not from fear, but from cold. Somehow, the air coming from the cells was cooler than in the hall. We reached the end of the corridor and headed left, combating the oppressive silence with nervous jokes about vampire bats hanging from the ceilings and corpses in solitary confinement. I was describing my favorite scene in Grandma's fifth movie, *Return to the Asylum,* when Oscar stopped and grabbed my arm.

"Listen."

I held my breath. A distant *beep, beep, beep* was just barely audible over my too-loud heartbeat.

Oscar glanced at me. "The crew?"

"Probably."

We set off at a faster pace, and the beeping grew louder. When the corridor ended, we stepped into a small foyer. I scanned it quickly—a window crusted with grime, a dilapidated staircase, and a pair of doors propped open with mic stands.

"There." My voice cracked a little as we hurried to the entrance. But my relief didn't last long.

The mess hall extended in front of us, row after row of heavy-looking steel tables. Rusted, broken chairs were strewn in the aisles, legs bent or missing. A lone, battery-powered fluorescent lamp stood on the other side of the hall, surrounded by cables, bags, and other gear.

But the crew was nowhere to be seen.

"Perfect," I muttered, stepping back when a rat scurried out from under a table and fled into the shadows. "Just perfect."

Oscar groaned. "I just realized what that noise is," he said angrily, heading down the aisle. "Aunt Lidia's phone alarm. *Again.*"

I hurried to keep up with him. "For her pills?"

"Yeah." We reached the lamp and began digging through bags, looking for Lidia's phone. Oscar grabbed a backpack with more force than necessary, knocking over the lamp. I caught it, raising my eyebrows at him as I set it upright.

"You okay?"

"No." Furiously, Oscar dumped the contents of another bag on the table. "You've seen how awful she looks lately. She keeps forgetting her pills—it's not like her. Jess is making us go home for a few weeks after this episode so she can rest."

"Well, that's a good thing, right?" I asked tentatively. "She needs to get better. And you'll come back."

"Yeah." Oscar shoved aside a few folders and a walkie-talkie. "But if we go home, I'll have to visit my dad. And if I visit my dad, I'll have to tell him why I got expelled. And I—I just can't. *Ha.*" Oscar slammed the bottle of pills on the table with a sort of savage triumph.

Glancing at him, I unzipped a small pocket on the outside of a dark green backpack. "Here's her phone." I swiped the alarm off. "No reception."

Slowly, Oscar started stuffing everything back into the backpack. I took a deep breath.

"I know how you feel," I said. "I can't go back to Chelsea, either."

"Because you're mad at your mom for getting remarried?"

"No." I squeezed Lidia's phone. "Well, yes. But it's not just that. When she went to Cincinnati, I figured she'd either come back like she did the first few times, or finally focus on her photography, like she kept saying she wanted. But now she's marrying some guy, and he has a—a *daughter*, and . . ."

My throat tightened. Oscar quietly stacked the folders and slid them back into the backpack. I took a deep breath.

"The thing is . . ."

The Thing. I never said it out loud, not to Trish or Mark or Dad or Grandma. Because I knew how they'd respond.

Your mom loves you, Kat.

"She loves me," I whispered. "But she doesn't *like* me. Everything I do disappoints her."

That's not true.

"The first time she took off, I believed her when she said it was to give a real photography career a shot."

And she changed her mind. She came back.

"But photography had nothing to do with it. The real reason she left is . . ."

Don't say it!

But the Thing finally broke loose.

". . . me."

For a split second, I thought I saw a shadow flicker near the entrance. Not rat-size. Human-size.

"I used to think maybe she just never wanted kids at all," I said, still gazing at the entrance. "She's always trying to change how I dress, what I eat, everything. She'd *hate* my hair like this." I touched the back of my head self-consciously. "But it's not that she never wanted a daughter. It's that I wasn't the daughter she wanted. That's why she kept leaving. And now she's getting married again—and she'll have a stepdaughter. Elena." I closed my eyes. "Mom seems to like *her* just fine."

For the first time ever, I saw the Thing clearly, face-to-face. It had my eyes and nose and mouth, my old, long braid hanging down its back. It wore a pretty sundress, no Crypt

Keeper in sight. It preferred fashion magazines to horror movies, and shopping to paintball. The Thing was exactly what my mother wanted.

The opposite of me.

"I'm sorry."

I blinked, startled. "What?"

"Sorry about your mom," Oscar said again, staring at the walkie-talkie in his hands.

"Oh." I let out a shaky laugh. "*Sorry.* That's it? Aren't you supposed to say, 'That's not true, she's your mother and she loves you no matter what, blah blah blah'?"

Oscar lifted a shoulder. "Maybe you're right, though. Maybe some parents just—"

Creeeak.

We both jumped, staring around the mess hall. I stepped away from the fluorescent lamp and tripped a little on a roll of cables. No movement, no sounds . . . but I had the overwhelming sensation someone was watching.

"We need to find Lidia," I whispered.

Oscar stuffed the bottle of pills in his pocket before picking up the walkie-talkie. "Lidia?"

Nothing. Flipping the dial, he tried a few more times. "I don't know which channel they're using."

"Keep trying while we look for them," I said, itching to leave. The mess hall was creeping me out.

We crept toward the entrance, arms pressed together. I half-expected a pair of hands to shoot out from under every table and grab our ankles. But we reached the foyer safely.

"Back the way we came, or upstairs?" Oscar asked.

I studied the rickety staircase. "Not upstairs. Let's try to find the courtyard."

We hurried back down the dark corridor, both of us glancing over our shoulders every other second. Oscar kept flipping channels on the walkie-talkie, listening for the crew. Goose bumps broke out on my arms—the temperature in the hall was dropping. The Thing was right on my heels. I could sprint for hours and I'd never outrun it.

"Oscar?"

"Yeah?"

"Why can't you tell your dad you got expelled for fighting?"

Oscar didn't respond right away, and I wondered if I should've kept my mouth shut. Then he sighed.

"Because he's going to ask why Mark and I got in a fight in the first place."

I squeezed Lidia's phone again, my eyes darting into each shadow-filled cell we passed. I couldn't shake the feeling that we were being watched. "So, why did you?"

"Because . . ." Oscar hesitated. "He was my best friend, right?"

"Right."

"Well, I . . . I liked him. And I told him, and he . . . kind of freaked out. And told *everyone*. And—"

"Wait, told everyone what?" I interrupted, confused. "That you liked . . ." I trailed off as I realized what he meant.

Not liked him. *Liked* him. A crush.

"Oh. Okay," I said. Oscar glanced at me uncertainly, and I tried to smile in a reassuring way. "So—"

Beep! Beep! Beep!

I gasped, nearly dropping Lidia's phone. Oscar leaned closer and we stared at the screen.

KEEP HER AWAY <3 KEEP HER AWAY <3 KEEP HER AWAY <3

The beeps bounced off the stone walls, unnaturally loud in the tomblike prison. Frantically, I pressed a bunch of buttons at random. Oscar grabbed it and popped the batteries out, and the beeping stopped.

"Okay, seriously," he said. "What's going on? The phone, the GPS in the taxi, the laptop . . ."

"It's the show's ghost. He likes me."

He stared at me. "I honestly can't tell if you're kidding, Kat."

"Neither can I," I said wryly. "Look, Sam said the ghost of a boy haunts the show. The one in the photo next to Lidia, remember?"

I started walking again, and Oscar kept up at my side. "Oookay . . . so what are these messages about? *Keep her away* . . . Who's *her*? Emily?"

"I guess . . ." I trailed off, picturing the way the ghost boy had reached for Lidia as she'd crumpled. Ever since we'd left Crimptown, he'd been trying harder and harder to tell me something. And Lidia had been getting sicker and sicker. "No. It's about Lidia."

"What? Why?"

We passed the entrance and headed down the other hall. "The most haunted show on television," I said, thinking out

215

loud. "It started with the dead air in the first episode—the séance. What if the show is haunted because the ghost from the lighthouse never left?"

The corridor dead-ended, another hall stretching out to our right. "Lidia passed out at the first séance, when the lightbulb exploded," I continued. "And then again in Crimptown—and she'd been with Sam right before that. The message says *the medium*. It's not that Sam is dangerous, it's that he contacts ghosts. He contacted the lighthouse ghost, he contacted Sonja . . ."

I stopped again, and Oscar faced me. "What?"

"Sonja *possessed* Lidia," I whispered. "Mi Jin said it takes a ton of energy for a ghost to possess a person or objects . . . but ghosts can manipulate *electricity*."

Oscar glanced down at Lidia's smartphone. "So?"

"The hearts," I said softly. "Her heart—*Lidia's heart.*"

"What do you . . . ?" Oscar trailed off, and I saw the realization dawn on his face before I said it out loud.

"Her pacemaker. That's why they can possess her."

Oscar exhaled loudly. The temperature had dropped so low, I could see a wisp of his breath. "Okay. And now she's running around a prison with hundreds of ghosts. Perfect."

We walked toward the end of the hall, neither of us speaking. I was so lost in my thoughts about Lidia that we were almost in front of the last cell before I heard the rhythmic *scrape-scrape-scrape*.

Abandoning all pretense, I grabbed Oscar's hand. We exchanged a terrified look before taking the last few steps and peering inside the dark cell. A filthy cot was bolted to the wall on the right, directly below the sad excuse for a window letting in a weak ray of moonlight.

But my eyes went straight to the figure crouched in the corner, scraping at the floor.

CHAPTER TWENTY-ONE
THE RETURN OF
RED LEER

P2P WIKI
Entry: "Cold Spots"
[Last edited by beautifulgollum]
Cold spots are various spots in a haunted location with cooler temperatures, often thought to indicate the presence of ghosts which have not materialized.

MY skin felt like ice. All my instincts screamed at me to run, but my feet were frozen to the ground. It was a woman—a woman with long hair hanging in her eyes, head bowed, sliding something over a board lying on the ground . . . a board with letters, numbers, and a tiny light flashing red . . .

Oscar squeezed my hand so hard I cringed. "Aunt Lidia?"

My knees nearly buckled in relief. He was right—it was Lidia, crouched over Mi Jin's Ouija board. But she didn't stop moving the planchette when Oscar said her name. He approached her slowly, letting go of my hand to kneel down next to her. "Can you hear me?"

Scrape-scrape-scrape.

"You forgot your medicine again." Tentatively, Oscar touched her arm. I stared down at the board, a chill of dread slowly creeping down my spine.

"Oscar . . ."

"Look, it's right here." Oscar handed me the walkie-talkie and pulled the bottle of pills out of his pocket. "Aunt Lidia, can you stop for a second, please?"

"Oscar."

"What?"

I pointed at the board. "Look at what she's spelling."

FREETHEMEN—FREETHEMEN—FREETHEMEN

"Free the men?" Oscar glanced nervously at Lidia. "What's that supposed to mean?"

I swallowed. "Remember the Ouija board? *Gather the women.* And the other one—*free them.*"

"So?"

"Oscar, think about it." My voice cracked with fear. "She's been sick ever since Crimptown."

"Yeah . . ." Oscar stood slowly, lowering his voice. "Wait. You think Sonja is still possessing her?"

"Not Sonja." Kneeling down, I grabbed both of Lidia's hands with mine. The scraping stopped, and suddenly the cell felt too quiet. Lidia didn't look up, though I could see her shoulders rise and fall with each quick, shallow breath.

"Who are you?" I whispered, then let go of her hands. I knew the name she would spell before the planchette slid over to the first letter.

REDLEER

The scraping stopped. Oscar and I backed away as Lidia lifted her head. Slowly, her lips stretched into a wide, wide smile.

But not Lidia's smile.

She lurched forward, shoving us aside with freakish strength. I slammed into the wall as Lidia burst out of the cell and took off down the corridor.

"Wait!" Oscar struggled to his feet and sprinted after her. Dizzy, I stumbled out after him. Tiny spots of light danced in my vision as I ran down the dark corridor. I could just make out Lidia racing around the corner, and Oscar put on a burst of speed. When a shadow lunged at him from one of the cells, I shouted a warning a second too late. The mess-hall chair slammed into Oscar's head with a sickening sound.

THUD.

I screamed as Oscar crumpled to the ground. His attacker tossed the chair aside, then stepped over his motionless body and walked toward me. Terrified, I stood rooted to the spot, unable to focus on anything other than the glint of the knife in her hand.

Emily Rosinski smiled at me. "Hello, Kat."

Without waiting for a response—my vocal cords seemed to have seized up, anyway—she grabbed my arm. I tried to call Oscar's name, but all that came out was a small, strangled cry as she pulled me past his body and down the corridor. Even in the dark, I could see a giant lump already forming on his forehead.

Emily's nails dug into my arm, and I winced. She pushed through a set of double doors, and I stumbled half a step behind her, dimly aware that we were outside. I was so fixated on the knife swinging back and forth at her side, several seconds passed before I realized I was still holding the walkie-talkie. I couldn't call for help now, of course—no one could get to us in time. Glancing at Emily, I tucked it into my jacket pocket. We crossed a small, walled courtyard, heading straight for the guard tower.

"Hope you brought your camera!" Emily said cheerfully, kicking the door open. The DO NOT ENTER sign fell to the ground. "This'll make quite a post."

The steep staircase twisted like a snake inside the tower structure, just wide enough for one person. Emily nudged me forward. "Up you go."

Weak with fear, I began to climb, Emily right on my heels. I glanced down every other second, my eyes seeking out the knife. By the time I reached the top, my legs burned and my heart hammered wildly in my ears. I hurried to the railing and stared down at the compound. The electric fence cast a long, jagged shadow that circled the courtyard. And there, huddled right outside the entrance to the main building with the rest of the crew, was Dad.

My knees nearly buckled with relief. I opened my mouth to yell for help and felt cool metal press against my neck.

"Don't interrupt," Emily said softly. "They're filming."

After a few seconds, she pulled the knife away. My breath came out in a shaky whoosh, and I gripped the railing until my knuckles were white.

This wasn't the fun kind of horror. This was really, truly horrifying.

I could barely make out Dad's voice as he slowly walked backward in front of Jess, her camera up and filming. Sam drifted along next to them, while Mi Jin trailed behind, glancing over her shoulder every few seconds. Probably wondering about Roland and Lidia, I realized, and almost laughed at the hopelessness of the situation. Roland was locked in the van, Lidia was possessed and doing who knew what, I was stuck in a tower with a lunatic, and Oscar . . . I felt sick when I remembered the way we'd left him lying unconscious.

"Almost midnight," Emily whispered, her gaze locked on the crew. "The fans will love this, won't they? Another host, gone. The curse continues." Grabbing my wrist, she tugged me over to a grime-covered control panel with a single, rusty lever. "Bunch of morons. You figured it out, though."

Confused and terrified, I watched her examine the lever. "Figured what out . . . ? That Roland got rid of all the hosts?"

Emily's eyes widened almost comically. "*Roland?*"

"Well, y-yeah," I stammered. "He got you fired, he framed Carlos with that exposé, he sent Bernice death threats . . ." I trailed off as Emily started giggling, a high, tinkling sound that made the hairs on my arms stand on end.

"Well, at least you got the first part right," she tittered. "Roland couldn't stand that Sam and I were in love. He told Jess I was unstable. Unstable! Can you believe the nerve?" Eyeing the knife in her hand, I decided now wasn't the time to be a smart aleck. "So Lidia fired me. And after I kept her secret, too! But I promised Sam I would come back. *I* set Carlos up, *I* sent Bernice those letters. I *made* this 'the most haunted show on television'—the host curse was all because of me." Emily slammed the knife down on the console. "Just one more host left to get rid of, right, Kat?"

Before I could respond, she grabbed the lever and pulled hard. I covered my ears at the resulting *screech*. When I lowered my arms, the air vibrated with a soft, deep hum.

"What . . ." I stopped, a jolt of terror ripping through me. "Did you just turn on the fence?"

"Your dad could use a few tips on being a real reporter," Emily told me, pulling out her phone. "After he interviewed that tourism-board member yesterday, I followed her to a bar and bought her a drink. Just talking about Daems had her all worked up. She told me—in the strictest confidence, of course—that even the city officials are so superstitious about this place, they never deactivated the fence. They think it keeps the ghosts in. Isn't that funny?"

Giggling, Emily held up her phone and started to record a video. "It's going to be an exciting episode, Kat. We should get a little extra footage. Don't," she added warningly when I stepped up to the railing. Dad and the others were crossing the courtyard, still filming, slowly making their way toward the fence. I spun around to face Emily.

"They don't know it's on!"

She snickered. "That's kind of the point, isn't it?"

"But—but what if Sam touches it?" I said frantically. "You don't want him to die, do you?"

Anger flashed in Emily's eyes. "He stopped responding to my e-mails. All he cares about is communicating with the dead," she snapped. "He might as well be one of them."

Okay, Roland was right. Total nutjob.

Without giving myself time to think about what a dumb move it was, I smacked the knife out of Emily's hand. It clattered across the floor toward the edge, and she dove after it with a cry, dropping her phone. I seized the lever and yanked as hard as I could.

It wouldn't budge.

"Come on, come *on*," I said frantically, throwing all my weight into it. But the lever was jammed.

Emily scooped up the knife and spun around just as I grabbed her phone. I lunged for the staircase, taking the steps two at a time without looking back to see if she was following.

CHAPTER TWENTY-TWO

FLIGHT OF THE INVISIBLE PRISONERS

WARNING! High Voltage

I sprinted across the small courtyard, half-expecting to feel a knife slash across my back at any second. Bursting through the doors, I ran straight to the end of the corridor and took the first right, then a left, then another left. Finally, I slowed my pace and listened for the sound of footsteps. But all I heard was my own quick, shallow breathing. I was alone.

Any relief I felt at having escaped Emily vanished when I remembered the crew wandering through the courtyard, clueless about the live electric fence. Fingers shaking, I swiped Emily's smartphone on as I retraced my steps back to where I'd left Oscar.

"No reception. Perfect." I tried cramming the phone into my pocket, but there wasn't room. "*Oh!*" I pulled the walkie-talkie out as I hurried around the last corner. "Dad? Jess? Is anyone . . . ?" I trailed off, coming to a halt. Oscar was gone.

"Okay," I whispered. "Okay. Now what."

Emily's phone suddenly blared with sound, startling me so badly I almost dropped it. I stared at the screen in disbelief. A video had started to play. And not just any video.

"Are you ready?"

"Shh!" I hissed, pressing buttons frantically as the lighthouse footage played. But the phone wouldn't turn off. I glanced around, terrified Emily would hear it and find me.

On the screen, Lidia's eyes flew open. This was the same video that Anonymous—Emily, not Roland—had posted in the forums. Lidia stared right into the hidden camera, right at me. Then the bulb exploded, and the scene went dark until Roland flung the door open. I watched him hurry to Lidia's side, check her pulse, slump over with relief when she responded. He ignored Emily's question about the fake lightbulbs and ordered her to turn off the camera. But this time, the clip continued.

Emily pulled the camera off the tripod, her eyes glued to Sam, whose head was in his hands. A few seconds later, Jess burst into the room.

"Lidia!" she cried, hurrying over to the table. Sam lowered his hands, and Jess glared at him. *"You did it anyway, didn't you?"* she said bitterly. *"You tried to contact Levi. I told you she couldn't handle it."*

"Excuse me." Lidia lifted her head. *"It was my decision, not Sam's. I wanted to speak to my brother, Jess."*

"I know, but . . ." Jess's face crumpled. *"Lidia, your heart's not strong enough for this."*

Lidia ignored her and started to stand. Roland took her by the elbow and slowly, they shuffled out of the room. Jess and Sam followed, eyes downcast. Emily waited until they were gone before hurrying over to the hidden camera—the phone I was holding. Her hand stretched toward the screen, and a moment later, it went black.

I exhaled shakily. Sam had contacted Lidia's brother in the lighthouse. Lidia's brother, who had died when they were teenagers. Levi.

The boy ghost.

I looked up, half-expecting to see him, and just barely managed not to scream.

At the far end of the corridor, Lidia stood silently, glowering at me.

"Lidia?" My voice shook. "I want to help you. Can you hear me?"

Creeeeeeeeeak.

My breath caught in my throat. Lidia slowly raised her arms, and all down the corridor, each and every cell door opened as if attached to her wrists with string.

"Levi," I whispered desperately. "What do I do? I don't know how to *help her*." Even as the words escaped my lips, images flickered through my mind like a slideshow. Lidia's eyes flying open as the lightbulb exploded, Lidia collapsing when I snapped her picture, Sonja's spirit leaving her body crumpled on the ground . . . the lights, the flash . . .

Strobe lights can trigger my seizures, so that meant no concerts or haunted houses. Not that that stopped me.

"Oh!" Cramming Emily's phone and the walkie-talkie into my jacket pockets, I pulled out the Elapse and held it up.

Flash.

Blinking, I could just make out Lidia slumping against the wall. I glanced at the viewfinder and sucked in a breath. Because Lidia wasn't the only person in the picture. In front of each cell was the outline of a man.

The prisoners were free.

At the end of the hall, Lidia pulled herself up and fled around the corner. A chill blew through the hall after her as the ghosts followed.

I raced down the corridor and turned the corner just as Lidia burst through a set of doors. The courtyard—Red Leer was leading the ghosts to the courtyard to make their escape. The electric fence couldn't hurt a ghost.

But it would kill Lidia.

I burst through the doors into the courtyard, my lungs aching. I might be able to save Lidia from Red Leer. But not if she reached the fence first.

Distant shouts reached my ears, and I squinted across the expansive field. For a moment, everything seemed to move in slow motion as I took in the scene.

Lidia, running flat out for the fence. Jess, throwing her camera aside and sprinting after her from the opposite end of the courtyard, Dad right on her heels.

Sam backing up to the fence near the entrance as Emily approached him, knife in hand.

"*The fence!*" I shouted at him. "*The fence is on!*" But I was still too far away. No matter how fast I ran, there was no way I could reach Sam in time. But I was much closer to Lidia than the others.

My leg muscles screamed in protest as I tore after her. She'd nearly reached the fence, but I was closing in. A shriek almost caused me to trip, and for one horrible moment, I was positive Sam had been electrocuted. Then movement to my right caught my eye, and I glanced over just as Roland tackled Emily.

Relief washed over me, and I put on another burst of speed. Three yards to go, two, one . . . I grabbed Lidia around the waist and we both fell to the ground with an impact that knocked the wind out of me.

She rolled over with unnatural speed, but I managed to hold her down. My elbow stung, and I felt blood trickling down my arm. Struggling to pin her with one arm, I aimed the camera at her face.

"*Let me go.*" The low, growling voice wasn't Lidia's any more than the grotesque smile twisting her lips.

"I'm trying to," I gasped. Then I pressed the shutter button and held it down.

Lidia's eyes rolled back in her head as the flash pulsed like a strobe light, and her body went limp. Through the neon spots dancing in my vision, I glimpsed the hulking outline of a man with a curled mustache just before he vanished in a light gust of wind.

CHAPTER TWENTY-THREE

HOW TO TRAIN YOUR DEMONS

ERROR!
Cannot save images because memory card is full.

DANGLING my legs out the back of the ambulance, I watched through drooping eyelids as Dad and Jess talked with a few police officers. Next to me, Oscar sighed impatiently while the paramedic continued fussing over the lump on his head.

"I'm *fine*," he said for probably the hundredth time in the last hour. The paramedic rolled her eyes and, adjusting his bandage one last time, headed over to check on Sam.

"You were out cold," I reminded him, tugging the blanket the police had given me tighter around my shoulders.

"Yeah, but only for, like, a minute."

I offered him a section of blanket. Oscar shook his head just as a particularly chilly gust of wind hit. "Oh, fine," he muttered, tugging the blanket around his shoulders. Smiling, I scooted closer to him.

Dad kept glancing over at me, like he was worried I might disappear. After everything that had just happened, I figured he was mentally booking our one-way tickets home. I'd already told my version of tonight's drama to three different police officers. And it wasn't exactly a truthful version.

I mean, the part about Emily attacking Sam was true. The part about Roland wrestling her off him and getting a knife slashed across the face for his efforts was true, too. So was the part about Mi Jin pinning Emily to the ground and refusing to budge until the police arrived. And the part about Jess giving Lidia CPR and crying when she finally came to. And the part where Dad hugged me so hard I thought my ribs would crack, then promised I'd be lucky to be ungrounded before I was fifty.

But I didn't tell the police about Red Leer. My last decent photo was of Lidia standing at the end of the corridor, which was blurred with transparent outlines. The constant flash I'd used in the courtyard turned the pictures of her face into a warped, overexposed mess. I thought about how it would sound if I explained the whole thing to the cops: *Well, she's been possessed by the ghost of a pirate we picked up back in Rotterdam, and he tried to use her to free all the ghosts of the prisoners here at Daems. Luckily, Lidia's dead brother helped me save her with my camera.*

I figured that would just convince the police I had some sort of head injury, so I kept it to myself. But the *P2P* fans were going to hear all about it in my next blog post.

Which honestly would probably be my *last* blog post.

"Hanging in there, you two?"

Oscar and I looked up, startled. Roland smiled, then winced and touched the bandage stretched along his cheek.

"I keep forgetting about this thing."

"How bad is it?" I asked, holding out my arm. "Because I think I lost a few layers of skin on my elbow. It's pretty epic."

Roland chuckled. "Mine's a shallow cut. Although they said it might scar."

"Scars are cool," I assured him. "Um . . . I'm sorry about, you know . . ."

"Locking me in a van with a psychopath running around?"

"Well, yeah," I admitted. To my relief, Roland looked amused.

"You really thought it was me pulling all that host-curse garbage?" he asked, and I nodded. "Why?"

"Er . . ." I wrinkled my nose. "I thought you were jealous."

Roland's eyebrows shot up. "Jealous? Of what?"

"Well, that Emily was so obsessed with Sam. Because, you know . . ." I glanced at Oscar for help. He leaned away from me, palms flat as if to say, *Leave me out of this.* Sighing, I turned back to Roland. "I guess I thought you were in love with her."

For a second, Roland gaped at me. Then he burst out laughing.

I rolled my eyes. "Okay, so I got that wrong."

"A little bit, yeah." Roland shook his head, still grinning. "I've had my eye on her for a while, but believe me, that isn't why. She struck me as a little off from the very beginning."

"So you got her fired?"

"Yeah, but that was before I realized she genuinely needed help. And Sam . . ." Roland glanced over to where Sam stood a little apart from the others, his expression lost. "He's just clueless. I kept trying to tell him Emily's behavior was getting obsessive, but he didn't want to listen. Eventually, everyone but Sam could see it, and we fired her."

"When did you realize she'd set Carlos up?" I asked.

"Not until recently," he admitted. "Sam started getting letters from her again, and the writing reminded me of the threats that scared off Bernice. None of us thought . . ." His face tightened a little. "We didn't realize how bad it had gotten, or we would've done something sooner."

"Roland!" Jess called, waving for him to join her, Dad, and the policemen. One was still examining Emily's smartphone. I'd given it to him after deleting the dead-air footage. I figured there was enough evidence against Emily without it. Lidia didn't want fans to know about Levi's ghost, and the crew had kept her secret. I could keep him a secret, too.

"I guess it's my turn." Roland pulled a sucker from his pocket and ripped off the wrapper. "Not that there's much to tell, since I spent most of this whole ordeal locked in the van."

"I said I was sorry," I said, exasperated. "And besides, Oscar let you out eventually."

"Yeah, how about a thank-you?" Oscar added pointedly.

Roland crunched down on his sucker and, giving us an insolent look, headed off to join Jess without another word.

I glanced behind us, where Lidia was fast asleep on the gurney. I'd managed to get a few minutes with her before the paramedics arrived. She'd shown me the picture of Levi in her locket. He had the same sharp nose and amber eyes.

"Is he still here?" she'd asked sleepily.

"Yes," I'd told her. I didn't have any way to prove Levi was still here, but I believed it. As long as Lidia was near Sam—as long as she was a ghost hunter—she would be in danger of being possessed. And Levi would stay, to try to protect her.

So I would do what I could to help him help her.

"Thank you."

Glancing up, I realized Oscar was watching Lidia, too. "What? Why?"

"You saved her life," he said. "Thanks."

"Oh. You're welcome." It certainly hadn't felt like saving her. In fact, the way Lidia's eyes had rolled around in her head as I'd flashed the camera in her face would probably haunt my nightmares for a while. But it had worked—when she'd regained consciousness, she was herself again. Red Leer was gone. (*Where* he'd gone was something I was currently too tired to contemplate.)

"So . . ." I paused, adjusting the bandage on my elbow. "How long do you think you'll be in Oregon?"

Oscar made a face. "No idea."

We fell silent for a few seconds, swinging our feet over the concrete. I gave Oscar a sidelong look. "Think you'll visit your dad?"

His legs fell still, and he took a few seconds to respond. "I don't know. I guess so."

"Oscar, it'll be . . ." I stopped. *It'll be fine.* But how could I say that, when really I had no idea? Maybe Oscar's dad would understand when Oscar told him he'd been bullied because he liked a boy. Maybe not. Maybe my mom would start treating me like a daughter she actually wanted in her life. Maybe not.

"Whatever," I finished decisively.

Oscar's lips twitched. "It'll be whatever?"

"Exactly."

We smiled briefly at each other, then went back to swinging our legs and watching the crew.

Our last few days in Brussels were relatively quiet. I wrote a lengthy e-mail to Jamie and Hailey, detailing the entire Daems ordeal, and a much shorter version to Trish and Mark (after all, I'd be able to tell them the whole story in person soon enough). My blog post had a few hundred comments—some flattering, some insulting, but hey. As Roland had pointed out when he and the rest of the crew read it, the important thing was that people were talking about *P2P*.

Obviously, most of the buzz was about Emily's arrest. The forums had exploded with new members all looking for gossip about the former host and the way she'd sabotaged the show, all because of her obsession with Sam. Ratings for the Brussels episode were bound to be incredible, thanks to the media hype alone—even people who didn't care about ghost hunting would tune in just to see all the stuff with Emily. Fright TV wasn't canceling *Passport to Paranormal* any time soon.

And the host curse was officially broken. After a long discussion with Jess, followed by an even longer discussion with me, Dad had decided to stay with the show. But first, we were going back to Chelsea.

"The whole crew's taking two weeks off after the Brussels episode airs," I told Grandma, twirling the phone cord around my finger. "I think everyone needs a break after the whole Emily thing. But Fright TV is sending us to South America at the end of November!"

"Excellent!" Grandma exclaimed. "Does that mean we'll be having our annual Thanksgiving Freddy Krueger marathon?"

"Of course!" I paused, wrinkling my nose. "Unless you were planning to spend Thanksgiving with . . . I mean, I'll be with Dad, and I don't know if . . ."

"I'm sure we can work something out with your mom," Grandma said reassuringly, then yawned. "I hate to say it, but it might be time for me to hit the sack," she added. "Have a safe flight, okay? Tell Sam I said hello."

I laughed. "Not gonna happen." Hesitating, I stared at the laptop screen, where the *P2P* forums were still open. "Hey, Grandma?"

"Yes?"

I took a deep breath. "There's something that's been bothering me. I know the whole Sumner Stalker thing is just supposed to be a joke, but I . . . well, I don't think it's very funny. Emily . . ."

I paused, unsure of what I wanted to say. The truth was, Emily had terrified me far more than any horror movie or haunted prison ever could. I'd woken up at least once every night since Daems from nightmares filled with her high-pitched giggle, her hollow face, the gleam of her knife. She'd gone from being Sam's fan to something much, much worse, all because she couldn't let go of the bitter feelings eating her up.

"Emily was a real stalker," I finished. "I guess I just don't want anyone calling you one. Even if it's just a joke."

Grandma was silent for a moment. "You're absolutely right, Kat," she said at last. "I won't call myself that anymore. Or anyone else, for that matter."

I smiled, relieved. "Thanks."

After we hung up, I closed the forums and started to log out of my e-mail. Then I noticed my chat contacts list and, after a second of hesitation, opened the window.

MonicaMills [Mom]
Unblock this contact?

"Kat?"

I glanced up to see Dad in the doorway. "Yeah?"

"Lidia's cab is here."

"Coming." I clicked YES, then closed the laptop and followed Dad out into the hallway.

The whole crew had gathered in the lobby to say good-bye to Lidia. A few days of possession-free rest had done wonders—she still looked a bit drained, but much more like her old self. Still, Jess hovered around her with a nervous look, as if she expected Lidia to collapse again at any given moment.

I spotted Oscar standing off to the side as the others took turns hugging Lidia good-bye. He smiled when he saw me.

"Jekyll?"

I glanced down at my T-shirt. "Yeah. If I wear it inside out, it says *Hyde*," I told him, and he laughed.

"Nice."

"Thanks." I glanced outside, where Dad and Roland were loading luggage into the cab. "So . . . I'm going to meet my mom's fiancé this weekend. And his daughter."

Oscar made a face. "Well, maybe it won't be that bad."

"Famous last words," I said dryly. "If we were in a slasher movie right now, you'd be the first one the maniac attacked with a chainsaw."

"Probably." Oscar's smile faded, and he stuck his hands in his pockets. "I'm, um . . . I'm going to see my dad. Lidia said she'd set up a visit when we get home."

I nodded, unsure of what to say. We stood in silence, watching as Jess, Sam, and Lidia started heading out the entrance.

"I'm glad, though," Oscar said suddenly. "I'm tired of worrying about it, you know?"

"Yeah." I tried to sound optimistic. "And hey, the bright side is, no matter how good or bad things go, at least we'll see each other again in a few weeks."

"That's a bright side?" Grinning, Oscar dodged a light punch I aimed at his arm. "Just kidding."

"Oscar, let's go!" Lidia called, and he picked up his backpack.

"Good luck," I said, sticking my hand out. Oscar took it firmly in his, and we shook.

"You too, Doctor Pain."

Outside, Dad slipped his arm around my shoulders as Lidia and Oscar climbed into the cab. We waved until they pulled out of the parking lot and disappeared around the corner.

Roland stretched his arms over his head and yawned hugely. "I'm starving."

"Well, we've got a few hours to kill," said Jess. "Want to grab something to eat before the twenty-four hours of nasty airline food begins?"

"You should order the vegetarian meals," Sam told her mildly as we started walking. "The tofu curry I had on the flight to Rotterdam was delicious."

"It *was* pretty good," Roland agreed, exchanging an amused look with Mi Jin. "Probably because that was pork, not tofu."

I lagged behind, pulling my camera out of my pocket. Dad glanced over his shoulder.

"You all right?"

"Yeah." I waved the Elapse at him. "Just wanted to get some pictures, if that's okay."

Dad smiled. "Of course."

I slowed down, taking in the cobblestone street, the cluttered shop windows, the tiny tables set up under colorful awnings. Up ahead, Dad and Jess were chatting away about the architecture (judging from their animated gestures to the surrounding buildings), while Roland and Sam watched

Mi Jin drop a few coins into the case of an accordionist squeezing out an upbeat polka. For a moment, all five of them stood still as crowds of people hurried by.

Kneeling, I held the camera up to my eye. "Okay," I murmured, adjusting the lens until they were in focus. "Lots of motion around them, a slower shutter speed would give the crowd a really cool blur . . . wider aperture, shallower depth of field and . . . perfect."

Click!

PASSPORT TO PARANORMAL
EPISODE GUIDE
SEASON 1

1

Oct 10 • **Emily Rosinski**

Cannon Beach, OR • *Limerick Bed & Breakfast*

Creator and producer Lidia Bettencourt grew up in this coastal Oregon town, and her childhood fascination with the haunted lighthouse led her to choose it as the location for *P2P*'s first episode. The pilot episode included the infamous "dead air"—90 seconds during which viewers lost sound/audio. Fright TV could not explain the disturbance, leading to the show's slogan: "The most haunted show on television."

2

Oct 17 • **Emily Rosinski**

Seattle, WA • *Oxford Hotel*

The crew investigated room 610 of this hotel, where the ghost of a local author terrorized visitors by attempting to re-create scenes from her horror novel, *The Woman in the Mirror.*

3

Oct 24 • **Emily Rosinski**

Las Vegas, NV • *Burning Love Wedding Chapel*

This episode featured one of *P2P*'s most popular scenes, in which Sam Sumners attempted to contact the ghost of the Elvis impersonator who haunted the chapel and ended up entertaining the crew with a rousing rendition of "All Shook Up."

4

Oct 31 • **Emily Rosinski**

San Diego, CA • *Sandoval Studios*

This art studio claimed the spirit of a troubled artist haunted its gallery, occasionally making small changes to paintings, such as adding small clouds or extra stars.

5

Nov 7 • **Emily Rosinski**

Tucson, AZ • *Silver Rush Mansion*

The crew spent the night in this mansion, said to be haunted by the disgruntled original staff from the early nineteen hundreds.

6

Nov 14 • **Emily Rosinski**

Santa Fe, NM • *Dragonfly Dance Hall*

The spirit of a ballroom dancer betrayed by her partner lingers in the dance hall, occasionally trying to tempt visitors into a waltz.

7

Nov 21 • **Emily Rosinski**

Austin, TX • *The Asylum*

The crew investigated claims that this popular Halloween haunted house was actually haunted by a restless spirit year-round.

8

Dec 5 • **Emily Rosinski**

Dallas, TX • *OCH Recording Studio*

A fire claimed the lives of seven musicians at this studio over a decade ago. The studio was rebuilt and outfitted with new equipment, but occasionally, engineers report the song the band had been recording when the fire started begins playing through the speakers.

9

Dec 12 • **Emily Rosinski**

Lake Quivira, KS • *Crowing Farm*

The crew explored the cornfields surrounding this abandoned farm, once the ritual site for an eerie cult.

10

Dec 19 • **Emily Rosinski**

Madison, WI • *Stet News*

The owners of this local paper claim headquarters are haunted by the spirit of a disgruntled copy editor responsible for sneaking typos into articles just before the paper goes to print.

SEASON 2

11

May 8 • **Emily Rosinski**

Evanston, IL • *Saint John's Cathedral*

The crew investigates local claims that this church is haunted by the spirit of a young nun who tried to run away to enter a beauty pageant but was hit by a motorcycle and died on the front lawn.

12

May 15 • **Emily Rosinski**

Fayetteville, AR • *TW Hart Bridge*

Local legend says this bridge is haunted by the spirit of a bank robber in the mid eighteen hundreds, who sought refuge in the Ozark mountains and, when trapped by authorities, leaped off the bridge to his death.

13

May 22 • **Emily Rosinski**

New Orleans, LA • *Blacksmith Bar*

A fan favorite, this episode includes the infamous scene where Roland tries to conjure Bloody Mary in the mirror of the women's bathroom.

14

May 29 • **Emily Rosinski**

Charlotte, NC • *Dusty Wind Backcountry*

Those who venture out onto this difficult trail sometimes claim to see the ghost of a hiker who perished in the backcountry decades ago.

15

June 5 • **Emily Rosinski**

Charleston, WV • *Pelotaid Factory*

The fire which raged at this factory half a century ago didn't destroy the building—but it did claim the lives of eleven workers, who still roam the facilities today.

16

June 12 • **Emily Rosinski**

Oakton, VA • *Frostproof Gardens*

The crew spent the night in a greenhouse haunted by what locals referred to as an "agent of darkness" responsible for squeezing the juice from its still-ripening fruits.

17

June 26 • Carlos Ortiz

District of Columbia • *The White Whale*
In the first episode with new host Carlos Ortiz, the crew investigates a popular club haunted by the spirit of a guitarist. Some visitors claim to see colorful auras when there's a guitar solo during a show.

18

July 3 • Carlos Ortiz

Baltimore, MD • *Clementine Cottage*
The crew explores the former home of a local poet who believed the spirit of his deceased wife remained with him as his guardian angel. Even after his death, locals claim her ghost still haunts the cottage.

19

July 10 • Carlos Ortiz

New Hope, PA • *Brew Ha Ha*
This café is famous for two things: its delicious fried rabbit sandwich and the spirit of the woman tried and hung for witchcraft in the sixteen hundreds, who now haunts its kitchen.

20

July 17 • Carlos Ortiz

Park Ridge, NJ • *Bottle of Jinn*
More commonly known as "the one where Carlos got a tattoo," this episode features a bartender with a supposed third eye whose bar is haunted by a genie-like spirit capable of granting wishes.

21

July 24 • Carlos Ortiz

New York, NY • *The Alcazar*
This elegant theater claims to be haunted by the spirit of its first producer, who expresses his dissatisfaction during performances by flickering the lights and causing prop malfunctions.

22

July 31 • Carlos Ortiz

Monroe, NH • *Sacred Heart Church*
Locals claim a particularly wicked poltergeist haunts this church's cemetery, raising blood and bone from the dirt.

Crimes and Covers

Also available by Amanda Flower

Magical Bookshop Mystery
Verse and Vengeance
Murders and Metaphors
Prose and Cons
Crime and Poetry

Magic Garden Mystery
Mums and Mayhem
Death and Daises
Flowers and Foul Play

India Hayes Mystery
Murder in a Basket
Maid of Murder

Appleseed Creek Mystery
A Plain Malice
A Plain Disappearance
A Plain Scandal
A Plain Death

Andi Boggs
Andi Unexpected
Andi Under Pressure
Andi Unstoppable

Living History Museum Mystery
The Final Vow
The Final Tap
The Final Reveille

Amish Candy Shop Mystery
Lemon Drop Dead
Candy Cane Crime
Marshmallow Malice
Toxic Toffee
Premeditated Peppermint
Lethal Licorice
Criminally Coca
Assaulted Caramel

Amish Matchmaker Mystery
Marriage Can Be Mischief
Courting Can Be Killer
Matchmaking Can Be Murder

Piper and Porter Mystery
Dead End Detective

Farm to Table Mystery
Put Out to Pasture
Farm to Trouble

Crimes and Covers

A MAGICAL BOOKSHOP MYSTERY

Amanda Flower

NEW YORK

Copyright © 2022 by Amanda Flower

Published in the United States by Crooked Lane Books, an imprint of The Quick Brown Fox & Company LLC.

Crooked Lane Books and its logo are trademarks of The Quick Brown Fox & Company LLC.

Library of Congress Catalog-in-Publication data available upon request.

ISBN (hardcover): 978-1-64385-596-7
ISBN (ebook): 978-1-64385-597-4

Cover design by Stephen Gardner

Printed in the United States.

www.crookedlanebooks.com

Crooked Lane Books
34 West 27th St., 10th Floor
New York, NY 10001

First Edition: January 2022

10 9 8 7 6 5 4 3 2 1

For my husband David

"Books are the treasured wealth of the world and the fit inheritance of generations and nations."
—Henry David Thoreau, *Walden; or, Life in the Woods*

Chapter One

"Violet, we have to talk about the wedding!" Sadie said as she bounced through the front door of Charming Books. Bouncing was Sadie's main mode of movement. She wore a red dress with white faux fur trim and a matching red beret on her head. No one since the 1920s has loved a beret as much as Sadie. She was basically Tigger in a Mrs. Claus outfit.

In my arms, I held a stack of new fiction releases to be shelved as Sadie excitedly told me everything we needed to do for the big day.

"And then there is the cake, and the favors—you have to have favors because you don't want to look cheap—and the candles—"

My head began to spin. I set the stack of books on one of the couches in front of the large fireplace, which ran at full steam in the middle of the winter. Charming Books was the bookstore I owned with my Grandma Daisy in the small village of Cascade Springs, New York. The village was only a fifteen-minute drive from the majestic Niagara Falls, and Decembers here were bitterly cold. The fireplace had been going around the clock since Halloween.

Faulkner, the shop crow, flapped his wings from the second lowest branch on the birch tree that grew in the middle of the bookshop. It was just after ten in the morning, and Faulkner liked a quiet snooze after his breakfast of fruit and peanuts. Being awakened by a bouncing Christmas elf was not on his agenda.

The birch tree was the soul of the bookstore and the heart of the its magic. Some might think all bookshops have magic because the books found on their shelves can transport readers away to new places. But, in the case of Charming Books, I meant it quite literally. The shop could talk... sort of... It was complicated.

Sadie twirled, and her skirt kicked out around her in a red ring. I was happy to see she was wearing leggings underneath her dress.

Emerson, my tuxedo cat, wound his way around my feet. I scooped him up and set him on the back of the couch. "Sadie, what do I have to do for the wedding? You and Grandma Daisy told me all I have to do is show up." I was to marry my fiancé, Chief David Rainwater of the Cascade Springs Police Department, the weekend before Christmas. Rainwater was everything that I could want in a partner and husband. I couldn't wait to spend the rest of my life with him. I still called him by his last name all the time, even though we were engaged. Old habits die hard and all that.

However, neither of us was excited about planning a wedding. After I offhandedly mentioned to my grandmother, Mayor Daisy Waverly of Cascade Springs—yes, my fiancé was the police chief and my grandmother was the mayor—she and Sadie took the wedding planning into their own hands. Rainwater and I had just held on for the ride.

"I know," she said. "But the wedding is three days away. We have to get you ready."

"Get me ready?" I squeaked.

"There's your hair, makeup, nails. A juice cleanse is not out of the question."

I tugged on the hem of my red Charming Books sweatshirt. "Oh, it is definitely out of the question. Trust me on that."

She stopped twirling and dropped her arms, looking like a little girl who'd lost her balloon. Sadie was six years younger than me and was petite with silky black hair and a bright spirit. She had the best vintage wardrobe in the state since she owned Midcentury Vintage, the clothing boutique that was across River Road from Charming Books. She was the one of the first people to befriend me when I moved back to Cascade Springs and was like a younger sister to me. Making Sadie frown was never a goal of mine. I would have to compromise.

"You can paint my nails," I said, hoping my lacquered olive branch would put an end to the juice cleanse conversation.

She clapped her hands. "Excellent!" She paused. "What juice flavors do you like the most? Lemon packs the biggest punch to rid your body of toxins."

"As much as I love you, I'm still saying no to the juice cleanse." I walked over to the sales counter and leaned against it.

"Okay, fine," she conceded. "But Violet, you *are* getting married, and you're acting like it's no big deal."

I might be *acting* like it was no big deal, but it was a *huge* deal. Massive. Colossal. The proof of it sat on the ring finger of my left hand. The bright green emerald glittered in the morning light streaming in from the skylight above the birch tree. Rainwater had told me that he knew I needed something unique, and the stone was as green as the leaves on the birch that I held so dear. It was his way of saying he not only accepted but supported my connection to this place and the tree. It was the perfect choice.

Sadie put her hands on her hips. "Aren't you excited about the wedding?"

"I'm excited about being married to David," I said. "The whole day is intimidating. Any time you and Grandma Daisy talk about it, it seems to grow bigger and bigger. We just wanted a small ceremony."

"You know the whole village is invited, right?"

How well I knew that. We would get married here at Charming Books, but since we couldn't possibly fit all the guests that my grandmother felt she was obligated to invite, we would be having the ceremony on the front porch of the bookstore. Grandma Daisy, in her capacity of mayor, would be officiating. Sadie was my maid-of-honor and Rainwater's younger sister Danielle was his best woman. At least they let me keep the wedding party small like I'd wanted. I'd won a few small battles in the plans. I wasn't naïve enough to think I'd won the war.

There was one more potential member of the wedding party—Fenimore James, my father. But I hadn't spoken to him in months, and I didn't know if he would attend. I didn't even know if I wanted him to be there.

Sadie sighed. "Vi, we are so different. I want a huge wedding. It's the one time in your life that you truly are the center of attention. When I get married, it will be a giant blowout and I won't make apologies for that."

I smiled. "And no one is asking you to." Sadie's dream might not be that far away. After years of chasing the wrong man, she had finally found a good and decent guy, Simon Chase, who was stable and over-the-moon in love with her. I wouldn't be the least bit surprised if she got a ring for Christmas.

"Now back to that manicure. My friend at the salon has an opening tomorrow morning. She can give you a hair trial too."

I raised my brow. "An opening this close to Christmas?" I asked.

Sadie nodded. "We got lucky, two people just canceled. Don't worry, no one else will snap it up. I already grabbed it and talked to Daisy about watching the store while you're out. It will take a few hours."

"Hours?" I squeaked, realizing that I squeak a lot when it came to listening to Sadie and Grandma Daisy's plans.

"Well, we couldn't do it before this because you were busy at the end of the semester. We have to cram everything together in one day. Don't worry, we will get it done. I have an itinerary."

I knew this was true. December was always a crazy time for me between the shop and the end of the semester at Springside Community College, where I was an adjunct English professor.

Before I could ask Sadie what exactly was on the itinerary, the front door of Charming Books opened and a delivery man walked inside.

He had so many boxes stacked in his arms that I couldn't see his face, but I knew it had to be my delivery man.

"Hank!" I cried, and ran over to help. "What are you doing carrying all those boxes in at once? They are all books. You could throw your back out." I took the top two boxes from the stack. When I did, I could see most of his narrow face turn into a wide grin.

Hank was a congenial man, close to Rainwater's age, so somewhere near forty. He had a beard and wore the insignia jacket of his delivery company, NY Box. He was an inch or two shorter than I was and had a thin frame like he had run cross-country in high school.

He has been delivering to my store since early September. He told me once that he'd taken the delivery job to make some extra money for his family, especially for his ill daughter, and now planned to continue after the new year.

He placed the three remaining boxes on the hardwood floor by the sales counter. "Aww, you know I have to keep pushing myself to carry more. The more boxes I can deliver all at once, the more stops I can make and the more money I can earn. Also, you know I love coming here the most." He rubbed his hands together. "What do you have for me today?"

I chuckled. "I've got a new teen romance in I know Abby will enjoy." I walked to the stack of books that I had left on the couch and picked up a hardback with a glossy silver cover.

"I know Abby will love it. She has loved every book that you've given her," Hank says. "We are so grateful to you for them. The books are huge comfort to her during treatment."

I smiled. Hank's fifteen-year-old daughter Abby had been in treatment for lymphoma for over a year. I knew how hard it was on Hank and the entire family. On a personal level, I knew how hard it was to watch because my mother died of cancer when I was close to Abby's age.

"She will probably read the whole thing in one sitting." Hank's eyes glimmered. "How much is it?"

"No cost. It's yours." I held the book out to him.

Hank waved me away. "Violet, you can't keep giving me books."

I just smiled.

He sighed. "Someday I'll be able to pay you back for all that you've given me.'"

"Just think of it as a tip for your great service delivering all the supplies we need for the shop."

He chuckled. "Nice try, but my company doesn't want us to take tips."

"Okay, it's not a tip then. It's just a Christmas gift for Abby." I held it out a little further.

He accepted the book. "I guess I can take a Christmas gift for my daughter. That's different."

"It's very different," I said, but as I spoke, Hank was already reading the dust jacket closely.

"This sounds like something she'd love. I don't know how you find all these authors that she likes so much. You always know what she wants to read." He held onto the book tightly. "It's like some kind of magic."

Something like that, I thought as I glanced at the tree.

"Violet is the book whisperer," Sadie chimed in. "Every time I come into the store, I leave with books to read. Violet really knows her stuff."

"Imposter," Faulkner cawed from the branches. Leave it to Faulkner to call me out.

Hank's whole body jerked at the sound of the bird. "I will never get used to that crow looming overhead. There are a lot of scary animals on my route, but your crow takes the cake. Are you sure he won't attack someday?"

"Faulkner is harmless. He talks big but would rather nap than cause any real trouble."

"False," the large black crow countered.

I shot him a look. He wasn't doing himself any favors by proving me wrong.

Hank rubbed the bottom of his beard. "It's like he understands you."

"He might understand a little. Crows are very smart—on par with dolphins and pigs even."

Hank wrinkled his brow and removed the scanner from his belt and held it out to me. "Just sign here with your finger, and we are good to go."

I did as I was told.

"Thanks." He clipped his scanner back on his belt and held up the book. "Thank you for this. I have a lot more stops on my route today, but I can't wait to give this to Abby as soon as I get home."

"Sounds like a perfect December night," I said with a smile.

"You bet it is." He grinned and headed for the door. "Sadie, I left a package outside your door too."

"Oh, thanks. I'll go grab it now. I think Violet needs a break from my wedding talk."

He paused. "Wedding talk?"

"Oh, Violet and Chief Rainwater are getting married on Saturday. You didn't know?"

"They are?" His eyes went wide.

"Violet, you didn't tell Hank?" Sadie's question was bordering on an accusation.

I wrinkled my brow. "Should I have?"

8

"Of course." She reached into the pocket of her Mrs. Claus dress. "Here's an invite, Hank. If you are free, you should come. It will be the party of the year!"

He took the invitation and tucked it into the front cover of the book I had given him. "Well, if I'm not on the route, I'll try to come. I'm never one to turn down free cake."

"You're a guy after my own heart, Hank," Sadie said and turned to me. "Violet, we can go over your beauty regimen later."

Regimen? Who said anything about a regimen?

"Sounds like your wedding will be quite a big to-do. I thank my lucky stars every day that my wife agreed to elope."

At the moment, I wished I had done the same when Rainwater brought it up right after we had gotten engaged.

Hank waved, but as he went out the door, a woman blew in with a gust of snow, blocking his path. "Excuse me," Hank said and tried to maneuver around her, but she didn't budge.

Another gust of cold air, snowflakes, and a few stray leaves blew into shop. The wind was enough to make the large birch tree sway, and Faulkner complained from his perch. He puffed up his feathers to fight the cold.

When the snow settled, the small woman in a long skirt and a giant coat stood in the doorway. A stocking cap was pulled far down over her face, covering her eyebrows. A scarf hid the lower half of her face. We could not see anything but her bright blue eyes.

"Excuse me," Hank said.

She glanced at him and moved to let him by.

Sadie and I stared at her. Her skirt was so long it even covered her shoes, making her look like she was floating.

"What do I have to do to get some customer service?" the woman asked in a high-pitched voice.

I stepped forward. "I'm so sorry. How can I help? Can we help you find a book?"

Her icy blue eyes turned to me and narrowed. "I'm not here to buy a book. I'm here to sell a book. I'm looking for a woman named Violet Waverly?"

My eyes widened. "I'm Violet. We don't have a very large used book section, but I will be happy to talk to you about whatever it is that you wish to sell."

"You most certainly will," she said in an almost threatening tone.

Sadie must have heard the threat in the woman's words as well because she stepped closer to me. I don't know how she thought she was going to protect me in her red velvet dress and high-heeled boots, but she would surely try. Sadie picked up Emerson like she would protect him too. This did not sit well with the little tuxedo cat, who tried to wriggle out of her grasp.

Emerson was not a timid cat. He jumped to the floor and circled the strange woman like a cheetah on the hunt. My guard was up. When my cat didn't trust someone, it was noteworthy.

I walked over to the counter. "I'm happy to see what you have, and we can take it from there."

The woman shuffled across the shop's old floorboards as I slipped behind the sales counter. Typically, I never sat there unless I was ringing up a sale. I liked to be out on the floor where I could interact with the customers. I encouraged the two part-time clerks I had recently hired to do the same. This time, I felt more secure with some space between the woman and me.

"You said you had a book?" I questioned. There was nothing in the woman's hands.

She unzipped her massive coat and reached inside to pull out a package wrapped in brown paper.

Standing on her tippy toes, she set the package on the counter. With an air of reverence, she unwrapped a very old book, one I couldn't believe I was seeing with my own eyes, in my shop.

I stared at it. It couldn't be...

She removed her hat, revealing a curly mop of reddish-gray hair underneath. As she removed the scarf, I saw she had a tiny nose and pointed chin. "How much will you give me for that?"

I couldn't put a price on it. I was speechless.

Chapter Two

"Well, are you going to answer me?" she asked in a much harsher tone. Since her attitude already bordered on troll under the bridge, that was saying a lot.

"I can't put a price on this." I wanted to push the book back toward her, but I was afraid to touch it. "You would have to speak to a rare book dealer. They would be able to assess the real value."

"I don't want to speak to a rare book dealer. I'm here to speak to you. You're supposed to be the expert on this sort of thing."

I looked up from the woman's copy of Henry David Thoreau's *Walden* on my counter. As a scholar in nineteenth-century American and particularly transcendentalist literature, I had read the book so many times that I could recite full passages from memory. I had spent my entire adult life studying the work and wrote my dissertation on it. "How do you know that?"

"I have my ways," she said. "This is a first edition. I believe that you are familiar with the work." She eyed me as if waiting for me to deny my knowledge of Thoreau's work, which I couldn't and wouldn't. I knew *Walden* almost as well as the author did. In fact, I might have known it better, having spent so much time studying it and writing about it for my dissertation.

"I *am* interested in the book, but I'm not a rare book dealer or an archivist who could authenticate it for you."

"I don't need it authenticated. I know it's real. I just need you to buy it."

It was a simple brown leather book with a decorative design embossed on the cover. The spine read "Walden; or Life in the Woods" and "Thoreau." It looked like it was a first printing, but I had never been this close to one before. This book was originally published in 1854, meaning that if I was right and this was a first edition, it was over one hundred and sixty years old. My hands hovered over the book.

"You can touch it," the woman said.

If it was the real thing, I definitely should *not* have been touching it, at least not without gloves. The oils from my skin could ruin the book's surface over time. Even so, I couldn't resist lightly brushing the cover with my fingertips. The leather was very old and had a bumpy surface.

I flipped to the cover page and to the back of that page. The publisher was right. It read "Ticknor and Fields." The date was right—August 1854. Could this be real? Only two thousand copies were made for the first printing.

It was possible, of course. Copies of the book were out there. It had been reprinted and copied so many times over the years. Being in the public domain, it was impossible to know how many editions of Thoreau's work there were in circulation or in how many languages. There was nothing to stop a new edition of the book. In my own library in the small apartment on the second floor of Charming Books, I owned five editions of *Walden*. The oldest was a 1901 edition my grandmother gave me when I picked my dissertation topic. It was old, but not worth anything close to what this first edition was worth.

"Look at the first page."

Frowning, I flipped past the title page and almost fainted. The book was signed, and it appeared to be in Thoreau's hand. I recognized the dramatic "y" on "Henry" and the right-leaning slant from pouring over his letters in my studies of the writer.

"Well," the woman said. Clearly, she was bored with my enchantment with the book.

"Where has it been all this time? It's like it came straight from the printer. Is it a replica?" I asked.

I thought my question was one to be expected, but she grabbed the book from the counter at that and snapped it closed. "How can you ask me such a thing? If it was a replica, do you think I would be here? I need to get this into the hands of a person who will truly appreciate it. I was told that person was you."

"Who told you that?"

"It doesn't matter. Are you interested in buying it or not? If you don't want it, I'll leave. There has to be someone else who will take this off my hands."

Off her hands? I wondered if she was selling it because something was wrong with it.

Before I could answer her questions, Sadie chimed in. "How much do you want for it?"

"Seven thousand," the stranger said without blinking an eye.

I sucked in a breath. That was a lot of money, and with a busy small business to run and a wedding a few days away, not to mention the student loans that I would be paying off for another decade at least, I didn't have a spare seven thousand dollars lying around. However, if it *was* real, I knew that I would be able to sell it for twice that, especially with Thoreau's signature, if it could be authenticated.

Sadie whistled. "That's a lot of money."

"Does that mean you're not interested?" the woman asked.

"I'm interested," I said quickly.

Sadie's eyes bugged out of her head. Since she and Grandma Daisy had begun planning my wedding, she knew how careful I was with my money. I had turned down some of their most expensive ideas—one of which had been a Broadway-like play reliving Rainwater's and my love story. Since we had met for the first time over a murder, I didn't believe it would hit the right chord for a wedding reception. Grandma Daisy went along with my decision, but made sure to tell me that I had no vision.

Right now, I was grateful that the woman had her eyes on me. I didn't want Sadie to tip her off that I would probably never work up the nerve to buy it even if it was autographed by Thoreau. I only wanted to learn more about it. Like where had it come from? How had it remained so pristine all this time? What was the name of the woman standing in front of me, and how had this treasure come to be in her possession?

I shook my head as if it completely slipped my mind to ask. "You know, I'm Violet, and this is my friend Sadie Cunningham."

Sadie held out her hand to the woman. "I own Midcentury Vintage across the street. I would love for you to stop by. I could give you a consultation."

If I had been closer to Sadie, I would have stepped on her foot. I didn't think insinuating that the woman needed a wardrobe update was the way to convince her to give me the information I wanted.

When the woman didn't shake her hand, Sadie dropped it to her side. "I'm also a published writer. My first novel came out earlier this year."

The woman sniffed. "What does that have to do with anything we are talking about here?"

Sadie's face fell.

I frowned. "What is your name?"

"My name is meaningless to you if you won't buy the book."

But this couldn't be the real thing, could it? The last first edition of Thoreau's masterpiece that had come up for auction sold for over fourteen thousand dollars. Perhaps the copy that sold for such a high price was a fluke bought by a one-time collector who just had to own it, but a signed first edition of *Walden* was certainly worth more than the seventh thousand dollars the woman was demanding.

"Where did you get this?" I asked. Maybe she would tell me that.

"That doesn't matter either. What matters is whether you'll buy it or not. I told you my price. Now make your choice."

Alarm bells went off in my head. "I can't make a decision like that in a split second," I said. "It appears to me to be the real thing, but I need some proof such as a letter of authenticity to show the provenance of the book."

"Yes, you can. Just decide."

"She really can't," Sadie said. "Violet takes forever to make a choice. You should have heard her hem and haw over the wedding flowers. It was painful to watch."

"Sadie," I muttered under my breath.

"I don't care about any of that. If this is something you want, you have to make that choice now. Time is ticking away."

I frowned. Something was off. In my experience, people wanted you to make big choices fast for one of two reasons: they were in a hurry to get away from you or they were trying to trick you. I had a feeling that this woman just might have been trying to do both. "This is a valuable book. Clearly you know that or you wouldn't be here, but without some proof of ownership, it would be risky for me to buy it."

She straightened up. "What are you implying? That it's stolen? That's outrageous."

I held up my hands. "I didn't say that."

In so many words, I mentally added.

"I have to check the path of the book to see how it came into your hands. That's something that has to be done to make sure it's an authentic first edition."

"I'm telling you it's a first edition. That's all you need to know."

I shook my head. "I'm sorry, but I can't just take your word for it. I would need to have it authenticated before I would buy it. That would take a few weeks to get done, but I'm interested. There is a rare book dealer in—"

"A few weeks? Are you insane? I don't have a few weeks. I don't even have a few days. You need to buy this book. Now. Today. In cash."

Sadie wrinkled her nose. "That book is really old. What's the hurry? And who has seven thousand dollars in cash lying around?"

The nameless woman glared at her. "I don't expect some pixie dressed as the mistress of Christmas to understand."

"At least I have Christmas spirit," Sadie shot back with her hands on her hips.

The woman raised her fist in the air. "You lost your chance. This is the last time you will ever hear from me!" And she stormed out of the shop.

Sadie folded her arms over her red dress. "Was she trying to say she didn't like my outfit?"

I ignored her. "Something very strange is going on here. Why was she being so shady about that book?"

I peered out the window, expecting to see the woman making her way up the street, but she stood in front of Charming Books, talking to Hank. He must have been walking back to his silver van after making more deliveries to the many small businesses on the street when she stopped him. Hank pointed down River Road in the direction of the Niagara River and the village's ill-fated courthouse, which had been in disrepair since May. She nodded at something he said and then marched down the street.

Hank shook his head as he watched her go before climbing into the van and driving in the opposite direction.

"I know a lot of super weird things happen in this shop," Sadie said. "But I'm not wrong in thinking that that was extra weird, even for Charming Books, right?"

I turned to Sadie. "You're not wrong. It was weird. Super weird indeed."

Chapter Three

"What's super weird?" a male voice asked from the direction of the door that led to the kitchen at the back of the shop.

Cascade Springs Chief of Police David Rainwater stepped through the kitchen door. It was a miracle I didn't swoon right there on the spot.

He was the handsomest man I had ever seen. I still pinched myself in disbelief that he was my soon-to-be husband. It was surreal. He was Native American and a member of the Seneca Nation that had lived in the Niagara region for hundreds of years. He had brown skin, chiseled features, and stunning amber eyes. If I didn't know better, I would have said that the magic of the shop had somehow brought the two of us together because it seemed that only the mystical forces of the shop could have brought me such a man.

Rainwater walked further inside the room carrying two cardboard boxes. "Do you have somewhere to put these?"

I raised my brow. Rainwater was in the middle of moving into my apartment. It had been happening bit by bit over the last several weeks. Every time he showed up with another suitcase or cardboard box, he would assure me that he wasn't bringing anything more, as the apartment had become a maze of boxes and suitcases.

"Maybe the storage room by the kitchen? Or if you think you can find room for them on the stack of boxes upstairs, have at it. We will find a place for everything after the honeymoon." My plan was to get through this wedding and then focus on combining our households.

Rainwater grinned. "I'll add them to the stack then. This is the last one." He paused. "I think. My sister keeps finding other things she thinks I will need when I move. Truth be told, I think she's just excited about the massive increase of closet space in the house. I saw her on Pinterest looking at closet organizing tips. She's having the time of her life." He chuckled. "So tell me about this weirdness. I have been packing and doing departmental paperwork all day and could use some interesting news."

Sadie waved her hand as if Rainwater was a teacher and she was waiting to be called on. "A witch came into the shop and yelled at Violet."

"That is interesting," Rainwater said.

I appreciated the fact that he didn't get all caught up in her use of the word "witch" or really react to the news that I had been yelled at. We had come a long way in our relationship. "Sadie, she was not a witch."

"She looked like one. If she was in a lineup, I'd pick her as the witch any day, even if the whole cast of Harry Potter was in it."

"Are there witches in Cascade Springs?" Chief Rainwater asked, sounding a bit concerned. He glanced at me as if he expected me to have the answer. I guessed he looked to me for answers because of the shop and the tree. He thought I would know about all magical and mystical things that might come up in the village.

In the middle of the shop was the birch tree that was over two hundred years old, at least one hundred years older than a birch tree should live. When my ancestress Rosalee, who was an herbal healer, moved to Cascade Spring and built her home around the birch tree, she discovered that if she watered the tree with mystic water from the natural springs that the village was named after, the tree would thrive. She was the first Caretaker of the tree. The role was passed down from mother to daughter through the generations after.

Over time, the mystic power infused itself beyond the tree into the house and bookstore. Through the books, it reveals messages to the Caretaker. Right now, the Caretaker was me.

When I told Rainwater the truth about the shop months ago, he was more accepting than I'd expected. The shop's essence still caught him off guard from time to time, especially since he was over six feet tall and had to acquire the skill of dodging flying books. He was learning—he hadn't been hit by a flying book in at least a week. That was a record.

"Not as far as I know," I said, looping back to his first question about witches in Cascade Springs.

Sadie fluffed her skirt. "She did insult my outfit. How could she do that? I think it's festive."

"It's very festive," I said. "But Christmas is over two weeks away. I thought you would save an outfit like that for Christmas Eve or Christmas Day."

"This?" Sadie shook her head. "For real Christmas? No, thank you. This is just a warm-up outfit. I have things much more Christmasy to wear closer to the date."

21

Rainwater's brow went up, and I did my best to hide my smile. Fashion was as important to Sadie as books were to me. I wasn't going to tease her about it, and truth be told, she looked adorable in anything she wore.

"I need to get back to my shop," Sadie said. "I've left it too long. So many people are coming in looking for outfits for the wedding and for Christmas too." She said Christmas like it was clearly a secondary event. "It's going to be incredible. We have so many surprises in store for the two of you. Daisy and I are going to blow your socks off."

When Sadie had left, Rainwater said, "Do you really think we want to have our socks blown off?"

"Hard to say."

He laughed and enveloped me in a hug. Then, he looked around.

"There aren't any customers here right now," I said with a chuckle.

"Oh good," he said and promptly planted a kiss on my lips.

"Get a room!" Faulkner cawed. He was no longer in the tree, but on his perch by the front window where he could glower at every passerby.

"Is the crow staying after the wedding?" Rainwater teased.

"Sure is. It's a package deal, David. A wife, magical bookshop, sarcastic crow, and escape artist tuxedo cat. No backing out now."

He grinned. "I guess I'm stuck then. Now tell me about the witch." He followed me over to the two sofas in front of the fireplace. The flames snapped and crackled in the hearth. Emerson curled up in his cat bed in front of the fire, but he wasn't asleep. He watched Rainwater and me so intently, I thought he could understand our conversation. There were times with Emerson and with Faulkner when I thought they understood every word I said. More than once, Emerson has helped Rainwater and me solve a murder case. The question was whether had he been part of it by chance or if the little tuxedo cat knew exactly what he was doing. I was already dealing with the shop's mystical properties. I couldn't really entertain the thought that I had a magical cat too.

I sat in the sofa facing the front door, so I could jump into action if any customers came in. Even though it was Wednesday, I expected the shop to grow busy as the day went on since we were so close to Hanukkah and Christmas. Was there really a better holiday gift than a book? I certainly didn't think so.

"She's not a witch," I said, repeating what I told him earlier. "At least, I don't think so. She's a book dealer, I imagine."

"A book dealer? What's so scary about that? You have book dealers come into the shop all the time. Why was Sadie's dander up over it?"

"This one was different." I went on to tell him about the *Walden*, maybe-signed first edition, and the price tag. "But if it's real, it would be worth twice that. Maybe more. It's rare to see a book that old in mint condition. To be honest, I could hardly believe my eyes. I wish she had stayed longer so I could have had a better look at it. Even more, I wish she'd let me call a rare book dealer to get their take. I know someone who has a shop in Camden."

Camden was the next village over from Cascade Springs.

"Do you think she will come back?" he asked.

"My guess is yes. She really wanted me to buy the book."

"Then next time she's here, see if you can get a name or any personal information. I can look her up and make sure she's not some kind of criminal."

"Or witch?" I asked.

He shook his head. "Sorry. Law enforcement doesn't have a database for witches."

"Too bad."

He shifted in his seat. "I know I said I don't have any more boxes to bring over, but what about my recliner? Do we have the room? The only furniture you have to sit on in your living room is that horribly uncomfortable couch."

I raised my brow. "It's not *that* uncomfortable."

"I had to see a chiropractor after taking a nap on it." He folded his arms.

"We'll find a place for your recliner."

He grinned.

Rainwater would be moving into Charming Books with me and would rent his house to his sister Danielle and ten-year-old niece, Aster. His sister worked as a waitress at a local café and was a single mom. He was giving her a much better rental rate for a house in Cascade Springs than anyone else could or would in the village. Of course, he was right. And it was a bit of extra money coming in.

When we got engaged, where we would live involved many long conversations. Rainwater had been living in his house with his sister and niece for a few years. After a messy divorce, Danielle had moved to Cascade Springs three years ago to escape her ex-husband, and Rainwater wanted her to live with him so he could give his sister and niece extra protection. However, Danielle's ex-husband was now completely out of the picture, and the whole family could breathe a sigh of relief.

Even so, he hadn't wanted to ask Danielle and Aster to move. They were just beginning to find their place in Cascade Springs.

Danielle was a waitress at Le Crepe Jolie, the best café in the village, owned by my high school friend Lacey and her husband Adrien, and Aster was thriving and making friends at school.

We considered me moving into that house with them, but the truth was I didn't want to leave Charming Books. I was still getting used to being the Caretaker for the shop. There was so much more I needed to learn. Also, to be honest, as much as I loved Danielle and Aster, I didn't want to start my married life living with my husband's family looking over my shoulder. I just knew that that was a recipe for disaster.

Thankfully, Rainwater had understood how I felt and agreed to move to Charming Books. It was the perfect solution for now. I didn't know if we would always live above the bookshop, but I wasn't ready to leave yet. Now, I just had to find a place for his massive recliner, and married life would be just fine.

I held his hand. "We'll find room for your stuff. Don't worry. We have all January and February to get settled. It's usually quieter around the shop at that time anyway. I don't want you to worry about me making space for you here because I will. I want this to be your home just as much as it's mine or Emerson's or..." I looked at the perch in the window. Faulkner was glowering down at me. "Or Faulkner's."

The large crow smoothed his feathers. I didn't think for a moment that I'd get away with not saying Charming Books was his home too.

Rainwater smiled and grabbed me around the waist, pulling me close. "I'm not worried. Things aren't important." He looked into my eyes. "And it already feels like home because you're here. Wherever you are is home to me. You're all I need. I've been waiting for this for so long."

25

I smiled at him. He made it sound like he had been chasing me for ages, but Rainwater and I had only been seriously dating since January and we were marrying in December. To me, that was a whirlwind romance. However, I think we both wanted this to be the way our love story would go, even if it had taken me a bit longer to figure it out than him.

Rainwater was steady that way. I never for a moment wondered who he really was. He had no secrets from me. I was the one who had been holding back for all those months. I had secrets, and some of them were downright unbelievable. When he learned the truth about this shop and my part to play in it, he accepted it. He accepted me.

He proved to me I would be the Waverly woman to break the chain of unsuccessful romances. Every Caretaker before me, including my mother and my grandmother, had had a string of failed love affairs. I'd thought for a long time that would be my destiny too, but then I realized the difference was that none of these women had trusted the man they'd loved enough to let him in on their secret. When I'd told Rainwater the truth, I broke the cycle. I had to believe that. It was the only way forward for us. It was a way forward in trust and belief in our relationship. I think every Waverly woman before me had lost that trust somewhere along the way. I thought of my parents. They were no exception.

I pulled back from his embrace. "In any case, we have so much to do. I want to find this mystery woman. But I'll wait until after the wedding to dig into it. I have a feeling that if she really wants to sell this book to me, she will be back. What's a few days to wait?"

Just then, a book appeared on the coffee table in front of us. I would have sworn that a moment ago, the table was completely clear. I hadn't yet picked the coffee table books that I wanted to display on it for the day.

"It's *Walden*," Rainwater said in a hushed tone.

The book fell open and its pages fluttered until it stopped on a particular page.

I rubbed the pressure point on the side of my temple. "Of course it is."

Chapter Four

I didn't want to read the page that the shop so obviously wanted me to read. I didn't want to receive some cryptic literature-laden message from the shop. Couldn't I just have a week off from my duties as the Caretaker of the shop for my wedding? Was that too much to ask? Apparently it was.

When I made no move to look at the pages, Rainwater picked up the book. As soon as it was on his lap, it snapped closed as if in anger. The shop might be all right with me sharing my secret with Rainwater, but it surely didn't want anyone else trying to communicate with it or decipher its messages.

"Geez," Rainwater said. "I'm lucky I didn't get a paper cut." He held his hands in the air as if he was afraid the book would bite him. Considering how hard the book had closed itself, he wasn't far off the mark.

I held out my hands. "Give it to me."

He shook his head. "You're going to have to take it. I'm afraid to touch it."

I moved the book from his lap to mine. As soon as I lifted my hands from the book, it opened to a page. My eyes fell on the line:

The cost of a thing is the amount of what I will call life which is required to be exchanged for it, immediately or in the long run.

This couldn't be a good sign.

Rainwater peered over my shoulder. "What do you think the essence is trying to tell you?"

The essence was what we called the power in the shop. It ultimately came from the mystical springs that were in the park behind the bookshop. Every other day, I had to go into the woods and collect water from those springs. When I watered the birch tree with the mystical spring water, the essence of the spring became infused into the tree and the shop. It was able to communicate with the Caretaker—me—through messages in books just like this. I would be lying if I didn't say that sometimes I've lain awake at night, pondering how incredible it all was.

"What I think it means is there will be a price for the woman's visit. I don't know if she's the one who will pay it or me."

"You can tell that from one little sentence?" He shifted in his seat on the couch. "And that's not the only line on that page. How do you know that's the phrase the essence wants you to read?"

I looked at him. "Well, it's certainly not his marveling at the cost of a house being eight hundred dollars, which is the next line."

Rainwater wrinkled his smooth brow.

I touched his arm. "I'm sorry. I don't know how I know what line the essence wants me to read. I just do. I guess I've never questioned it before."

He covered my hand with his. "Okay, but it still doesn't mean that something bad is going to happen. She was trying to sell you *Walden*. I'm sure the book is reminding you of the possible cost a rare book's first edition would be."

I sighed and wished I could be as sure as he was, but I had had too many strange experiences with the messages from Charming Books to believe that the shop's essence was speaking to me in such a literal sense. "I think it's something more than that."

"Could it be that you just want something else to focus on?"

I looked at him. "What do you mean?"

He put his hands on my shoulders. "Could it be that you have pre-wedding jitters? We have a lot going on right now, and this woman's surprise visit just added to your already full plate. It would make sense if you fixated on it."

I looked up into his amber-colored eyes. They looked more golden than amber in the light coming in through the skylight and windows than they normally did. "No, it's not that. I mean, yes, I'm a little apprehensive about what Grandma Daisy and Sadie have in store for the wedding day, but not about marrying you. I have never been so sure of something in my life."

He smiled. "Okay. Then, let's put the woman and *Walden* out of our heads until after the wedding. If that woman, whoever she was, really wants to sell you the book, she will be back just like you said."

"And if she doesn't come back?" I asked.

He shrugged. "Then it was just another strange day at Charming Books. Where, let's face it, strange is kind of the norm here."

Faulkner cawed from his perch by the front window as if he were trying to emphasize on Rainwater's point. "Rather than love, than money, than fame, give me truth."

I rubbed my forehead. "I knew I never should have taught him Thoreau."

Rainwater looked up at the bird. "Yeah, that's going to backfire."

* * *

Over the next several days, putting the encounter with the woman out of my head proved to be easier than I expected, but that was mostly due to the fact that Grandma Daisy and Sadie had packed my days with wedding preparations. I had been plucked, fluffed, exfoliated, and detoxed within an inch of my life. By the time the morning of the wedding came around, I was exhausted.

I woke up at four and stared at the ceiling of my bedroom. I was getting married today. The gravity of that hit me all at once. I didn't know what to expect from the day, and I was seriously regretting my hands-off approach when it came to planning. Letting Grandma Daisy and Sadie handle all the arrangements seemed like a great idea months ago when Rainwater and I had gotten engaged. Now, I wasn't so sure.

Most of all, I wanted to remember this day and, no matter what happened, burn it in my memory forever. It didn't matter that a videographer and photographer would be there. I had a fear that the busyness would turn the most important day of my life into a blur and that I would miss all those little moments that made it special.

I groaned and covered my face with the back of my arm. A loud purr began in my ear. Emerson was here to comfort me. I lowered my arm and squinted at him. All I could make out of his lithe body were the white patches on his tuxedo that glowed in the dim street light coming in through the window.

He meowed in my face.

"I know. You have no worries about today, do you? Oh, to have the life of a housecat."

Emerson arched his back and hissed softly. It wasn't in anger, but it was most certainly to remind me that he was much more than a mere housecat.

I scratched him between the ears. "I know, Emerson. You're special."

The purring resumed. Emerson was never one to turn down a compliment. He was certain he deserved all the praise.

The cat moved away, and I made out the shape of a book where he had been sitting. It wasn't unusual for me to fall asleep with a book or three in my bed. Last night, I had gone to bed so late after the wedding rehearsal and dinner that I passed out as soon as my head hit the pillow. I hadn't brought a book with me to bed. I knew that for certain.

I scooted up into a sitting position and reached for the light on my nightstand. When I turned on the light, there was a volume of *Walden* on top of my quilt.

I exhaled. Part of me hoped I'd brought this book to bed with me. That would mean the shop's mystical essence had nothing to do with it, and certainly hadn't put the book in my bed to bring to mind the peculiar woman who'd stormed out of my shop earlier in the week.

I rubbed the back of my neck. I felt a headache begin to form at the base of my skull. "Maybe," I said to no one but myself because Emerson had already left the bedroom, "maybe I grabbed it last night on the way up."

By the look of it, it was a mass-market paperback edition that I had in the shop for sale.

"Yes, that must be it," I said, still talking to only myself. "I'm sure I just absentmindedly picked it up in my sleepy state." Feeling better, I started to snuggle back into bed, hoping to catch a little more sleep.

The shop's essence wasn't having it though. The book fell open, and the pages fluttered to life. At last, the pages stopped moving, and they settled wide open on the bed.

I squinted at the page and then looked up at the ceiling. "Come on. It's my wedding day. You won't even give me a break on my wedding day?"

As if to make a point, the volume scooted one inch closer to me. If I hadn't seen this happen before, I would have screamed.

Instead, I grimaced and a large part of me didn't want to look at the pages to see what the shop wanted me to know. I doubted it was best wishes on my upcoming nuptials.

I peered at it. Wedding or not, I was far too curious not to look. Not to mention, I knew the shop's essence wouldn't leave me alone until it believed I had absorbed its message.

I picked the book up and set it on my lap. My eyes fell on the line that read:

Be it life or death, we crave only reality. If we are really dying, let us hear the rattle in our throats and feel cold in the extremities; if we are alive, let us go about our business.

I looked up at the ceiling again. "Nice. A cheerful passage for my special day."

The book snapped closed. It seemed to me that the essence did not appreciate my attitude.

I sighed. There was no going back to sleep now. I got out of bed.

It was a losing battle to try to put the lines out of my head. Was the passage trying to tell me to get on with the business of the day, or was it telling me of a death?

I dressed in jeans, a thick hooded sweatshirt, and wool socks. Over that, I put on snow pants and my winter coat and topped it off with a hat and a scarf. The scarf covered most of my face. Only my blue eyes could be seen in my bedroom mirror. That reminded me of the mystery woman again. When she had stepped into the shop earlier this week, all I could see of her were her eyes. My eyes were blue with a tinge of gray. Hers were the brightest blue I had ever seen. They almost looked artificial, like she was wearing colored contact lenses.

I groaned. There was I was again wondering about the mystery woman when I should have been heeding the shop's advice and going about my business.

And my business was my duty to the birch tree. Part of that duty was to water the tree every other day with water from the springs in the park. The waters were special—mystical even. They had kept the birch tree alive for over two hundred years, and make no mistake, this was no ordinary birch tree.

I left my apartment and paused in the middle of the children's book loft that was just outside my apartment door. It was decorated as a fairy forest with toadstools for seats and a mural of fairies peeking out around the bookshelves lined with the bright spines of picture books. Kids and parents alike loved the children's loft. It was my favorite room in the house when I was growing up at Charming Books. I used to spend countless hours there daydreaming and praying that my mother's cancer would magically disappear. It never did.

I padded in my stocking feet to the top of the spiral stair-case that wrapped around the birch. Faulkner was asleep on his favorite branch. His long black beak was tucked under his left wing. Moonlight that came into the shop through the skylight above his head glistened on his ebony feathers, making him look more like a stone sculpture than a living, breathing bird.

I grabbed my snow boots by the front door and carried them into the kitchen. I perched on the kitchen stool and put them on. Emerson appeared at my feet. He had a knack for doing that, and I rarely ever saw him coming. He looked at me with expectation on his black and white face.

"Nope," I said as I laced up the second boot. "Not happening. No way."

He cocked his head so that the white side of his face caught the light.

"Double nope."

His ears went back and he gave me the most pitiful expression he could muster, which was saying a lot because Emerson was the most expressive cat I had ever met.

My shoulders slumped forward. "Emerson, I can't take you with me to the springs this morning. I can't risk you running off today."

He lowered his head and stared despondently at his two white forepaws. His thin black tail beat a staccato rhythm on the floor.

I groaned, not knowing why I bothered to argue with him. The tuxie always won, and to be honest, there was no way for me to stop him from coming along or following me. He had a history of sneaking out of the house. Many times, I found him out in the village, prancing up and down the streets like he owned the place. My guess was Emerson believed just that. It was pointless to tell him otherwise, just like it was pointless to tell him to stay home.

"Fine," I said, "but it's very cold outside, which means you have to let me carry you and keep you close. I can't have you getting frostbite."

He lifted his head and a smug cat smirk curled his lips. He knew as well as I did that my resistance was futile.

I pulled my stocking cap down further over my ears and went out the back door of the house. It was still early and as dark as midnight in the back garden.

Before I went through the garden gate that led to the woods and the park, I stopped to grab my grandmother's watering can from a shelf in the garden shed. One full can of water every other day was all the tree needed to stay alive and vibrant. Normally, I watered the tree at night, but because of the wedding, I didn't know if I would be back in time tonight. It was more important to water it every other day than the time of day. At least that's what I had found over the last couple of years.

Goodness knows I have tried shortcuts along the way, thinking I would make it easier on myself if I cut a few corners. One time, I'd gathered up gallons of the spring water and stowed them in the kitchen. My hope was that it would be easier to water the tree without having to run back and forth through the woods quite as often. It was a good plan. Sadly, it didn't work. It seemed that the water lost its mystical essence if it sat around for any length of time. It didn't matter how long I held the water— be it one day or just a few hours—by the time I poured it into the ring of dirt surrounding the birch tree, it had lost its power.

I knew because the birch tree's leaves would turn brown and fall off. It happened more times than I would like to admit, and I wasn't going to let it happen again.

I had to go to the springs. There was no alternative. I knew I was taking a risk by watering the tree earlier than usual. I didn't even know if it would work. Perhaps Rainwater and I would have to go into the woods after the wedding to collect more water.

I was going through the garden gate when I heard something in the snow behind me. I turned to find Emerson leaping through the deep snow like an arctic fox in the tundra. "Are you sure you want to do this? It's awfully cold out."

He meowed softly as if to say his mind was made up. I was certain it was.

"All right. Let's go. Sadie said she would be at Charming Books at nine." Apparently, even after all the beauty treatments I received this week, it was still going to take a lot of work to get me ready for the wedding, or so I'd been told.

Emerson looked down at his snow white chest as if taking in his handsome tux that was always a perfect fit. He purred.

"Yes, you are already wedding ready. It must be difficult to look so dashing all the time."

I patted my shoulder, and the cat ran at me, jumped onto my arm, and pranced up my body until he perched on my shoulder like a parrot. Usually, I would have made him walk to the springs and back, but it was dark and cold. I didn't want to worry about him wandering off in the forest. Today was going to be stressful enough.

Chapter Five

There was a well-worn path from the back garden behind Charming Books that led to the woods and the village park where the springs flowed. Generations of Waverly women walked into those woods year after year to collect water for the tree. So many times, I wondered how my ancestress Rosalee had known what to do with the water. How did she know that watering the tree would lead to the essence? Did she find out accidently? There was no record of how she made the discovery. It was a secret Rosalee took to the grave.

But she must have had a feeling that the springs were special. Rosalee was a naturalist and a healer. She came to Cascade Springs from Ohio after her husband died in 1812 because she had heard of the healing waters. Somehow, even before she arrived, she had known the place was special.

An owl hooted above in the canopy, and Emerson's claws dug into my thick coat. He was a small cat, and a strong hawk could carry him off if given the chance, but Emerson would give them one heck of a fight if they tried. I placed a gloved hand onto his black back, hoping that would soothe him.

I could hear the owl, but not see it. A second owl answered the call, but I couldn't pinpoint where either were hiding in the trees. It was just two hours before dawn, but it felt like the middle of the night in the dense wood.

Wind rustled bare branches overhead, causing them to knock together in a *clack, clack, clack* that made me shiver. The air was bitterly cold, but the forest broke the worst of the wind. Emerson shivered, and I turned on the small flashlight that I kept in my coat pocket.

I didn't need the light to find my way to the springs. I had walked that path so many times that I could do it on the darkest night, but the flashlight gave me a sense of security during those early morning hours in the woods. Last week, a large snowstorm had blown into the village off of the Great Lakes, and as the temperatures in the days after never rose above freezing, the sixteen inches of snow was still there. For the first few days after the storm, I had to use my snowshoes to walk to the springs. It was my only hope of making it, but now it was packed down enough to walk in just snow boots.

I now saw other boot prints on the path. I reminded myself that it was a public park and visitors and residents alike could come and go as they pleased. This was the exact reason I got water from the spring in the dark whenever possible. I didn't want any nosy neighbors asking uncomfortable questions.

The owl hooted again, and I picked up speed. There was no time to delay. The sooner I completed this most important errand, the sooner I could turn my focus to the day ahead and marrying the man of my dreams.

The springs were in a clearing, surrounded by birch trees. The springs were a series of basins carved into the rock face of a steep hill. Pure groundwater bubbled up in the basins, where it could break through the snow and ice. The birch trees that circled the large pool glistened with a coating of fresh snow. If I had to conjure up a mystical place in my mind, this would be it. It was made even more so by the stillness and clarity of winter.

A large rock with a deep fissure was to my right. The healing water bubbled up through that crack and down the side of the rock. The water's source was an aquifer connected to the Niagara River. Until recently, I'd thought the aquifer was confined to this little section of the woods, but that all changed when the village hall had been excavated and fresh spring water was discovered all around the structure's base.

When I reached the water's edge, I kneeled down and stared at its icy surface. The light was just beginning to soften the sky, telling of the sunrise to come. It danced and sparkled across the iced surface, but the pool wasn't completely frozen because the water was always on the move. Sometimes, when it was very cold, the entire pool would freeze. Even Niagara Falls itself had been known to freeze when the temperatures dropped well below zero. It was cold this morning but in the high teens, so the water continued to run.

However, as far as I could reach from the safety of the bank, the water was frozen. I wasn't going to risk walking out onto the ice to reach open water. Instead, I was going to have to break the ice. Emerson knew the drill and jumped from my shoulder as I picked up a fist-sized rock that I always left at the side of the pool. Taking the rock, I hit the surface of the ice until it cracked enough to let me dip the watering can into the frigid water. I shivered as the icy liquid soaked through my gloves to my fingers, even though I took care to keep them out of the spring.

Soon, the watering can was filled and my fingers were cramping from the cold. I stood on my stiff legs. "It's time to go."

Suddenly, a loud crack rang out from somewhere in the forest. It wasn't like a tree branch cracking from the wind. It was as if someone had taken a log and whacked it against the trunk of another tree. I let out a breath. It was probably a large buck making noise. Whoever was causing the ruckus, I didn't want to meet them in the woods in the dark.

I held the watering can close to my chest, taking care not to spill any of the precious water. "Emerson, let's move."

When I looked down, the little cat was gone.

My heart began to race. It was just like the little tuxedo to go missing at a time like this.

"Emerson," I hissed. "Now is *not* the time to play games."

There was a flash of light to my right one hundred feet away.

I turned off my own flashlight and tucked it in my pocket. It took a moment for my eyes to adjust to the darkness. I could see the sky brightening through the trees. I didn't see another light other than the beginnings of the sunrise in the east. I began to believe that I had imagined the flash, but I knew I had not imagined Emerson's disappearance or the cracking sound.

I was just about to call for my cat again when I saw the light a second time. There was no doubt the beam was coming from a flashlight sweeping back and forth through the woods. It was almost as if the person was looking for something—a cat, perhaps?

I should stop the person and find out what was going on, but what good would that do? It could just be someone out for an early morning walk even though the park was technically closed to the public from dusk to dawn. It was a rule I consistently broke every time I got water after dark.

Again the loud crack came, and I saw a tree near the beam of light jolt. I jumped at the noise and some of the precious spring

41

water sloshed out of my watering can. It was time to leave. I didn't want to have to explain to Rainwater that I was late for our wedding because I had been attacked by Bigfoot, assuming Bigfoot needed a flashlight to make his way through the forest.

And I knew what he would say if he knew I was in the woods so early on this cold morning. He would have insisted that he come with me. Maybe I was being superstitious, but I didn't want him to see me before the wedding.

I watched with rapt attention as the shape of a person, or at least what I thought was a person, appeared to walk among the trees. It was too dark to know for sure, and the beam of the flashlight was pointed far out in front of them, making it impossible to see the individual more clearly.

It was time to go, but I couldn't leave without Emerson. He could take care of himself as he had proven so many times, but he was still my cat. I loved him. You don't leave people or animals behind. It's always been my motto.

"Emerson," I whispered as the figure threw something else against the tree. Were they trying to break something open?

There was a soft meow, and I spotted my cat about ten feet away from me. The white markings on his chest, face, and paws gave him away as he crouched low to the ground.

Carefully, I inched toward the cat. He has been known to run away on more than one occasion, and I couldn't afford to play hide and seek today. "Let's go home."

Emerson growled low in this throat.

Whoever or whatever was in the woods throwing objects at the trees froze. My heart was in my throat—we'd been heard. There was no reason to be quiet any longer. I grabbed the cat, held him and the watering can close to my chest, and took off down the path toward the bookshop. I skidded on the slippery packed snow.

Hearing footsteps behind me, I ran faster, and I was grateful that I either walked or rode my bike everywhere in the village. If it hadn't been for that physical conditioning, I would have never beaten my pursuer home.

I dashed through the garden gate and through the backdoor, which I had left unlocked. Rainwater hated when I left the backdoor unlocked, but in this case, it worked to my advantage. Had I had to use the key, I wouldn't have been safe inside the house when the unknown figure came out of the woods.

The person was bundled up in a black winter snowsuit. I couldn't determine if it was a man or a woman, but at least now I could rest assured that it wasn't Bigfoot. It was a small comfort. They stood outside of my garden gate and stared at the house as if debating whether they wanted to come into the garden or not.

Emerson complained in my arms. I was still clutching him and the watering can as I stared out the window. I set the watering can on the kitchen island and Emerson on the floor. He looked up at me and yowled as if he felt like he needed to protest his mistreatment.

When the person looked up at the kitchen window, I jumped back from the pane. After a few seconds, I peered out again but the dark form had gone.

I checked to make sure the back door was locked and the deadbolt was in place. I picked up the watering can, and before I watered the tree, I double checked the locks on the front door as well.

With the doors secure, I turned my attention to the tree. As soon as the water hit the roots, nothing happened. I wished

I could say that the tree sparkled, began to sway or sing, or did something even remotely interesting. It did none of those things. I knew the tree would react only if it was *not* watered.

With the watering can empty, I knew what I had to do next. Call Rainwater.

"What's wrong?" he asked.

"Why do you think anything is wrong?" I asked.

"Because you specifically told me I wouldn't be hearing from you until I saw you at the wedding this afternoon." Even at this early hour, he sounded as if he was wide awake.

"Oh, I did say that, didn't I?"

"So something must have happened."

I sighed and told him about my trip to the natural spring and the mystery person in all black who had followed me back to Charming Books.

On the other end of the line was silence.

"David?"

Still nothing.

"David, are you still there?"

"I'm here. I'm just texting two of my officers to get over to Charming Books and search the area including the woods behind your shop." There was a pause. "Why would you go to the springs so early in the morning? Even more, why would you go to the springs without telling me?"

"I needed to water the tree today."

He sighed. Maybe he knew he couldn't argue with me when it came to the birch tree. "This is the second mystery person who you mentioned just this week."

"You mean in addition to the woman with the copy of *Walden*?"

"Was there a third mystery person sniffing around Charming Books?"

"No, just the two," I said as cheerfully as possible. Rainwater was frustrated with me and I didn't want to make it worse. I was beginning to regret calling and reporting being followed. However, I knew if I didn't tell him and he found out another way, it would be a whole lot worse. Entering into marriage with a lie—even by omission—probably wasn't the best way to go.

He sighed again.

"And even though I couldn't see this second person's face, I know it's not the woman that came to the shop the other day. Whoever this was, they were a lot bigger." I took a breath. "It was probably a hiker wondering why I freaked out and ran out of the woods. They probably wanted to see if I was okay."

"It could have been, but I'm still sending two officers over there to check it out. I need you to be safe."

"I know, it's our wedding day."

"Not just on our wedding day. I need you to be safe every day. If something had happened to you, Violet, I don't know what I would have done. I don't know if I'd survive it." His voice shook.

"Don't say that."

He was silent for a moment. "The officers are on their way now. Just stay inside. I don't want to have any more surprises before the wedding."

"Neither do I," I said.

Chapter Six

It seemed that Rainwater and I were going to get our wish for no more surprises. Hours later, I stood in front of a full-length mirror that Sadie had propped up against the tree and gawked at my reflection. I was a bride.

I'd be lying if I said I had been waiting for or expected this moment my whole life. Marriage had never really occurred to me as a possibility. Perhaps it was because I had been too invested in my research and scholarship in nineteenth-century literature. Or perhaps it was because I hadn't had an example of a successful romantic relationship to aspire to. Both Grandma Daisy and my mother only had a string of failures to speak of, just as every Waverly woman before them. Nothing predicted that I would be standing here today in a wedding gown, and yet, here I was.

The dress was one of the few decisions that Grandma Daisy and Sadie had left up to me. Like my grandmother said, if I didn't feel good in my wedding outfit, she was certain that I would show up in jeans and a T-shirt. She wasn't far off the mark about that.

I'd tried on many dresses, but as soon as I'd put this dress on, I knew it was the one. It had cap sleeves and a scoop neck, and it was embellished with tiny sequins and pearls sewn in the pattern of leaves all over the skirt. They reminded me of the birch tree's waxy leaves. No other dress truly stood a chance after that.

The problem was that the dress was way over my budget, but when the bridal gown attendant said she had a sample of the dress for sale that she would sell me for a fourth of the price, I snapped it up.

Except for fittings, today was the first time I was seeing the dress. Sadie kept it safe and locked in her dress vault at Modern Vintage all these weeks. She was afraid that Faulkner or Emerson would harm the fabric.

My hair was swept to one side and assembled in a loose braid with what seemed to be four hundred bobby pins that the hair dresser had stuck in my strawberry blonde hair.

Grandma Daisy put her hands on my shoulders as she stood behind me in the mirror. "I have never seen a more beautiful bride."

I smiled. "And I have never seen a more beautiful mayor."

Grandma Daisy tugged at the hem of her forest green silk jacket. As always, there was a silk scarf around her neck. This one shimmered with rhinestones and glittery tassels. "I do clean up nicely, don't I?"

Grandma Daisy had on a sharp pantsuit and somehow looked official and mischievous at the same time. My grandmother's silver bob glimmered in the bright light coming into the shop through the windows. It was cold outside, but that sun made a miraculous debut for the afternoon outdoor wedding. Guests were already sitting in the sixty-some wooden folding chairs in the front yard and more people, standing or bringing their own chairs, spilled out onto the sidewalk and street. Using her mayoral authority, Grandma Daisy had closed the section of River Road in front of Charming Books for the entire afternoon. She loved to wield her mayoral power. Thankfully, she typically used that power for good.

"I have something for you." Grandma Daisy removed a box from the pocket of her jacket. "Here."

I blinked at her. "What is it?"

"Let's just say it's something old."

I opened the box and inside was a brooch in the shape of the birch tree. I looked at the tree and at the brooch and back again. They were the same. "Where did you get this?"

"It was Rosalee's, and it's yours now. It's been passed down through the generations all the way to you. I've been meaning to give it to you ever since you moved back to the village, but I am now happy I dragged my feet so I could give it to you on this special day." She took it from the box. "You can wear it on your clothes or in your hair. I think hair is best for the wedding, don't you?"

I nodded because I was unable to speak.

She clipped the brooch on my hair. "There. Now you are ready."

"Thank you. I will treasure it."

"I know you will." Grandma Daisy kissed me on the cheek, and there were rare tears in her eyes. "I wish your mother were here for this day."

I felt my own tears begin to well up. "Me too." I rubbed my bare arms. I was going to freeze on the front porch. I shivered.

"I have something to keep you warm," Sadie said and appeared at my side with a deep green fur bolero that matched my emerald engagement ring. "This will keep you warm during the ceremony and at the reception too. And don't worry. It's faux fur. I'd never buy or sell the real thing."

I put it on and felt like a movie star, or more accurately, like a bookseller who was pretending to be a movie star for a day. "Thank you, Sadie."

"Don't worry, Violet," Grandma Daisy said. "We are at Charming Books. The shop will make sure everyone is comfortable during the ceremony. I put in a special request. Sometimes it still listens to me." Grandma Daisy headed to the bathroom. "I'm going to powder my nose one last time. I want to look my best too."

"What did she mean by that special request stuff?" Sadie asked.

"Who knows," I said nervously.

Seeming to forget about it, Sadie bounced to the window. "Looks like the whole village is here."

Knowing my grandmother, I was sure that was the case.

"It's about time!" Sadie exclaimed as she was barely able to contain her excitement.

"I should go out there and stand with your groom," Grandma Daisy said, reappearing from the bathroom.

I reached for her hand. "Before you go—have you heard from my father?" I asked. I did my best to sound like it wasn't a big deal. I didn't fool Grandma Daisy, though.

She pressed her lips together. "I haven't heard a thing, and that wasn't for lack of trying. You know Fenimore is a nomad. He travels around the country and Canada playing his guitar and scraping together just enough money to get by. I've tried every phone number and address I had for him, but no luck. My guess is he's wandered somewhere down south for the winter."

I nodded. "Thank you, Grandma."

She touched my cheek. "The rest of us—the whole village—are here for you today. And you have a man standing outside who can't wait to spend the rest of his life with you. Focus on that."

I nodded again, but a tiny part of my heart cracked.

Grandma Daisy went out the front door and as she went, I could hear the excited murmur of the crowd outside. It really did sound like the entire village was there.

Not to have either of my parents with me on my wedding day was a difficult truth to accept, even if I knew it was impossible for my mother to be there and very unlikely for my father.

My father was a traveling troubadour. He met my mother thirty-some years ago while he was playing and traveling through Cascade Springs at the height of tourist season in the village. He'd had no plans to stick around our tiny village, but when he met my mother, he stayed for the summer.

I was the result of their summer romance. At the end of the summer, my mother told him to go. She hadn't been planning to ever get married. And it wasn't until after he was gone that she found out she was pregnant with me. She raised me as a single mom and kept my father's name a secret. I never knew who he was until he showed up on my doorstep a little over a year ago, claiming to be my dad. It was a shock. In the time since, Fenimore and I tried to have a relationship of some sort, but I wouldn't call it a father-daughter relationship. I doubted that he would ever be in a place where he was comfortable with the title of dad, and I wasn't comfortable calling him that, anyway.

I had mixed feelings about him missing the wedding. On the one hand, it was the biggest day of my life and I wanted him there, especially since my mother couldn't be. But on the other hand, it didn't seem right to me that he be there and not my mother. I hardly knew him.

"Wedding!" Faulkner called so loudly from his perch on the front porch that I heard him inside the shop.

I looked at my phone, and he was right. It was time to get married. I put the phone in my pocket. The pockets were the most amazing feature of this dress.

Sadie stood at the kitchen door with Emerson in her arms. "We're going out the back door, Vi, so that you can walk up the aisle."

I knew this from the wedding rehearsal the evening before. "Right." Even knowing that, I couldn't resist peeking out the front window one last time.

My grandmother stood at the gate and greeted guests. My stomach tightened and my nerves began to get to me. Faulkner was on his perch and flapped his wings to the left of the front door. He snapped his beak when the photographer got too close. The young woman yelped and ran away. She would need to use her zoom lens if she wanted any photos of the crow.

I found myself searching the crowd for the woman with *Walden*. Even though this was the most important day of my life, I couldn't get that encounter out of my head or the passage that the shop's essence made me read very early that morning:

Be it life or death, we crave only reality. If we are really dying, let us hear the rattle in our throats and feel cold in the extremities; if we are alive, let us go about our business.

"Violet, step away from the window," Sadie said in a high-pitched voice. "We don't want anyone to see you before your big moment." She put a hand on my arm. "Let's go. It's time for you to get married."

I swallowed hard. "I'm ready."

Outside the back door of Charming Books, I stood in my heels with my fancy dress and the faux fur jacket Sadie had given me. The jacket was the only thing that was keeping me from freezing to death. Sadie was in a 1940s gold dress and matching cape.

We heard music playing from the front of the house.

She set Emerson in the snow. "He will lead the way."

As if he knew his job, Emerson pranced around the house with his tail high.

"Did Grandma Daisy hire a string ensemble?" I asked.

Sadie smiled. "That's just the first of many surprises you will see today. It's time to go." She started around the house. "Count to thirty, and then follow me."

I shivered, but I couldn't tell if it was from nerves or because I was freezing.

She disappeared around the side of the house, and I began to count. I waited as I was instructed, and then I started walking. My knees wobbled.

As I came around the side of the house, I was shocked at what I saw. The crowd was even larger than what I had seen through the window. It stretched up and down the street, but in a village as small as Cascade Springs, their faces were all familiar even though I was completely blanking at that moment and couldn't remember any names, including my own.

One of those faces stood out. It was the woman in the long skirt and giant coat who'd come to Charming Books just a few days before—the same woman who had tried to sell *Walden* to me. She was still in the village? She stood there in the middle of the street with other smiling faces, but she wasn't smiling. She was glaring at me.

I shook my head and glanced along the sidewalk, and then I saw another face I didn't expect. It was my father's. I gasped. I didn't know who I was more shocked to see.

"Vi!" Renee Reid, a friend and colleague from the community college, sat in the last row of folding chairs. "They are waiting for you."

My attention turned from the two surprise guests to the porch, and there he was. David Rainwater, my soon-to-be husband, was beaming at me. That smile was just for me.

Everything I had done or seen that morning and in those last few moments fell away. All I could see was Rainwater's smiling face. He didn't cry. He just looked happy. Radiant. I walked toward him as if we were attached by an invisible string. He took my hand and helped me up the porch steps. I held on tight. I would never ever let go of that hand.

"Let us begin," Grandma Daisy said.

* * *

After the wedding, Rainwater and I stood at the garden gate saying goodbye to guests as they made their way to the reception in a tent down the street along the river. Rainwater and I stayed behind for the time being for a few wedding photographs. I watch from the front yard as the photographer got a picture of Rainwater and his young niece Aster alone. The little girl adored her uncle. I knew this photo would be my favorite out of the entire wedding album. We had a small wedding party, and the pictures would not have taken long if it had not been nearly impossible trying to get a crow and a cat to cooperate.

I appreciated Rainwater's patience as we captured all the photos that I wanted.

Then something hit me. Maybe the photographer had gotten a picture of the mystery woman. But when I went to ask her, I found that she had already left to set up at the reception.

Grandma Daisy was the last to leave. She hugged Rainwater and then me. "I can't think of a time I've been happier."

"Thank you, Daisy. The service was perfect," Rainwater said.

She shook her finger at him. "No, no. No more calling me Daisy or mayor or anything else but Grandma Daisy. You're my grandson now."

His amber eyes sparkled. "Okay, Grandma Daisy."

"Now, you two freshen up," Grandma Daisy said with a wink. "Your ride to the reception will be here any minute. I should head there now and make sure everything is ready for your arrival." She kissed us both on the cheek. "Welcome to the family, grandson."

After Grandma Daisy left, we warmed up inside the bookshop while we waited for our ride. Rainwater asked, "What had you so distracted before you walked down the aisle? Was it Fenimore? I know you weren't unsure about marrying me."

I hugged him around the waist and leaned my head against his strong chest. "I never for a second had any doubts about marrying you. And yes, seeing Fenimore was very distracting." I frowned. "He didn't come up to greet us. I know crowds make him anxious. Or maybe he didn't want to wait."

Rainwater squeezed my hand. "He'll be at the reception."

I nodded. "He wasn't the only surprise guest. Remember that woman I told you about on Wednesday? She was in the crowd."

He raised his brow. "Really?"

I nodded. "I wonder if she will be at the reception. If she is, I will have to talk to her. Who she is remains a complete mystery to me."

Rainwater shook his head. "Only you would want to solve a mystery at your own wedding."

Outside the window, a white carriage stopped in front of the bookshop. The carriage was trimmed in twinkle lights and greenery. The horse was white and had a red velvet ribbon braided into its mane, and the driver wore a riding coat with a tail and a black top hat. There were many carriages in Cascade Springs that drive tourists around the village, but not one as fancy as this. "Is that our ride?"

"I would not expect anything less from Grandma Daisy."

The ride to the reception was short since it was just to the giant heated tent set up along the river across the street from the dilapidated village hall, but when we were within one carriage-length of the tent, and Rainwater tapped the driver on the shoulder. "Can you stop here?"

The drive pulled the reins. "Here, sir?"

"Yes," Rainwater said. "Thank you so much for the ride." He climbed out of the carriage and helped me out as well.

"David, what's going on?" I asked as he led me toward the river's edge.

"I just wanted to be alone with you for a moment more before we face everyone."

"All right." I squeezed his hand, and he led me toward the river.

"I have a gift for you."

"David, you didn't have to buy me anything." I blinked. "You already gave me a ring."

"We gave each other rings. I wanted to give you something uniquely yours, something that was only made for you."

He started to reach into his suit coat pocket and then stopped. He was facing the river, and I was facing him. His eyes went wide. He tucked whatever it was back into his pocket and ran toward the river at full tilt.

"David!" I called after him. I lifted up my skirt and followed him. I wasn't nearly as fast moving in my dress, but I was grateful that I'd insisted on wearing sneakers to the reception part of the evening. If I had still been wearing the heels from the ceremony, I would have fallen down for sure.

Rainwater was in the icy river, pulling a woman from water. I covered my mouth.

"Call for help!" Rainwater shouted over his shoulder.

I pulled my cell phone out of my dress pocket and called 911.

Rainwater pulled the woman onto the bank, but we both knew there was no hope. She was blue. Even so, Rainwater started CPR.

I stood there shivering, relaying to the dispatcher what was happening.

It was the woman from the shop. She had on the same giant winter coat that she had been wearing when she came to the shop and when I saw her at the wedding just two hours ago. Could it be that the book was inside of her coat? As I thought this, I noticed something else.

Her hand lay open, and there was something written on her palm. I lifted my skirt out of the snow and shuffled over so I could get a better look. All the while, I was still on the phone with dispatch.

The cold water had washed away some of the message scrawled in blue ballpoint ink, but it was still legible: "They stole my book."

My heart sank to the soles of my shoes. I knew immediately what book had been stolen. Someone had killed this poor woman and stolen the first edition of *Walden*.

Chapter Seven

Police officers who were dressed in suits and dresses for the wedding came running down to the riverbank. I recognized two EMTs and the coroner as well. Rainwater was the chief of police, so it made sense that all of these people were guests at our wedding. The sound of an ambulance cut through the winter evening air.

The two EMTs gently guided Rainwater to the side. He shivered as he gave orders through chattering teeth.

I grabbed an officer's arm as he ran by. "Chief Rainwater needs medical attention. He could get hypothermia from being in the water."

"Right." The officer removed his coat and ran over to him. Rainwater tried to refuse, but in the end, he accepted the coat and put it on.

More EMTs arrived. They had been on duty and were in uniform. Two of them whisked Rainwater up the riverbank and into the bay of an ambulance. I ran up the slippery bank with the hem of my dress in my hands.

A female EMT put her hand out. "Ma'am, you can't be here."

"I'm his wife," I pleaded.

She jerked back.

"She is," Rainwater said from inside of the ambulance.

The EMT stepped aside and let me climb into the ambulance.

His soaked tuxedo jacket was on the floor in a heap. He was wrapped up in a solar blanket. The heat in the ambulance bay was going full blast.

"One of my officers should be here soon with a change of clothes for me and another coat. I always have an extra uniform at the station," Rainwater explained.

I nodded as the surreal aspects of the last few minutes hit me. It was my wedding day. I should be inside of that heated tent celebrating with friends and family. Instead, here I sat in the back of an ambulance with my new husband who had almost frozen to death pulling a dead body from the river.

I shook my head. I shouldn't feel sorry for myself. A woman was dead. "It's her."

His brow wrinkled. "Her who?"

"The woman from the shop," I said and then lowered my voice. "The one with the first edition of *Walden*."

He sat up. "Are you sure?"

"I'm positive. I first recognized her by her coat. It was the same one she had on in the shop and at the wedding."

He nodded. "You still don't know her name?"

I shook my head. "Did you see her hand?"

Rainwater nodded. "It said 'They stole my book,'" he said.

"It has to be *Walden*."

"So this could very well be the reason she was killed."

An EMT tried to get Rainwater to lie back down, and Rainwater waved his hand away.

"I know it was her," I said.

"We can't jump to conclusions just yet. The coroner will determine if it was murder. She just as easily could have slipped on the ice and drowned."

"I know that," I said softly.

"Oh, Violet, does this remind you of Colleen?"

My childhood friend Colleen Preston died that very same way—drowning in the river. Some of the people in the village believed that she had been murdered. I was questioned and subsequently fled the village to escape their scorn even though I was completely innocent. It was only when I came back to Cascade Springs as an adult that it was proven her death was accidental. So yes, I knew very well how an accident could look like a murder.

Even so, I said, "I don't think it's an accident, and if it is murder, the motive was to steal that book."

"Who would do this?" he asked.

"I don't know." I started to shake.

Rainwater reached out a hand to me. "Are you okay?"

"Yep," I squeaked.

He smiled. "That's what I thought." He paused. "When my clothes get here…"

"I know. You have to investigate."

"I can get the investigation rolling. My officers and the coroner can process the scene. I'll be at the reception as soon as I can."

"Should we even have the reception? It doesn't seem right. A woman is dead."

He nodded. "Yes, we should still have it because we got married today. It's still a meaningful day." He studied me. "What is it? You have a strange look on your face."

"There's a dead body outside of our wedding tent. I think it would be odd if I didn't have a strange expression on my face."

"What—" He was cut off by his officers.

"Chief," Officer Wheaton stepped into the ambulance with a duffle bag. "We have your clothes." Officer Wheaton, who never had much use for me, shot an irritated look my way.

"Thank you, Wheaton." Rainwater tried to stand up but couldn't because of the low ceiling. He took the bag from Officer Wheaton. "Any new developments?"

Officer Wheaton glanced at me.

"You can speak frankly in front of my wife, Wheaton," Rainwater said.

"A water-logged matchbook for the Starlight B&B was discovered in the woman's pocket, sir."

Rainwater nodded. "Good. Check that out. Also talk to the wedding photographer and see if she got any photographs of the woman. Violet saw her at the wedding ceremony, so there might be pictures of her."

"Right." Officer Wheaton gave a stiff nod.

"Tell the group by the scene that I will be there in five minutes."

Officer Wheaton scowled at me once more and left the ambulance.

"Violet, go to the reception tent and get warm. Find something to eat while you're there too. I'll be there as soon as I can."

I frowned.

"Please." He stared at me with those amber eyes, making it impossible for me to look away.

I sighed. "Okay, but I'm going just to see if anyone at the reception saw anything."

"Whatever it takes. I'll send a couple of the officers over to speak to the guests too."

"What about Grandma Daisy? What do I tell her?" I asked. "She is going to want to know what is going on."

Rainwater let out a resigned sigh because he knew this was true.

"Tell her we have everything under control."

I could tell her that, but it didn't mean she would believe it.

I stumbled out of the ambulance and looked toward the river. There was a tight circle of emergency staff and police officers around where Rainwater had left the body. Red and white lights from the ambulance reflected off the ice-laden trees and trampled snow.

I started toward the reception tent, but I didn't get very far when my grandmother came running toward me. "Violet, my girl, are you all right?"

Her glossy silver bob blew about her face in the wind and her long cape fluttered around her shoulders. She looked like a queen who was sorely disappointed with her subjects. All that was missing was the crown. Faulkner was on her shoulder, which was a nice touch, though.

She crushed me with a hug.

"I'm okay," I managed to wriggle free despite the tight hold she had put me in.

She dropped her arms. "What's this about a dead body? Did you really find a dead body on your wedding day? Are you trying to set a record for finding dead people at the most inconvenient times?" She stepped around me and pointed to the officers by the river. "Is that where you found the body?"

Before I could answer any of those questions, my grandmother started off to the river's edge.

I sighed and followed. Rainwater wasn't going to like this.

"Excuse me, excuse me. Mayor coming through. Step aside," my grandmother said as she forced her way toward the crime scene. "Mayor and her crow coming through."

Officers backed away, but I thought that had more to do with Faulkner's beady eyes than my grandmother's words.

I wove through the crowd behind her.

Grandma Daisy stopped abruptly. "Oh my land, Roma Winterbourne! How did she come to an end like this? What a terrible fate for her. I can't say I'm surprised though. It seemed like luck was never on her side."

Rainwater, who appeared at my side in new dry clothes and a warm coat, asked, "You know her?"

"Yes, I do," my grandmother said. "I would recognize Roma Winterbourne anywhere. Some people change, but never enough for me not to know who they are. A person's face doesn't transform that much with age, at least in my opinion. And as you know, my opinion is always right. This doesn't include the people who get plastic surgery, of course. They cheat."

"This woman was in the shop a few days ago," I said. "She never mentioned she knew you."

Rainwater put a hand on both of our shoulders and directed us away from the riverbank. "We need to give the emergency responders room to work."

Grandma Daisy nodded. Faulkner bobbed his head along with her.

"Grandma Daisy, why didn't she mention you when she was at Charming Books?" I asked. "It's your shop."

She shrugged. "How am I to know? Besides, it's your shop, my dear. You're the Caretaker now."

As soon as she said this, she looked around to see if anyone might have overheard her. No one appeared to be listening.

"And she wouldn't ask after me in the shop because I had already spoken to her that day."

My mouth hung open. "What?"

"Grandma Daisy," Rainwater said. "You had better start at the beginning."

My grandmother tucked her hands into her cape. "I already had a conversation with her earlier in the day. She had been looking for someone to buy a copy of *Walden* from her, and I told her to go to Charming Books. I was quite proud when I said that my granddaughter had her PhD on that very author." She wrinkled her nose. "I have to say Roma wasn't as impressed as I would have liked her to be, but she said she would talk to you all the same. She was desperate to sell the book."

"How do you know her? How do you know her name?" My questions came out in a rush.

Grandma Daisy fluffed her coat. "She was my college roommate way back in the stone age. Until this week, I hadn't seen her in over fifty years. Let me tell you, it was a shock when I ran into her on the street. I'm sorry to say that she looked like she had fallen on hard times." She looked in the direction of where Roma Winterbourne's body lay. "The last time I saw her, she was a chipper and motivated coed planning to start a job in journalism in the big city. I was a little jealous, I will admit, because I knew there was no big city in my future. My future was coming back to Charming Books and tending to the bookshop and the tree."

I didn't know my grandmother had wanted a life other than caring for the shop. She had never let on that she had once wanted something more. It was hard for me to come back to Cascade Springs to accept my inheritance, but I always thought that struggle was unique to me.

I shook my head. "You had a friend come to my shop and you didn't tell me she was coming? All you had to do was shoot me a quick text message."

"I didn't say she was my friend. She was my roommate for one year, my freshman year. We were assigned to live together. We got along okay. She was an odd duck, but sometimes people say that about me. They're wrong, of course. I'm as normal as it comes considering the magical inheritance and all."

Rainwater and I shared a look.

"What? You don't believe me?"

Faulkner cocked his head as if to say he was ready to come to Grandma Daisy's defense if needed.

"Why didn't you ask me if the woman had stopped by, though? I have seen you dozens of times since her visit, and you never once brought it up," I said.

"And you never told me that she came to the shop. I assumed that she changed her mind about talking to you. I didn't want to give you one more thing to worry about this close to the wedding. I knew that if there was some rare edition of *Walden* floating around out there, you would try to find it."

Now, I had plenty to worry about because Roma was dead at my wedding. Somehow that was better?

Chapter Eight

I stepped into the reception tent. Everything was beautiful and glittery. Guests were seated at their tables and were eating. I was relieved to see that. The decorations were appropriate for the season. The room shimmered in deep greens, whites, silvers, and golds. An empty dance floor was in the middle of the tent, and a three-tier cake sat by the empty sweetheart table. It was decorated to look like birch tree bark. The string quartet playing in one corner of the tent wasn't loud enough to block out the nervous whispers and, I assumed, gossip that swirled around the room. All of it brought tears to my eyes.

Sadie threw up her hands. "Violet, only you would find a dead body at your wedding!"

I wrinkled my nose. I didn't think that was a compliment. "Does everyone in the tent know?"

"Yes," she said with a sigh. "It's all anyone can talk about. What should we do? Should we tell everyone to go home?"

I shook my head. "Rainwater is sending two officers in to ask the guests if they saw anything. I think we should get on with the reception as best we can despite the sobering tone."

"Oh, Violet!" Lacey Dupont hurried over to me with her hands stretched out. "You poor bride. After that beautiful wedding, this terrible thing has to happen."

Lacey was a rosy-cheeked, cheerful woman who, as far as I knew, never uttered a bad word about anyone. Her husband Adrien, who was also the chef at Le Crepe Jolie, placed his hands on her shoulders. Where Lacey looked like she was made of cotton candy and everything sweet, Adrien, who did body building as a hobby to work off the kitchen stress, looked like he was made of solid granite. Le Crepe Jolie had catered the reception.

"I hope it's all right that we went ahead and fed the guests," Lacey said.

"Yes, that was the right thing to do." I smiled at her and Adrien in turn. "It all looks so wonderful. I'm sorry tonight's events put a damper on it."

Adrien shook his head and said in his French-Canadian accent, "Do not worry about us. We worry about you."

I hugged them both.

"You need something to eat," Lacey said. "Let me fix you a plate. We have all your favorites from the café here. I made sure we had everything that you like." There were tears in her eyes.

"Lacey, it's perfect. You did an amazing job. And you're right, I should probably eat something. I was too nervous to eat much before the ceremony." I looked at the sweetheart table with its silver and gold accents. It was lovely, but not somewhere I'd want to sit by myself. "Is there another spot where I can eat? I don't want to sit at the sweetheart table alone."

"You won't have to," a deep voice said.

I turned to see Rainwater step into the tent followed by two officers. "My officers are going to quietly speak to the guests table by table. That should give us enough time to eat and have a first dance."

I looked up at him. "Really?"

"Really," he said. "I'm doing my best to give you the wedding you deserve."

I touched his arm. "I already had the perfect wedding. This is just the party."

"We will go fix up some plates!" Lacey clapped her hands, and she and Adrien hurried to the serving table.

"Violet," he said as his amber eyes pleaded with me, "I'm so sorry."

"There's nothing to be sorry about."

He shook his head. "There aren't many women who would say that on their wedding day."

I looked up at him. "I would think by now, David Rainwater, you would know I'm not like many women."

He took my hand, and we walked to the sweetheart table. Guests clapped for us. The next half hour felt surreal. We ate, cut the cake, and danced our first dance as a married couple, but all the time, I was aware of the two police officers moving around the room asking guests if they knew anything about the dead woman outside.

Rainwater led me off of the dance floor, and Officer Wheaton walked up to us. "Sir, the coroner is about to leave and wants to talk to you before he goes." He frowned at me.

If I had had any hope of Officer Wheaton being more accepting of me now that Rainwater and I were married, it was dashed. He was determined to dislike me, and it looked like a permanent condition.

"Tell him I will be there in a moment," Rainwater said.

Officer Wheaton nodded and left the tent.

Rainwater looked at me. "Violet, I'm—"

I placed a hand on his cheek. "Just go. You have to go. It's your job."

"This is not how I imagined spending our first night together."

I smiled. "It wasn't on my list of possibilities either. However, the sooner I get used to the idea of being married to a cop, the better, right? This isn't the first time that I've worried about you."

"I don't want you worrying about me."

I arched an expertly manicured brow at him. "I'm your wife now. It's sort of my job."

His face broke into a grin. "Okay, wifey."

I wrinkled my nose. "No 'wifey,' thanks."

He laughed. "It doesn't suit you at all. How about I call you Violet—my Violet?"

I smiled. "I'll take that. Now go, you have a case to solve."

He chuckled. "Yes, ma'am. You're almost acting like you don't plan on getting involved. We might be married now, but I know you haven't changed." He kissed me and then said in a low voice, "Make a point not to change, okay?"

"I will," I promised.

He turned to leave.

"David," I said, stopping him. "We have to find the book."

He turned back to face me. "We have to find out what happened to Roma first."

"I believe if we find one, we'll find the other." He nodded thoughtfully, then left the tent.

A moment later, Grandma Daisy walked over to me. Faulkner was still perched on her shoulder like it was something he did every day.

"Has Faulkner been here the whole time?" I asked.

Faulkner narrowed his eyes at me as if he were waiting for the answer to my grandmother's question as well. "No, I guess I didn't think about it."

Faulkner groomed the feathers on his right wing with his long pointed beak.

"Well, all I have to say is I'm glad we got through the ceremony before all of this chaos." Grandma Daisy picked up my left hand and looked at the wedding ring. "Yep, locked and loaded. There are no take-backs for this one."

"Grandma."

"Not that I think David would do that, but I personally could not have endured any more delays before this wedding. I have been waiting for this day for so long. I knew you and David were a perfect match from the moment you met. Now the only problem is this murder stuff is really going to put a damper on me getting a great grandchild."

I blushed and looked around. "Grandma! How can you talk like that? Roma was your friend."

"I never said we were friends. We were roommates. It wasn't anything more than that, but yes, I'm very sorry she was murdered."

"Stop saying murder," I hissed. "We don't know it was murder. It could just as easily have been an accident," I said, very nearly repeating Rainwater's words.

"Oh, I don't think so. Roma Winterbourne was the type to attract trouble. It would not be a shock to learn that she was killed."

"What do you mean?"

"Let's just say that she wasn't the most honest person. Maybe it's not fair for me to say that since I haven't seen her in so many years, but if she was anything like she was in college, she was a cheater and would cut corners to get what she wanted. On tests, with boyfriends. You name it. She found a way to cheat."

"How did she get the copy of *Walden*?" I asked.

"I have no idea, but if she had it, she must have cheated to get it somehow. I would bet my scarf collection on that."

Maybe Grandma Daisy was right, and it was murder. Perhaps that's what Rainwater was hearing right now from the coroner. If that were true, and if my grandmother wasn't careful, she was going to start sounding like a suspect.

Chapter Nine

The next morning, I woke up after Rainwater had already left for the police department. He had stuck a note on the bathroom mirror saying that he had to go in early to deal with the case and that he hoped to be home at noon. I wasn't holding my breath that he would be back by then.

Because Rainwater had to work, I felt I should get back to work as well. Our Vermont honeymoon was on hold. Rainwater couldn't leave the village until Roma's case was solved. I understood, but I was also in need of a vacation.

Until then, I would work. I spent the morning trying to shoehorn David's clothes into my very full closet. When late morning came around, I was more than happy to abandon the project and get the shop ready to open. I opened Charming Books just as I normally would on a Sunday afternoon. It was a beautiful December day. Bright sunlight danced on the snow, making it sparkle with that special snow blue hue. As I swept a fresh dusting of flakes from the porch steps and the walk, all I could think about was Roma and the book. What had happened to *Walden*? A part of me felt guilty that I was as preoccupied with the whereabouts of the book as with Roma's death.

I had only spoken to her briefly on Wednesday morning, and I didn't hear from her after that. Had she been in Cascade Springs this entire time? Had she been planning to come back and talk to me about the book again after the wedding? Why was she at the wedding? It was impossible to know the answer to the last two questions, but I was certain that Rainwater was working on the first one.

I stood on the shop's front porch. I didn't have a coat on and the chill in the air cut through my sweater. Motivated by the cold, I made quick work of sweeping the steps.

The rental company had already come and collected the chairs and decorations from the wedding. It was like it never happened. While I was alone all morning, I wondered if it all had been a dream.

I leaned my broom against the porch post so that I could use it later to clear the walk again because more snow was predicted for later in the afternoon. As long as the snow remained light, I could keep the path to the sidewalk clear with just a broom. However, the meteorologist promised a night of heavy snow. I would be using the shovel by the evening.

When I turned back to go inside, I stopped short at the sight in front of me. Emerson was sitting on a book that lay on the threshold. When I had gone outside to clear the sidewalk, there hadn't been a book there—I knew that for sure. Again, the shop was not so subtly trying to get my attention.

I leaned over, Emerson hopped off the book, and I picked it up. The book, *Walden*—no surprise there—was opened to a page. My eyes scanned the text, and as I wondered if they knew all along where they should look, they landed on:

Books are the treasured wealth of the world and the fit inheritance of generations and nations.

It seemed to me that the shop's essence was confirming what I already thought, which was that I had to find *Walden*. The special volume was truly a treasure that needed to be protected. Best case scenario, it would be donated to a library or museum now that Roma was gone. That was assuming that it belonged to Roma. I couldn't get out of my head what my grandmother had said about Roma's cheating past. It made me wonder if Roma had stolen the book from someone else just to have it stolen from her.

I carried the book into the shop and set it on the sales counter, keeping it open to that page as if I needed a reminder to keep working at it. I needed to reach out to my contacts in the rare book world. If someone had stolen the book and wanted to sell it, that person would be most successful trying to sell it to a rare book dealer. Maybe that's why I was so surprised that Roma had come to me. I was a bookseller, but I didn't work in rare books. Was it because she had no provenance records that rare book dealers had turned her away?

The closest rare bookstore was just one town over in Camden, called Tattered Spine. If I had stolen a valuable book, that is where I would go first. The shop was owned by Heathcliff Howell. As far as I knew, he was the only person who worked there too. Although I'd never been to the shop before, I knew Heath from bookseller association events in the region. He was an academic man with a precise beard and wire-rimmed glasses. He looked exactly how you might imagine a rare book dealer to look. I didn't know if he acquired the look due to his profession or if he acquired the profession due to his look. In any case, his store was the place to start my investigation.

Rainwater could concentrate on Roma's death. I would focus on her book.

I called Tattered Spine, but my call went straight to voice-mail. This wasn't altogether surprising. Many of the smaller shops in Western New York weren't open on Sundays. Even so, I was disappointed. I had half a mind to close my shop for an hour or two to run over there and knock on the door. However, that idea was quickly put out of my head as some last-minute Christmas shoppers came into Charming Books.

The shop was still bustling when Sadie stopped by a little past noon.

I handed the customer standing in from of me his receipt and thanked him for his purchase.

After he left, Sadie came over to the counter. "Vi, how are you?"

I cocked my head. "That seems like a loaded question."

"It is," she said. "You should be on your honeymoon right now."

I sighed.

She gave my hand that rested on the counter a squeeze. "Chief Rainwater will figure this all out, and you will be on your trip in no time."

The truth was that I wasn't in as much of a hurry to go on the honeymoon as I was to find out what happened to that copy of *Walden*.

She shook her head and her ponytail bounced. "Anyway, I have all your wedding gifts over at my shop. I figured that, with everything going on, you and David wouldn't want to deal with them last night."

"Thank you, Sadie. I completely forgot about the gifts."

She grinned. "I knew you would. They can stay there until you get back from your honeymoon, and we can open them together. It will be fun."

I smiled. I wished that I was as confident as Sadie that there would actually be a honeymoon. At this point, I just didn't know. Thankfully, the shop was busy which kept me from dwelling on it for too long.

Christmas was on Friday, and everyone who came into the shop was desperate to find a book for someone they loved. The good thing was Charming Books never disappointed in this regard. It was the shop where the books literally picked you.

The shop's essence had the ability to put the book that someone needed, whether it was for themselves or for someone else, right in front of them. At times, books flew across the store behind customers' heads—that was always nerve-racking for me—and other times the book just appeared close by so the customer couldn't possibly miss it.

By the time the sun began to set after four, I was exhausted. Every customer who had come in the store left with one or more books that they'd needed. But I had spent the last three hours playing interference between customers and the shop's mystical essence so the patrons wouldn't catch on to how I knew what their next read should be.

After the last customer walked out of the shop, I sat on the couch by the fire and sipped my tepid coffee that I had forgotten on the counter while I was working. It had been a good day monetarily for the shop, but it certainly wasn't how I'd expected to spend the day after my wedding.

Right now, one of my assistants or Grandma Daisy should have been managing the store while I was away in a Vermont cabin with my new husband. We'd planned to stay there for the week and come back after Christmas. It would have been my first time leaving the village for any substantial amount of time since I'd moved back. I had been looking forward to it, but any time I felt sorry for myself, I reminded myself of the woman who'd died.

It seemed the shop believed I needed a reminder of what really mattered too because the volume of *Walden* that had been sitting on the sales counter flew across the shop and landed in my lap.

I rubbed the tense spot between my eyebrows that seemed to grow more painful by the second.

The book fell open and my eyes were drawn to the words:

There are a thousand hacking at the branches of evil to one who is striking at the root.

I turned my gaze to the tree. "So you are telling to get to the root of the problem?"

As usual, the tree said nothing in return, but Faulkner said, "Strike at the root!"

I rubbed my forehead again. "Please don't tell me you can read too. I don't know if I'd be excited or horrified at that news."

Before Faulkner could answer me, the front door of Charming Books flew open with a bang. A cloud of snow blew in behind an elderly woman holding a cane. To me, the cane appeared to be more of an accessory than a necessity as she was holding it a foot off of the floor. Her hair was tethered in a long silver braid. She looked around the shop, and the braid that ran all the way down her backside whipped back and forth like a rope. It made me wonder how long her hair was when it was unbraided. On the top of her head, she had on a royal blue beanie that was tilted at an angle.

Faulkner cawed and flapped his wings in protest. If anyone was to be making loud and disruptive noises in Charming Books, he wanted it to be him.

I set the copy of *Walden* aside to stand up, and I smiled at the woman. "Can I help you?"

"You!" The woman said and thrust her mittened hand in my direction. She must have thought the mitten wasn't effective in assigning blame because she ripped it off and pointed her sharp nail at me. "You're the one who has *my* book!"

Faulkner flapped his wings in the tree branches above our heads. Emerson was nowhere in sight, but I was certain that the tuxedo cat was looking on from one of his many hidey-holes in the shop. Emerson could move around Charming Books and the entire village of Cascade Springs without being seen if he wanted to.

"Excuse me?" I asked.

"You have the book! I demand you give it back. I'm the rightful heir. It's mine. It needs to be returned to the family."

"What book are you talking about exactly? This is a bookshop. There are thousands of books in here." Even as I said it, I knew what she was going to say.

She shook her finger even harder at me. If she wasn't careful, she might hurt herself. "Don't mock me. You know the book I mean. *Walden*! You have my copy of the book that had been passed down in my family for generations. It's mine!"

"I have copies of *Walden* for sale." I was stalling her. She was so visibly upset that I wasn't sure what she would do.

"Don't you play dumb with me." Her lip curled in disgust. "It's a very unattractive quality. I know that woman came to you with the intention of selling the book. The troll. She abused our friendship and turned her back on me. She stole my book and then tried to sell it for her own gain."

"Do you mean Roma?" I asked.

"Roma Winterbourne. Yes. Yes, that's who I mean," she snapped. "She told me she sold the book to you. She had no right to do that. She stole it from me, and now, you have to give it back."

I took a small step away from her just to make sure I was out of the range of her cane if she chose to drive her point home with it. "I don't have the book. Roma did come to the store and offer to sell it, but I didn't buy it."

"Liar!" she cried.

Emerson leapt onto the counter and hissed.

I moved behind the sales counter. Being called a liar shredded my last nerve. "It's the truth. And who are you? How would you know if I was lying to you or not?"

She straightened her shoulders and tapped the end of her cane on the wide plank flooring for good measure. A silver ID bracelet clattered on her wrist each time the cane hit the floor. "I'm Imogene Thoreau, and that book is mine. It was written by my great-great-great-great-grandfather Henry David Thoreau."

"That's impossible."

She glared at me. "Are you saying that Henry David didn't write that book?"

"No, I'm saying it's impossible that you are a direct descendent of Henry David. He didn't have any children."

She threw her cane at me.

Chapter Ten

So, telling someone that they are misinformed about their own lineage wasn't the best idea I'd ever had, but Rainwater had me enrolled in a self-defense class last summer. My last lesson had been on dodging flying objects, so I put it to good use when Imogene hurled her cane at me and was able to jump out of the way. A vase that had held some of the wedding flowers had not been as lucky and lay shattered on the floor.

Imogene covered her mouth. "Oh my word! I'm so sorry about your vase. I—I don't know what came over me."

Now that she no longer had the cane on her, I felt more comfortable walking around the sales counter. "I'll get a broom and some paper towels."

Faulkner was in the tree, squawking and crying. "Off with her head! Off with her head!" It was his favorite proclamation when he was upset. Emerson, for his part, was on top of the mantle. It seemed that he had jumped straight up in the air and landed there next to a portrait of Emily Dickinson.

"Faulkner, calm down. Emerson, jump down from there."

They must have sensed that my tone meant business this time because the cat jumped to the couch and Faulkner fell silent.

"Why don't you have a seat on the sofa there while I clean this up, and then we can talk?"

She nodded dumbly and shuffled over to the couches. She sat in the one facing the front of the shop and watched the entrance as if she expected someone to stride in at any moment and drag her away.

I hurried to the kitchen to grab another broom, a dust pan, and some paper towels.

After cleaning up the mess, I sat across from Imogene on the opposite couch. To my right, the fire crackled in the hearth. "Imogene?" I asked when she didn't say anything.

"I'm so sorry about your vase." She picked up her cane.

"You're forgiven, but what happened?"

She shook her head slowly as if the act of shaking it was made more difficult by its incredible weight. "It's just what you said." She took a breath. "I have heard this so many times. No one believes that Henry David was my ancestor, but he was." Her dark eyes flashed. "He was! The book that you and Roma stole was proof of that."

I held up my hands. "I don't have your book." I paused. "As for Henry David Thoreau, he never married nor had any children. There is no scholarship on it. If he'd had a child, someone would have found out by now. It would have been a huge bombshell in American literature."

She opened her mouth as if she was going to argue with me again.

I forged ahead. "Furthermore, none of his three siblings married or had children either. There are no direct descendants of the Thoreau family. When his younger sister Sophia died in 1876, it was the end of the family line."

"How would you know?" She sat up in her seat, and some of that fire in her demeanor that I saw before was back.

I scanned around her seat to make sure there weren't any heavy objects near her that she could hit me over the head with.

"How can you question what I know to be true about my family?" Her face was as red as a strawberry.

"I've spent my entire adult life studying Thoreau. I've written countless papers on him. It's because of my knowledge of the author and his family that Roma came to my shop to try and sell the book to me. But, for what I hope is the last time I have to say it, I didn't buy it."

She glared at me. "You're one of those scholarly types who isn't able to see the truth. If he didn't have any children, why would there be a story in my family that we descended from him?" As if it were even more proof, she went on. "Why would I have the book if it weren't true?"

"I'm not saying that the book wasn't passed down as a family heirloom, but I'm saying there are no direct descendants of Thoreau. To say there are is a very serious claim."

"It's not a claim. It's the truth."

"If it's something that you want or need to prove, you should also contact the author's society. They would take a claim like this very seriously because it would have a huge impact on Thoreau's story and what they know about him."

"Don't you think I've tried? But those uppity weasels won't even listen to me. They stopped taking my calls. They told me I was wrong."

I bit my tongue to stop myself from saying that she probably was wrong. Being Thoreau's descendent was her hard and fast belief. Just like politics has turned into a religion for many, this was her truth now, and there was nothing anyone could say or show her to make her think differently.

"I don't need you to believe me. I just need you to return the book." She held out her bejeweled hand. "Give it to me."

"I don't have it. Roma offered it to me, but I didn't buy it." I felt like a broken record.

"She said she sold it to you."

"When did she tell you this?" I asked.

"Yesterday morning."

Before I saw her at my wedding then.

"And when did she supposedly sell it to me?"

"Sometime before that. She didn't say the exact time." She folded her arms. "If you won't cooperate, let's just call Roma and prove you wrong."

My eyes widened. Either Imogene didn't know Roma was dead, or she was a very good actor. "You have her number?"

"Yes, I do. She was my dear friend for many years until she turned on me. What I have learned in this life is that everyone turns on you after a time. You can't trust a single person—not even your blood."

I winced. That was a very sad statement. "If the book was stolen, I think that you should speak to the police about this."

She scowled. "I'd rather not. I have no use for cops. They aren't trustworthy either. They are just another group that wants to stand in my way from proving the truth."

"You've had run-ins with the law?"

She pressed her lips together. "I have been arrested a time or two. Nothing serious. Just when those uppity professors refused to listen to me about my ancestry. I set them right, and the spineless academics that they were called the police."

I was itching to call Rainwater. He would want to speak to a witness who not only knew Roma but claimed to have a history with the missing book. Also, Imogene had spoken to Roma not long before she'd died. Rainwater would want to talk to her about that as well. However, I didn't know how to do it without her noticing.

"The police will be able to help you with your missing book. Let me just make a quick call." I removed my cell phone from my pocket.

Imogene picked up her cane from where it leaned on the sofa and pointed it at me. "If you make that phone call, I will wallop you. And this time I won't miss. I don't want to talk to the police. They just make things more difficult."

I put the phone back in my pocket. Imogene was unstable at best. One minute, she was lamenting, throwing her cane, and then apologizing to me. The next minute, she threatened to do it again—and worse. The only thing I knew for sure was that her belief that she was Henry David Thoreau's great-great-great-great-granddaughter wasn't an act. She actually believed it.

"Now, just hand over the book, and I will leave."

"I told you. I don't have it." Okay, this was enough. I wasn't going down this path again.

She stood up with the cane in hand.

How dumb of me. I should have hidden the cane when I had had the chance. I jumped to my feet. I really didn't want to get beaten up by a batty old woman. I knew I could defend myself, but I didn't want to hurt her.

The front door of the shop opened, and the law strolled in. Rainwater filled the doorway.

"David," I said with a sigh of relief.

84

"What's going on in here?" Rainwater wanted to know.

Imogene spun around.

Rainwater was in uniform today, so there was no question he was a police officer. She pointed her cane back at me. "I told you not to call the police."

"I didn't! That's my fi—husband. He lives here. He also happens to be the chief of police."

She wrinkled her nose. "I should have known there was some kind of collusion with the authorities. If not, you would have been arrested and thrown in prison for stealing my book. It must be nice to be sleeping with the cops. Makes your life of crime that much easier, doesn't it?"

"What's going on?" Rainwater asked in a much sterner voice.

"Well, since you're here, I might as well tell you." Imogene thumped her cane on the floor. "Your wife stole my book. I want it back, and if she doesn't give it back, I want to press charges. Not that I have any hope at all of the system being fair to me."

"What book is this?" Rainwater asked, looking at me.

I raised my brow. "*Walden*, the copy that Roma Winterbourne had."

Rainwater's stance changed just a little. He was more alert. With a dead body sitting at the county morgue, he went into full cop mode.

"When was the last time you saw Roma?" Rainwater asked.

"Ye—yesterday," Imogene stuttered as if she changed her mind about what she said next. "Yesterday morning. She'd had the book for three weeks, and I wanted it back. I had let her borrow it because she was going to help me prove my pedigree. She said that she had the connections to do it. What I didn't know until later was that she wasn't trying to help me at all. She was trying to sell my book to your wife." She pointed her finger at me again.

That was really starting to get old.

"Pedigree?" Rainwater asked.

"Yes, this is Imogene Thoreau," I said.

"Thoreau like…"

"Just like."

Imogene straightened up. "I am the great-great-great-great-granddaughter of Henry David Thoreau."

When Rainwater shot a look at me, I shook my head ever so slightly to the negative, but I decided to wait until this conversation with Imogene concluded before I told him what I knew of Thoreau's family tree. I really didn't want to get smacked with that cane.

Rainwater took a breath. It was clear that he was deciding how to proceed. "Ms. Thoreau."

Imogene perked up when he called her that. So far, so good.

"May I ask where you were between four and six o'clock last evening?"

Imogene blinked. "Where I was? I was at home. I was at home worrying about my book!"

"Was anyone with you?"

"My son stopped by briefly to drop off dinner. He thinks I can't feed myself. He's a good son even if he becomes frustrated with me at times. I know he cares."

"And when was that?"

"Five thirty, I guess. What does this have to do with her taking my book?"

"I can assure you that Violet does not have the book," Rainwater said in a measured voice. "But you are right, it is missing. We believe that Roma is the last one who knew of its whereabouts."

"Well, find her and arrest her!"

"I'm afraid we can't do that. You see," Rainwater paused. "Roma Winterbourne is dead."

Imogene crumbled to the floor.

Chapter Eleven

R ainwater looked at me. "Can you do something?"

"What do you want me to do? She threw her cane at me earlier." I held my hands up.

Imogene rubbed her eyes. "I'm sorry. I'm sorry. What you said came as a shock. It's just, if Roma is dead, I have no hope now of proving the truth about my family. She was the only one who was willing to do it. No one else will listen to me."

It could be just me, but I'd postulate that her habit of throwing things at people when she didn't get her way might be the reason why no one took her seriously.

"Because you're one of the last people to see Roma alive, I would like to talk to you," Rainwater said. "We can do it here or at the station."

Her eyes widened almost to the size of the lenses in her glasses. "Why would the police want to talk to me? How did she die?"

"Ms. Winterbourne fell into the Niagara River last night and died. It seems she hit her head when she fell and drowned."

"That's terrible, but I don't know why you are questioning me. I already told you that I was home last evening and that my son was there. If you don't believe me, you can ask him."

Rainwater nodded. "What's your son's name and phone number?" He whipped out a small notebook from the pocket of his winter coat.

"His name is Edmund Thorne," she said and then rattled off a phone number.

"His last name isn't Thoreau?" I asked.

"He has his father's last name," she snapped at me. "It's the only thing that man ever gave that boy."

"Did your son know Roma?" Rainwater asked.

"I don't think he ever met her. He had no reason to, but I did tell him about her." Then she muttered, "Not that he wanted to hear about it."

"Why didn't he want to know about her?" I asked.

"If you must know, it was because he didn't want to hear anything more about Henry David. He seems to accept the lie that we have been told over and over again from others like you—that Henry David didn't have any children."

Rainwater and I exchanged a look.

"And where do you live, Ms. Thoreau?" Rainwater asked.

She pressed her lips together. "I live in a small apartment on Goldfinch Street. It's the second floor of a townhouse. I have a horrible neighbor in the first-floor apartment who thinks he can play the violin. He can't."

"And the address?" Rainwater asked.

She told him her address, and when he asked for her phone number, she told him that too. Despite her prickly attitude, Imogene didn't refuse to tell Rainwater anything that he needed to know. It made me wonder if she was really telling the truth. Also, why would she hurt Roma when Roma likely had the book? If she did that, she might never see the book again.

"Can I leave now?" Imogene asked.

Rainwater closed his notebook. "You may, but don't be surprised if you get a call from me later today or tomorrow after I speak to your son."

She glared at us in turn and then stormed out of the shop. Her cane never touched the floor.

After she left, Rainwater fell on one of the couches. "That was Henry David Thoreau's great-great-great-granddaughter?"

"She said she was his great-great-great-*great*-granddaughter, but it's simply not true."

"Why?" He rubbed the back his neck and looked terribly tired.

"Thoreau never married nor had children. None of the four Thoreau children did. They lived most of their lives in New Concord, Massachusetts, and their lives were well-documented by themselves and by others."

"I don't think she knew she was going to be telling her story to a transcendentalism scholar."

I frowned. "It doesn't matter if I am a scholar or not. It's well-documented that the siblings didn't marry or have children in or out of wedlock. It would only take a quick Internet search to verify that on a number of reputable websites. All of them died relatively young too, except for his youngest sister Sophia. She had a longer life. Henry David was forty-four when he died."

"So he didn't marry," Rainwater said, talking through each point to make sure he had the facts right. "That never stopped anyone from having children before."

"If it were really true, someone from the family would have come forward much sooner than this. His work has been published thousands of times in countless languages. Yes, it's in the public domain now, but it wasn't for a long time. Don't you think an heir would want to cash in on that?"

"Not if they didn't know they were an heir until after the work was in the public domain."

I frowned. "I suppose, but why wait until now to reveal who she is? If someone had come forward and said they were related to Thoreau, it would be major news in literary circles. She would be wanted for interviews and talks at colleges all over the country. The Thoreau Society would definitely want to talk to her. I just didn't buy it. I knew she said she'd already spoken to some scholars, but which ones? I'm sure there would be some out there who would want to hear her story, even just so they could write a paper to tear her claim apart. A paper like that could help them secure tenure at their college or university."

"Is academia that conniving?"

"More. That's nothing." I sat next to him on the couch. "It's just too far-fetched."

Another copy of *Walden* flew across the shop and landed gently in my lap.

Rainwater raised his brow at me. "Too far-fetched? Like a magical bookshop, perhaps?"

He had me there.

"I actually came here with some news about the case," he said, "but it seems you have been doing a much better job detecting than I have."

"I didn't do anything," I said. "Imogene literally stormed in here and accused me of buying the book from Roma." I scooted closer to him. "What do you have to tell me?"

"The coroner has ruled her death an accident. There is no evidence that she was pushed or kicked into the river. He thinks that she simply slipped on the ice and fell in. Tragically, it happens at least once or twice every winter somewhere along the river."

"I know," I murmured, thinking of my friend Colleen again.

Rainwater squeezed my hand.

"But what about the book? What about the message that was written on her palm?"

"Even though the coroner ruled the death accidental, some things don't add up. There was some unusual debris under Roma's fingernails."

"What was it?" I asked excitedly.

"It was brownish green cloth. The coroner said that he had only seen nail scrapings like this one other time, and they were from—"

"The cover of a book," I interrupted him.

He nodded.

"It has to be *Walden*. Maybe someone was stealing it from her, and she scratched up the cover as she was trying to get it back."

"That was my thought too."

"If she did scratch the book so deeply to have some of the leather under her nails, the value of the book, even being signed, will drop by thousands. It would no longer be in mint condition. Most collectors don't want books with any tears on the covers."

He leaned back on the couch and sighed. "This is not how I wanted our first few days as newlyweds to go." He sat up again. "There are questions about the case, but since it's not technically a homicide, I can leave for our honeymoon. I will put Officer Wheaton on the case. He can follow up with Imogene and her son."

I shifted away from him. "You would put Wheaton on this case? He's the last person who could possibly understand how valuable that book is."

Rainwater frowned. "He has the most seniority in the department. And it's no longer a homicide case."

"Yes, but we don't know what happened. We still have to find the book!"

Rainwater rubbed his forehead like our conversation was giving him a headache. I didn't doubt for a second that it was.

"Okay, I'll give it three more days, but I do want to spend Christmas in those mountains in Vermont with my new bride. Is that too much to ask?"

I took his hand. "It's not."

"So, we have a deal? We will look for the book three more days and then let Wheaton take over."

I didn't like the idea of Wheaton taking over anything, but I said what only seemed fair, "Deal."

Chapter Twelve

Since I only had three days to find the book, I didn't waste any time. On Monday morning, I called one of my backup assistants and told him I needed him to cover the shop for me, even though I was technically still going to be in the village.

Charles Hancock stepped into Charming Books twenty minutes after I'd called him. He was an eighty-something gentleman, who had an irrepressible crush on Grandma Daisy and also was just a tad eccentric. He called himself a knight, and just like Don Quixote, it seemed that he really believed it. Instead of going on quests with Sancho Panza, his knightly energy was put into admiring my grandmother.

I met him at the door. His bald head was bare. The only nod to winter in his attire was a wool coat over his 1950s business suit.

"Charles, where is your hat?" I asked as soon as he walked into the shop.

He wagged a crooked finger at me. "Don't you mother me, Violet Waverly. When I get a call that my beloved Daisy is in need of my help, I rush to her side. I had no time to find a hat. What kind of knight would I be if I cared about my own creature comforts above hers?"

I winced. I may have implied that Grandma Daisy wanted him to work in the shop that day so I could go snoop. I told myself that it was the only way I could get him to come to the shop.

"Where is Daisy?" He looked around the shop.

"You know that she's working on the village hall restoration project. That's why we need your help to watch the shop today."

He gave a solemn nod. "Oh, yes, she works so very hard. As much as it pains me that her work keeps the two of us apart, I know that she has her own responsibilities to this village. I may be a knight, but I'm a modern one at that. I know Daisy is a great leader, and her subjects need her."

"I'm sure she appreciates that," I said as I put on my coat.

"Do not worry. I will take good care of the shop while the two of you are away. You can rest assured."

On that note, I left the shop and walked to the river. I thought I might get some inspiration as to where to turn next if I went back to the place where we'd found the body.

There was a melted patch in the snow where the tent for my wedding reception had been. My heart sank a little when I saw it. The wedding had not gone as planned, but neither had the honeymoon. I'd agreed to leave with Rainwater for Vermont in three days, even if we didn't find the book before then, because I knew my husband was as disappointed as I was by the way things were turning out.

There wasn't even any crime scene tape there where Roma had been found, more proof that the police, including Rainwater, thought it was an accidental death. I wasn't so sure. I looked around the street at the village hall where my grandmother used to work as mayor until the foundation crumbled some months ago.

No one went in there now because the building was unstable. Once a majestic building, it was now surrounded by cones and hazard tape. Grandma Daisy insisted its condition was temporary.

The village hall had once been a stopping point on the Underground Railroad, and when my grandmother was elected mayor, she'd made it her mission to recognize that history of Cascade Springs. Grandma Daisy raised hundreds of thousands of dollars to put a new Underground Railroad museum in the least used massive building outside of the handful of village offices housed there. During the project, foundation cracks came to light, which led to the excavation. My grandmother had to raise even more money to restore the building and save it from collapsing. Unfortunately, those measures weren't quite enough. Not with the aquifer waters seeping into those cracks and eroding the foundation at such an accelerated rate. The building collapsed under its own weight on the weakened foundation, and now it sat in a sad heap at the top of the hill overlooking the Niagara River. Thankfully, though, due to the excavation and my grandmother's efforts, no one was harmed. I shuddered to think what might have happened if the grand old building's flaws had gone unnoticed. Many people could've been injured, and the collapse could've been far more damaging.

Even with the building in ruins, Grandma Daisy was not discouraged. She immediately started planning a fundraiser to restore the building over that last few months that rivaled a presidential campaign. To date, she has raised over one million dollars. The civil engineers working on the project said it would take at least one million more just to make the building safe for use again.

The cost would daunt most people, but not my grandmother. She believed in the history of Cascade Springs and was doing everything she could to preserve it. Because of that, I hadn't seen her much these last few months. Just last month, she was in New York City for five days speaking to millionaires and nonprofits to raise money. No one in Cascade Springs doubted her success.

Next to village hall was Le Crepe Jolie. Even in the snow, it looked like a café right out of a French magazine. The few tables that were usually outside had been put away for the winter, but the gilded window frames, pinstriped awning, and antique door still stood out brightly.

I hadn't found anything new at the crime scene, but that didn't mean I didn't deserve a breakfast crepe.

As I stepped into Le Crepe Jolie, the enveloping aromas of fresh bread, fennel, and berries filled my nostrils. The inside of the café was warm, both from the furnace and the ovens going full blast in the kitchen. I quickly shed my winter coat, hat, and gloves.

"Violet," Lacey cried. The silver barrettes that she always wore were slipping out of her smooth hair. "Adrien and I have been so worried about you since the wedding. What a terrible way to start your life with the police chief. Can I get you anything? Crepe? Coffee? Lemon madeleines?"

"All of those sound good."

She snapped her fingers. "Coming right up. You came at a good time. Most of the breakfast rush is gone. I can sit with you for a minute or two as long as it stays slow in here. Your favorite table by the front window is open." She went through the swinging door by the kitchen.

I sat at the table she indicated and looked out the window. I had a perfect view of where the wedding reception tent had been and where Roma had died.

Lacey came out of the kitchen a moment later with a small tray, holding two glass mugs of coffee, some cream and sugar, and a plate of Le Crepe Jolie's lemon madeleines. The pillowy cookies were Grandma Daisy's absolute favorite treat.

"I'll pack up a little box for you to take to Daisy," Lacey said as she arranged everything on the table. "Danielle will bring out your crepe just as soon as Adrien finishes making it. We made it with mushroom and Swiss cheese—your favorite."

I wrapped my cold hands around the coffee mug to warm my palms and fingertips. "You are all too good to me."

"Don't be silly. We treat you just how you treat anyone who walks into Charming Books."

I wished that were true, but I would never be as naturally kindhearted as Lacey. When we were kids, she'd had a tough time in high school. She was bullied and belittled, but she kept a smile on her face through it all. I was sure she'd go home some days after school and cry herself to sleep, but she never showed how hurt she was. I still kicked myself all these years later that I didn't defend her more when I had had the chance.

She sipped her coffee. "Officer Wheaton came into the café for a latte this morning. He said that the woman's death was ruled an accident and that the case was closed. I thought, with that news, you and Chief Rainwater would be off to your honeymoon this morning."

I bit the inside of my cheek to keep myself from saying what I really thought of Officer Wheaton spreading that news throughout the village. If he'd said it at the café, everyone would know it by the end of the day.

"David still has some work to do on it. We will leave for the honeymoon as soon as we can."

She beamed at me. "I'm so glad. I remember my honeymoon with Adrien. It was the most magical time. It gave us a chance to get away from it all. When you own a café, that is rare." She sighed. "Maybe someday we can take time off to go again. Danielle could easily fill in for me, but who would cook? Adrien is such an exacting chef. He would not want anyone sending out subpar food from his kitchen."

"Here's your crepe, sister," Danielle said as she set it in front of me. "I can call you that, right?"

Danielle Cloud was as beautiful as her brother was handsome. She had jet black hair that hung down her back, and today it was plaited in a long braid. She had the clearest skin I had ever seen and the same sparkling eyes as her brother, although hers were a deep brown that bordered on jet black.

"You most certainly can." I smiled at her. "I know David and I have a few more things to get out of the house and move to Charming Books. I hope it's not crowding you out too much."

She waved away my concern. "The little house feels massive now that David has moved out. Aster and I walk around in awe at all the space we have. Please don't feel rushed."

I smiled. "Thanks. We just haven't had time to really decide where everything is going to go in our apartment."

She smiled. "I can imagine. Anytime Aster and I have moved, it's been such a chore. It's nice to finally feel like we have a home." She looked over her shoulder. "I had better get back to the kitchen. Adrien wants to come out and say hello, but someone needs to watch the leek soup like a hawk. It's today's lunch special." She went back to the kitchen.

I cut into my crepe and the melted Swiss cheese oozed out. A cloud of steam hit my face. It felt better than the facial Sadie had made me get before the wedding.

"I can completely understand having trouble finding a place for everything when you combine homes," Lacey said. "In our case, it's hard to find places for all the food and supplies for the café. It's not a big building. We store things everywhere. We have three deep freezers in the basement and another at our house in the garage. Anywhere we can put a freezer, we do it."

The mention of the café's basement caught my attention. Le Crepe Jolie was next door to the village hall that had collapsed. Was Lacey's basement and her entire café in danger of that happening too?

I asked her as much.

"It's funny you mention that because I've been thinking about that a lot lately too. I even had a basement expert come out, but he said not to worry because the basement was bone dry. The foundation is sound too. He didn't find any evidence of water under the building."

"Does that seem odd to you?" I asked.

"It does." She picked up a lemon madeleine from plate and set it on a napkin in front of her. "I mean, the village hall was right next door and on a hill. The entire basement filled with water when the building collapsed, but we have nothing. The basement guy said it was strange but didn't seem too overly concerned. He said there are pockets of spring water from the aquifer all over the village, but until there is an in-depth study of the entire town, it's hard to pinpoint where the water will show up. He said it was something he could do."

"Don't tell Grandma Daisy about him because she would want to do it. The village budget is already stretched too thin this year for a ground study."

Adrien stepped out of the kitchen. He had on a blue apron over his white T-shirt and black jeans. "Violet, I'm glad you're here. How is the crepe?"

I looked down at my plate that was two-thirds empty. I hadn't even realized I'd eaten that much. "It's amazing, as always."

"I'm glad." His French-Canadian accent seemed more pronounced today. He sat at the table next to Lacey.

I raised my brow. There were still customers in the café. It was unheard of for Adrien to do more than come out and say a quick hello when he was cooking. His craft was all encompassing.

Lacey rubbed her husband's shoulder. "Adrien, Violet is our friend. We can trust her."

"What's going on?" I asked.

Adrien pressed his lips together, and Lacey continued to rub her husband's shoulder.

"You guys are scaring me," I said finally, after a long moment of silence.

Adrien patted Lacey's hand on his shoulder. "I had a visitor this morning, and she said that she spoke to you."

"Who was it?"

"Imogene," Adrien said in a clipped voice.

My mouth fell over. "You know Imogene Thoreau?"

"I know Imogene, but her last name wasn't Thoreau when I first met her. It was Thorne."

I raised my brow. That was her son's last name. Hadn't she said that that was her son's father's surname?

As if he could read my mind, Adrien said, "Her maiden name was Harter. She married and changed it to Thorne. When she got divorced, she changed it to Thoreau."

"Is Imogene a regular here?" I asked. I had never seen her at the café before, and I ate here almost every day. But I wasn't here every second of every day. I could have missed her.

Adrien shook his head. "It was the first time. She'd learned that we were friends, and she wanted me to try to convince you to give her book back to her."

"I told her I don't have the book."

He nodded. "That's what she said. So, I told her that if that's what you said, it must be true. I have never known you to lie. She didn't believe me and stormed off."

"I don't know how she thought she could convince you to tell me anything if you didn't know her."

"I didn't say I didn't know her. I don't know her well, but that doesn't change the fact that Imogene is my aunt."

I stared at him. "Come again?"

He relaxed, but it did little to hide his chiseled muscles under the shirt. He might want to think about getting a larger size. It didn't look like a comfortable fit. "She's my aunt on my mother's side."

"I thought you were French Canadian."

"I am, but my mother was American. She moved to Quebec when she was twenty. She was a French major in college and went to Quebec for a study abroad program. She fell in love with the place and never came back to the States. When she left, her American family thought she was turning her back on them.

Maybe she was, in a way. She and Imogene were never close, but I don't know why. I think the Thoreau story was part of it. I can't ask my mother now, though, because she passed away ten years ago."

"I didn't know that. I'm so sorry." As I said this, I wondered what else I didn't know about Adrien.

"After my mother died, I was ready to leave Quebec and see where she was from. It was this village. The moment I set foot in Cascade Springs, I felt connected to it. Have you ever visited a place before and known it's where you belong?"

I had. Even though I would have denied it at the time, when I came back to Cascade Springs from Chicago, I think a large part of me knew that I would never live in the Windy City again.

He gazed at his wife. "I met Lacey, and the rest is history. I never thought of going back to Canada other than to visit."

"He may have found out about the village because of Imogene, but he stayed for me." Lacey said. "It was the most romantic thing he could have done, which is saying a lot because Adrien is one of the most softhearted and generous men a person could ever meet."

"I knew Imogene and her son still lived in the village, but I didn't reach out. I felt like I'd be betraying my mother somehow. Instead, I turned all my attention to the café. And once I met Lacey, all my attention went to her. Although, after Lacey and I got married, I did run into my cousin."

"Edmund?" I asked.

Adrien nodded. "You've met him?"

"No, but Imogene mentioned him yesterday."

"Edmund and I are friendly, but we're not buddy-buddy. He stops in here for lunch when he's working for the village."

103

"Edmund works for the village?" I asked.

"On and off. He's a freelance civil engineer. I think he's working with Daisy now, trying to decide what needs to be done to save what's left of the village hall."

I blinked at him. "Does Grandma Daisy know that you're cousins?"

"I don't see how she would know that. I never told her, and I can't think of a reason why Edmund would bring it up." He shrugged. "I have been wrong in the past though."

"So you have an aunt and a cousin who live in this tiny village, and you never see them?"

"I have no reason to unless they stop by the café. You'd be surprised how many people have blood relatives walking the earth who they never speak to. Sometimes it's because of a falling out, or sometimes due to a sheer lack of effort. In my case, Imogene was furious with my mother because my mom wouldn't support Imogene's claim about Thoreau."

"Your mother didn't believe the story about Thoreau?"

He folded his hands on the table. "She'd heard the same stories that Imogene had, but she always said that there was no way to prove it. She just thought they were nice stories."

"Have you ever asked Edmund what he thought?"

Adrien shook his head. "No. I didn't think it was worth bringing up an old feud between our mothers. We've never discussed it."

Lacey placed a hand over Adrien's folded hands. He smiled lovingly at her.

"Did you know Roma?" I asked.

"Who's that?"

I looked around the café and was happy to see that no one seemed to be paying any attention to our conversation. Even so,

I lowered my voice. "She was the woman found dead by the river on Saturday evening."

"Oh, I never knew her name."

"I don't know if she was a friend or just someone your aunt knew, but Imogene came to my shop because of Roma. Roma had tried to sell me Imogene's *Walden*, but I didn't buy it."

"No wonder Imogene was furious when she asked me about you. That book is her whole world." He sighed and stood up. "I'm sorry to hear about Roma and even sorrier that she is connected to Imogene. I might have no relationship with my aunt, but I still wouldn't want her to be in any kind of trouble."

"You're a kind man," Lacey said and smiled at her husband.

He squeezed his wife's fingers. "I should get back to the kitchen. I just wanted to warn you. Imogene is a loose cannon, so keep your eyes open."

Great.

"Adrien, before you go," I said, "I have one last question."

He stood just beside our table.

"Why didn't you ever say anything about this to me? I did my dissertation on Thoreau. I certainly would have been interested if you'd had some sort of connection to such a famous author."

"You did?" Adrien asked. He clearly had no idea what I'd earned my PhD in, just like I'd had no idea that his mother had died a decade ago. I realized that that was likely for a good reason. I couldn't recall a single conversation over the past two years that I'd had with Adrien about my scholarship. Typically, we talked about food and recipes. Well, he talked about his recipes, and I ate his food.

I shook my head. "Never mind. Thanks for letting me know about Imogene."

He nodded. "Remember to watch your back while you look into this. I don't believe for a second that you won't investigate. Lacey and I don't want you getting hurt. You're more like family to us than any of my blood relatives are."

"I'll be careful," I said.

"Be sure that you are."

His words felt like a warning.

Chapter Thirteen

If Imogene's son, Edmund Thorne, worked with my grandmother, I wanted to know more about what Grandma Daisy and Edmund were working on. After I left the café, I decided to go to the source—Grandma Daisy. The temporary city offices were in an old Victorian house that was similar to Charming Books in size. The house was also on River Street, but closer to the livery where the village carriage drivers began their workdays.

River Street was the longest road in the village. It was also the main way in and out of Cascade Springs. The road was so long, in fact, it traveled through Cascade Springs, through the neighboring village of Camden, and right into Niagara Falls. As it drew closer to Niagara Falls, the road widened and traffic picked up.

My grandmother felt very strongly that the seat of village government needed to stay as close to the village hall as possible. The closest place that wasn't occupied either by a resident or a business was the narrow Victorian home. It was brown with black trim. Most of the shutters were missing, and the front door looked like it could be breached with just a gentle nudge.

Grandma Daisy turned a blind eye to all these "minor" issues, as she'd called them, and set up shop there.

As I reached the house, the front door opened and the delivery man, Hank, stepped out. "Violet!" He grinned at me. "Coming to check on your grandmother? I can say that she is hard at work inside." He clipped his package scanner to his work belt. "I have never in my life seen a person who works as hard as her. Is it true that she thinks she can bring the village hall back?"

I laughed. "It's true, and don't you go telling her anything different. I can assure you that will not go over well with Grandma Daisy."

"I never would!" he said cheerily. "I'm sorry to hear about all that fuss at your wedding reception. I was at the ceremony but missed the reception. Too many packages to deliver right before the holidays, you know? I heard about it from the rumor mill."

I nodded. "The rumor mill is strong in Cascade Springs."

He laughed. "Well, I had better be off. So many packages to deliver! It seems everyone did their Christmas and Hanukkah shopping online this year." He waved good-bye and jogged to his van parked just up the road.

When I walked into the house, my grandmother personally came out to greet me at the door. She sat at a metal desk with blueprints spread out in front of her. Her glasses hung on the tip of her nose, and her silver bob framed her face.

My grandmother lost her secretary in the spring and had yet to replace her. Honestly, I would be surprised if she did replace her. Grandma Daisy liked to do everything herself, so not having a right-hand person to delegate to was a plus in her eyes.

At the wedding, my grandmother had looked like a silver siren in her suit and scarf, but now she was back to her typical attire of jeans and a sweatshirt. Clearly, I'd gotten my fashion sense from my grandmother. A fuzzy, snowflake-patterned scarf was wrapped around her neck. She gave me a hug. "There's my girl! What a special honor that you would stop by. Who's at the shop?"

"I asked Charles to come in for the day, so I could take care of few things," I said.

"Charles!" Grandma Daisy put her hands on her hips. "Violet, you know by calling him in, you're just encouraging his crush on me, don't you?"

"Umm," I said.

Grandma Daisy groaned. "So you asked Charles to help so you could wander around the village and get a little snooping in."

"I don't snoop," I said defensively.

Grandma Daisy laughed. "Oh, all right. We won't call it snooping. That's far too childish anyway for what the essence is making you do. Any word from the books?"

"Grandma, someone will hear you," I whispered.

"I'm the only one here. It's Christmas week. Most of the staff took the week off, and the rest are working from home."

"Shouldn't you take some time off too? I don't think you have taken a day off since you were elected."

"A mayor never rests, especially now that we have such a massive project ahead of us." Her eyes glowed.

There were very few things that my grandmother loved more than a massive project. When I first moved back, it was just as much of an adjustment for her as it was for me. I became the Caretaker of the tree and the shop. She'd passed on the torch, so to speak. In doing that though, the shop's essence no longer talked to her. She started to feel obsolete, which did not sit well with Grandma Daisy. Naturally, to remedy that, she decided to run for public office.

Grandma Daisy patted her hand on the desktop. "We have a lot of work to do, but if all goes well, the village hall will be put back together again like Humpty Dumpty."

"I'm pretty sure the poem said Humpty Dumpty couldn't be put back together again."

"Bah, that's all right. You know what I mean."

I set the box of lemon madeleines that Lacey had given me on her desk next to the blueprints.

"Are those my favorite cookies?" she asked. "I can smell the lemon from here." She opened the box and popped an entire treat into her mouth.

"Grandma, you need to be careful. You could choke on that. Just take one bite at a time."

"I'm fine," she said as she chewed on her madeleine. "And these are amazing. I don't know how Adrien does it. I've tried to bake them so many times, and they've never come out quite like this." She swallowed. "It's very kind of you to bring me these, Violet, but I can tell that you are here to ask me something."

"Why do you say that?" I sat perched on the edge of the desk, taking care not to sit on the blueprint.

"Because you're shifting from foot to foot and keep glancing out the window like you have somewhere else you need to be. I'm not offended, even though I am your grandmother."

"There's nowhere else I'd like to be." I shook my head. "But I *am* here to ask you something."

She grinned and took another madeleine from the box. "See? Told you." She took a bite this time, instead of devouring it all at once. She did listen to me... Sometimes.

"Does Edmund Thorne work for the village?"

"Sure. The village contracted his private company to help rebuild the village hall. Why do you ask?"

I hadn't seen my grandmother since the wedding, so I quickly filled her in on Imogene's visit and what I'd learned from Adrien just moments ago.

"I had no idea that Edmund and Adrien were cousins. Neither of them has ever mentioned it."

"They aren't close," I said.

"Hmmm, still seems like it would come up sometime. This is a very tiny village."

I didn't argue with her on that point because I felt the same way.

"As for Edmund, you're in luck. He will be here any minute. I was just going to go over the latest plans from the architect with him to see if they will work for the hall. Edmund has a good eye, and he will catch anything that the architect or I missed."

The front door of the house opened and a tall man with blond, curly hair and a beard walked in. I guessed he was somewhere close to fifty years old. He wore a navy pea coat over a dark gray suit. The suit stood out because no one in village government wore suits. My grandmother was the perfect example of this.

"Edmund!" Grandma Daisy said. "I'm so glad you're here. Have you met my granddaughter, Violet?"

Edmund gave me a polite smile. "I haven't had the pleasure. You're the one who just got married. Daisy often spoke about your wedding in our meetings. Congratulations."

I thanked him.

Grandma Daisy chuckled. "Other than the restoration of the village hall, it was the biggest event of the year. However, now that the wedding is over, I can give my full attention to the restoration."

"I'm glad to hear it," Edmund said. "I know everyone is eager to get the project going. You did an amazing job raising money for the restoration. Even if we are not able to fit everything on your punch list into the budget, I am confident that we will make the building safe and stable to use again."

"Oh, I will get everything on my punch list," Grandma Daisy said. "I always do."

"You will need to raise another two hundred thousand dollars."

"Oh, is that all?" my grandmother asked.

I shook my head. Sometimes I really wished I had my grandmother's confidence.

"I thought it was one million more," I said.

Grandma Daisy smiled like Emerson when he knew he was getting away with something. "I had a very successful trip to New York City and was able to raise eight hundred thousand from some very well-to-do donors."

I gawked at her. "Grandma Daisy, that's amazing."

"Isn't it, though?" She beamed and then turned back to Edmund. "Now before we get started, Violet needs to talk to you."

Edmund looked to me. "Can I help you with something?"

"Maybe. I met your mother yesterday. She stopped by Charming Books."

He nodded. "Yes, I heard about that visit both from my mother and from the police. I can assure you she's harmless."

"She threw her cane at me."

"She has a short temper, but you weren't in any real danger."

Tell that to my vase and wedding flowers. Rather than argue, I asked, "Did you hear about the death of your mother's friend, Roma Winterbourne?"

"Yes, I heard about that as well from both my mother and the police. I can promise you that my mother has nothing to do with it. The death was ruled an accident. It's a tragedy, but I'm not sure why the police are still looking into it."

"It's because your mother claimed that Roma stole her book, and after Roma died, she accused *me* of stealing it or buying it from Roma."

He rubbed the back of his neck. "That book. I've lived my entire life hearing about it. I love my mother, I do, but I hate that book."

"You hate *Walden*?" Grandma Daisy asked. "But it's an American classic. Violet here spent her adult life studying it."

"I suppose that explains why my mother thought you might have it. I'm sorry if she caused you any discomfort. If anything was damaged, send me an invoice."

"Have you read it?" Grandma Daisy asked.

"No," Edmund said in a clipped tone. "And I don't plan to. I have heard enough of it my entire life. There is no need."

"If the book was stolen, the police have to investigate it," I said. "It's still a crime. Since it can be tied to a woman's death—accident or not—it makes it that much more important to look into."

He shook his head. "I wish it would all go away. My mother needs to let the book go. The only sad thing about this is its value. I wish that hadn't been lost. I would have loved for her to sell it. She's on a fixed income, and the extra money would have been a great help to her. For that reason, I'm upset that it was stolen, assuming that that's what happened. However, I know my mother well enough to know that she was never ever going to sell it. There was never going to be any amount of money that she would have accepted. If someone had offered her one million dollars for it, she would have turned it down. I just wish she would finally let it go. Maybe this will force her to do so."

"I don't think your mother is willing to let it go. She seemed very adamant that she needs that book back because it is her proof."

He groaned. "I'm not surprised. Did she tell you that ridiculous story that Henry David Thoreau is her great-great-great grandfather?"

"I think she said four greats, but yes. You don't believe that you are a descendant of Thoreau?"

"I don't know. It doesn't matter if I am or not. There is no way to make any money off of his work. It's all in the public domain and has been for a very long time. Maybe that sounds callous that I just look at it from a monetary perspective. She doesn't care about the money. Her mission is to prove her relation to Thoreau. She's tried to do it her whole life, but I will say it's only been in the last five years that she's really gone to such extreme lengths. She's contacted museums, scholars, and colleges. None of them will give her the time of day. I think that, because she entering her twilight years, she is seeking validation. She truly believes that getting some sort of proof of her ancestry will give her that."

"Where did she get this idea about Thoreau?" I asked.

"There have always been stories in my family that we were related to Thoreau somehow, but that's all they were, just stories. I think, as time went on, my mother lost more and more of her grasp on reality, but she held onto the family lore. It became the most important thing in her life. She even sued the state of Massachusetts a few years ago because Walden Pond is a state park. She said that it rightfully belonged to her as Henry David's great-great-great-great-granddaughter. The whole thing is ridiculous. She even went so far to ask me to change my name to Thoreau. I refused. I'm not going to buy into her lunacy."

I cringed when he said that. Mental illness could have such painful impacts. Somehow I didn't think he'd appreciate my sympathy. I changed the subject. "Did you know Roma?"

"I met her a while back. She was one of the very few people who took my mother seriously. I can't say I was happy about it. My mother was in a fragile mental state, and I think it grew worse with Roma's encouragement."

"She admitted to giving Roma that book," I said.

"She did?" Edmund asked.

"Roma claimed she had a way to prove that Imogene was related to Henry David."

"I can see why my mother gave her the book then. After so many years of floating around in her own alternate reality, my mother is desperate for proof. She took a risk and gave the book to a person she trusted, probably the last person on this earth that she trusted."

"Your poor mother," Grandma Daisy said. "It sounds like she has been torturing herself for years trying to prove this."

"Torturing herself and others," Edmund said like he spoke from experience.

Before I could ask him what he meant by that, he added, "I do apologize for all this, but my mother is unstable. She has always been. I have been the parent for a long time. There are times I wish I could just wash my hands of the whole thing, but she is my mother. I have no choice but to deal with her."

I bristled at the way he spoke about his mother, and my heart filled with compassion for Imogene. She wasn't well. She was confused, and her condition might be made worse by lack of love from her only child.

"I can tell by the look on your face that you're judging how I feel about my mother. If you lived through some of the challenges that I had faced as a child, you would think differently— not that I would ever wish that on another person."

He was right. I didn't know what it was like to grow up in such strange circumstances. However, I had grown up in very strange circumstances of my own. The bookshop was all the proof I needed of that. However, not knowing what Edmund had been through, I tried my best to give him the benefit of doubt.

"If she's sick, she needs help," I said.

He looked at me like I didn't have a clue. "She's also an adult, who is mostly functioning. In that case, she has to choose to take the help. We've tried so many things from counseling to medication. Nothing has worked. There's nothing more I can do but to make sure she eats and stays out of trouble. The doctors don't think her condition is bad enough that she needs to be in a facility." He pressed his lips together as if he disagreed. He rubbed the back of his neck again. "I know I sound cold, but I do love her. She's my mom. She was a single mother. I never knew my father. I'm doing the best I can to take care of her. I always have, even when I was a child. You can't know what it's like to take care of a parent at a young age or how that changes you as a person."

I bit the inside of my lip. I did know. My experience was different, of course, but my mother died of ovarian cancer when I was thirteen. When she was ill, I spent countless hours caring for her. However, I knew physical illnesses and mental illnesses were very different. It wasn't fair to compare my experience to his, but at the same time, he also had no way of knowing what I had been through in life.

I sensed Grandma Daisy bristle. She knew better than anyone what I had been through. She'd been there too.

"If your mother needs help…"

"I've tried." He looked to my grandmother. "Daisy, can we go over these plans?"

Grandma Daisy looked to me, and I gave a slight nod. It seemed I had gotten all the information that I was going to get out of Imogene's son for now.

Chapter Fourteen

I left my grandmother and Edmund to their meeting. I had a
little better understanding of Imogene and how important
proving she was a descendent of Thoreau was to her. I couldn't
help but wonder if it was important enough to kill for, though.
It might have been given that she'd needed to retrieve her book,
but the book was still missing.

Since I had Charles covering for me at the bookshop, I was
reluctant to go back to Charming Books. Instead, I decided to
go to Springside Community College and visit a friend. The
campus was a little too far away to walk to, and the snow was
packed down enough that I thought I could ride my bike.

I retrieved my aqua bike with the bright pink basket from
the garage. As soon as I strapped on my helmet, which my
grandmother had decorated with hand-painted violets, Emerson
appeared in front of the front tire. "No, Emerson, you are not
going with me to school."

He cocked his head.

"Emerson, college is no place for you."

He cocked his head the other way.

"Okay, get in," I groaned.

The little tuxedo cat jumped from the icy gravel driveway into the bicycle's pink basket. He snuggled down into the towel I kept in the basket for him and began to purr.

I climbed on the bike and pushed off. "One of these days, I'm going to win one of our arguments. Mark my words."

His purring only got louder.

The fastest way to reach campus was through the woods. I was a little apprehensive riding there after being chased away from the springs the morning of my wedding.

With everything that happened since then, I had put the encounter in the back of my mind. Pedaling over the frozen ground brought it back to the forefront of my mind. I passed the springs. It was yet another day that I would have to fetch water for the tree, but that would have to wait until I returned from campus. The water couldn't hold its mystical powers for that long and explaining why I had a watering can of spring water in my bicycle basket while on campus could lead to an awkward conversation.

I made it through the woods without incident, rode passed the village bike shop that was closed for the season, and pedaled onto campus. My first indication that the campus was deserted for winter break was that none of the sidewalks had been shoveled. The parking lot had not been plowed either. It seemed to me that the college was hoping the snow would melt before the students returned in January. There were a few cars in the lot, and I hoped for the sake of the drivers that they wouldn't need to move them anytime soon.

Bringing the bike was a much better idea than taking the car. At least I could push the bike through the snow until I reached the library, which is where I was headed.

Emerson sat up in his basket as I hopped off and painstakingly walked my wheels through the snow to the library's front door. I leaned the bike against one of the pillars, and the cat jumped to the steps that, despite the overhang of the building, were dusted with an inch or two of snow. Emerson pranced up the steps and waited at the door for me. Shaking my head, I followed him.

The automatic door didn't open, and the sign on the door said the library was closed. I should have expected this. It was only a few days before Christmas, and clearly no one was on campus. Why would the library be open?

I was about to leave when a face appeared in the door's window. I screamed.

Emerson hissed and ran down the steps.

I was about to follow him when the doors opened, and the college's head librarian and my friend, Renee Reid, whom I hadn't seen since the wedding, stood in the doorway. "Sheesh! It's just me, Violet. There's no reason to scream bloody murder."

"I'm a little bit on edge." I gave her a wobbly smile.

She arched her brow at me. "A little bit? Is that what you're calling it? Get your scaredy cat and come in."

Emerson ran up the steps and then strolled into the library with his head and thin black tail held high as if he hadn't been spooked at all.

Renee laughed.

Most of the lights were off inside.

She must have noticed me looking around because she said, "The library is closed. I can't turn all the lights on. Then, someone would know I was here and ask me to help them with something. It's my winter break too. I just happened to be looking out the window at the snow when you rode up, so I knew it was you at the door. Had it been anyone else, I would have hidden."

"How do you know I'm not going to ask you for something?"

"Oh, I'm certain you're going to ask me for something, but you're my friend. Besides, you ask much more interesting questions than the rest of the faculty. Let's go to my office."

Renee's office was tucked in the back corner of the library near the stairwell that led to the basement, where the boiler room and the college archives were. Books sat on orderly carts in her office, waiting to be reviewed and shelved. Everything was organized and in its place. Even her houseplants on the windowsill sat in a straight line. Seeing all the organization soothed my soul. It was something that I longed for at Charming Books. A couple things held me back in achieving such a streamlined existence. The first of these was the shop's essence, which moved the books to any place it deemed fit, and the second was my grandmother. Grandma Daisy's idea of tidiness was a bit more higgledy-piggledy. Even now, when Grandma Daisy was only in the shop a couple days a week because of her many mayoral duties, she still managed to make a mess. Over time, I had learned to roll with it more or less, but being in such a tidy space made me long for what could be. I sighed.

Renee sat in her executive chair behind the desk. "What's with the big sigh?"

"Your office is so pristine."

Renee grinned. "I've had some say it was stark. That's why I added the plants. I want to give the impression that I have a soft side, even if it's not true."

"You do have a soft side. You just don't let most people see it."

She rolled her eyes. "And I would like to keep it that way too."

I might have imagined it, but for just a second, Renee almost looked sad. It wasn't an expression that I had ever seen on my friend's face. Renee could be irreverent, sarcastic, annoyed, and certainly hilarious, but I had never seen her truly upset.

She shook her head, and the fleeting expression disappeared, making me question if it had ever been there at all. "I'm guessing you're here about the body?"

Emerson jumped into the windowsill and batted at one of the plant leaves. I started to get up to shoo him away.

"Oh, you can leave him be. The plants are fake. He can't hurt them," she chuckled.

"They are? They look so real."

"I only buy the very best fake plants." She grinned. "Am I right about the body?"

"Yes," I said grudgingly.

She leaned back in the chair. "Tell me. I was at the wedding, of course, but didn't get more than the rumors swirling around the reception."

I gave her a brief summary of what we knew about Roma's death. I didn't feel bad about telling her it was ruled an accident since Officer Wheaton had already announced that to everyone at Le Crepe Jolie.

"That's not the weird part."

She arched her brow at me. "A woman tries to sell you a rare book, and then dies at your wedding. You say that's not weird?"

"Okay, it's not the weird*est* part," I said and went on to tell her about Imogene Thoreau. "Imogene thinks the book is proof that she is a direct descendent of Henry David Thoreau."

"The best way for her to find out if she is related to Thoreau is do one of those DNA tests that you can get in the mail now. You know, the one where you can find everyone you're related too."

"But someone has to have some DNA from Thoreau to test too," I said.

"Maybe his museum or one of his archives has a fingernail or even a bone of his. Maybe even a hair. It doesn't take much."

I wrinkled my nose.

She held up her hands. "Hey, I'm just saying. I read this article about brilliant people being dug up so people could collect their DNA in hopes that they could be cloned and come back. That way the brilliant clones could help them take over the world."

"That can't be true."

Renee shrugged.

"Even if it is true—which I doubt—I'm not sure Thoreau would be on that list. He would just tell everyone to live simply and below their means. To let each person live their life the way they chose."

"Good point. This is the first that I've heard about an heir to Henry David Thoreau running around the village. If someone had come into the library saying something along those lines, my staff would have told me. They are horrible gossips." She rolled her eyes.

"I knew it was a long shot," I said.

"You should talk to Richard. If she didn't come to the library for help to prove her lineage, she could have gone to the English department."

She had a good point. Richard Bunting was chair of the English Department, which made him my boss since I was an adjunct for the department. I taught two to three classes every semester, and since I was the newest hire, I usually got the classes that no one else wanted like Freshman Composition. Not only was Richard my boss, he was also Renee's boyfriend. After having a terrible crush on Renee for a year, he finally worked up the courage to ask her on a date.

I wrinkled my brow. "If Roma or Imogene had spoken to Richard about Thoreau, I'm surprised Richard didn't mention it to you."

She folded her hands on the top of her clear desk. "Richard and I aren't exactly speaking at the moment."

"What?" I stared at her.

"We broke up," she stated this with the same amount of emotion she would have had if she had been telling me the weather for that day.

"What? How? When did this happen?" I yelped. I had been a big encourager of Richard's to make a move with Renee, so if their relationship had failed, I felt in some way responsible.

"It was about a month ago. It's really not a huge deal, and I'm doing just fine. To be honest, I'm better without him. His nerves got the better of both of us at times. It's good to be away from that kind of energy."

I studied her face as if to reassure myself that she was telling the truth, and she really was okay with the break up. "Why didn't you tell me?"

"You were in the middle of fall semester and about to get married. I didn't want to add to your stress. Besides, I don't like to wallow when stuff happens because it always does. I just got on with my life."

Now that she mentioned it, I remembered that it had struck me as weird that Renee and Richard hadn't sat together at the last several Red Inkers meetings. The Red Inkers were a writing critique group the met biweekly at Charming Books. And now that I thought about it, I hadn't seen them together at the wedding. I was so distracted by the day going smoothly, and then Roma's death, that I hadn't really even registered how strange that was. Renee and Richard had never been ones for public displays of affection, but they used to attend events together as a couple. However, the more I thought about it, the more I realized that they had hardly spoken of each other in the recent weeks.

Tonight was the last Red Inkers meeting before Christmas. Since we were supposed to be on our honeymoon, Rainwater and I hadn't planned on attending. David had written some children's books that he wanted to publish. Since the meetings were at my bookshop, I usually went. Even though I wasn't a writer, I appreciated the craft and loved to hear about each author's process.

"I'm so sorry, Renee," I said. I couldn't think of anything else to say.

She sighed and shrugged. "It is what it is."

"Can I ask what happened?" I held up my hand in a stop sign. "You don't have to tell me if you don't want to."

"The thing is that I don't know. It was Richard's idea to break up. I thought we were in a good place. We hadn't been dating long." She shrugged again.

My heart sank. "I'm so sorry. I was really rooting for you two."

"I know, and I appreciate that. I do. This could be just a bump in the road in my story or the end of a chapter entirely. Maybe I will be like Henry David and just run away to the woods. Although I'm not much for the idea of becoming a vegetarian like he was when he lived on Walden Pond. I do love a good cheeseburger." She stopped speaking but looked like she was thinking of saying more.

"What is it?"

"What's what?"

I gave her a look. "There's something that you're not telling me."

She wouldn't look me in the eye. "I actually started to see someone else."

I blinked at her. "Really? Who is he?"

"He had been coming into the library a lot, doing research on the history of Cascade Springs and the village hall. You know how everyone is eager to bring the history of the village back better than ever after you destroyed the village hall."

I folded my arms. "I didn't destroy the village hall. The aquifer underneath it did. I just happened to be there at the time."

She gave me a look like she didn't believe me.

"What's his name?"

A light blush shone on her cheek. "Edmund Thorne. He's such a smart guy, Violet. You would love him. We have the best conversations. I've learned a lot more about Cascade Springs and architecture from him. He's so interesting."

I stared at her. Edmund Thorne was Imogene's son—a son whom I'd found to be exasperated with his eccentric mother.

"What?" she asked.

I shook my head.

"No, you can't pretend like nothing is wrong. You wouldn't let me do that. There's something *you're* not telling *me* now."

"He's her son," I said.

She squinted at me. "He's whose son?"

"Imogene's. Imogene Thoreau's. You're dating her son."

Chapter Fifteen

"What?" Renee cried so loudly that she spooked Emerson, who jumped off the windowsill and dashed out the office door.

He was going to be so hard to find in the large library with all its nooks and crannies. I tried not to think about it for the moment. It would only stress me out.

"I just saw him an hour ago with Grandma Daisy," I said. "They were going over the plan to fix the village hall. He confirmed that Imogene was his mother."

Renee pressed a hand to her head. "Why do I find all the men with baggage? There must be a stamp on my forehead or something to let men like that know that I will go out with them. I wonder if I can get it surgically removed."

"He never mentioned his mother or Thoreau?" I asked.

"No, he didn't. We've only been on a couple of dates so far. It's not like we got to the point where we'd talk about our family trees. Wacky relatives are date five information, at the very least." Renee rubbed her forehead as if trying to erase that sign she'd mentioned earlier. "Listen, I will make some calls to other libraries and museums and find out if they have heard of or heard from Imogene. When I know something, I'll call you."

"You're not coming to the Red Inkers meeting tonight?" I asked.

"I emailed the members of the group to say that I'm withdrawing. I think it's the best thing to do under the circumstances. It's just too difficult to sit in the same room with Richard and listen to him talk about his writing. It's bad enough seeing him on campus, but I'm going to continue to do that because I love my job and need the paycheck and the health insurance that comes with it."

"I'm sorry, Renee." I didn't blame her. I wouldn't have wanted to be in a small group with an ex-boyfriend either. "We'll miss you at the meetings."

She smiled. "I'll miss them too, but this is for the best. I know it is. Now, you go look for that book, and I'll see what I can find on my end. This search for *Walden* is a much welcome distraction."

As I'd expected, it took me forty minutes to find Emerson in the large library. Both Renee and I searched for him. We finally found the cat sitting at the front door with his sleek black tail curled around his pristine white paws. He meowed as if to ask us where we had been all that time.

I put my hands on my hips. "Let's go."

He scratched on the door as if he had been waiting to leave for hours.

I knew I needed to head back to the bookshop soon to relieve Charles, but I wanted to make one more stop on campus before going home.

If Renee was taking advantage of the quiet campus to get some extra work done, I knew Richard was likely doing the same.

The English department offices were in the humanities building, just across the courtyard. I left my bicycle at the library and took Emerson with me on a walk across campus.

Even though I was an adjunct, Richard had given me a key to the building. Some of the classes I taught were at night, and he'd wanted me to be able to get into the building if I needed to without calling security.

Although I had yet to use it, I was glad I had that key now. The building was locked for winter break. The English department was at the end of the hall on the first floor. I didn't see any lights under the door. I used my master key again to get into the office.

The main office space was dominated by a large window that looked out over the college courtyard. Right now, there wasn't much to look at other than snow.

Richard was notorious for being in his office at all hours of the day and night. The last several months, he'd been there even more often to work on his promotion portfolio. The portfolio process to become a full professor was grueling, and when I was in grad school, I saw more than one talented professor crack under the pressure.

Richard's personal office was in the back of the shared area. I knocked on the door. There was no answer. I tried the doorknob, but the office was locked.

Emerson sat at my feet and placed a paw on my pant leg.

I sighed. "You're right. It's time to go home. I can ask him this evening at Red Inkers why he broke up with Renee." And I would certainly ask. Maybe it was none of my business, but I felt partly responsible for Richard and Renee getting together in the first place. I wanted to know what had gone wrong, and how I'd failed in setting up a match.

I turned around to leave the office when the outer door flew open. Emerson jumped on a chair. I wasn't sure if he did so out of fear or to get a better look at the person who came in.

"Ahh!" There was a scream and envelopes flew in all directions.

I put a hand to my chest. "Mary Alice, what are you doing here?" I asked just as soon as I realized it was the school of humanities secretary.

"Oh Violet, you scared me half to death. What on earth are *you* doing here on winter break? And aren't you supposed to be on your honeymoon?"

I sighed. I was growing tired of honeymoon questions. "I'm so sorry if I scared you. I happened to be on campus and dropped by to see if Richard was in." I bent down to help her collect the envelopes that were all over the floor.

Emerson batted one of the envelopes under the desk. I fished it out and handed it to her along with the others that I had gathered up.

"Thank you." She stacked the envelopes on her desk. "Richard isn't here as far as I know. I just came in to get a little work done. There was some paperwork I couldn't complete before the end of the semester and the best time to do it is when no one is here." She grinned. "Plus, my three teenagers are home for the holidays. I needed a break from them. That's my story."

Mary Alice was the secretary for the English, music, and art departments. In a school as small as Springside, most of the staff wore many hats. I was sure she had other responsibilities on campus that I didn't even know about.

"I hope the college isn't overworking you," I said.

131

She chuckled. "That's the Springside model. Work your staff to death until they are so exhausted that they don't have the will to leave."

I grimaced. It wasn't a glamorous take on academia, but it wasn't an unusual story for a small school with a tight budget. I wanted to tell her that coming into the office on her day off was only proof to the college that she would get her work done no matter the cost to her personal life and health, and by doing that, she was inadvertently encouraging the college to pile on more duties and responsibilities. It proved that she not only could handle it but also that she was willing to. In a way, she was agreeing to the mistreatment. However, I bit my tongue from saying any of it. I'm sure she had heard it all before.

"Did you get married?" Mary Alice asked, slightly alarmed. "Are you working because the wedding was called off?"

"The wedding happened." I held up my hand to show her my ring as proof. "My husband has been caught up in a case, and we can't leave the village right now."

"You're talking about the woman who died by the river, aren't you?" She sighed. "That was such a sad story. I didn't hear if she was from here or not."

"She was a visitor," I said, leaving it at that.

She nodded at this too. Living in a village, visitors and tourists could almost be blamed for anything by the locals.

"To be honest, I'm surprised Richard isn't on campus," she said. "If you're looking for a person who never leaves work, he's your guy. I'm pretty sure he sleeps in his office from time to time. It's not like the man has a long commute. He can walk from his townhouse. Yesterday, I came in to use the scanner—I don't have one at home—and he was in his office. It was seven in the morning during winter break."

"But you were also here at seven in the morning," I pointed out.

"Yes, but I already told you. I have teenagers that I needed to get away from." She pressed a hand to the side of her head. "Between the music and their bickering, I'm going to lose my mind. I don't know how any mother has any Christmas spirit left after her child turns thirteen years old."

"How old are your kids?" I asked.

"Thirteen, fifteen, and seventeen. I'm right in the thick of it. My mother told me I will start to like them again when they are in their twenties. That feels like eons away."

"Did Richard say why he's been working so much over break?" I asked. "Is it a new research project or something?"

"He hasn't said, and I offered to help. He turned me down, though. I'm sure it's because he's embarrassed." She clicked her tongue in disapproval.

"Embarrassed about what?" I asked, thinking she was going to mention his break up with Renee.

"Because he applied for full professor and didn't get it."

"What?" I yelped. "Richard has been here for fifteen years. And he always gets great evaluations from his students."

"That may be so, but he's still only an associate professor. He can't go up in status or salary until he's a full professor at this point in his career."

"Did the promotion committee say why he didn't get it?"

"Lack of scholarship," she said in a low voice, as if she were saying something gruesome and didn't want anyone else to overhear.

"Lack of scholarship?" I whispered back, following her lead.

"The committee said he didn't have enough proof of conference presentations and published articles to be promoted." She shook her head. "I saw the letter. The dean had me type it up. It was pretty harsh. They gave Richard one more academic year to increase his scholarship and reapply for full professorship. If he can't prove that he's actively working on it, he won't be allowed to apply again. They can't just let him keep applying over and over. The application process is too time consuming for him and the committee."

"But he is tenured."

She shrugged. "Tenure is based more on how long you've been a professor, your involvement on campus, and your student evaluations. Scholarship is one piece, but it's not as important when you apply for tenure as it is when you apply for full professorship."

Emerson wove around my feet as if he were trying to be comforting. If Mary Alice thought it was off that I'd brought my cat to campus, she didn't say anything. She had been a college secretary long enough to know that college professors do all kinds of odd things. None of their antics had ever seemed to bother her, as far as I knew.

"Surely that's more important than making full professor?" I picked up Emerson and cradled him in my arms.

"For job security, yes, but it won't save him from being embarrassed when the rest of the faculty learns of this at the start of spring semester. And being full professor is worth the work. It's an impressive bump in pay, but I think for Richard it's more about the title. The prestige that comes with being a full professor is important to him."

I frowned because what she said reminded me of Imogene. She wasn't trying to prove Thoreau's book was real for the money. It was the principle of the matter that motivated her to continue.

"How many people know?" I asked, certain that Renee would tell me if she knew.

"Not many yet. He received the letter right after finals but before grades were due. The campus was mostly deserted at the time. I believe the dean did that out of kindness to Richard. It gave him time to get used to the idea before classes were back in session."

"So you think he's been on campus working on research?" I asked.

"That would be my guess. I know making full professor is all he's ever wanted. He talks about it constantly."

That sounded odd to me. Richard had never mentioned that to me, but on campus, I was his employee. Richard was pretty old school when it came to office hierarchy. I could see him believing it was inappropriate to speak about such a matter with someone under his charge.

"Richard needs to make a big splash with his research. This is his last shot. If he doesn't make full professor now, he can't apply again. I'm not sure what will happen to him then," she said.

That sounded ominous.

She shook her head. "He's been pretty tight-lipped about everything since he got the news."

I set Emerson back on the floor. Poor Richard. Between breaking up with Renee and this latest news, he had to be in a bad place. He and Rainwater were friends. Maybe I should ask David to talk to him. Perhaps he'd be more comfortable talking to my husband than to me, especially since I technically worked for him.

Mary Alice cocked her head. "Now that you've brought it up, I did pick up one hint about his research, even if he wouldn't tell me what was going on."

"Really?" I asked.

"An elderly woman with a cane came here right before finals. She said she was looking for an expert on American literature. I know you teach many of those classes, but you weren't here that day, so I introduced her to Richard. The two went to talk at the college café, I believe."

"Did she give her name?" I asked.

Mary Alice scratched her head. "It was an old-fashioned name like Marjory or Gertrude."

"Imogene?" I asked.

"Yes!" She smiled. "Yes, that was it!" she said like I'd won some kind of prize. "And I found another clue."

I took a breath because a part of me was loath to hear it. "What was that?"

"He left the title page of a paper he was writing in the printer. The title is what caught my eye."

I waited.

"I believe the article was called 'The Descendent of the Great Transcendentalist.'"

My heart sank.

"I found that to be a little strange because I thought that was your area of study," she went on to say. "I wanted to ask him about it, but he's been so closed-mouthed lately that I decided to let him be. Maybe I should have asked more questions."

Maybe she should have.

"He's seemed depressed and bitter in recent weeks. Honestly, I think he would do anything to satisfy the committee's requirements for promotion."

"Anything?" I whispered.

"Anything." She was emphatic.

Richard was my boss, my colleague, and most of all, my friend. He was the person who had welcomed me to Cascade Springs and offered me the job at Springside. He was also head of the Red Inkers and a close friend of Rainwater's. Knowing all of that, could I really believe he hid knowing about the first edition of *Walden* from me?

The answer was yes, and it broke my heart.

Chapter Sixteen

As I waited for the Red Inkers meeting to begin that night, I paced the floor of the bookshop like a caged tiger. How could Richard be working on an article about transcendentalist literature and not tell me about it? He certainly could research and write about any topic that he wished, but wasn't it professional courtesy to tell your colleague when you ventured into their particular area of study?

I felt betrayed, and then guilt washed over me for feeling that way. Surely, Richard hadn't told me because he'd been embarrassed about not making full professor.

I made one more lap around the shop when I heard a thud behind me. I spun around and saw Faulkner walking on the floor. Faulkner never walked on the floor. Staying high in the tree on his perch or on one of the high bookshelves was a great joy for him, especially when he could get to a spot that Emerson couldn't reach.

Emerson was snoozing in his cat bed by the fire after our visit to campus. He opened one green eye and glowered at Faulkner. It was clear he found it odd, too, that the large crow was walking around.

"Faulkner, are you hurt?" I asked.

The big bird squawked at me. "The price of anything is what you're willing to give in exchange for it."

I folded my arms. "So you are paraphrasing Thoreau now?"

He cawed and leaped into flight. In the blink of an eye, he was back on his favorite branch at the top of the tree.

"Glad to see you're all right," I said, intent on resuming my pacing when I saw a book on the floor where Faulkner had been. It didn't take a genius to guess what the book would be.

"You're working for the shop's essence now too?" I asked the bird.

He didn't even deem my question worthy of a response. Instead, he snuggled his beak under his right wing like he was settling in for a nice nap.

I glanced at Emerson. The little tuxedo cat had lost interest. His expressive eyes blinked once, then slowly once more. I sighed. "I guess I'm on my own here," I said. Not that they were listening since they were both fast asleep.

Knowing what was going to come next, I picked up the book.

In preparation for the Red Inkers meeting, I set a circle of folding chairs in the middle of the shop. It was how the meetings had been set up long before I returned to Cascade Springs. I sat in one of those chairs and put the book in my lap. As soon as I moved my hands away, the book opened. This time to an early page. I read:

I went to the woods because I wished to live deliberately, to front only the essential facts of life, and see if I could not learn what it had to teach, and not, when I came to die, discover that I had not lived. I did not wish to live what was not life.

I shook my head. "He's working late at the station again tonight."

Sadie sighed. "You guys have not had the greatest start to married life. Have you even seen him all that much since the wedding?"

I bit the inside of my lip. "He's just busy at work right now with…"

"The dead woman. We know." Sadie grabbed Simon's hand and squeezed it tight. "David is an amazing man, and I'm happy you're married, Violet. However, I don't know if I would be cut out to be married to a cop like you are." She squeezed her boyfriend's hand a little tighter. "That's why I'm glad you work insurance, baby. Your nine to five schedule suits me just fine."

He chuckled. "Yep, I'm nice and boring."

I couldn't help but notice that Richard seemed to grow more and more uncomfortable as this conversation went on.

"We're going to have such a small group tonight with David absent and Renee leaving the group," Sadie said. "Did anyone else think that email came out of the blue? I mean, she was here last week and seemed to really enjoy the meetings."

"I thought it was odd too," Simon agreed. "But she said she had a lot going on at work right now and didn't have as much time for writing. I think we all go through periods like that. Sometimes life gets in the way."

"Richard, did she discuss it with you before quitting?" Sadie asked.

"She—she—" He started coughing and cleared his throat. "Frog in my throat. If you will excuse me, I'm just going to get a glass of water."

I waited a full ten seconds before I said, "Why don't you two pull out what you're planning to read tonight. I'm going to go see if he needs help finding the glasses. You know Grandma Daisy. She never puts anything back in the same place twice." I forced a laugh.

I went into the kitchen and found Richard standing in the middle of the room, gripping the edge of the island's counter as if his life depended on it.

"Richard?" I said softly.

He jumped and knocked over the kitchen stool that was next to him. Quickly, he set it back on its legs. "Oh, Violet, it's you."

"Do you need any help finding the glasses?"

"Glasses?" He stared at me like I'd spoken a different language.

"Yes, for the water you came in here to get," I said in my most helpful voice.

"Oh. Oh, yes, I do need water. That's why I'm here." He started to look around as if searching the air for water glasses.

I stepped around him, opened a high cupboard door, removed a glass from it, and filled it with tap water. I left the glass in front of him on the island.

"Thank you. That's just what I came in here for. It's just what I needed." He couldn't have sounded less convincing if he tried.

I sighed. "Richard, what's wrong?"

"Wrong? Nothing is wrong." He forced a laugh. "I'm dandy."

I leaned back on the kitchen counter and folded my arms. "I don't think anyone who has ever said they were dandy actually felt that way."

"You've spoken to Renee, haven't you?" He looked at the back door as if he was thinking about bolting.

"I was on campus today and stopped by the library. Even with everything closed, Renee was there working."

"She is so dedicated to her job," he said with a pained expression. "I'm convinced she was born to be a librarian. She is the most organized person I have ever met. She's helped me so much with my research over the years."

"You're talking about her like she's just a coworker, not someone you dated."

He clasped his hands together and wrung his fingers. "Dating a work colleague was ill-advised. I realized it would interfere with our work. By breaking it off, I did what was best for both of us."

I wasn't sure he really felt that way because Richard appeared to be in physical pain, and if he twisted his fingers any harder, he might have dislocated them. I couldn't watch it anymore. I picked up the water glass. "You need a drink. Here."

He didn't argue with me. Taking the glass from my hand, he took a long drink. When he was done, he asked, "How is Renee? Did she seem..." he trailed off as if he couldn't find the right word or realized his question was inappropriate. In a way, the question was. After breaking up with her, Richard didn't have the right to ask if Renee was okay anymore.

Even so, I answered, "She's all right. She's tough."

He nodded. "I always knew she was resilient."

"Why'd you break up with her? Renee said she didn't know."

He wouldn't look at me. "I just had to focus on my research. My relationship with Renee was taking me away from my work."

"Any relationship is a distraction," I said. "You don't believe yours was worth the distraction?"

"I—I care about Renee. She's an amazing woman and a phenomenal librarian. I just have to focus on my work. Sometimes work has to come first."

This was true. I've felt that way many times in my own life. When I was in grad school, I never dated. I didn't want anything or anyone getting in the way of my goals. However, I also knew that that period was temporary. Someday grad school would end, and I would care about other aspects of my life again. And not just my love life, but my health and friendships too—everything that I put on the back burner in my all-encompassing quest to earn my PhD.

"Richard, what's going on? You have been acting strangely for weeks. You've been avoiding me. Even at Red Inkers meetings, you have hardly said one word to me over the last couple of weeks."

He wouldn't look me in the eye. "I don't know what you're talking about."

"You know exactly what I'm talking about, and I think it has to do with Imogene Thoreau."

Richard stared at me, and then chugged the rest of the water to give himself time to think about his answer. "Who?" he squeaked.

I folded my arms. "I saw someone else when I was on campus today. Mary Alice. She told me all about Imogene visiting you and the article you are writing about her claim of being descended from Thoreau."

He forced another laugh. "That's ridiculous. I wouldn't do any research on Thoreau without consulting you."

"Why's that?" I asked.

"Well, it's your area of expertise. It's just courtesy between professors to consult one another when it comes to concentrations."

"But you didn't do that," I said.

He looked out the window again like he was really ready to make a run for it.

"Listen, Richard, I didn't come in here to give you a hard time. It's fine that you're writing an article about Thoreau. It will help your career."

He dropped his eyes. "Mary Alice told you that I didn't get full professorship, didn't she?"

I nodded.

He shook his head. "I love working at the college, but what I hate most about our campus, and any campus for that matter, is the gossip. It won't be long before everyone on the faculty learns what a failure I am. How will I show my face at the faculty assembly? I know they will all be talking about it."

"You're not a failure. You were just missing some of the requirements for promotion. You will get them when you apply again."

He balled his hands into fists. "I *have* to have everything I need when I apply again. There is no third chance. If I'm not promoted, I will languish as an associate professor forever."

I don't think Richard realized how offensive that might sound to a non-tenured adjunct professor. I would love to be a tenured associate professor. Talk about job security. Not that I needed job security, really. I had that in my bookshop with its mystical essence. That was the ultimate job security. I didn't say anything about it to Richard. I saw no point in making him feel worse than he already did.

"I understand," I said. "I just wish you had told me about it. Then I would have been forewarned when that woman came into Charming Books wanting to sell me a signed first edition of *Walden*."

"What? Imogene *never* would sell that book. She wouldn't even let me take it out of her sight. As I looked it over, she watched me like a hawk. She made me wear gloves—which I understood—but also a face mask so that I wouldn't even breathe on it. I cannot believe she tried to sell it. When was this?"

"Why don't you tell me how you met Imogene, and then I will tell you my story?"

I was sorry to admit it, but I no longer fully trusted Richard. We had worked together in the English department for the better part of two years. I thought I knew him, but seeing what he was willing to do when he was desperate to be published disturbed me. I think it upset me the most because I wouldn't have cared. If he had come to me and said that he'd met someone with a first edition of *Walden* and that he wanted to write an article about her so he could reapply for a promotion, I probably would have offered to help him. He should have known that about me. Instead, he assumed that I would be upset or territorial, so he tried to hide it. Didn't he think I would find out eventually? I read all the same journals. And every professor's publications are listed in the faculty newsletter. What was he thinking?

I realized that he hadn't been thinking. He'd panicked. Panic was what had caused him to break up with Renee as well. It made me sad that someone so brilliant would let fear rule their life like this.

"Very well," Richard said. "I spoke to a woman at the end of the semester. She called herself Imogene Thoreau. She'd said she had a signed first edition of *Walden* that had been in her family for over one hundred and fifty years. I was shocked. She was looking for someone to authenticate it. I'd suggested libraries and auction houses to go to about her book, but she shot all my ideas down. Her reluctance to go to one of these reputable authenticators made me suspicious. Normally, I would have turned her away and told her to speak to an expert on the matter." He swallowed. "However, I had just learned about not getting the promotion. I was in a weak state, so I agreed to meet with her in hopes of getting something to help me when I reapplied."

I nodded.

"At the meeting, she told me why she wouldn't go to those other archives and libraries. She had already tried, and they'd all turned her away because of her claim of being a direct descendant of Thoreau. As you would know even better than I do, this is close to blasphemy in American literature circles. Scholars don't want to be told that they missed something from a non-scholar even if the non-scholar is telling the truth."

"Do you believe that she was telling the truth?" I asked.

"I believe that she believed it," he said. "There was no question that she thought she was related to Thoreau. However, I told her I didn't know if I could prove she was related to Thoreau, but I promised her that I would try."

"How were you going to prove that?" I asked.

He hesitated. "I don't know. I hadn't thought that far ahead."

"Didn't she ask you how you were going to prove it?"

"No." His Adam's apple bobbed up and down. "All I said was that I would try. That's all I could do. That I'd try if she would let me write two articles on her claim and about the provenance of the book. I knew she didn't like my terms, but she agreed. I really believed she was at her wit's end." He paused. "I did mention you and the store. I said you might know more. She didn't seem interested in Charming Books, and I can't say that I tried to push her in that direction. I really needed a paper topic, so I didn't mention it again."

"But she never came to my store."

He stared at me. "But you said she came to your shop and tried to sell the book."

I shook my head. "It wasn't Imogene. It was another woman named Roma Winterbourne. I met Imogene later. Imogene claimed that Roma had stolen the book from her. She'd let her borrow it because *Roma* had said she could prove she was related to Thoreau."

He stared at me in shock. "She asked someone else for help?"

I nodded. "It seems to me she will talk to anyone who is willing to take her seriously about being descended from Thoreau. I can't blame her for trying so many different tactics to prove she was right. She has been trying to prove this was true most of her life. She had to be feeling desperate." I thought about what her son Edmund had said that the book had become the most important thing in Imogene's life. By his tone, I would guess he felt that it was more important to Imogene than even he was.

Richard nodded. "She was looking for validation." His face clouded over. "There was no way to prove what she wanted to prove as far I knew. That doesn't mean I wasn't going to get an article or two out of it. I used her—or planned to use her—and her book. Believe me when I say I have never been more disgusted with myself than I am right now."

I wasn't sure what I could say to that. That he had a right to be disgusted with himself? That I was disappointed? That he didn't really do anything morally wrong, just ethically wrong?

"Richard, honestly, if Imogene's story is proven false, do you really think articles about her will increase your chances of making full professor?"

He stiffened. "The college just wants to see a certain publication credits in reputable journals for promotion. They don't expect me to prove anything. My article will focus on the delusions that people like Imogene have when it comes to famous writers. She's not the first one to make such a claim about being a descendant of a great writer. My thesis is looking at how people go from adoration of a writer to obsession. Such an article will improve the reputation of the college. If I do that, yes, I will be awarded full professorship."

Sadie popped her head into the kitchen. Her black ponytail hung over her shoulder like a tassel. "Are you guys ever going to come back in for the meeting? I really love Simon, but we can talk to each other all the time about our writing. We would like your opinions on our latest work. Simon has written the most gorgeous Christmas poems, but I love everything he writes. I don't think he's taking my critique too seriously. We need the input of real literary scholars like the two of you."

"Right. Let's start," Richard said. As he brushed passed me to leave the kitchen, he refused to look me in the eye.

Chapter Seventeen

After the Red Inkers meeting, I went into the woods to get water for the birch tree. Surprisingly, Emerson didn't want to come along even though I'd invited him this time. Instead, the tuxie decided to stay home curled up in his warm cat bed. Perhaps the last trip to the springs had taught him a lesson. I can't say I was thrilled to have to go out on another cold night after dark to fetch water. It was only eight thirty in the evening, but it was as black as midnight. I knew it wasn't even Christmas yet—that was still a couple days away—but a large part of me was already longing for spring. Winter in Western New York was long and deep. It wasn't likely that we would see grass again until late February, and even after that snow melted, it could and most likely would snow again through the beginning of April.

Walking along the forest path, I was on edge. Every rustle of bare branches or snap of a fallen twig made me jump. I made it to the springs and back in fifteen minutes flat, which was the fastest time I had ever clocked. I didn't stop to take in the beauty of the springs or look around for animal tracks like I normally would have. The man chasing me through the forest that morning of my wedding day had thoroughly spooked me.

I let out a deep breath when I walked through the garden gate. I opened the back door to the shop and cried when I saw a shadow in the kitchen. "Ahh!"

I hugged the full watering can to my chest. I wasn't going to lose one drop of water, even if I was murdered in the process.

The overhead light came on and Rainwater stood in the middle of the kitchen in sweatpants and a T-shirt. His feet were bare, and he had a glass of water in his hand.

"David!" I cried.

"Who did you think it was?"

"I—I don't know."

He set his glass on the counter.

"I guess I'm still not used to having you around."

He smiled. "Well, I haven't made that any easier on you since I haven't been around much since we got married." He took the watering can from my vise-like grip, set it on the kitchen island, and gave me a hug.

I didn't disagree with what he said.

"I wish that you waited until I was home to get water for the tree. I don't know how I feel about you going into the forest at night."

"David, it's part of my job."

He sighed. "I know, but I can go with you."

I bit my tongue to keep myself from reminding him that he wasn't around enough to go with me. The birch tree needed to be watered when it needed to be watered. I couldn't just work around his schedule.

"Just with you being chased out of the forest the other morning," he said. "It doesn't feel safe." He frowned.

I gave him a squeeze, and my heart softened a bit. I picked up my watering can. The sooner I watered the tree, the better it was for the shop.

Rainwater followed me into the main part of the store. "I have just about everything set up to get away for a few days. Wheaton is thrilled. I think he's been waiting for his chance to be in charge. I won't be surprised if I get back and learn that he was after my job."

I glanced at him. "Are you worried about that?"

He laughed. "Not as long as Grandma Daisy is the mayor of Cascade Springs. I'd say my job is safe while she is in office."

I knew he was right. Grandma Daisy had been a great champion of Rainwater being the chief of police in Cascade Springs even before I'd met him and before she'd been elected mayor.

"I'm just not sure Wheaton is the right officer for this job." I poured the water into the ring of dirt around the birch tree. I shook the last few droplets from the can. Not a drop should be wasted.

"He's a good cop, even if he has a sour personality," Rainwater said, defending his choice.

Sour personality was putting it lightly. I pressed my lips together. I surely wouldn't want Officer Wheaton to be the face of the department. No one would like the police in Cascade Springs if he were.

"You still think the case will be closed by Christmas Eve?" I held the empty watering can to my chest.

Rainwater sat on the arm of one of the couches. "It's closed now. At least as far as the death is concerned. The only reason we're sticking around is to find that book. It may have been stolen, and that's still very much a crime." He held out his arms, and I walked over to him. I was still in my winter coat, hat, gloves, and boots. I must have looked a fright. However, from the smile on Rainwater's face, he didn't think that in the least. He put his hands on my hips.

"Speaking of the book, I learned some new things today." I went on to tell him about meeting Edmund, my visit to campus, and the conversation with Richard during the Red Inkers meeting. I bit my lower lip. "I suppose all that proves is how much Imogene wants her idea of being Thoreau's great-great-great-great-granddaughter validated. We are no closer to knowing what happened to Roma along the river or the location of Imogene's book."

Rainwater nodded. "I think we already knew that about Imogene from meeting her."

"Still, Richard can't be the only person she asked for help. We know she asked Roma too of course, but I'm betting there were others. I'm going to check in with the rare bookstore in Camden tomorrow. I tried to call a few times today, but there was no answer. The store might be closed for Christmas week, but I'm going to check it out anyway. I'll just go there tomorrow and knock on the door. My guess is that the bookstore owner is there even when the door is locked."

"Can someone make a living off of being a rare book dealer?" Rainwater furrowed his brow.

I frowned. "If they have the right rare books that serious collectors want, they can. If they have books worth collecting, like this particular copy of *Walden*."

"Then I'm coming with you."

I cocked my head. "David, if I show up with a cop, he's not going to want to talk to me."

"It's in Camden. No one knows I'm a cop there. I'll go undercover." He wriggled his eyebrows at me. "I'll blend in."

I gave him a look. "You never blend in." I smiled. "You're just too good-looking."

He grinned. "You think I'm handsome."

"Very."

His grin widened, and he kissed me.

Faulkner flapped his wings in the tree over our heads. "Rather than love, than money, than fame, give me truth. Give me truth!" he cawed.

"Why did you teach that crow *Walden* again?" Rainwater pulled away and asked.

"I didn't," I said.

* * *

The next morning, Grandma Daisy came into Charming Books. She took off her puffy winter coat and tossed it onto the coat tree with a flourish. "Violet, my dear, I have news!"

I was on my second of cup of coffee that morning even though it wasn't yet nine o'clock. I hadn't slept well the night before. My brain had been whirring over the missing *Walden* and where it could be. I finally gave up trying to sleep at four in the morning, left Rainwater in the bedroom, and went into the living room to read from Thoreau's classic text. I'd hoped the shop's essence would give me a new clue to what may have happened to Roma and the book. But I got nothing. It seemed the shop's essence was as fast asleep as Rainwater, the cat, and the crow.

"News?" I asked around a yawn.

Grandma Daisy stopped smoothing her silky silver hair and squinted at me. "Did David keep you up late?" She wiggled her eyebrows.

"Grandma!"

"What? I'm over sixty, but I'm not dead."

I rubbed my right eye to head off the twitching that was bound to start any minute. "I was up late reading."

She walked across the room and sat on one of the sofas. "You know, dear granddaughter, I advocate for reading as much as any other bookstore owner, but that's not going to give me great-grandchildren."

"I've been married for four days," I said.

"And you're *reading*?" She sighed.

I suppressed a groan. "Can you just tell me what your news is?"

She clapped her hands. "Yes. The village hall will reopen in April."

"That's just a little over four months away."

"I know! And it's less than a year from the foundation collapse of the building. Everyone said I couldn't do it, but I proved them wrong again." She pumped her fist in the air.

"That's amazing, Grandma Daisy. But I thought you still had a lot of money to raise before work on the village hall could begin?"

"Oh, I do. I can't be lax on that, but Edmund said we have enough to make the building safe again, and work can begin the Monday after Christmas. I told him, 'Let's do it!'"

I gave her a hug. "I'm proud of you. You've worked so hard."

She glanced at the birch tree. "I have. When you became the Caretaker of this shop, I felt obsolete. I had been the Caretaker

156

for so long that I didn't know what else to do. Like I said, I'm not dead yet, and I need a purpose. It's good to have a project. Everyone needs something to work for. It keeps you young."

"It's certainly kept you young, Grandma."

"What's kept Grandma Daisy young?" Rainwater asked as he came down the spiral stairs that led to our apartment on the second floor.

"There's my handsome grandson," Grandma Daisy crowed. "What's this about Violet staying up all night reading? I'm not sure that's what a new wife is usually doing just days after her wedding."

"What?" Rainwater asked, clearly confused by Grandma Daisy's hints. "Violet is always reading, just like you."

"Ignore her," I told Rainwater. "Grandma Daisy just told me the village hall should reopen in April."

"Not should, Violet. *Will*. It will open in April. Nothing can stop it."

"Well, congratulations, Grandma Daisy," Rainwater said. "If anyone can get that done, it's you. No one in the village should have doubted you could get it done."

"Thank you, grandson. Now talking to you as your mayor, where are you on this awful death of Roma Winterbourne? I need a report." She stood up a little straighter and smoothed her jingle bell-clad scarf over her shoulders.

"It was ruled an accident," Rainwater said.

Grandma Daisy waved her hand dismissively. "I know what the coroner said, but it can't be the end of it. If I had to nominate anyone for most likely to be killed, it would be Roma Winterbourne. My guess is there is foul play afoot."

"Why do you say that?" Rainwater stood a little straighter, now giving Grandma Daisy his full attention.

"Because she was always cheating someone. She cheated on grades all the way through college, and she cheated at work. I made a few calls to old college friends who I thought might know a thing or two about Roma."

"And?" Rainwater asked.

"Well, she's been able to keep herself from being arrested, but just barely every time. She has been involved in several scams in which she fleeced senior citizens." Grandma Daisy smoothed her scarf again. "A friend of mine invested with Roma on some multi-level marketing scheme of hers. The scheme failed, and my friend never saw one red cent. Roma took her money and ran. When my friend called the main number to complain to corporate, they said they'd never heard of Roma Winterbourne and that Roma must have been impersonating one of their sales representatives. Can you even imagine?"

"Why didn't your friend sue?" I asked.

"After she'd handed over the money to Roma, she couldn't afford a lawyer. Also, she couldn't sue the company because Roma had lied, and they weren't involved at all. She had to reverse mortgage her house to live after that."

"Poor woman," I said, but I thought this was a good suspect too. "Where does your friend live? Would she have been in Cascade Springs on Saturday?"

Grandma Daisy perched herself on the stairs around the birch tree. "I know what you're getting at, and my friend would make an excellent suspect to be sure, but she retired to Florida. She hasn't been back to New York State in over twenty years. She left soon after Roma ripped her off. She lives in one of those planned senior communities down there. I wish she had reached out to me for help. I had no idea. She said she was too embarrassed to tell anyone what had happened. I believe the only reason she told me now was because Roma died."

I sighed at the idea of a viable suspect lost.

"Well, that does coincide with what Imogene claimed." I looked at Rainwater. "She said that Roma convinced her she could prove Imogene was the descendent of Thoreau if she lent her the book."

"Which she did," Rainwater said.

"Another scam." Grandma Daisy clicked her tongue. "What I have learned in this life is that once a person is shady, they're always shady. I don't like to be such a naysayer like that, but it's been proven time and again. I like to give people the benefit of the doubt and believe that they can change, but that's just not realistic, especially when it comes to Roma."

"So, like Imogene says," I said. "She gave Roma the book, hoping Roma could prove her lineage. Meanwhile Roma was trying to sell the book to the highest bidder and make a quick seven thousand dollars."

"We don't know if she wanted to sell it to anyone else but you," Rainwater said.

"We will soon. Grandma, can you watch the shop for the morning? David and I are making a stop at Tattered Spine, the rare bookshop in Camden. If she wanted to sell the book around Niagara Falls, that would have been the place to go."

Grandma Daisy fluffed her jingle bell scarf. "Sure thing, but I didn't even know Tattered Spine was still open. If it is, it must be some kind of miracle."

"Why do you say that?" I asked.

"Because Heath has been desperate to get out of the business for years. Before you moved back to the village, he tried to talk me into buying his entire inventory. I declined. First, I could never afford it. Many of his books are very expensive, much more than retail. Second, I had no place to store thousands of rare books, and third, that's not what Charming Books is about."

I wrinkled my brow. This was news to me. The few times I had spoken to Heathcliff Howell, the owner of Tattered Spine, he had said that business couldn't be better. I realized even then that he might have been lying. Working any specialty retail store had its fair share of challenges. By the way that Heath had put it to me, though, it was a breeze.

"I guess we had better ask him about that," Rainwater said.

"We should," I agreed.

Chapter Eighteen

My car was a Mini Cooper that Rainwater could barely fit into, and his car was a department-issued SUV. Neither was a great option to drive to Camden. However, when Grandma Daisy offered her old, two door sedan, we decided to make do with the SUV. I told Rainwater to park it in the community lot two blocks from Tattered Spine. There was no reason to tip Heath off that Rainwater was a cop until we knew what was going on. I'd been of a similar mindset about calling to see if the store was open. It wasn't a far drive, and if Heath was still in business, then David and I would use the element of surprise when we interrogated—er, questioned—him.

Camden was the only town between Cascade Springs and the city of Niagara Falls, making it a short drive. Tattered Spine was in an old, free-standing building that looked out over the town square. There was a full suit of armor standing by the door, holding an axe. Even though the axe was dull, I was certain it could still do some damage.

Rainwater eyed it. "That's... welcoming."

"I think Heath wishes he'd lived in medieval England. Instead, he's in Western New York. It must be a great disappointment to him."

"Anyone who knew what the medieval times were really like would *not* want to live back then," Rainwater said. "It was dirty and smelly, and it's likely you wouldn't have lived passed fifty."

He had a point. I put my hand on the door handle and was surprised when the door opened easily.

The bell over the door rang as we stepped into the shop. It took a moment for my eyes to adjust to the dim light. There were just a few florescent lights hanging from the old beams overhead. If Rainwater reached up, he could have touched the light without fully extending his arm.

When I could see clearly, I sucked in a breath. For a much as I complained about the disorderly state and disorganized book-shelves in Charming Books, the shop was nothing compared to the tightly packed bookcases at Tattered Spine.

"All it would take is one match, and this place would go up like a tinderbox," Rainwater whispered into my ear.

"Shhh," I hushed him because I heard a man clear his throat. I couldn't see anyone though.

"I'll be with you in a moment." There was a pause. "On second thought, I could use some assistance if you would be so kind. Can you come to me?"

"Where are you?" I asked.

"Walk toward the cuckoo clock on the south wall."

Rainwater and I looked around the shop. Sure enough there was a nonworking cuckoo clock high on one wall above one of the overfull bookcases. The cuckoo bird dangled from a stretched-out spring under the clock. It was like everything else in the shop—worn down and broken looking.

We wove our way through a sea of shelves and piles of books to the designated location. We found Heath sitting on the floor surrounded by a five-foot-tall ring of books. There was no telling how long he had been in there.

"If you could just help me to my feet," Heath said. "I have been sitting here cross-legged for so long that my legs have fallen completely asleep. I was just going to wait until the delivery man came so he could help me up."

Rainwater and I moved the books that were stacked all around him. Heath gave Rainwater his hand, and my husband pulled the bookseller to his feet.

Heath dusted off his hands and stumbled a bit. "Oh, thank you. I was doing some inventory of the lower shelves back here and got carried away. It was too late when I realized I had trapped myself. It wouldn't be the first time, and I would have been able to dig my way out eventually. However, it was made far easier with your assistance." He wobbled a little bit. "Oh, I hate that feeling you get when your feet fall asleep. It's all pins and needles." He grabbed onto a bookcase for support.

"Maybe you should sit down," Rainwater said, offering the other man his hand again. "In a chair."

"That's a fine idea. There's a chair behind the cash register."

I stepped back as Rainwater guided Heath to his seat. When he was seated, the bookseller rubbed his calves. "Oh my. That's terrible for my circulation. I just get carried away in the work, you know?"

Heathcliff Howell was a man who lived up to his name. He was refined in a dusty sort of way and a transplant from a bygone era where being a footman was a common job for the working class. Although Heath would not have been a footman. No, he would have been the intellectual lord of a manor, spending his days collecting books and pouring over old manuscripts written in Latin and Greek.

A cat hissed and jumped onto the counter behind me.

"Precious, you need to calm yourself." He shook his head. "She's not much for strangers."

Precious was a grey Persian cat who looked like she enjoyed tormenting the mice she caught before eating them. I say that being a cat person.

"Every bookstore needs a shop cat," Heath said. "I'm just afraid Precious is not a people person. In fact, I can't think of one person that she likes, and that includes me too. She does enjoy ruling over all the nooks and crannies of this shop, so she lets me live. Besides, I need her to protect the books from any mice that might make their way into the shop. They take one look at her and run the other way."

I'd probably run away from Precious if I were a mouse too. Rainwater looked at me with wide eyes as if to ask who this guy was.

"Heath, I don't know if you remember me, but I'm Violet Waverly of Charming Books."

"Oh right. Daisy Waverly's shop. I heard she is the mayor of Cascade Springs now. How is she doing? I was always so fond of Daisy when we met at book association meetings."

"She's fine," I said. "She's very busy being mayor."

"Hmmm, I suppose that means she doesn't have time for coffee with an old friend, then?"

"Probably not," I said.

He looked to Rainwater. "Thank you for your help a moment ago, young man. Who are you?"

"I'm chie—I'm Violet's husband, David."

"Oh, David Waverly then? That seems modern. Now women won't take their husband names and insist they take theirs. The world has turned upside down. That's why I stay out of the fray here with Precious and all my books. Life is so much simpler in the world of fiction."

"David's last name isn't Waverly," I said. "But mine still is. I guess you would call me one of those modern women. You have a lovely shop." I decided it was best to change the subject.

He studied me. "I'm not sure lovely is the word that you really wanted to use. It's too small, and I know it. The thought of moving out of here is just too overwhelming. I have been in this place for forty years. It might look like chaos, but I know where each book is. If you asked me right now, I could pull the book for you in less than five minutes. Go ahead, try me."

"Try you?" My brow went up.

"Yes, tell me a book title and I will pull it." He folded his arms and lifted his chin as if in a challenge.

"I don't know the titles you have."

"You're a bookseller. You know there are certain titles that we all have all the time, and don't cop out and say the Bible."

"Umm, how about *The Old Man and the Sea*?" I said, throwing out the first title that came to mind.

He snapped his fingers and ran into the stacks. Precious whipped her tail back and forth on the counter. She watched Rainwater and me like we were mice she was sizing us up for supper. Even though she was much smaller than me, I guessed she could take me if it came down to it. That cat was a tough cookie. Rainwater must have thought the same because he sidestepped away from the cat and bumped into a shelf.

"I have it!" There was a muffled call from somewhere in the shop.

I looked this way and that, trying to determine which direction he was coming from, but I couldn't see him amid all the shelves and stacks of books.

He reappeared with a bright smile on his face. "Did you time me?"

I winced. I had forgotten to time him since I had been so focused on not being attacked by his lion cat. "Umm, under two minutes."

He grinned from ear-to-ear. "See? I told you I could do it under five minutes." He held a paperback out to me. It was a 1980s edition of *The Old Man and the Sea*.

When I didn't reach for the book, he dropped it on the sales counter, and Precious put a commanding paw on it. I wasn't going to attempt taking anything from the Persian.

That was something I couldn't even do at Charming Books, but in my defense, my bookshop's mystical essence moved the books wherever it saw fit.

"That was impressive," Rainwater said. "But we are here about another book."

"You came to the right place. That's what I'm about—books, books, and more books. If it's an old book, I'm sure I can help you. The new books you will have to go elsewhere." He said this like newer books weren't nearly as desirable to have.

"We are here are for a particular book," I said. "A first edition of *Walden*. Signed."

What little color there was in his pale face drained away.

Rainwater must have noticed it too because he said, "Does that sound familiar to you?"

"It's funny that you mention it because a woman came to my shop not that long ago with such a book. Before that, I had never seen a first edition of *Walden*."

"What was her name?" I asked.

166

He was quiet for a moment as if he was trying to decide if he wanted to answer my question. Finally, he said, "Roma Winterbourne."

Rainwater and I shared a look.

"She said she had a signed first edition of *Walden* and was looking to sell it. I was very much interested. First editions are my passion, and I do most of my business dealing them. However, I am very picky about the condition. She had it with her and allowed me to examine it. It was the real thing, so I told her I would buy it."

"Did you?" I asked excitedly. "Do you have it here in the shop right now?"

He shook his head. "I wish I had. I really do. I made her an offer—and a generous one at that—but she said she had to think about it. She gave me a phone number before she left, but when I called it to up my offer, I found that the number she'd given me was out of service."

"Do you still have that number?" Rainwater asked.

Heath gave him a strange look as if he was beginning to question who Rainwater was.

"I know someone who could look it up and find whose number it was before it went out of service," Rainwater explained. "We are very interested in the book too."

Heath frowned but opened a drawer under the cash register. He removed a small notebook, and flipped through it. Finding the page he was looking for, he grabbed a stub of a pencil, scribbled the phone number on a piece of paper, and handed it to Rainwater.

Rainwater thanked him and tucked it into his coat pocket.

"Did she ever come back?" I asked.

Heath turned to me. He still had the curious look on his face as he studied my husband. "Roma?"

I nodded.

"No, she never came back. I was greatly disappointed. I very much wanted that book. It would have been a great boon for my business. I know at least five collectors I work with who would have wanted to buy it. Those would have all been in private sales. If I could have taken it to auction, I would have had a bidding war on my hands. It really would have been good for my business."

I was about to ask for the names of those private collectors when the door to the shop opened, and a man carrying three cardboard boxes stepped in. "Hey Heath, do you just want these by the door?"

To my surprise, I saw that it was my delivery man, Hank.

"Well, I didn't expect to see you here, Violet," Hank said with a smile.

"Is this bookshop on your route too?" I asked.

"Sure is. I deliver wherever my route takes me. It's usually in Cascade Springs and Camden. Sometimes I venture out. I had a delivery close to the big falls the other day. That was a treat. I couldn't resist getting out and snapping a few pictures. It doesn't matter how many times I see the falls, the majesty of it all gets me every time." He made a muscle move as if to show off his bicep, but his thick winter coat concealed any muscle movement. "Carrying all these books around the area is making me strong. I keep telling me wife that, but as of yet, she's not impressed." He laughed at his own joke. "Hey, Chief Rainwater, are you two out on the town for your honeymoon? I can't say I'm surprised that Violet would want to spend time in another book-shop, and it must be nice for you to have a break from the beat."

"Chief Rainwater?" Heath asked. "The beat? What on earth are you referring to?"

"You didn't know that Violet married the chief of police from Cascade Springs last Saturday?" He pointed at Rainwater. "He's standing right there."

"You're a cop?" Heath asked. "Why didn't you say so when you arrived? You just came in here asking about *Walden*. I thought you were into books."

"I am into books. I love books," Rainwater said.

"Oh, if he was asking about *Walden*, he must be here about the dead lady. Man, that was terrible. It was all anyone wanted to talk about on my route on Monday morning."

"What dead woman?" Heath cried.

Rainwater straightened his shoulders and his amber eyes narrowed just a hair. It was like he was changing from my husband to a cop right before my eyes. "Roma Winterbourne drowned in Niagara River on Saturday night."

Heath slapped a hand over his mouth. "No. That can't be. What happened to *Walden*?"

"We don't know," Rainwater said. "That's why we are asking people who might have been in contact with Roma about the book."

I made a mental note that Heath seemed more upset that something might have happened to the valuable book than the fact that a woman had died. I was also certain that that hadn't been lost on Rainwater.

"Wait, wait, wait," Heath stuttered, standing up. "You're asking me about this because you think *I* have something to do with the woman's death? Is that what you think?" He started to hyperventilate. "I don't know anything about the dead woman. I already told you that I spoke to her once. Once! I don't even have her phone number. She gave me a fake number." He jabbed his forefinger into the cover of his address book.

Precious, who was still on the counter, hissed. She made it clear that she was on her owner's side on this.

Rainwater held up his hands. "Now, Heath, you're getting yourself worked up. I want you to take a deep breath. There you go. In and out. In and out."

"How can I take a deep breath if I'm being accused of murder?" His eyes darted around as if he thought the entire Cascade Springs Police Department was about to burst into the bookshop and arrest him.

"You're not," Rainwater said. "Roma's death was ruled an accident. There is no murder."

All the air left Heath's body in a *whoosh*.

"However," Rainwater added, "we are looking for that copy of *Walden* because the owner of the book reported it missing. She's afraid it might have been stolen."

Beads of sweat gathered on Heath's forehead. "Isn't Roma the owner?"

"No," Rainwater said. "The owner is named Imogene."

I noted that he didn't say Imogene's last name. That had to be intentional.

"Does that name ring a bell for you?" Rainwater relaxed his hands at his sides.

"Imogene, Imogene," Heath muttered to himself. "No, not at all. I would remember if I had met anyone by the name Imogene."

"I have to get to the next stop on my route," Hank said. "I really wish I could stay, but duty calls." He headed for the door.

When he left, I said, "You guys continue with this. I just want to catch up with Hank. I have a question about, umm, a package." I hurried through the maze of bookshelves and out the door.

I emerged from Tattered Spine just as Hank was starting up his delivery truck. I waved.

He lowered his window. "Do you need something, Violet?"

I peered into his van. There were dozens of packages piled up in the front seat and on the floor. It looked to me like Hank still had a lot of stops to make before the end of the day.

"Actually," I said, "I just have a quick question. Do you remember last Wednesday when you came into my shop, and there was a woman there who wasn't happy with me?"

"Oh yeah! She was mad. She almost knocked me over when she left the shop. It's hard to believe a woman that small could be so strong."

I nodded. "Right. That was Roma Winterbourne."

"Oh, the woman who was in your shop that day is the dead lady? I had no idea. Yikes. She was pretty upset with you."

"She was," I agreed.

"I hope the argument that she had with you didn't give her a stroke or something. She was awfully red in the face."

My heart sank. I hoped that that wasn't true either. I wondered why I hadn't thought of that before.

"After she left, I saw that she stopped you on the sidewalk outside of Charming Books. What did you talk about?"

He stared at me, rubbing his chin. "Now that you mention it, I guess that she did. I don't remember exactly. I was probably giving her directions. For whatever reason, people believe that delivery people know where everything on the map is. We don't. We just know our routes and the GPS takes care of the rest."

"Oh," I said dejectedly. "I was just hoping that she had said something that would give us a clue about what she did after she left the shop."

He shrugged. "Sorry. Well, I'd better go if I want to finish my route on time. This close to Christmas, everyone is working doubles."

I nodded and stepped away from his truck.

Chapter Nineteen

The next morning, I was dusting the shelves at Charming Books when my cell phone rang. It was Renee.

"I called in favors to every library I knew that had a connection to Thoreau," she told me. "You owe me big time. All these people want to do is talk about him. I mean on and on and on. They are worse than you. You should have seen the level of rivalry between the libraries about who had what on him. I knew librarians could be competitive with statistics, like who has the best circulation and whatnot, but nothing like this. I thought I was starting a turf war or something."

"I'm surprised you were able to get through this close to Christmas," I said.

"The people I spoke to live and breathe Henry David Thoreau. Christmas is meaningless to them."

"What did you learn?" I put my duster on the shelf and spied Emerson eyeing it from his cat bed by the hearth. I picked it up again. "Had any of them heard of Imogene?"

"Had they ever. They all had a lot to say about her too."

I waited, even though it killed me not to ask more questions. I knew Renee wanted to tell her findings in her own way.

"Apparently, Imogene has been harassing them on and off for years. She would go to the libraries saying she wanted to research Thoreau, and then she would try to talk them into believing her story. I think at first they were curious about her and wanted to know more. That didn't last long."

"They don't believe it?" I asked.

"Not even a little bit. Not a single expert I spoke to believes that Henry David had children out of wedlock. And we know for a fact that he didn't have any kids in wedlock."

"What did they tell Imogene when she shared her story?"

"The same thing you told her, I assume. That it couldn't be true. But she was relentless. One museum banned her from the building completely after she'd chained herself to the archive doors, saying she wouldn't leave until they accepted her story as fact."

"It seems odd to me that I didn't hear about this in an academic bulletin or something like that. I mean, that would be news."

"According to the archivist, they kept it hush-hush by request of the university. You know the administration balks at the possibility of any bad publicity."

I did.

"Imogene signed a letter promising she wouldn't visit the campus again or contact any faculty or staff member. From what the archivist said, she's kept her word so far."

I wrinkled my brow and leaned back on the sales counter. "So she thought she would have better luck here in Cascade Springs. We're hundreds of miles away from Walden Pond."

"I don't know the answer to that one," Renee said. "I'm just reporting back on whether you have a loose cannon on your hands—and you do."

I ended the call with Renee and bit my lower lip. This case was growing stranger by the day and time was running out. I had promised Rainwater I would let the case go by Christmas Eve.

I needed to learn more about Imogene. The easiest way to do that would be to speak to her, but I didn't know where she lived. The one person who would know was her son, and I knew Edmund and Grandma Daisy had a meeting scheduled to walk around the village hall this morning. There was one problem. I didn't have anyone to watch my shop so I could go find them. It would be foolish to close the shop just a few days before Christmas, even for just a few hours. This was the season when Charming Books made almost half of its annual revenue. And I had a wedding to pay off, so that money was valuable. I could only think of one person who could help me out.

A half hour later, Lacey walked through the door. "Oh, it smells like Christmas in here," she said.

I grabbed my coat from the back of the tall stool behind the sales counter. "Lacey, thank you so much for coming on such late notice."

"Are you kidding? This is such a treat. It's not often that I can get away from the café, and this is the perfect time to. We just finished the breakfast rush. Danielle will be able to handle the customers until I get back. I do have to be back for lunch though."

"No problem. I just wanted to run to the village hall and catch up with Grandma Daisy."

"Oh! Daisy popped in the café this morning and told everyone there that the village hall would open in April. She was overjoyed about it."

I wrinkled my nose. I was sure that my grandmother was excited about her new timeline, but I wasn't so sure it was a great idea to tell everyone about it. What if she wasn't able to deliver? It seemed to me that she could be setting herself up to look bad. However, this was one of the many ways that Grandma Daisy and I differed. She liked to make announcements about what was to come. If she didn't reach those goals, she could explain why the changes were better. I, on the other hand, preferred to say nothing and let the work speak for itself when the time came.

"I'm actually hoping I will have a chance to speak to Adrien's cousin too. Did you know he had a cousin so close?"

"I knew that Adrien had family nearby, but not *in* the village," she said. "You can be sure I asked him about it that night. Adrien and I are partners in life and in business. We need to be honest and open with each other. We discussed it, and all is well between us. In marriage, communication is the key."

"Your marriage is what I want our marriage to emulate. In my own family, I haven't seen many successful examples of what real love and partnership should look like, so you are that example for me."

She squeezed my hand. "You don't know how much that means to me, Violet. Growing up, I looked up to you and Colleen so much. You were both so pretty, smart, and popular. I felt like the dowdy friend that two nice girls were letting hang around out of pity."

What she said was like a small stab in my heart. Because there had been times growing up that Colleen, who was like a sister to me until she died much too early, and I hadn't wanted Lacey around. Sometimes we used to feel exactly what Lacey was describing. This also signaled to me that Lacey was a lot more observant than Colleen and I ever gave her credit for.

"I'm sorry if we ever made you feel that way," I said. "I'm sorry for how I treated you at times. I know Colleen would be sorry too."

She smiled. "It was a long time ago, but I do appreciate your apology. Now, please don't talk about it anymore because you will make me cry."

"Okay," I said with a smile of my own.

She cleared her throat. "Before you go, I have one more thing to tell you. You might want to ask Edmund about her cabin in the woods."

I stopped in the doorway and turned back. "What did you say?"

"Imogene lives in a cabin in the woods."

Of course she did. That's exactly where someone with the last name Thoreau would live.

"At least that's what she told Adrien the last time he saw her," Lacey added quickly. "Neither of us knows where the cabin is, and we didn't ask."

Outside of Charming Books, I hurried down the sidewalk in the direction of the village hall. I was eager to talk to Edmund and learn where his mother's cabin was. Could it be in the park behind Charming Books?

I supposed it was possible. There were four little cabins in the park that were rented out in summer, but I had never heard of anyone staying there in winter.

I let out my breath. I felt like I had had a breakthrough in finding the book as one of the clues that the shop's essence had wanted me to pay attention came to mind:

I went to the woods because I wished to live deliberately.

It was an early line in *Walden*. It seemed clear to me now that the shop had wanted me to take that passage quite literally and go into the woods. And not for spring water, but to find Imogene.

However, it would be helpful to be pointed in the right direction by Imogene's son first. I decided to start with a conversation with him.

Even with how preoccupied I was over Roma's death and Imogene's missing book, I still took in the beauty of the village at Christmas. A fresh layer of snow had fallen overnight. In doing so, it covered up the ugly part of winter—the brown tire tracks and piles of gray ice, slush, and snow. Now, the village looked like a painting you could buy in any of its own gift shops or art galleries.

Fresh green garland and white twinkle lights wrapped around every gas lamppost. Each piece of garland was topped with a silver bell. A white carriage pulled by a tall white horse with a red ribbon braided through its mane passed by. The carriage driver was telling the elderly couple in the back of the carriage the history of the village.

"Cascade Springs has always been a special place. It was first settled by Native Americans for the healing powers of the springs. They were followed hundreds of years later by French trappers and then English settlers. Everyone who came here wrote letters home about the waters and spoke of miracles brought on by the water." The driver waved at me as he continued to speak.

The couple appeared to be engrossed in his every word. It was a fantastical story, and I guessed for them that's how it would always remain—just a story. For me, it was real life. The water from the springs did have powers. My family tree and the birch tree inside of Charming Books was all the proof I needed of that.

The oddest aspect of winter in the village was the river. Along the banks, it would freeze solid when the temperatures dropped well below zero at night. But that just made the current in the middle of the river that much more powerful, and the water would splash over the frozen parts beneath it. Some of it would then freeze in place while most of it pushed on toward the falls. It was almost like it was in a hurry to fall over the steep cliff a few miles away.

Grandma Daisy stood on the hall steps in a purple, knee-length winter coat and gray hat with a bright green pom-pom on the top. She gestured wildly as Edmund, in his pea coat and classic leather gloves, made notes on a clipboard. He didn't wear a hat despite the cold bite in the air.

I pulled my own stocking cap farther down over my ears. I hated it when my ears were cold.

"This village hall has to come back better than ever. There is so much history here. We need to honor the people who struggled to make it to this last stop on the Underground Railroad before freedom in Canada," Grandma Daisy said, projecting her voice so loudly, that I wouldn't have been the least bit surprised if Lacey could hear her inside Charming Books. I also wondered if Grandma Daisy was testing out her words for a future speech for when the museum finally opened.

Edmund said something back, but I couldn't make it out.

I wasn't sure this was the best time to speak to them. They both looked very intent on the project at hand, but the clock was ticking and I needed to get back to the bookshop so Lacey could leave and help with the lunch crowd at Le Crepe Jolie. Besides, I knew that my grandmother wouldn't mind if I butted into the conversation. Edmund was another story.

"How's the project coming?" I asked from the foot of the hall steps.

Grandma Daisy and Edmund turned around to face me. Grandma Daisy smiled, but Edmund frowned.

"Violet, my girl, come up here, so we can tell you my vision."

I noted that Grandma Daisy called it her vision, not their vision. I knew the word choice had been intentional. Grandma Daisy was proud of this project, and she was taking ownership of it. She deserved to, really. She had almost single-handedly raised all the money with countless meetings and creative fund-raisers. Like Rainwater had said, no one in the village doubted that Grandma Daisy would get the job done.

I walked up the steps and stood a few feet away from them. "I hope I'm not interrupting your meeting."

"We do have a lot of work to do," Edmund said. "Your grandmother has this project on an ambitious timetable."

"Bah!" Grandma Daisy. "What good does it do to take your time? We will get it done and up to code. Before you know it, the Cascade Springs Underground Railroad Museum and the village hall will number as one of the biggest attractions in the region."

I didn't think it was worth reminding my grandmother that Niagara Falls was only fifteen minutes away. She really did believe the museum would be more popular than one of the natural wonders of the world.

"All we have to do is prop up the building and throw some spackle on the cracks, and it will be as good as new," my grandmother said. "If the hall looks a little rough around the edges, that's all right. She is almost two hundred years old after all."

"She?" Edmund asked. "The hall is female?"

"Of course she is," Grandma Daisy said.

Edmund pressed his lips together as if stopping himself from saying something more about the building's gender. "It is a little more complicated than just propping up the building, but it is doable."

"That's all I need to hear." Grandma Daisy clapped her mittened hands together like it was a done deal. "Did you need something, Violet?"

"Actually, I wanted to talk to Edmund."

His brow rose but he did not speak.

"Have you seen your mother?" I asked him.

"I haven't seen her in a few days." He scowled. "To be honest, I think she's avoiding me. She's got it her head that I'm somehow involved with her book going missing."

"Oh?" Grandma Daisy asked. "Why would she think that?"

"Because I won't buy into her story about Thoreau. She has completely lost her grip on reality now. It's all she talks about. I told her I didn't want to hear it any longer and have not seen her since. She then accused me of telling Roma to steal the book." He closed his eyes for a moment. "As much as I hate that book, I would never do that. It's too valuable."

It was interesting to me that he said he would never tell Roma to steal the book because of its monetary value, not because it would hurt his mother to lose her beloved copy of *Walden*.

"Poor woman," Grandma Daisy said. "It must be so hard to feel like no one believes you."

"No one believes her because her idea is crazy," Edmund said sharply.

Grandma Daisy and I shared a glance.

"Look." Edmund ran his hand through his thick hair. By some miracle, every strand of hair fell right back into place. "I know that I sound awful."

"You don't sound great," Grandma Daisy agreed. "But maybe one small step up from awful."

He sighed. "I know, but if you'd had the same fabrication shoved down your throat your whole life, you might feel the same. In the last few weeks, she has gotten so much worse. She keeps telling me this is something that she must prove in order to legitimize our family before she dies. Like it's her dying wish or something."

"Is she sick?" I asked. "Is she worried about dying?"

"No," he said. "She's fine. She's just being morbid."

"Oh, I can understand that," Grandma Daisy said. "You reach a certain age, and you start to think about your mortality. You can't help it. You want to know what legacy you are leaving behind. She wants this to be her legacy."

I frowned at the thought of my grandmother contemplating her mortality.

"Yes," Edmund said. "I do believe it's something like that."

"Do you know where she is now?" I asked.

"No. She's not at her place. I stopped by on the way here." He rubbed the back of his neck. "She might not want to see me right now, but I'm still her son and have to make sure she's all right. She's my responsibility." He said this as if this was a responsibility he was not thrilled to bear.

Even with my gloves on, my hands were beginning to become painfully cold from standing outside for so long and not moving. I shoved my hands into my pockets. "Lacey Dupont mentioned that she'd said to Adrien, your cousin, that your mom was living in a cabin in the woods."

"Ahh," Grandma Daisy said. "I knew that the parks department had gotten a request for a winter stay in one of the cabins. They'd told me about the request, but I said it was up to them to approve it or not. I have enough on my plate with the village hall to save. Imogene must have been the one who asked and they granted it. However, my understanding was that she wasn't sleeping there because of the cold. I could be wrong."

"Why would they let her do that?" He groaned. "I told her not to go there. The cabin has no insulation. She could freeze to death if she spent the night there. Do you understand what I'm dealing with now? She would rather have a Walden Pond experience, no matter how uncomfortable, than just accept that she's a normal person with no legacy to leave behind. I have my doubts about the story that she is living there. Why would she tell Adrien and not me? She barely knows him."

I shrugged. "Maybe she wanted to tell you but was afraid of your reaction."

"Afraid of my reaction? She *should* be afraid of my reaction. She needs to let this crazy idea of hers go. She has no legacy."

Grandma Daisy shook her head. "Everyone, no matter how humble, has a legacy to leave behind." She glanced at me. "Some are more unique than others. That is all. Besides, how do you know her story isn't true?"

"Because everyone she has ever asked told her it *can't* be true." He sounded like a stubborn child, and I was liking Edmund less and less by the second.

"That doesn't mean anything," my grandmother said. "If I believed every person who told me that something I said or believed wasn't true, I wouldn't say or believe anything. Just think of how many contractors told me this building should be demolished because it could never be saved. I didn't believe them. I kept trying to find someone who would listen to me, and I found you. Now, the building will be saved. Your mother is just looking for that one person to believe her. That's all she needs."

My grandmother made a good point.

Chapter Twenty

I left Edmund and my grandmother on the steps to the village hall. Grandma Daisy spoke about flooring tile and paint colors for the exhibits in her museum. Edmund cautioned that she was getting ahead of herself. I could have warned him that Grandma Daisy always got ahead of herself, but I thought that was something he could figure out on his own. Perhaps I was still a little miffed by how he'd talked about his mother too, so I would let him fend for himself when it came to dealing with my grandmother and her big plans.

I had roughly forty minutes before I had to be back at the bookshop to relieve Lacey. It wasn't a lot of time, but I knew I had to visit the cabin in the woods. If I didn't go now, it would drive me crazy for the rest of the day.

I crossed the street to the side of River Road that ran along the Niagara River, just a few feet away from where Roma's body had been.

Did I really believe that Roma's death had been an accident? I knew the evidence pointed in that direction and that Rainwater believed it, but I couldn't forget the remnants of a cloth book cover discovered under her fingernails.

Then, there was the shop's essence. The shop had never led me astray before. If it wanted me to look into something, it had always been before a crime was committed or because something was very wrong and needed to be corrected. I didn't believe that this time was any different.

A path ran along the river that led to Cascade Springs Park. The river turned away from the park at that point and the area around me grew more wooded and quieter. I could no longer hear the rushing water to my right.

When I used to get the spring water for the tree at night in winter, the woods felt close and foreboding. The branches looked like reaching arms and crooked hands, and the sounds were amplified by my thundering pulse.

But in the late morning light, the woods now welcomed me. Squirrels jumped from tree to tree. Birds twittered in the high branches, and fresh snow glistened on every surface.

It was like walking into Narnia. It felt magical. If I didn't believe in the power of the springs before, I would believe it now. I also would not be surprised if Mr. Tumnus, the faun, hopped out from behind the birch trees and offered to play his flute for me.

The cabins were a short walk from the entrance of the park. Charming Books was on the west side of the park, and I was coming into the park from the south. The cabins were in the southeast corner.

During the summers, this part of the park was constantly busy, especially this last summer. Grandma Daisy had advocated renting campsites out to visitors, and to begin renting the four cabins out there for week-long and weekend rentals.

At first the village council had been against the idea. They'd liked the fact that many people couldn't stay in Cascade Springs because vacation housing was limited to high-priced bed and breakfasts that dotted the village. They said they wanted to keep it that way to keep trouble out, to make sure there wouldn't be a drinking problem caused by tourists, and to keep the woods and springs pristine.

Grandma Daisy said in no uncertain terms that they were being elitist and that she wasn't going to stand for it. It was a tense few weeks, but in the end, Grandma Daisy prevailed. The camping licenses and the cabin rentals became a major fundraiser for the village hall project.

As I grew closer to the campground, the snow-covered dirt path changed to a snow-covered gravel path. I couldn't see the division between dirt and gravel because of the snow, but I felt it under the soles of my boots.

I could see all four cabins from where I stood. During the summer, because of leaf cover and vegetation, I wouldn't have been able to see the cabins nestled in the trees so easily.

Now, the question was about which cabin Imogene was using. They were all one-room log cabins and looked like they could have been made by Thoreau himself.

"Are you here looking for me?"

I spun around. "Fenimore! What are you doing here?"

My father stood in the snowy parking lot with his guitar gig bag slung over his arm. His beard was grayer than it was when I'd seen him last summer, and he wore an oversized stocking cap that covered most of his thin ponytail. He wore a flannel-lined denim coat over his usual patchwork jeans. For the last couple of years since he'd revealed to me that he was my father, he spent summer in the Niagara region—mostly in Cascade Springs because it was a popular tourist trap and the tips were good from people touring the wineries.

"I thought that you didn't want to talk to me after you saw me at the wedding," he said. "You looked so upset."

I had been startled at the beginning of the ceremony because I'd spotted Roma, but he was right, I had been taken aback when I saw him there as well. The truth was, I had never expected him to come.

He lowered his eyes. "After I saw your reaction, I didn't bother to go to the reception."

My heart ached that he had felt like he was unwanted. Now that he mentioned it, I hadn't seen him at the reception. I had been so preoccupied with Roma's death that I hadn't realized it at the time. It was more proof of how distant I was from my own father that I didn't even notice his absence at my own wedding reception.

"Are you here looking for me?" he asked again.

"I…" I trailed off.

"Because that does my heart good to think that you were. I was afraid that, after how you reacted at the wedding, you never wanted to see me again. I know I haven't been a great father to you." He shook his head. "That's wrong. What I really mean to say is I know that I haven't been a father to you at all."

I didn't correct him because what he said was true.

"But I want to make a more of an effort. You being here encourages me to think that you want to make an effort too."

Again, I didn't correct him or tell him that I had come to the cabins to look for Imogene. He seemed so happy about it that it seemed cruel to tell him the truth. To be honest, if I had known that I would find him there, I would have come looking for him, if for no other reason than sheer curiosity to find out what he was doing in my village in the middle of winter.

A thought struck me. "Fenimore, are you living in one of these cabins right now?"

His face turned bright red. "Just through the end of the year, and then I will be on my way south. I have to work some odd jobs and save up some cash to make bus fare. There's not much need for a troubadour in the middle of winter like this. I've been going to Niagara Falls when I can to play around there where the tips are better."

"You came back for my wedding," I said softly.

His face flushed red. "I got one of the messages that Daisy had left about the wedding for me three days ago. I was in Texas, close to El Paso actually. It was a long journey, and I spent every cent that I had to make it up here in time. I—I wanted to see my only child on her wedding day. I didn't think about it. I just came." He swallowed hard as if he were choking up.

I searched his face. Was he going to cry? I had never seen him cry before, not even when he spoke of my mother, whom he still claimed he loved.

I didn't know what to say. I hadn't even known that he ever thought of me when he wasn't in Cascade Springs for the summer tourist season.

"I'm sorry if my reaction scared you away. It wasn't my intention. I was just so surprised. A large part of me thought that you wouldn't come. I asked Grandma Daisy several times if you'd planned to be there. Every time she said that she hadn't heard from you."

"You wanted me there?"

"I think every child wants their parents at their wedding. You're the only parent I have left." I looked into his dark eyes. "Yes, I wanted you there. Mom couldn't be there." I closed my eyes for a moment. I had been so caught up in Roma's death and the missing book that I hadn't allowed myself to grieve the fact that my mother hadn't been at my wedding. It suddenly washed over me as an acute and piercing pain.

When I was in college and graduate school, and friends and classmates were planning their weddings, I remembered so many of them complaining about their mothers vetoing decisions and generally trying to micromanage their ceremonies and receptions. I could understand how that would be frustrating. At the same time, I used to want to tell them that they didn't know how lucky they were to have their mothers there. But I never did. It was not their fault that their mothers were alive and mine was dead.

I licked my cold dry lips. "I'm glad that you came. I'm sorry there wasn't time to speak before the wedding. I think if I had been a bit more prepared for you being there, I wouldn't have reacted in that way. I am sorry if it upset you. I just was so surprised."

His shifted the strap of his gig bag on his arm. "I should have expected you to be surprised. That was my mistake. I just wanted to get here in time for the wedding I didn't think of anything else." He paused. "And I did try to talk to you before the wedding."

I stared at him. "When?"

His face flushed bright red. "Ummm…"

My mouth fell open. "You were the one in the woods banging on the trees early in the morning."

His Adam's apple bounced up and down.

"What were you doing there? Looking for me?" I squeaked.

"No, no, I wasn't. I didn't know you were there until I saw you."

I took a step back from him. "Then what were you doing there, and why were you hitting the tree?"

He tugged on the side of his stocking cap until it covered one of his eyes, making him look like a hippie pirate. He pushed the hat back above his hairline. "I was spooked. I thought I had seen a bear in the woods, and I was trying to scare it off. It wasn't until after I had made all that noise that I saw it was just a buck. However, I was glad to scare that away too. Deer can be dangerous."

His story was plausible, but I wasn't sure that I completely believed him. Fenimore had a history of stretching the truth when it worked in his favor. It had taught me to be leery of his stories.

"Okay," I said. "But why were you there that morning?"

"I couldn't sleep. I was nervous about the wedding, about seeing you." He swallowed. "And about how you would react. I thought a walk in the woods would be the best remedy for all of that. Imagine my shock when I saw you on the path. It almost frightened me more than thinking there was a bear there in the woods." He cocked his head. "I saw you and just thought it was so odd that you would be walking in the woods that early on your wedding day. What were you doing out there?"

"When did you see me?" I rocked forward onto the balls of my feet as if I was getting ready to run away from this conversation. It was tempting to flee. That had been my modus operandi when dealing with Fenimore in the past.

"When you were walking back down the path on the way to Charming Books," he said.

That meant he hadn't seen me collect water from the springs.

I certainly wasn't going tell him I was getting mystical spring water for my magical birch tree so I could receive literary clues from the shop's essence. I let out a small sigh of relief.

"Why did you chase me?" I asked.

"I wanted to talk to you, but you ran away so fast," he said. "So I just followed you."

"You could have called my name out," I said. "You could have told me who you were. You scared me to death."

"I—I guess I was afraid. When I saw you run, I thought that you knew it was me and you were running away from me because you didn't want to see me. Then when I saw you at the wedding and you had that scared and shocked look on your face, I thought I was right. I thought I made a mistake coming here for your wedding after all."

"How would I have known that it was you? You were so bundled up that I couldn't possibly see your face. And it was dark. "

"I guess I wasn't thinking straight."

I made no comment on that statement. "Honestly, I'm still not happy that you chased me out of the woods like that, but I'm relieved to learned it was you and not..."

"And not what?" he asked.

"And not a murderer," I said.

"Is that a reference to the woman who was killed back by the river?"

"Her death was ruled an accident." I studied my father's face. "Do you question that? Is there something you know that you're not saying? Because if there is, you need to tell my husband."

Fenimore frowned. I knew that he didn't have a liking for the police. He had spent too much of his life living on the fringes of society to completely trust law enforcement.

"If you won't tell the police, you need to tell me."

He glanced at the cabins. "I'll just say I'm not the only one living in these cabins."

"You mean Imogene. I know that she's living in one of these cabins too."

"Well, that woman who died had been here. She and Imogene were friends, or so I thought."

"She was living here?"

He shook his head. "No. But she was here. That's all that I will say about it." He took a breath. "When I raise my bus fare, I will be out of your hair. Come summer though, I do want to try again. I want to try to mend things between us, if not as father and daughter, then as friends."

"I'd like to try that too," I said quietly.

I watched as he shuffled away. His gig bag tapped a gentle rhythm on his back as he walked. I wished things could be different between Fenimore and me, and maybe they could, someday. At the moment, we were both too hurt by the past. But my heart lightened a little to know that he had come back to Cascade Springs to see me get married. I think that was truly the first ray of hope that I had ever had that someday we'd have a real father-daughter relationship. And maybe someday I would even have the nerve to call him "Dad."

Time was running out. I had spent too long talking to Fenimore and I needed to get back to the shop, which meant I needed to make up my mind as to which cabin to start with. I was just about to head to the one closest to me when I heard a "Meow!"

I spun around and saw Emerson sitting as sweet as can be on one of the footpaths leading to the cabin to my far right.

He meowed again and then began licking his paw.

"Emerson, what are you doing out here? It's the middle of winter. You're supposed to be napping at the shop. That's what a normal cat would do when there is snow on the ground."

Emerson paused his grooming and looked at the paw he held up as if he was seriously considering what I had said. Then, he turned and began walking toward the far cabin.

When I didn't follow him, he peered over his shoulder and meowed a third time.

I looked heavenward to gather myself, and then I followed the cat.

Emerson sat in front of the cabin door and batted it with his paw.

"Okay, okay," I muttered. "I get your point. She's staying in this one, Great All-Knowing Cat."

Emerson rubbed my legs and began to purr. Clearly, he approved of this new title.

Each cabin in the wood had a hand-carved sign on the door with its name inscribed. This one read "Holly." It was hard for me to believe the Imogene had picked it because of its Christmasy name. Perhaps it was just the most comfortable cabin of the lot.

I knocked on the door, but there was no answer. I knocked a second time, a bit harder. Still nothing.

I looked down to consult Emerson on this matter, but he was gone.

"This disappearing cat game is super old," I grumbled.

There was a muffled meow in response. Where on earth had he gone in such a short period of time?

A *tap, tap, tap* rapped on the window to the left.

I jumped and then looked through the window. My cat was on the windowsill on the inside. Of course he was.

I shook my finger at him. "You're in so much trouble. Someday I'm going to figure out how you do that all the time, and it won't be as fun for you anymore."

He yawned, showing all his little pointy teeth. Clearly, I was boring him. Maybe that was why he was always running off and getting into trouble because he found Charming Books too boring. If he didn't like being the shop cat of a magical bookshop, he would have hated being a regular housecat.

I went back to the door and tried the doorknob, which opened easily. Oh, I should have tried that first.

There was a single light bulb hanging overhead, and I pulled the chain. I gawked at what I found. It was like a serial killer's layout to take out Henry David Thoreau. However, instead of plans to kill the already dead author, it was plans to prove Imogene's relationship to him.

An elaborate family tree was thumbtacked to the cabin wall. On the kitchen table were dozens of photocopies of what looked like letters written by and to Thoreau. A magnifying glass lay on the table next to an empty white teacup.

There was evidence that the tea was recent. An electric tea-pot on the counter was unplugged from the wall but still warm. Imogene had been here not too long ago.

Henry David Thoreau would not have had electricity in his cabin in the woods, so I was a bit surprised to see that Imogene was using this modern convenience when it wasn't exactly his-torically accurate. However, I reminded myself she was trying to prove that she was related to Henry David, not be him.

Emerson walked around my feet.

"We shouldn't be here. This is an intrusion."

He meowed at me. I didn't know if his response was in pro-test or agreement. I knew I had to leave. I didn't want Imogene to catch me here. It was too private. That being said, I wasn't above slipping out my cell phone from my pocket and taking photographs of the family tree on the wall and the letters on the table.

Before I left the cabin, I squinted at the family tree one more time. It began with Thoreau's grandparents, then moved to his parents, and then down to Thoreau and his three siblings—one brother and two sisters. Next to Henry David, there was a line that indicated a relationship. The line led to a woman's name: "Elsey Hampshire."

There was a small note written in tight print next to the woman's name. "Local farmer's daughter near Walden Pond." I rocked back on my heels. So this was her theory. She believed that Thoreau had had an affair at Walden Pond. It would have been a scandal—one that would have ruined Elsey for certain. However, it might have ruined Henry David too. For all of his talk about doing good and upholding virtues, an affair would not have reflected well on him.

Then, another line went from Elsey to a man named Devon Crumpet. This was the man that Elsey had married. They'd had a son, Maxwell Crumpet. There was another note next to Maxwell's name. "H.D.'s son. Passed off as Devon's son."

"What are you doing?" a scratchy voice asked.

I spun around to see a red-faced Imogene Thoreau standing in the cabin doorway.

Chapter Twenty-One

I mogene looked so small in her knee-length winter coat, large stocking cap, and thick mittens. The lower half of her face was swallowed up by her wide scarf. However, her dark eyes were full of anger. "I asked you a question."

"I—I'm so sorry. I live on the other side of the woods and was out for a walk. I didn't know anyone was staying in this cabin during the winter." That was sort of true.

"You were not just out for a walk. You came here to spy on me." She shook a mitten-covered had at me. The mittens were bright purple and looked like they had once belonged to Barney the dinosaur. It was a bit hard to take her pointing seriously.

I tried to ignore the mitten. "Spy seems like such a strong word."

"But it is the right word." She removed her mittens and hat and dropped them on the table, covering the letters. "For someone who doesn't believe me, you are quite interested in the life I lead."

"I think I shut you down too fast when you told me your story earlier. I'm here to hear you out."

She gave me a dubious look and sat in the kitchen chair. She didn't remove her winter coat. It was cold in the cabin—only a few degrees warmer than the outdoors. The wood stove was not on. Did Imogene use the stove at night? If she didn't, how did she stay warm?

"So you weren't just out for a walk after all."

She caught me.

"May I sit?" I asked, pointing at the chair across from her.

After a moment of hesitation, she nodded.

I slipped into the chair. I was trying to decide how to ask her to tell her story again when she began to speak.

"My grandmother was the one who told me the truth about our family. She heard it from her grandmother, the woman who'd had Henry David's baby. My great-great-great-great-grandmother Elsey was only eighteen when she fell in love with Thoreau. She was a simple farm girl, but loved to read. She'd walk several miles every few weeks to get books from the library. When Thoreau came to Walden Pond, she was excited that such a learned man would be humble enough to live a simple life like her own. Her father sold food to Thoreau and offered to help him with his kitchen garden. Elsey went with her father as often as she could to escape chores at home.

"My grandmother said that Henry David loved Elsey too, but they could never be together. They were from different positions in life. Henry David, for his part, told Elsey that he was dedicating himself to a simple life of study and had no plans to marry. Elsey left him and married another man, a local farmer by the name of Devon Crumpet." Imogene stood up and walked over to the family tree tacked to the wall. "Devon was the man my grandmother knew as her grandfather. She said he was a kind and simple man. A good farmer who worked hard for his family. He loved Elsey dearly." She played with the ID bracelet on her wrist. It had something engraved on it, but I couldn't read what it said. "When her husband died, Elsey told my grandmother the truth. Devon never knew Maxwell, my grandmother's father, was not his son. Maxwell never knew either. Elsey told my grandmother not to tell another soul, and she didn't until she told me on her deathbed. At the same time, she gave me the book as proof." She shook as she spoke.

I sat back in my seat. "Thoreau never knew he had a child."

She nodded. "Elsey kept it a complete secret from him. She would have been ruined if the truth had come out. Her husband, even though he was a good man, might have turned her out of the home. What choice did she have but to keep the secret? They were happy enough. I think the only reason Elsey told my grandmother was because she wanted to make peace with her past before the end.

I shivered because Elsey's story was so much like my mother's. She had a relationship with my father when he was passing through the village as a traveling musician. She got pregnant, but she never told him. Instead, she had me alone and raised me with Grandma Daisy's help. It wasn't until she was dying that she reached out to my father and told him the truth. She died when I was thirteen, but my father didn't come looking for me until many years later when I was adult. I did not welcome him into my life at first.

"I kept my promise to my grandmother and didn't tell anyone until after she died. However, when she passed, I told my mother, and I told my husband at the time. I was planning to tell the world. They discouraged me. They said it would only embarrass the family. They were wrong, though. It will lift the family up."

"My mother refused to speak to me about it, and my husband left me over it. He claimed I had become obsessed with a lie. It wasn't a lie. It was the truth." She pounded her fist onto the table.

"Do you have any other evidence?" I asked quietly.

Her dark eyes snapped in my direction. "What do you mean?"

"Do you have any proof that Elsey's story was true?" I asked quietly. Surely, she had to have something more than a story if she wanted to prove this was conclusively true.

"I have—had—the book! That should be the only proof that is needed."

"But that's not true," I said as gently as I could. "You need more proof. The book is not enough."

"It's signed."

"But it is only signed with *his* name. It's not even made out to Elsey. You have to see why people would have doubts. Thoreau was bound to have signed copies of the first printing of his book. There are copies out there in libraries, archives, and even private collections."

"He wouldn't have put her name in the book if he didn't want anyone to find out about the affair. They had to be careful!"

"I'm sure that's true, but it doesn't help your case as it stands today."

Tears gathered in Imogene's eyes. "You don't know how much I have lost because of this. In the end, my mother would not speak to me. My marriage was ruined. My son barely tolerates me and only continues to check in with me out of a sense of obligation and duty. He does not love me as a son should love his mother. I have lost so much." She clasped her hands together on the table and gripped them so tightly that her knuckles turned stark white.

I leaned across the table. "What do you gain by proving it?" I asked.

She looked at me. "Validation." Her breath caught. "Because sometimes—just sometimes—I think my son and the others are right. That I am losing my mind. I need to prove this story is true to prove that I am not."

Her last comment was the first grasp on reality that I had seen from Imogene. In essence, she was far too invested into her tale about Henry David Thoreau to turn back now. If she took it all back now, she would have destroyed all those relationships in her life for no reason. She would rather hold onto a lie—if it was a lie, I didn't know anymore—with all her might than know it was all for nothing.

"There is a way to settle this once and for all, true or false."

She looked up at me with hope in her eyes.

"I don't know if you can do it, but if you had a piece of Henry David's DNA, you could test it and yours and see if you are related. I don't know how you would get that DNA, and the test would be expensive, but at least you would know."

"You are not the first person to tell me that," she said, sounding disappointed that I hadn't come to her with a brand-new idea.

"Who else suggested it?" I asked.

"It does not matter because it can't be done. It just can't," she said.

"How did you meet Roma, Imogene?" I asked.

She scowled at me as if this was abrupt change of subject. Maybe it was, but I was grateful when she answered the question.

"I met her at a conference on Thoreau." Imogene smoothed one of the photocopied letters with her hand. "I went in hopes that someone there would listen to me."

"Roma was one of the scholars?" I asked.

She shook her head. "No, she worked in a booth, selling trinkets and souvenirs to the attendees."

I must have made a face because she went on to say, "That didn't mean she didn't know a lot about literature. She explained to me that she had a degree in American literature but never went to graduate school because academics weren't open to new interpretations."

In some cases that was true, I mentally admitted. "But Roma was?"

"Yes." Imogene's eyes sparkled. "She listened to me. She believed me."

I bit my tongue to stop myself from asking if that was really true, or if Roma had lied to her to get her hands on the book. "How was Roma going to help you prove your grandmother's story?"

"She said she needed the book to do it. She said if she could authenticate the book as signed by Thoreau, it would prove my story."

I wanted to tell her that authenticating Thoreau's signature would prove nothing about her ancestry. It would only prove that Thoreau had signed the copy of *Walden* that she owned.

"You gave her the book then and there?" I asked.

She shook her head. "No, no. We met over two years ago. I said that I wanted to try myself. I thought I could get someone in a position of authority to take my story as the truth. They should. It *is* the truth!" She lifted the photocopied letters from the table and ran her finger absentmindedly along the edge. "I stayed in contact with her over time. She changed jobs. She was no longer selling souvenirs. She told me that she worked for an archive and had the connections to people there who could prove my story."

"Did you go to that archive?" I asked.

"N—no, Roma said that she could handle it all on her own. I believed her. Nearly a month ago, she came and collected the book. It was hard to let it go, but I trusted her. She was my friend, and I knew she'd do right by me."

Imogene must have been so desperate and naïve to give her book, her most precious belonging, to Roma. Perhaps she was at her wit's end, not being able to prove what was true. Her son Edmund did say that she'd been thinking about her own mortality a lot as of late.

To be honest, it was hard for me to believe that so many scholars and libraries had turned her away so cruelly. Libraries and archives exist for education and discovery. Even if someone were to come in with a wild idea, they had an obligation to help the person. Typically, the only reason a person would be turned away or asked to leave is because they'd caused a disruption of some sort. It made me wonder how Imogene had approached these institutions for help.

"How did you learn that Roma was trying to sell the book?" I asked.

"I didn't know about it until the day she died. I spoke to a book dealer, and he said it was strange because there had been a woman in his shop trying to sell him a book that sounded almost identical to mine. When I asked him to describe her, I knew it had been Roma. I had never felt so betrayed in life. I felt worse than when my husband left me."

"I'm so sorry," I said.

She looked at me. "You are the first person to say they feel sorry for me about what Roma did. Everyone else thinks I'm overreacting."

"Who's everyone else?"

"My son, of course."

"And anyone else?"

She didn't answer my question. Imogene murmured, "I went to the woods because I wished to live deliberately, to front only the essential facts of life, and to see if I could not learn what it had to teach, and not, when I came to die, discover that I had not lived." She looked at me. "That's why I am here in this cabin in the cold and snow."

"How long have you been here?" I asked.

"Two months. I am not here without permission. I know that's what you think. I paid the rent on it with every last penny I had."

I frowned. If Imogene had been here for so many weeks, she was likely here the morning of my wedding. "Have you heard any strange noises in the woods?"

"What do you mean? It's a forest. There are many noises here at night."

"Like someone hitting the trees."

She paled. "I don't know what you're talking about," she said sharply.

I interpreted that to mean that she knew exactly what I was talking about. I wasn't going to be dissuaded so easily. "Very early Saturday morning, I was in the park."

She narrowed her eyes at me. "Why were you in the park so early?"

205

I internally grimaced. "I was getting married later that day. I came into the woods to clear my head. You and Thoreau aren't the only ones who go into the woods to find solace."

She frowned like she didn't believe that was the whole truth. I didn't tell her that she was right. "When I was in the park, I heard someone banging on a tree with a large stick or log. I left, and the person followed me out. Did you hear anything?"

She wouldn't look at me. "No. It must have been too far away."

But it hadn't been too far away, and we both knew it.

Instead, she placed a hand to her forehead. "I should lie down. I feel a headache coming on."

I stood up. That was the least subtle hint to signal the end of the conversation that I had ever received.

She looked up at me. "Are you looking for my book?"

I didn't see any reason to lie to her. "I am."

Tears welled up in her eyes. "If you find it, will you give it back to me? It's all I have."

"I will," I promised, hoping it was a promise I could keep. Even though I knew she was lying to me about not hearing anything on Saturday morning, I felt compassion for her. If *Walden* was a shovel, she'd dug a hole so deep for herself that she may never get out.

I looked around the cabin but didn't see Emerson. I consoled myself that the cat had gotten into the cabin. He'd probably already got himself out of it.

Imogene didn't get up when I'd stood, so I let myself out. As soon as I stepped outside, I spotted Emerson on the gravel, cleaning his paws. "You're quite pleased with yourself, aren't you?"

He purred.

"Come on. Let's go home."

He trotted in front of me, leading the way. Even though we were in another part of the park, the little tuxedo cat seemed to know exactly where he was going. I followed him along the path to the springs.

In the winter daylight, the springs sparkled as more light reached the water's surface through the bare trees. I knew I had to get back to the shop to relieve Lacey, but I took a moment to gaze at the shimmering water as it trickled down the side of the rock and up from the ground below. The only word to describe how it looked was magical.

At my feet, Emerson arched his back and hissed at something behind me.

I spun around just in time to see a dark shadow disappear behind a tree. I let out a breath. "Emerson, it was just a deer looking for food."

He hissed again.

"It was a deer." This time I said it with less confidence.

Chapter
Twenty-Two

"Oh, Violet, you're back. I wish I could stay and chat some more, but I have hurry back to the café." Lacey grabbed her coat from the coat tree. "I'm sure the rush is already starting."

I shook snow off of my winter coat into the dirt around the birch tree. I knew it would have no effect on the shop's essence, but in the dry winter, a little extra water wouldn't hurt.

"I'm so sorry for holding you up," I said.

"Don't be silly, I had a great time." She held up a tote bag. "I have four books in here right now I'm dying to read. I left you a list on the counter. I'll come back later with my credit card to pay for them."

"Don't be ridiculous. You and Adrien give Grandma Daisy and me free food all the time, and you took time out of your day to help me this morning. You're not paying for those books."

"Are you sure?" She bit her lip.

"Yes," I said leaving no room for argument.

"Oh, thank you. I'm excited to read them. The odd thing about Charming Books is that, every time I come in here, even when I don't know what I'm looking for, I find exactly what I want to read. It seems I find a book I didn't know I wanted at every turn."

"Charming Books is the store where the perfect book picks you. A little bookshop magic, I guess," I said with a shrug and then looked at the tree out of the corner of my eye.

"Must be. All right. I'm off. Stop by the café later to get a bite to eat. Adrien is in a quiche mood today. He's made dozens. You'll want to stop by and grab one. Oh, there are a few people browsing, and I made four sales!" she said and went out the door.

"Thank you," I called after her, and then I looked down at Emerson. "Maybe we should hire Lacey. She's good for business."

The rest of the day was busy. It was the day before Christmas Eve and it seemed everyone needed a last-minute gift or two. I was happy to help them, and the shop's essence worked overtime to put the right book in front of each customer. I planned to keep the shop open an extra hour that night to catch any shoppers on the way home from work. When I had a short break, I glanced out the window and saw Midcentury Vintage, Sadie's shop, had a healthy amount of business too.

Sadie had done so much for me leading up to the wedding, and I hadn't had time to thank her properly. Hurriedly, while Charming Books was quiet, I ran over to her shop with her maid of honor gift, which I had forgotten to give her when I saw her at the Red Inkers meetings. It was a cappuccino maker that Sadie had been talking about for weeks. I think she'd secretly been hoping her boyfriend would get it for her for Christmas, but I told him my plan. He would just have to get her something else.

I stepped into Midcentury Vintage and smiled. Sadie was in her element as she held up different party dresses in front of her teenaged customer. The girl standing in front of her was very thin and there were bags under her eyes. I set Sadie's gift on her sales counter. She could open it when she had the time. It was clear her shop was busy. There were several customers milling about, looking at all the beautiful vintage clothes that were so well displayed against the simple white and chrome walls and furnishings.

"Violet! You're just in time to see Abby pick her Christmas dress," Sadie said.

The teenager blushed.

A middle-aged woman looked on. "I like the blue one."

"Me too," Sadie said. "It matches your eyes, Abby."

The girl smiled shyly. "I'll go try it on." She stepped behind the curtain into the changing area.

"Marie, this is Violet from Charming Books. She knows Hank too," Sadie said. "Vi, this is Hank's wife."

"It's nice to meet you," I said.

"It's so nice to meet you. Thank you for all the books that you've given Abby. If we had more time, we'd stop over and take a look." Worry creased her forehead. "But I think that Abby will be too tired for that."

"I completely understand," I said. "Another time."

Marie nodded.

Abby stepped out from behind the curtain. Now that she was in the dress, her whole demeanor had changed. She stood up straighter and smiled wider. Her skin even looked brighter and rosier.

"Gorgeous," Sadie exclaimed.

Abby beamed. "I think it's this one."

"It was made for you," Sadie said with a sigh.

I smiled and backed away quietly, letting Abby relish the moment.

When I returned to my shop, I picked up a copy of *Walden* and perched on the warm hearth next to Emerson's cat bed. The little tuxedo cat snuggled down into the bed as if he intended to take a nice long nap. I couldn't blame him. I wanted to curl up and fall asleep in front of the fire too.

I lay the book on my lap and waited, but nothing happened. I waited a little longer. Still nothing. I looked up at the birch tree. Its waxy leaves glistened into the sunlight pouring in through the skylight above.

"Oh, come on!" I complained to the tree, to the shop's essence, to anyone who could hear me. "If you want me to find *Walden*, you have to give me something. Some sort of clue."

Faulkner cawed in the tree. My shout had woken him up from his afternoon nap, and he wasn't too happy about it.

Just when I was about to give up and go back to work. The book in my lap fell open. I looked down at the page:

The mass of men lead lives of quiet desperation. What is called resignation is confirmed desperation. From the desperate city you go into the desperate country, and have to console yourself with the bravery of minks and muskrats. A stereotyped but unconscious despair is concealed even under what are called the games and amusements of mankind. There is no play in them, for this comes after work. But it is a characteristic of wisdom not to do desperate things.

"Do you have a minute?" a timid voice asked.

I looked up from the book to find Richard Bunting standing in front of me. If there was ever a man living in quiet desperation, it was him. I closed the book and tucked it behind Emerson's cat bed before Richard could see the title.

After last night, I hadn't expected to see him before the next Red Inkers meeting. In fact, I'd had my doubts that he even planned to come to that meeting after he'd fled Charming Books the second the meeting had ended the night before.

Richard held out an eleven by seventeen piece of paper. "Would you mind hanging this in your shop?" He swallowed. "With Renee leaving the group, the rest of us have been saying that we need another member. In fact, we are looking to add three new people. I think we are all looking for new opinions and critiques of our work to make us stronger writers."

It was a flyer asking for applicants to join the critique group. I took the paper from his hand. "Sure, I'll stick it in the window. We get a lot of writers, both published and unpublished, who come into the shop. I hope some good candidates will want to apply."

He nodded. "Thank you. Sadie is putting it online too, but I thought we'd get some better applicants if they were local and already knew Charming Books."

"I'll hang it up right now." I stepped around the sales counter, grabbed a small roll of tape, and walked over to the front window to hang the poster.

Faulkner cawed.

I glanced over my shoulder. "Don't worry, Faulkner. I'm not going to block the view from your perch."

He flapped his wings as if to say he wasn't sure that he could trust me on that.

"There, see? It's not blocking your view at all."

Faulkner snuggled down into his feathers as if he was about to take a nap. I knew he was just stewing over what else he could be irritated by.

Another customer approached me and said he was ready to check out. As I rang up the customer, I expected Richard to leave, but he stayed in the shop. He shuffled from bookshelf to bookshelf, yet he didn't appear to be looking at anything in particular.

After the customer left, I walked up to him. "Is there something that I can help you find, Richard?"

He jumped as if he hadn't known that I was there. He cleared his throat. "I just want to apologize for not telling you about Imogene talking to me about the book. You should have been involved with the research. You would have added value to what I'm working on. I know you wouldn't have tried to steal the byline from me." He shook his head. "Or, I should have known that. It's hard to explain why I did it."

"You wanted to write papers on it," I said.

He wrinkled his brow. "It sounds terrible when you put it like that, but yes, that's why I didn't tell you. Her story is extraordinary. Even if it's not the truth, she believes it. I'm writing an article about her claim and another about obsessions that some people have with long-dead literary characters. She's not the only one. There are people who are in love with the greats, from Shakespeare to Hemingway, to such an unhealthy extent that it impacts their lives here and now."

"I suppose it's possible to become obsessed with just about anything if you let the desire for that thing to take over your mind," I murmured.

"Exactly. That's what Imogene has done. However, her story is just the very tip of my research in that area. I've interviewed seven other people with the same feelings but for other authors. Some are like Imogene and unequivocally believe they descended from these authors without any real proof. Others

213

are in love with them—and when I say this, I mean in actual, romantic love. They feel the same way about their author as you do about David."

That was hard to comprehend. However, I believed what Richard was saying. Delusion, if given permission, can take over the mind. I had even seen it in my own life to a much lesser degree.

"I had research to do and I needed that research to be promoted. I didn't tell you about it, not only because I feared that you'd take some of the credit, but also because I was so ultra-focused on it. Imogene is ultra-focused on Henry Thoreau. I'm the same when it comes to my research."

"And Renee?" I asked. "Where does she come into play in all of this?"

"I care about Renee. I truly do. She's a good woman, but she is a distraction from what I need to do. I'm just in a place where I need to concentrate solely on my work. Maybe a day will come when I can settle down, and then I might be able to reach out to her again."

But by then, Renee would be gone. I knew this about my friend without a shadow of a doubt.

"Did you know that Imogene is living in a cabin?" I asked.

"What? What cabin?"

"A cabin in Cascade Spring Park. It's one of the summer cabins that the village rents out to tourists during warmer months."

"But she is staying there now? That can only mean that her delusions about being connected to Henry David Thoreau have grown so great that she is now trying to live like he did. She might be under the misguided belief that Thoreau lived in the cabin on Walden Pond for most of his life. But that's just not true. He was there less than two years and went in and out of society all the while. He was never completely closed off."

I thought of the family tree thumbtacked to the wall of the cabin, serial killer style.

"I'm glad you told me where she is." He tugged on the end of his beard. "My article is due just after Christmas. I have a few more questions for her, and she hasn't been answering my calls. In fact, the last time I called, an automated message said that the number was no longer in service. I thought she had left Cascade Springs for good."

"You plan to go talk to her?" I asked.

"I have to. This article is far too important to my career to take shortcuts. I must go to the source."

I cocked my head. "What are the questions you need answered?"

He licked his lips. "Well, I—I don't think it would be professional of me to discuss it with you before I asked Imogene about these issues first."

My heart sank. He still didn't trust me. He thought I would steal his research, even though I'd assured him I wouldn't. At that moment, I realized that all Richard Bunting cared about was getting that promotion to full professor. Nothing else mattered. Not his romantic relationship. Not Imogene's privacy. Not even our friendship, which I thought was as solid as it could get.

He believed that Imogene was obsessed with proving that she was related to Thoreau. And though he might be right, he was just as obsessed, as he'd admitted, to writing about it as she was to proving her truth.

215

Chapter
Twenty-Three

Rainwater texted that he had to work late again. He said he needed to finish up some paperwork before we left for our honeymoon. It was becoming more and more obvious to me that I might set out for Vermont and never find out what had happened to that mint edition of *Walden*.

The thought of not knowing ate me up inside. It was a valuable book, but it meant more to me to know the truth about what happened to it and to Roma Winterbourne. I had to find it for Imogene and return it for her. Yes, she was a little batty about the book, and her theory about being Thoreau's great-great-great-great-granddaughter was far-fetched at best, but she truly believed it. My conversation with her earlier that day proved that to me. I was afraid of what she might do to herself if she could not get her book back.

A quote from *Walden* came to my mind. This one was unheeded by the shop's essence, and one that I knew from my years of study. Thoreau wrote:

> *A man is rich in proportion to the number of things which he can afford to let alone.*

Thoreau would not be impressed by me if this was what he believed. I knew that. There was very little I could "let alone," and Imogene's book was not one of the things I could ignore—not by a long shot.

When they'd found Roma's body, I remembered overhearing Rainwater and one of his officers saying that there was a matchbook for the Starlight B&B in her coat pocket. It was a detail I had soon forgotten in all the uproar around me, but it came back now.

It may be a waste of time. In fact, I knew that it would be, but I decided to go check out the B&B. Maybe seeing it in person would help me brainstorm. When the shop closed at seven, I said goodbye to the last customers and locked the front door.

Faulkner flapped his wings high in the birch tree. "Let alone. Let alone!" he crowed.

I squinted at him. "You are contradicting the shop. I can't let the case alone when the shop's essence is telling me to find out what's going on. I thought you and the shop were on the same team."

"Let alone! Let alone!" he repeated.

I shook my head and got my heavy winter coat from the coat tree. It made me look like Violet Beauregarde, the blueberry girl from *Charlie and the Chocolate Factory*, but it was cold out and keeping warm was my number one priority on a Western New York December evening. I added a white hat with a pom-pom on top and a matching scarf.

Emerson appeared out of nowhere, looked up at me, and yowled. He would give anything to get his claws on the pom-pom on the top of my head.

"My hat is not a cat toy."

Emerson laid his ears back in disgust. Faulkner cackled in the branches of the birch tree. I didn't know if the crow was laughing at the fact that Emerson had been thwarted or at how ridiculous I looked. If it was both, I would not blame him.

I had to dress warm. The temperatures were in the teens and dropping fast. After the relatively mild weather around my wedding day, Cascade Springs was now gearing up for a very cold Christmas.

Driving a car didn't seem practical. In the time it took my Mini to warm up, I could walk to the B&B. And walking would give me time to plan a strategy. I didn't think I could walk up to the B&B owner and just ask him to tell me what he knew about Roma. It was a small town, yes, but they had to—or should—respect their guests' privacy.

When my snow boots were on, Emerson ran to the front door and waited. "No, not tonight. I'm not going into the woods. I have to run an errand." Maybe it was silly not to tell the cat exactly where I was headed. But by not telling him, I was implying that I believed he could understand English. And the truth was that he might. The shop's essence has taught me that anything was possible.

Emerson sat in front of the door with his thin black tail flicking back in forth, clearly annoyed.

"Emerson, move away from the door."

He didn't even blink.

"Fine! I'll go out the back door then." I spun around and ran to the back of the shop. Emerson took off and ran ahead of me. I made a sharp turn back around and flew out the front door, closing and locking it behind me before he had the chance to turn around again.

I skipped down the porch steps of Charming Books with a spring in my step. I'd outfoxed the cat this time. But it would likely be the last. I glanced over my shoulder and spied Emerson in the front window yowling. I frowned. Maybe I shouldn't be so cheery about tricking the tuxie. He'd find a way to get even. He always did.

A walk through Cascade Springs the evening before Christmas Eve was like a stroll through an old New England Christmas card. The homes were lit up and cozy. Swirls of smoke billowed out of chimneys all over the village, and evergreens were tethered in place with bright red velvet bows to every fence and pole.

A dusting of fresh snow covered every surface. It seemed like someone from above had sprinkled powdered sugar on the world to make it just a little sweeter.

Instead of walking toward the river, I walked away from it and into the village neighborhoods. Cascade Springs had a very rigid building code for any new home built in the historic district or any changes made to existing homes or buildings in that district. Although there were many styles and periods represented from Colonial to Victorian, each house had its own character.

Charming Books used to be one of those old homes until it was transformed into a bookshop. My great-grandmother had been the one who'd made the sprawling Victorian house into a bookshop nearly one hundred years ago. I don't think that the village committee on historic buildings would have let that happen today.

I walked out of my neighborhood into the bird neighborhood, which was called that because every street had been given a bird name. A new snow began to fall.

Cascade Springs had a thriving arts district that was established in the late 1800s. Even before Columbus landed in the Americas, people came to the hot springs in Cascade Springs for the healing waters. By the time my ancestress Rosalee arrived during the War of 1812—after her husband died in the Battle of Lake Erie—the springs had become a bona fide tourist attraction and a common side trip for travelers to Niagara Falls just a few miles away.

Rosalee had recognized that the specialness of the water went beyond the healing powers of a drink and a good soak. She began to water the birch tree and noticed the effects it had. Seeing that the water gave the tree powers, she literally built her house around the birch tree. Rosalee used her gift from the tree's essence to heal people of their aliments. It wasn't until my great-grandmother turned the house into a bookshop that messages from the essence became conveyed through books, and it wasn't until I'd become the Caretaker that those messages were used to solve crimes. With every generation, the water bestowed the Caretaker with a unique gift. None were exactly the same.

The snowflakes caught the light as they fell, and I could almost make out the unique patterns of the ones falling closest to me.

Mesmerized by the falling snow, the lights, and the glitter of the season, I didn't realize I was being followed until I heard a meow.

I spun around on the snowy sidewalk to see Emerson strolling behind me like I was the Pied Piper and he was a mouse. Not that I thought Emerson would like being compared to a mouse. He was a proud cat and certainly would find that analogy offensive.

"Emerson Waverly, what on earth do you think you're doing? I thought I told you to stay home."

He cocked his head as if he didn't understand what I was saying. Oh, sure, now my words didn't make sense to the cat. It was a clear case of selective understanding.

I pointed in the direction of Charming Books. "Go home."

He started walking toward me.

I shook my head, hoping I could hold my ground, but I knew it was a lost battle. I said, "Go home."

He kept walking.

I put my hands on my hips. "If you're going to insist on coming with me everywhere, I need to get you a leash and walk you properly."

He arched his back at the idea.

"Fine. It's too cold for you to be walking on the frozen sidewalk." I unzipped my enormous coat. "Jump in."

He ran toward me, jumped inside my coat, and settled in. I thought he might fall out the bottom, but he fit in quite snugly. It wasn't a good look for me. Between the puffy blueberry coat and the cat snuggled down right above my bellybutton, I looked about six months pregnant. Seeing as how I hadn't even been married for a week, the tongues would start wagging if people saw me now. For extra security, I held my right arm around my waist to hold the cat in place.

The sooner I finished this errand, the sooner I could remove the cat and the coat from my person.

I picked up the pace for the rest of the walk to the Starlight B&B.

It was a narrow, plain brick home reminiscent of Edgar Allan Poe's house in Baltimore. I stepped through the door, and a bell rang on the inner doorknob.

"Hello?" the elderly man behind the desk said. He wore a suit jacket over a stiffly pressed white shirt and ascot. To my recollection, I had never seen a person wear an ascot as normal everyday clothing before. Not even Richard.

"May I grant you some assistance?" His tone and manner of speech was as formal as his clothing. It made me wonder if the ascot brought it on or vice versa.

"Hi, I'm Violet Waverly from Charming Books." I had no idea why I thought this introduction would give me an in with the ascot-wearing man, but Cascade Springs was too small of a town to hide your identity anyway, especially if you were local.

"I'm Jameson Horner, the owner of the Starlight B&B, the most dignified B&B in Cascade Springs." He said this as if he were reading it off of a brochure. "Violet Waverly. Then that makes you the mayor's granddaughter." He shook his head. "I never thought I would see the day that a Waverly became the mayor of this town. Your people weren't that well-respected for a long time, you know."

From inside my coat, I heard Emerson hiss softly. He'd found the B&B owner's comment offensive too.

"Well, I for one am happy to see it," he continued. "I have always been fond of strong women, and the Waverly ladies certainly are. My great-grandmother was friends with your family, and the stories I could tell you about your great-great-grandmother being harassed by the other villagers would chill your bones. Not everyone is appreciative of other ways of life, and not everyone is open to let people live how they choose. I do, of course. It's not my place to judge."

I relaxed slightly. "That's a good policy."

"You're married, aren't you?" His eyes shone. "I thought I remember getting a wedding invitation from Mayor Daisy herself. I couldn't go, unfortunately. I'm not one for crowds or the cold, and that event had both."

"I understand," I said.

"You're not a Waverly any longer, then?" he asked.

"I am. I'm not changing my name. My husband doesn't mind. He knows my family legacy is important to me."

"Ahh, that's something else I like to see—these more modern marriages. It does my heart good to hear that." He pressed his right hand to his chest as if he were about to recite the Pledge of Allegiance. A large emerald ring sparkled on his ring finger. "Now, how can I help you? You aren't in need of a room at the B&B, are you? You have Charming Books. Or maybe you are? You need to find a nice place to get away with that handsome police chief husband of yours. He is the nicest looking man, and so strong and dignified too." He sighed. "A man like that isn't easy to find. You were wise to snap him when you did."

I smiled. "Chief Rainwater is a fine man. I'll make sure to tell him he has an admirer."

"Oh, please do." He blushed.

"I'm actually here about a guest you recently had staying with you." I lowered my voice to a conspiratorial whisper.

He peered at me over his glasses. "And who would that be? I always have a rotating door of guests. As you should know, Cascade Springs is a very popular tourist destination any season of the year, but Christmas is especially so. I've even had some celebrities from New York City stay here. Broadway stars, in fact!" He ended that statement by rattling off a list of names I didn't recognize. I did my best to appear impressed because I didn't want to offend him. They could have all been very famous stage actors, but I spent most of my leisure time on research for my next project, not on theater. It was clear that Jameson was not as concerned about his guests' privacy as I thought he would be. That might work in my favor.

"I'm looking for information about Roma Winterbourne," I said.

"Oh." He pressed a hand to his chest again. "The dead woman. My, what a shock when that very unfriendly police officer came in on Sunday morning, insisting that he see where Roma had been staying. He woke me up. I make it very clear to my guests that Sunday is my sleep-in day and breakfast will be a brunch served at noon. I think they really like that. Who wants to get up early on Sunday?" He wrinkled his nose. "I suppose if you have to go to church, but now I watch church online in my pajamas. My church has gone high tech. It's lovely. I watch the whole service, but don't have to make small talk or shake hands. I think that's how God intended religion to be, don't you?"

Not from my understanding of Christianity, it wasn't, but I wasn't one to judge. My religious education was loose at best since my grandmother was running a magical bookshop and all. She certainly saw things a little differently than other grandmothers.

"What was the officer's name?" I asked, even though I had a very good guess.

Jameson waved his hand. "Don't you worry. It wasn't your husband. He's nothing but a gentleman. It was Officer Wheaton."

I figured as much.

"Did Officer Wheaton find anything?"

I felt Emerson shift under my coat. I moved my arm to hold him tight. I didn't think Jameson wanted my cat running loose in his B&B.

"If he did, he didn't tell me. I showed him to her room, but he wouldn't look through her things until after I'd left. The nerve, you know? It wasn't like I was going to spy on him, and this is *my* business. I need to keep an eye on things." He sniffed. "I assume that he searched her possessions after I left. He didn't take anything that belongs to the B&B, which was what I was afraid of. Trust me, I went up there to check myself after he left. He looked questionable in character, if you ask me."

I'd thought that about Officer Wheaton a time or two myself.

"Would you mind if I went up to see the room?" I asked. "You can come with me if that makes you more comfortable. I don't mind."

"I suppose you could, but there is nothing there. I packed up all her things after the police were through. It's not rented out yet, but I hope someone makes a reservation soon. Sometimes people like to travel after the hustle and bustle of the Christmas season. I can't think of a better place to be after the holidays than Cascade Springs, can you?"

I shook my head.

"It's the perfect winter getaway," he said. "As for Roma's things, they are still here. I couldn't find anyone to take them. The police said she didn't have any relatives or close friends who they could find to take her things. And they didn't want them either. What were they going to do with a bunch of women's clothes? It didn't feel right to throw her things away, though, so I tucked them away up in the attic. It was a tight squeeze. There

225

is a lot up there. Whenever I don't know what to do with something, it goes into the attic. When I die, my nieces and nephews will have a treasure hunt up there. There could be valuable items—or not. I just don't know." He pressed a hand to his back. "I'd go up and get it for you, but I hurt my back yesterday. My housekeeper mopped the kitchen, and I didn't know that when I walked in there. Next thing I knew, my legs were in the air and my back was on the floor."

My eyes widened. "Oh no, did you get hurt?"

"I went to the doctor." He reached behind and rubbed his back. "It's just a bruised spine, but I have to take it easy, so no trips to the attic for me."

"I'm glad it wasn't more serious. I don't mind climbing up to the attic if you give me a general idea of where her things are," I said.

"Well, I don't think you'd run off with anything like Officer Wheaton might have. You are the mayor's granddaughter after all. But..." He pulled on his collar. "You don't think that's a good idea, do you? In your," he lowered his voice to barely above a whisper. "Your condition."

"My condition?" I wrinkled my brow in confusion.

His face flushed. "I would never ask a woman so noticeably with child to climb into that old attic. It would be cruel."

I looked down at my coat and the bulge. "I'm not pregnant." I unzipped the coat, and Emerson's head popped out like a jack-in-the-box.

Jameson fainted dead away.

Chapter
Twenty-Four

I ran around to the other side of the counter. "Jameson! Are you all right? Is your back hurt again?" It could not have been good for him to have landed on his bruised spine a second time.

He groaned and slowly sat up. "My smelling salts. I need them. They will revive me."

"What?" I asked, thinking I hadn't heard him right. Had he really asked for smelling salts?

"My smelling salts. They are in the drawer right under the registration book," he gasped.

I looked down at the registration book and saw a small drawer under it in the counter. I opened it. There were pens, paper clips, envelops with the B&B logo printed on the corner, and yes, smelling salts.

"Shouldn't you be lying down? What about your back?"

He rubbed his forehead. "Did you have a cat's head in your coat?" He stared at me in horror. "You're carrying around a cat's head?"

"No! I mean yes, but it wasn't *just* the head. It was the whole cat." I pointed at Emerson, who peeked around the side of the desk. "That's my cat Emerson. He followed me here, so I put him in my coat to keep him warm."

He rubbed his head a little harder. "Is that supposed to make sense?"

"Should I call for an ambulance?" I studied his face, looking for any signs of pain.

"No, no, no. I'm not going to the hospital this close to Christmas. That's when all the knuckleheads are there. Just help me up to that armchair, and I'll sit for a spell. I will be fine. My back doesn't hurt any worse than it did this morning."

"But it could hurt more later," I warned, thinking of injuries I had sustained over my lifetime. They always seemed worse on the second day.

"Well, I will be the judge of that later. Right now, I just want to sit on a soft chair. Can you lend me your arm?"

As carefully as I could, I helped him to his feet. I was happy to see that his legs appeared to hold his weight even if he winced as he straightened up. We shuffled around the counter and across the room, into the small lounge at the front of the house. A fire crackled in the hearth.

"Ahh, much better." He melted into the chair like a deflated balloon.

"I'm so terribly sorry." I bit my lower lip.

"It's not your fault. This happens to me often." He waved the smelling salts back and forth beneath his nose.

"Aren't smelling salts for someone who is still unconscious? To wake them up?"

He frowned at me. "I use them to keep myself alert. Why else would I have them at the ready like that?"

I wasn't sure how healthy it was to use smelling salts on a regular basis, but I wasn't going to argue with him when I was getting the chance to poke around his attic to look at Roma's possessions.

"The need for smelling salts happens often, though I can't say the same for a cat popping out of a person's coat," Jameson huffed and then inhaled deeply. "The salts do revive me so."

"Is there someone I can call for you?" I wasn't sure I should leave him alone in the chair. What if his back started to spasm, or worse?

"Don't be silly. The doctor gave me muscle relaxers. I'll take two and sleep like a baby tonight." He lowered the salts. "If you want to go to the attic, the pull-down ladder is just at the end of the hallway on the second floor."

"I think I will, if only to put my mind at ease that I didn't miss something when it comes to Roma." I was getting warm in my coat. I took it off and placed it on the coat rack in the corner of the room.

"My, you are much smaller than that coat implies. I know it's not my place to say, but that coat does nothing for your figure."

I sighed. "It's warm," I said a tad defensively.

"My dear, sometimes we have to make sacrifices in the name of fashion. Look at me for example." He set the smelling salts on a coaster on the table next to him and fluffed his ascot.

I had no comment on that particular fashion accessory. "Where in the attic can I find Roma's box of things?" I thought it was best to get back to the matter at hand. I didn't for a moment think I would have the upper hand in a conversation about clothing with Jameson.

"It's just at the top of the ladder. I wrote her name on the box—that way if someone came looking for it I'd know where it was. My memory isn't what it used to be, so I like to label when I remember to."

I could see the staircase to the second floor from where I stood and thanked him. Emerson ran ahead of me.

"Watch your step!" Jameson called after me.

The little cat walked confidently up the narrow set of stairs. I imagined trying to go up these steps carrying a suitcase. It must have been a struggle, but that didn't change the fact that the B&B was a charming building. There were spots in the wall where the plaster had fallen away, so the original brick walls were visible. By the varying shapes of the bricks, I could tell that they had been made by hand.

Emerson stood at the top of the stairs and meowed at me as if to say this was no time to admire the architecture.

"I'm coming. I'm coming," I muttered.

At the landing, a brocade runner ran to the length of the hallway, which was narrow and dark. There was only one very small window at the end of the hall and two antique wall scones to light the way.

Emerson dashed down the hall like he was in a race. I knew for a fact that the little tuxie was dying to get to the attic, which would have countless places to hide and explore. Getting him out of this house was going to be a challenge.

I found the cord that Jameson had mentioned. As I pulled down on it, the ladder came down slowly. I looked behind me to see if any of the bedroom doors opened. It was close to eight in the evening now. I supposed that some of the guests might have already turned in for the night or were at least relaxing.

No faces appeared in the doorways, and I let out a sigh of relief. Even though I had permission from Jameson to be here, I really didn't want any of his guests seeing me snoop around.

As expected, Emerson galloped up the ladder and his black tail disappeared through the hatch. I climbed up after him, and the ladder groaned under my weight. It looked like the ladder was original to the house. The wood felt dry and brittle under my hands. Not wanting to have the ladder hold my weight for too long, I hurried up the rungs and stepped into the attic. The flooring under my feet was squares of plywood that weren't all nailed in place.

It was hard for me to imagine Jameson coming up here with his bad back. A lone triangular window no bigger than a lunchbox let in the only natural light in the room. The window was covered in dust, and it was late, so there wasn't much light at all—just a faint glow from outside. I could barely see my hand in front of my face. I waved my hand around above my head, hoping to find a chain that would be attached to a lightbulb. I should have asked Jameson where the light was before coming up here.

I was about to climb back down and do that when the lights came on. I spun around and came face-to-face with a life-sized mannequin dressed as a clown. I screamed and fell backward into a pile of old blankets.

A cloud of dust enveloped me, and I couldn't stop sneezing. Finally, when the dust settled, I righted myself and scrambled to my feet.

If I'd hoped not to disturb any guests in the B&B, I had failed. I wouldn't have been surprised if Rainwater had heard me scream. Not that I knew exactly where my husband was at the moment.

I shivered. I hated clowns, mimes, and people dressed up like cartoons. They just creeped me out. I assumed the clown was supposed to be for children's parties, but he was scary. What made him look even worse was the clear plastic dust bag over his body.

I glanced around the attic. "Emerson."

The cat meowed. He was on top of an old dresser, standing as nice as you please next to a light switch.

"Are you telling me *you're* the one who turned on the lights?"

He purred. I shook my head. I'd worry about what all my little tuxedo cat was capable of later. I needed to find Roma's box and get away from the creepy clown.

Jameson had said the box was just at the top of the ladder, and sure enough there was a large cardboard box sitting there with little to no dust on it.

In neat lettering, the top of the box read "Roma Winterbourne" and below was the date he'd put it in the attic. I had not expected Jameson to be so precise. The box flaps were folded, not taped shut, so it opened easily. Inside, I found clothes, toiletries, shoes, and a notebook.

My heart skipped a beat when I spied the notebook. I flipped through it, but every page was blank. I should have known. If it had been important, Officer Wheaton wouldn't have left it behind.

I went through the box again. I took everything out of her toiletry bag, examined each item, and put the bag back. Other than learning that oral hygiene had been very important to Roma—she had two kinds of floss and three tiny tubes of toothpaste with her—I didn't see anything that stood out. The items could have belonged to any middle-aged woman staying at the inn. There was nothing that distinctively cried "Roma" to me. That could be because Officer Wheaton had taken all those things when he'd come to the B&B.

On a whim, I flipped through the notebook again, and a piece of paper floated to the floor. Emerson jumped off of the dresser and pounced on it as if we were playing a game.

"Emerson, give me that."

I reached for the paper. It was just a small scrap, but on it was a sentence from *Walden*:

If you have built castles in the air, your work need not be lost; that is where they should be. Now put the foundations under them.

It was a popular quote of Thoreau's and one of my favorites. It was about making big dreams first and then figuring out how to reach them instead of plodding along with no direction, hoping you will get somewhere someday.

I flipped over the piece of paper. She had written it herself—or maybe someone else did, actually. I didn't know Roma's handwriting. I folded up the scrap of paper and tucked it into my pocket.

"Emerson, it's time to go." I stood up.

To my surprise, the little tuxie allowed me to scoop him up as if he were ready to go home.

I turned toward the stairs and heard a creak. I saw a shadow. Maybe I was still spooked by the clown, but I held Emerson close to my chest with one hand and picked up a candlestick with the other, ready to strike.

"Hello?" Rainwater's head popped through the hatch.

I lowered the candlestick. "David, you scared me to death."

He continued up the ladder and then had to crouch not to hit his head on the low ceiling. "Were you going to hit me with that?" He pointed at the candlestick. "Ms. Waverly in the attic with the candlestick?"

"Very funny," I muttered. "I wasn't going to hit you specifically. I was just ready to wallop anyone who was going to mess with me. This is no game of Clue."

He laughed. "Remind me not to mess with you." He arched his brow. "I see you brought your cat on this adventure."

Emerson wriggled out of my grasp and sat on my shoulder like a pirate's parrot.

"I don't *bring* Emerson anywhere. He just comes."

"What are you doing here? You can imagine my surprise when I came here to have another look at Roma's possessions to learn that my wife was already in the attic rifling through them."

I put the candlestick back on the dresser where I'd found it. "First of all, I love hearing you refer to me as 'your wife.' Second of all, great minds think alike. Maybe we both thought to find the book. It was best to go back to the person who started all of this—Roma."

He frowned. "Did you find anything?"

I removed the scrap of paper from my pocket and handed it to him. "Just this. It's a quote from *Walden*."

"I know." He smiled. "You're not the only well-read one in the family."

"I would never presume that I was." I took the piece of paper from his hand and flipped it over.

"Do you think it's important?" he asked.

"I don't know, but it feels important." I frowned at the scrap of paper in my hands. "On the other hand, I could just be reaching because I *want* it to be important."

"That's a problem we police fall into as well during an investigation from time to time." He looked behind him and jumped. "Good Lord! That clown is hideous!"

"You don't like clowns."

He shook his head. "Someday I'll tell you about my one trip to the circus when I was four. It scarred me forever."

I wrapped my arms around him. "I knew you were the one. I dislike clowns too."

He laughed. "This scrap of paper is interesting, yes, but it's not telling us anything that will help us find the book." He paused. "I cleared everything with the department and Wheaton is ready to take over the open cases. He will do fine managing it all for a few days. You did promise…" He looked at me, hopeful.

I know I had promised that I would leave for the honeymoon even if we didn't find the book by Christmas Eve. Which was tomorrow. But… How could I leave now? I knew something was off. The shop's essence hadn't let up in sending me clues. This scrap of paper had to mean something too. Wouldn't those clues have stopped if it hadn't been important?

Rainwater's shoulders sagged, and a pang of guilt hit my heart. I didn't want to disappoint him. He rarely took time off, and he had been looking forward to this trip for months.

I took his hand. "We can go," I said. "I don't know if we will ever find Imogene's book. I suppose I can't spend the rest of my life looking for it."

"Why do you want to find it so badly?" He searched my face with those beautiful amber eyes.

"At first, I wanted to find it because, to be honest, I'm nosy. I wanted to know what happened. It was a puzzle that I wanted to find all the pieces to and put back together. The puzzle piece that has stuck with me the most was on Roma's hand when we discovered her body. I can't get that image of the writing on Roma's hand out of my mind. Did she write it? Did someone else?"

"We think she was the one who wrote it," Rainwater said. "It's similar to the sample of handwriting you have right here on this piece of paper, and it was written on her left hand. She was right-handed."

I nodded. "Why would she write that on her hand if it wasn't true? It implies someone *stole* the book, doesn't it?"

He nodded. "But it's not proof that that's what happened."

I thought about this for a moment, and as much as I didn't want to admit it, I knew he was right. Then again, why would someone write that on their hand as their last dying act, assuming that's when it was written, if it weren't true? Wouldn't that be a waste of her last moments in some way?

"You said that was your first reason. What's your second?"

"I became more concerned about the case because of Imogene. Not knowing where her book is torments her. I'm worried about her." I told him about my visit with her earlier in the day. "She's so focused on the idea that she is Thoreau's relative. It's all that matters to her now. She has alienated everyone in her life over it. I think her son, Edmund, is ready to write her off as well. He talked about having her committed for mental health issues. I'm afraid of what she might do if she can't get the book back and prove her story is true. Everyone who knows her says it's an obsession. Her son. And Adrien."

Rainwater's brow went up. "Adrien?"

"Adrien Dupont. He's her nephew."

"What?" Rainwater jerked back.

I nodded. "But they aren't close. I really don't know how much they interact with each other, if at all."

Rainwater frowned. "I wish that you or Adrien had told me this before."

"What difference would it have made? Adrien doesn't know where the book is." I sighed.

"Listen," Rainwater said. "Would it make you feel better to go to Imogene's cabin tonight to check on her? I know it's late, but if it would give you peace of mind to leave tomorrow as planned, I'll do it. I don't want us to be on our honeymoon and see you distracted over what's going on back here in Cascade Springs."

"It would make me feel a lot better." I looked into his eyes. "David, don't ask me how I know, but I can't get out of my mind that something bad is going to happen and Imogene is right in the thick of it."

Chapter Twenty-Five

Rainwater had parked his SUV at the B&B, and it was a two-minute drive to Charming Books. I wanted to stop at the shop before we went on to Imogene's cabin for two reasons. First, I wanted Emerson to stay behind for once, and second, I wanted to see if the shop's essence had anything else to tell me before I spoke to Imogene. I knew I was close to something, even if I couldn't identify what that something was. I hoped the shop would clear that up.

We stepped inside, and Faulkner flew from the top of the tree to his perch in the window. He cocked his head at Rainwater. "You're still here?"

"Faulkner, I'm not going anywhere." Rainwater pointed at the bird. "I'm your stepdad now."

The crow squawked and flew around the shop.

I shook my head at Rainwater. "Did you have to get him going?"

Emerson curled up in his cat bed by the hearth. It seemed the little tuxedo had had enough excitement for one day. I was happy to see that. Perhaps this time I would be able to go to the woods without him following me.

"Hello, you two!" Grandma Daisy called as she came down the stairs from the children's loft.

I looked up. "Grandma Daisy, I didn't know you were planning to be here tonight."

She smiled as she walked toward me and gave me a hug. "I wasn't planning on it. However, I have been so caught up in the village hall and everything going on with the restoration that I realized I haven't come to see how the two of you are." She gave Rainwater a hug in turn. "Do you still plan to leave for your honeymoon tomorrow?"

"Yes," Rainwater said and glanced at me. "If Violet is comfortable leaving the search for the missing copy of *Walden* in Officer Wheaton's hands."

"Wheaton's?" Grandma Daisy yelped. "Why would you leave such an important matter in his hands?"

"Thank you, Grandma." I gave Rainwater a pointed look.

"I can't win an argument if you are both against me," Rainwater grumbled.

"Oh, Violet, I knew you married a smart man." My grandmother grinned from ear to ear.

"We are going to visit Imogene one more time in her cabin in the woods," I said. "I just want to make sure that she's all right."

"Did something in the books suggest that she wouldn't be?" Grandma Daisy asked in a much more serious tone.

I walked over to the tree, half expecting a volume of Thoreau to be there. It wasn't. I walked all around the tree to make sure I didn't miss a book. Still nothing. "No," I said. "Not directly at least."

"Does it ever say anything directly?" Rainwater asked.

He had a point.

"And is there a reason why you are circling the birch tree?" Rainwater cocked his head to one side. "Is that part of your job as the Caretaker?"

"No. I was hoping that the shop would tell me more about Roma and Imogene, or what happened to that valuable volume of *Walden*."

"It hasn't?" Grandma Daisy asked.

I shook my head. "I thought I would feel more confident going to Imogene's cabin with more information."

"I think when you see her and see she's safe and sound, you will feel better." He took my hand. "Let's go for a walk in the woods."

"Yes, that's a good idea," Grandma Daisy said. "I'm going to go home to crunch some more numbers for the village hall budget. It's coming along swimmingly!"

"I'm sure it is," Rainwater said. "Everyone in the village knew that you could do it, Grandma Daisy."

"As they should."

"And Charles Hancock is her greatest champion," I teased.

Grandma Daisy scowled at me. "Don't you have a cabin you need to be getting to?"

I laughed. "Let me just put my coat back on." I grabbed the large blue coat from the arm of the couch.

"Honey, that coat..." Rainwater trailed off.

I held up my hand. "Stop. I already know I look like an engorged blueberry."

"Okay," he said. "As long as you know. That being said, you're the cutest blueberry I've ever seen."

We said goodbye to my grandmother and went out the back door of the bookshop.

At night, when I fetched water for the tree, these walks into the park felt everything from peaceful to foreboding. But that night, with Rainwater by my side and holding my hand, walking to Imogene's cabin felt like I was exactly where I needed to be. He was right. We were going to arrive at the cabin and discover Imogene was fine. Tomorrow we would leave for our long-awaited honeymoon.

I felt him looking at me.

"Why are you smiling so much?" Rainwater asked.

"Because I'm happy. I know we haven't been able to celebrate our marriage very much because of Roma's death, but I'm so very happy."

He leaned over and kissed me. "I'm happy too."

I hugged him tight, but then felt his body tense.

I pulled back, but he held me close to his chest.

"What is it?" I whispered.

"There's someone in the woods," he said in a hoarse whisper.

"Imogene?" We weren't far from the cabins now.

"Not unless she grew a foot and half taller and was a man." His voice was hushed.

"Do you think it was the man who chased me out of the woods on the day of the wedding? Because I know who that is."

He stared at me. "What?"

"It was Fenimore." I told him about my conversation with Fenimore outside of Imogene's cabin.

"Why didn't you tell me this before?"

I made a face. "I forgot."

He sighed. "I don't think it was Fenimore. Maybe—but it could also be a hiker."

"The park closes at sunset," I said.

"How many times have you broken that rule?" he whispered back. "Listen, I want you to stay here by this tree and do not move. I'm going to see if I can find out who this is."

"Why can't I come with you?" I fought the whininess in my voice.

"Because I don't know if it's dangerous. Now, stay here." Rainwater gave me one final squeeze and then stepped off of the trail.

I stood by the tree as he'd asked me to. It was an old birch. Of course it would be a birch tree. I could hear Rainwater moving through the forest in the direction that the man had gone. I waited one minute. Two. I started to tap my foot. I peeked around the side of the tree, but couldn't see Rainwater or the other person any longer. From where I stood, I could see the clearing that led to the gravel parking lot in front of the cabins.

"David," I whispered.

There was no response.

I glanced at the clearing and back in the direction that Rainwater went. I chewed my lip. He could be gone for a while, and I knew Imogene was just a few yards away.

He would have to know that's where I would have gone, right? I thought about texting him to tell him where I was going but I didn't know if he had the ringer turned on. If he did, whoever he was following might hear the sound.

I decided I would be quick. I would check on Imogene and come right back to this spot. I just had to make sure that she was okay, and with a strange man walking around in the woods, I needed that reassurance.

I left my post and walked into the clearing and the parking lot. There was smoke coming out of Imogene's chimney and light shone from the window. I began to relax. She was fine. Maybe she was just pouring over her family tree again with a cup of tea.

I felt silly to be knocking on her door so late at night. It felt intrusive and just might scare her. I hedged. Maybe this was a bad idea after all.

"You didn't stay by the tree," Rainwater said behind me.

I jumped a foot in the air and fell to the ground.

"Violet," Rainwater said, looking down at me in dismay. "Are you okay?"

"That's the second time you've startled me tonight." I shook the snow off of my gloved hands. "You need to stop doing that."

He held out his hand and pulled me to my feet. Then, he brushed the snow off of my backside. "At least we know nothing is broken thanks to all the extra padding you have in that coat."

"Very funny." I gave him a look. "I'm grateful for this coat. I'm toasty warm. Sometimes comfort is more important than fashion."

He rubbed his hands together. "I would say that's always true. Besides, you're better off than I am. I'm freezing. I'll stop teasing you about your blueberry coat."

I squinted at him.

"I promise."

I shook my head. "What happened? Did you find that man you spotted?"

He shook his head. "I never caught up with him. It could have just been a hiker." He nodded at the cabins. "I assume the one with the smoke coming out the chimney is hers?"

243

I nodded. "Now I'm wondering if we should even knock on the door. It's almost nine at night. I don't want to scare her."

"We can go back home," Rainwater said.

"No, let's knock. We came all this way. If we don't, I will just toss and turn all night, wondering if she's okay."

"We don't want that," Rainwater said.

I stepped up to the door with Rainwater at my side. I knocked. There was no answer. I knocked a second time, harder. Still nothing.

"She might not want to come to the door." Rainwater reached his arm around me. "Imogene. This is the village police. We're doing a wellness check."

"A wellness check?" I whispered.

"We do them all the time for the elderly who live alone, especially if someone reports a concern about them."

There was still no answer. I stepped away from the door and over to the window. The curtains were drawn, but there was a small gap through which I could see Imogene lying prostrate on the kitchen floor. Her face was turned away from me, and she wasn't moving.

"David, we have to get in there! Imogene is on the floor. She might be hurt."

Rainwater stepped back and kicked the door in. It didn't take much effort. The stiff wind alone might have been able to take that door out.

We rushed into the cabin. Rainwater knelt by Imogene's still body. "Call an ambulance!"

I yanked my phone out of my pocket. I quickly told the dispatcher where we were and what was happening. "Chief Rainwater is with me. He's trying to help the woman."

"Good, good," the dispatcher said. "We have EMTs on the way. They should be there in five minutes."

I held the phone away from my ear as I stepped into the small kitchen. "Is she..."

"She's still alive," Rainwater said. "Her tongue is swollen, so I turned her over to her side. It looks like she had some sort of allergic reaction. Since it's in her mouth and throat, it could be from something she ate or drank."

There was a DNA test on the table. The package said, "Find out who you're related to today! You could be descended from royalty. Don't you want to claim your birthright as a prince or princess? Take this test!"

A used swab lay on the table next to articles on Thoreau. I stared at it. "Or she could have put a swab in her mouth and been allergic to that."

"What?" Rainwater asked.

He couldn't see what was on the table from his position on the floor, so I told him about the DNA test on the table. I wasn't about to touch it and leave my fingerprints on it.

Two EMTs rushed to Imogene's side with medical kits and a stretcher.

Rainwater scrambled out of the way. "She needs an epineph-rine shot. Looks like an allergic reaction."

One EMT looked her over, and the other pulled a syringe from her case and jabbed Imogene in the thigh.

"We have an ambulance outside. We should get her to the hospital."

"Right," Rainwater said.

Officer Wheaton came into the cabin. The small, one-room building began to feel very small. "Chief," he said. "I thought that you'd left for your honeymoon and this case was mine." He shot a sideways glance at me. His eyes widened when he saw the blueberry coat.

I was certain that Officer Wheaton blamed me for Rainwater being there, and I was beginning to wonder if I should invest in a more flattering winter coat. Clearly, this one was doing nothing for me.

"Things have changed," Rainwater said. "I want every inch of this cabin searched. Pay special attention to that DNA test."

Officer Wheaton frowned but didn't argue. Despite his sour demeanor, he respected his boss.

The EMTs put Imogene on the stretcher. She looked so small and frail. They carried her out of the cabin as if she weighed nothing at all. Lights from the ambulance and police car came in through the crack in the curtains and doorway. The garish light reflected off of Imogene's tea cup, her papers, and the family tree on the wall. Rainwater walked over to it.

I stood beside him. "What do you think happened?"

"She had a severe allergic reaction and went into anaphylaxis."

"From what? From the swab?" I glanced back at the kitchen. Officer Wheaton took photographs of everything that was on the table.

"It's as good of a guess as any. We will have it tested." He balled his fists at his sides.

I touched his hand. I knew he was upset with himself for looking at Roma's death as an accident and not a crime.

An EMT popped his head back into the cabin. "We're headed to the hospital, Chief. Just thought you should know that Ms. Thoreau is wearing an ID bracelet. It says she is allergic to penicillin."

I remembered the engraved ID bracelet that I had seen on her wrist several times. I had never been able to read it or ask her about it.

I swallowed hard, and Rainwater and I exchanged a worried look.

Chapter Twenty-Six

The EMTs had whisked Imogene away on a stretcher almost forty-five minutes ago while Rainwater examined the scene and directed his officers for the next steps. He spun around. "We're going to the hospital to check on Imogene's status."

Officer Wheaton nodded. He was wearing gloves and weeding through papers on the small table. Every few seconds, he stopped to take a photograph with a digital camera.

"I want that swab and the entire kitchen tested for penicillin. Call in a favor and see if it can be done tonight," Rainwater said.

Two more officers arrived to help Officer Wheaton process the scene.

"I've used up all my favors with the lab, Chief," Wheaton said. "I don't think it will do much good for me to say that."

Rainwater rubbed the back of his neck. "Tell the lab director that his New Year's Eve drinks are on me."

"Okay, Chief."

"And find her cell phone," Rainwater said.

"Did she have one?" one of the other officers asked. "By the looks of it, there is no modern technology in this room at all."

"It's hard to believe that she didn't have a cell phone," Rainwater said. "I suppose that's possible, but let's assume she did. I want to know everyone she spoke to recently, who knew she was living out here, and how she got that DNA kit."

The three officers nodded and then got back to work searching and processing the cabin. It wouldn't take them very long. There was very little there. If Imogene had wanted to live the simple life like Thoreau had on Walden Pond, she'd certainly accomplished that.

Rainwater turned to me. "You ready to go?"

I nodded, and as we went out the cabin door, I took one last look at the family tree on the wall. Henry David Thoreau's austere face with his mutton chops looked back at me with a mild introspective expression. What would he think of all this? What would he think of someone trying to kill a woman because of him one hundred and fifty years after his death? That certainly wasn't living simply.

Rainwater was quiet on the way to the hospital. We were in one of his officer's cruisers who'd arrived at the scene. He had said he didn't want to waste time going back to Charming Books to collect his car. The officer promised to bring his SUV to hospital when they were done at the scene.

The closest hospital to Cascade Springs was in Niagara Falls. The tranquility of the village fell away as we merged onto the highway and drove toward the bright lights of the city.

Under normal circumstances, being this close to the falls, I would have wanted to stop and see them. There was something magical about Niagara Falls at night in the winter. The colored lights for the evening shows reflected off of the ice. Snow fell, and you felt like you were inside a snow globe made just for you.

When we arrived at the hospital, Rainwater parked the cruiser in the first available spot and didn't waste any time going into the ER. Inside, the waiting room was busy.

He went to the desk. "I'm Chief David Rainwater from Cascade Springs. I had a victim come in here a little while ago. Imogene Thoreau."

"Yes, she's already been moved to a room on the second floor." She glanced at her computer screen. "Room 212."

"Can we go up?" he asked in a businesslike voice.

The woman at the desk eyed me.

"She's with me," Rainwater said.

She pursed her lips. "You can go up to the floor, but you will have to stop at the information desk to see if you can enter her room."

Rainwater strode directly to the elevator as if he were afraid the receptionist would change her mind if he didn't leave just then.

When we were in the elevator, I studied him. His jaw was locked and tense.

I put a hand on his arm. "David, what's wrong?"

He looked at me and his usually sparkling eyes were clouded with emotion. His face muscles were tight. "This is my fault. If I had listened to you and taken this case more seriously, Imogene wouldn't be lying in a hospital bed right now. We would have found her book, and she would have gone back to her life. Instead, I was just so focused on going on vacation and escaping the stress of the job that I pushed your warnings aside."

I grabbed his hand. "That's not true. It's not your fault. We don't know who did this to Imogene, but you're wrong. She wasn't just going to go back to her life even if she had the book. Proving her story was her life. You saw the inside of that cabin.

It is all she thinks about." I paused. "If anyone is to blame, it's me. I'm the one who told her to get a DNA test to prove once and for all that she was related to Thoreau. Maybe she reached out to the wrong person after that to get a test." I looked down at my boots. "I wish she would have asked me. Maybe she didn't because I'd warned her that the test was meaningless if there wasn't any DNA for Thoreau on record. I mean, I didn't think that any library or museum with a his lock of hair or something like that would just hand it over to her."

The elevator doors opened, and we stepped out only to find Imogene's son, Edmund Thorne, pacing in front of the elevator.

Edmund glared at me. "What have you done to my mother? She told me that she spoke with you today, and you gave her the ridiculous idea of taking a DNA test. Now I get a call that she had an allergic reaction to the test! Are you trying to kill her?"

I opened and closed my mouth.

"Mr. Thorne," Rainwater said. "I know this is upsetting, but we don't believe a DNA test could do that to her. It had been tampered with. That's our suspicion. We will know more when the lab results come back."

He pointed at me. "Then *she* put something on it to poison my mother."

I held up my hands. "I didn't. I didn't even know that she was planning to take the test. I don't know where she got it. She certainly didn't get it from me."

He threw up his hands. "This has gone too far. I have tried to be a good son, but how can I keep this up when she continues to tell this ridiculous story about Thoreau? When it started, it was just a bedtime story that she told me at night as a child. I thought it was neat to imagine that I was related to someone famous, but I never really believed it. I don't even know if she believed it then either." He took a ragged breath. "Over time, it became an obsession that put a wall up between her and everyone else in her life, including me. I didn't abandon her like others would have and did. She is my mother. I couldn't do that, but I've finally had enough. I can't keep taking care of her if she takes this so far that she almost dies because of it." His chest heaved.

A nurse pushing a medical cart walked by and raised her eyebrows as if to ask if we needed help with the unruly man in front of us. I shook my head ever so slightly.

"Mr. Thorne," Rainwater said in a measured voice. "I have to ask you to take a moment and calm down. Violet is not responsible for what happened to your mother. We understand that you're upset."

"Of course you would say that Violet wasn't responsible. She's your wife. No one wants to know they just married a killer."

"Sir," Rainwater said, all business now. "We can continue this conversation at the station, if you prefer?"

Edmund backed off and cast a guilty glance at me. I didn't think he really thought I was a killer. He was scared and upset, and his relationship with his mom was a mess.

"Have you been in to see your mother?" Rainwater asked.

"No, they wouldn't let me," Edmund said in a quieter voice than before.

"Have they told you her condition?"

"She's stable and sleeping," he said. "The nurse told me that she's out of danger. That's all I know."

"All right. I will go find out what is happening with her. Why don't you sit in the waiting room across the hall?"

Edmund looked over his shoulder at the empty waiting room. He turned back as if he was going to argue, but then his shoulders sagged. "All right."

Rainwater looked at me after Edmund went into the waiting room.

"You go," I said. "I'll stay here with Edmund."

"Are you sure?" Rainwater asked in a low voice.

I nodded. "I'm sure. He needs to vent. It's better if he does that to me than to his sick mother when he can finally see her." I glanced over my shoulder to make sure Edmund had not overheard me. The man was on a short fuse and just about anything was bound to set him off.

Rainwater patted my arm and then walked down the hallway toward the information desk.

Edmund sat in the waiting room, bent at the waist, cradling his head in his hands. He was a man who had run out of patience.

I sat in the chair farthest away from him in the small room. I wanted to help him, but I didn't want to be within striking distance in case he lost his cool. He had proven just a few minutes ago that he was teetering on the edge.

"Edmund?" I asked.

He didn't lift his face from his hands. "Why are you still here?"

"Because I'm worried about your mother." I paused. "I'm worried about you too."

He lifted his head, and his eyes were clear. "Why on earth would you be worried about me? You don't even know me."

"That's true," I said softly. "But we have a friend in common. You're important to her, so that makes you important to me."

He frowned. "And who is that?"

"Renee," I said.

His face softened. "That's right. Renee mentioned the two of you were friends." He dropped his head into his hands again. "I can't imagine what she thinks of me now. We've only been dating a short while, but my family history has been exposed."

"Everyone has something about their family that they'd much rather keep secret." I thought of my own family and the birch tree. I was certainly speaking from personal experience in this case.

"That may be true, but it's sure to chase Renee away."

I shook my head. "I don't believe that. Renee likes you, and she's a lot tougher than you are giving her credit for."

He looked me in the eye for the first time that night. "Maybe you're right. Her self-assuredness and practical nature is what drew me to her in the first place. It's so different than what I'm used to."

"You mean different from Imogene."

He stared at his folded hands again. "I'm not sure my mother even knows what being practical means." He straightened up in his seat. "In any case, you don't have to worry about me. I can assure you of that. This is not the first time my mother has put me in a spot like this. I doubt that it will be the last."

"You've been your mother's guardian a long time."

"My whole life. I don't know if I can do it anymore. When the hospital first called me to tell me what had happened, I thought she was dead. I was heartbroken, but a small part of me was relieved. I wouldn't have to do anything for her anymore. No more checkups to see if she'd showered or eaten or left her home. I was relieved that that wouldn't be something on my daily agenda any longer. I felt horrible that the thought even crossed my mind, and I feel worse now repeating it to you. My façade has crumbled. I'm not a successful civil engineer. My true self is an ungrateful son." He covered his face with his hands, and his shoulders shook.

"I don't think Imogene would believe that about you. She's told me that you are a good son, and she knows you care about her."

He studied my face as if to gauge if I were lying.

"She needs help," I said.

"Don't you think I know that," he shot back. "If you know so much about my mother, why don't *you* try to help her? I've tried too many times to count. I've spent too much money on it and too much time. There has to be a point in life when you let the other person lie in the bed they made, no matter what that bed looks like." He ran his hand through his hair. "I know you think I'm awful for saying that, and maybe I am, but it doesn't change the fact that it's how I feel. I just need to get away from it. I took this job to rebuild the village hall as a break, and through me working for the village, she learned about the cabins in the woods and believed it was her calling to live like Thoreau—the real Thoreau, not the false name that she gave herself.

"Do you know how many strings I had to pull to convince the parks department to let her rent one of those cabins for the winter? She said that if I did that, she would lead a quiet life. She just wanted a quiet place to be for a few months like Thoreau. She promised that she would stop trying to prove her false story. She lied to me!" His face morphed from an angry grown man's to a hurt little boy's.

I didn't know what to believe. I didn't know if I should feel sorry for Imogene for the son that she had or for Edmund for the mother that he had. Maybe I needed to pity them both. Maybe they both were to blame for the fractures in their relationship.

Rainwater stepped into the waiting room, followed by a doctor and another police officer. They all looked so serious that Edmund and I both jumped to our feet.

"What's wrong?" I asked.

"Mr. Thorne, Officer Cutler and Dr. Ramer are going to ask you a few questions about your mother and her allergies. Imogene is doing better. I was able to speak to her for a minute."

"What did she tell you?" I asked.

Rainwater pressed his lips together. "Not much. She was too groggy and said she doesn't remember how she got the test," he said, as if he wasn't completely confident that Imogene was telling the truth.

I wanted to ask him more about it, but I thought it was best not to do that in front of Imogene's son.

"Now," Rainwater went on. "I have to leave, but Officer Cutler should be able to answer any questions you might have. I promise you that we will find out what happened to your mother."

Edmund sat back down. The doctor sat next to him and they spoke in low tones. Rainwater nodded to Officer Cutler, and the two stepped out of the waiting room.

I didn't know what to do. I was torn between wanting to know what the doctor had to say about Imogene's condition and wanting to hear Rainwater and Officer Cutler's conversation. In the end, I stepped out of the room too.

The two police officers were standing by the elevator.

"I want a guard posted outside her room. No one goes in to see her without being cleared." Rainwater's voice was tight.

Officer Cutler nodded. "We will get her phone to the tech team. They should be able to get into it and see her call log. We also have a judge subpoenaing her phone records. One of those will come through soon, and we can find out who she's been in communication with."

"You found Imogene's phone?" I asked.

Officer Cutler looked to me and then to the chief. She swallowed. "We did. The EMTs found it in her pocket when they were in the ambulance. It's password protected, and we can't get into it. We should be able to soon though."

"Can you use fingerprint or facial recognition?" I asked.

"No," the officer said. "It's a very old phone. It doesn't have biometric technology. It's just a passcode."

"Can I see it?" I held out my hand.

Officer Cutler looked to Rainwater, and my husband gave a slight nod. Officer Cutler reached into her pocket and pulled out an old smartphone. I tapped the screen, and it asked for a seven-digit passcode. I tapped in 7-1-2-1-8-1-7. The phone unlocked. I handed it back to Officer Cutler. "There you go."

She stared at the phone in her hand. "How…?"

"I read somewhere that people use important dates as passcodes. The date that I thought would be most important to Imogene is Henry David Thoreau's birthday, which is July 12, 1817."

Officer Cutler shook her head and started to flip through the phone. "Her most recent calls were to the same local number. My guess is it's in Camden by the first three numbers after the area code."

"Can I see that again?" I asked.

"Sure," the officer said with a sigh. She wasn't even hiding the fact that she was irritated with me for upstaging her in front of Rainwater.

I didn't touch the phone this time but looked at the number. It looked familiar.

I removed my own phone from my coat pocket and typed the number in. It was what I had suspected. When I pulled the number, it was for Tattered Spine, Heath Howell's rare bookshop. I showed Rainwater the phone.

"Looks like we need to get over to Tattered Spine and have another chat with Heath," he said.

"Yes, we do," I said.

Rainwater pressed his lips together. I knew he didn't like the idea of me going with him.

"I know Heath," I said. "Remember his reaction when Hank the delivery man revealed that you were a cop? He might be more willing to talk to another bookseller than a police officer."

"Fine," Rainwater said. "I don't have time to take you home anyway." He turned to his officer. "Is my car here?"

"It's out front, sir." The officer gave a brisk nod.

"No one goes into Imogene's room. Do you understand me?"

Beads of sweat gathered on the young officer's face. "Yes, sir. I won't let anyone in."

"And if she wakes up, and the doctors let you speak to her, see if she can remember when she took the test. Also if she can remember what she ate or drank. Any of those things could have been tampered with. We can't assume that she had an allergic reaction to the DNA test until we get some results back."

Officer Cutler's head bobbed up and down. "Right."

"Violet, let's go." Rainwater headed down the hallway.

I tripped down the hallway after Rainwater. I had worked on cases with him in the past, but none of them were this intense. I had a sense that Rainwater was expecting something else to happen, and whatever it was, it wasn't good.

Chapter Twenty-Seven

Rainwater's SUV was parked right outside of the emergency room like Officer Cutler had said. Rainwater hopped in, and I followed suit. I felt like if I wasn't quick about it, he might leave me behind. He was in that much of a hurry.

Rainwater grabbed his siren off the car's dash, reached out the open window, and slapped it on the roof. He then peeled out of the parking lot. I gripped the armrests on either side of me as he flew onto the highway. I had never been seen him drive this fast before. His jaw was clenched. Questions boiled in my mind, but I kept my mouth shut. It was obvious that he had a sense that something bad was about to happen. If I asked him to verbalize it, it might make things worse.

"Call Camden Chief," he ordered the Bluetooth system in his car.

The phone rang and a male voice picked up. "Chief Rainwater, what's shaking? Aren't you supposed to be on your honeymoon?"

"Technically yes. Listen Hal, I have a situation." He quickly relayed what had happened in the last hour and half. "I could really use your help on this. I think something bad might be going down at Tattered Spine."

"We will have an officer out there to meet you," Hal said. "And whatever else you might need."

"Thanks. I'll be there in ten."

Again, I wondered if I should ask the dozens of questions swirling in my head. Again, I held my tongue. I knew Rainwater was doing all he could to keep it together.

The passage the shop's essence had revealed to me early in the day rang in my head.

The mass of men lead lives of quiet desperation. What is called resignation is confirmed desperation. From the desperate city you go into the desperate country, and have to console yourself with the bravery of minks and muskrats. A stereotyped but unconscious despair is concealed even under what are called the games and amusements of mankind. There is no play in them, for this comes after work. But it is a characteristic of wisdom not to do desperate things.

Desperation. I thought it had been about Richard Bunting, but maybe I had been wrong? I knew Richard wasn't the killer, so was the "desperation" about the killer not Richard? When Imogene would be awake enough to tell us if anyone had been in the cabin with her before she'd collapsed, it would be all over for the killer.

It made me wonder why the killer hadn't stayed to finish the job. Did they think that Imogene was dead when they had left the cabin? If that was the case, Imogene was one lucky woman.

By some miracle, Rainwater and I got there at the same time as the Camden police officer. We met him at the door.

The middle-aged police officer held out his hand to Rainwater. "I'm Officer Archer, Chief. Nice to meet you. This business is on my beat, but I can't say I've ever had a reason to go inside. From what I've heard, the shopkeeper has a low profile."

Rainwater nodded. "We're following up on an attempted murder case. The victim most recently spoke to someone at this number several times today. Our hope is Heath Howell knows something about it."

Officer Archer nodded. "Well, I've been an officer in this town for close to thirty years, and the only ones I have ever seen go in and out of this shop are Heath himself and delivery people. He must do a great online business because he gets barely any foot traffic at all."

"Let's go in." Rainwater nodded to the door.

Officer Archer seemed to notice me for the first time.

"She's with me," Rainwater said in a clipped tone. "She's a bookseller like Heath. I think she can add to the conversation with him."

The officer shrugged and knocked on the door. Hard. It was long after the shop closed, and there was no answer. I think I would have been more surprised if someone had come to the door and opened it for us at the first knock. I had knocked on so many doors this week with no answers that anything else would have been strange.

Officer Archer knocked again with no luck.

The yellow light from the electric lamppost on Tattered Spine's olive green window awning cast a sickly green onto the sidewalk at our feet. All the lights in the bookshop were off.

The officer banged on the thick wooden door that looked like it has once been part of a Medieval castle for a third time. The knock resounded with a deep *thud, thud, thud*.

"I'll try and call him," I said, removing my cell phone from my pocket. I called Heath's cell and shook my head. "His number went right to voicemail."

Rainwater frowned.

"Chief, it's unlocked," Officer Archer said.

Rainwater stepped around him and pushed open the door with his hand. He and the officer went inside. I followed them inside.

The smell of dank and dusty books accosted us. When I had been studying literature at the University of Chicago for so many years from undergraduate all the way up to my PhD, I had once loved that smell. To me it had been the scent of research, promise of new discoveries, and a bygone time. Now, it smelled like danger. Something wasn't right. When Rainwater and I had visited Heath earlier in the week, the shop had been in disarray, but it was organized chaos. Now, it was a mess. Stacks of books were toppled on their sides. Entire shelves of books were in piles on the floor with their covers torn off and the pages bent.

"Looks like someone tossed the place," Officer Archer said.

It was the best possible description. I knew this wasn't Heath's doing. He would have never treated books so poorly. He loved books more than he loved people or animals or anything. As soon as that thought hit my mind, I began to wonder what had become of Precious. She was a disgruntled cat, but I didn't want anything bad to happen to her.

Officer Archer walked deeper into the shop, stepping over stacks of books as he went. When he made it to the sales counter, he gasped.

"What is it?" Rainwater asked.

I expected him to say Precious had swatted at him. What he actually said was a shock. "It's a body, Chief. A very dead body."

Rainwater and I hurried to the counter and waded through the books like Officer Archer had.

When I peered over the side of the counter, I gasped. "It's Heath." I immediately recognized his tweed suit, even though it was ripped and spattered with blood. His battered and bruised face made him hardly recognizable.

Rainwater knelt beside Heath. "Call an ambulance, now," he ordered Officer Archer.

His sharp command seemed to snap the officer out of his shock, and he ripped his radio from his shoulder.

"Violet, I want you to go to the front of the shop and wait for the ambulance," Rainwater said.

"But—" I stammered.

"Please." He looked me in the eye. "It's bad enough that you've seen this once. I don't want it burned into your memory."

I didn't say it, but it was already a little too late for that. The image of Heath Howell dead in his bookshop was burned into the memory bank of my mind and would be impossible to forget. Ever.

I stepped into the main room and fell into a stack of books. The paperbacks fell to the ground. I stopped myself from picking them up. I didn't want my fingerprints found anywhere in this place. It didn't make much difference to the state of the room either. It was a mess. There was clear evidence that there had been a struggle. Books and knickknacks lay torn and broken on the floor. A bookshelf had been knocked completely over and the cash register drawer stood open.

I inched my way over to it. All the money in the drawer was gone. Could this have been a simple robbery? Had someone come into this building and robbed Heath and killed him? Was it unrelated to Roma Winterbourne's death and the attempted murder of Imogene Thoreau? I shook my head. I couldn't believe that. The three events had to be related, and the glue that bound them all together was *Walden*.

If the valuable copy of *Walden* was somewhere in this shop, it would take days to find it among the chaos and thousands of other books.

I heard the sound of sirens in the distance. The ambulance was on the way, and by the sound of it, more than one. Camden was as small as Cascade Springs. When there was a crime like this, every officer and EMT in the village came running.

I pressed myself up against a bookshelf as five more officers came into the shop with an EMT who had a medical case. Even with all the bookshelves between us, I could clearly hear the conversation coming from the back of the room.

"He's gone," someone said.

I knew it was true. No one could have been still alive with the number of injuries Heath had sustained, but I gasped all the same. Who would want to kill a bookseller? That's all he did was sell books. What was the danger in that?

"The coroner is on his way."

I recognized Officer Archer's voice.

"Good," Rainwater said. "He is the one that worked my case last Saturday. Maybe he will be able to pick up similarities between the two bodies."

"Was your vic beaten to death?"

"No. Drowned in the river," Rainwater said. "It was ruled as accidental, but now I wonder."

"Drownings are always hard to determine in that way," Officer Archer said knowingly.

The group of officials continued to talk, but I couldn't get the phrase "beaten to death" out of my head. Heath had been beaten to death. What a terrible way to die. I shivered as the thought chilled me to my core. Yet I felt hot at the same time. Like all the heat in my body had rushed to my head. I stumbled out the front door.

Now the olive green awning looked even sicklier with the red and blue lights bouncing off its waxy surface.

Outside, I unzipped my coat and fanned my face. I felt hot and more than a little queasy.

The door opened behind me. "Violet, are you all right?"

I turned to see Rainwater walking toward me. His face was a mask of concern.

"I'm okay. It just felt so claustrophobic in there, I had to get out. Poor Heath. I just thought I might be sick."

"I know what you mean. It's a gruesome sight. I wish I could have kept you from seeing that. I wish I had protected you better," he said. He placed his hand on my forehead. "Are you hot? Your forehead is cool."

"I feel a little off," I admitted. "It was a horrible to see. It wasn't my first dead body. I thought I was used to this."

"It's the first dead body that you've seen like that, and I don't want you to ever get used to seeing this. You're a bookseller, not a cop. You shouldn't be in these sort of situations."

I fanned myself some more. I didn't think it was worth reminding me that my bookshop was what encouraged me to be in these situations. I didn't want him to ever have any reason to resent the shop's essence.

"You don't look well." He studied my face in concern. "I'll have one of the officers take you home."

"No, I will be fine," I mumbled. I really did feel queasy. I wasn't usually so squeamish about such things.

"You can't stay here all night standing in the cold. You may be hot now, but with these temperatures, that won't last long at all. It's too crowded inside for you to wait there either. It's late, and I'm going to be here for a long while. I'm asking you to go home for me. Please."

"But..."

"Violet, this is not my district. They're letting me stay because of the connection to the cases in Cascade Springs. It's a professional courtesy, but it does not extend to my wife."

I nodded, knowing what he said was true.

"If you want to drive yourself, take my car." He fished in his pocket and came up with the car keys, which he handed to me. "I'll be there as soon as I can. Just lock yourself in the shop with Emerson and Faulkner. If I know anything, I know those two will keep a close eye on you until I get home. When an officer frees up, I'll have them check on Charming Books. Between me being here, an officer guarding Imogene, and the others working the case, we are stretched pretty thin across the department."

I nodded. "I know."

"And don't wait up for me," he added before turning to go back into Tattered Spine.

I realized this was what it was going to be like to be married to a police officer. There would be long nights when I would be home alone waiting in the dark to hear his footsteps on the stairs, so I could finally fall asleep and not feel the crushing fear that something might have happened to him. I wondered if, as time went on, I would be able to sleep before he came home. Would I become used to it? Only time would tell.

Chapter
Twenty-Eight

I parked Rainwater's SUV in front of Charming Books a half hour later. It felt strange to be driving such a large vehicle. My Mini Cooper could fit inside this car. Okay, maybe that was an exaggeration, but after driving the Mini for so long, the SUV felt like a tank, especially since I didn't drive often at all. In Cascade Springs, I either rode my bike, if the weather allowed it, or I walked. So I was relieved when I finally parked the car, even more relieved that it was in one piece and I hadn't scraped his hubcap on the curb.

The hot flash that had overtaken me when I'd stood outside of Tattered Spine had all but gone away. But the nausea remained. I decided I would, for once, take Rainwater's advice and go to bed.

I walked up the path to the front door of Charming Books. Everything was quiet and still. Holiday lights twinkled along the street.

Tomorrow was Christmas Eve. My Christmas wish was to put this nightmare behind us. It would be the first Christmas that Rainwater and I spent as a married couple, but instead of a quiet day together, we would be on the trail of a ruthless killer.

It was someone who'd killed two people now, assuming that Roma's death would now be considered a homicide, and had attempted to kill a third—Imogene. That was if all the crimes were committed by one person. I wasn't so sure about that. It seemed to me that the deaths themselves were too different from each other. Roma Winterbourne had drowned. I shivered. I knew from my own experience that that death might have been an accident just like the coroner had said.

I would have thought it was an accident, too, on a cold and icy December night if it had not been for the signed first edition of *Walden* and the message written in pen on the palm of Roma's dead hand. *They stole my book.* If it had not been those two things, I would have argued the death was an accident because it was so similar to how Colleen died almost nineteen years ago now.

Next, there was the attempted murder of Imogene Thoreau, who was formerly a Thorne. Someone had tried to poison her. If she wore a bracelet alerting people of a penicillin allergy, I just believed it was too far-fetched to even consider she would knowingly take penicillin. Someone had given it to her. Through the DNA test? It was possible. In any case, that person had known of her penicillin allergy. Was it someone who knew her well? It was also possible that it was someone who had seen her bracelet. I prayed that Imogene would recover. If she was lucid enough to tell us who gave her that test, then she could at least reveal the person who'd tried to kill her.

And finally, there was the successful murder of Heath Howell. That death was a shock indeed. Heath had been beaten so badly, I wished that I had heeded Rainwater's warning and not looked at the body. I now would be haunted with those mental images of Heath bloodied and bruised for the rest of my life. It was something I knew would follow me into my nightmares.

Beyond the murder and the attempted murder, I couldn't forget that the first signed edition of Henry David Thoreau's *Walden* was still missing. Whoever had the book in their possession would have a tough time selling it now. We knew from the evidence underneath Roma's nails that the book had been scratched. There would be obvious marks on the cover. As I had thought so many times over the last few days, when we did find the book, we would find the killer.

The porch light hummed beside Charming Books' front door, and the sound seemed to be even louder in the quiet of a winter night. I wondered if Rainwater and I would ever get our honeymoon. It seemed to me that the events of the night were sure to cancel the trip completely, and, after this, there would certainly be other events in the village that would interrupt our lives. It was just the price of being married to the chief of police.

However, I did feel like we were close to the end of the investigation. My mind was on Imogene as I reached the door. I was glad that Rainwater had had the foresight to place a guard at Imogene's door at the hospital. The killer, again, assuming that there was only one, wouldn't have thought twice about attempting to kill Imogene again when they learned Imogene was still alive. The killer had successfully killed two other people. What was one more death to a person like that?

The key fit into the lock, and I stepped into the store. I reached for the light switch and turned it on, but nothing happened. I flipped the switch up and down a few times.

There was a tickle on the back of my neck, and I started to back out of the shop. I was sure it was all right, but after the last few days, I was jumpy. I decided that I would go back to Rainwater's car and call the police department. Then, I would call Grandma Daisy and wait at her house until Rainwater got home. I hesitated because Faulkner and Emerson were in the shop. Shouldn't I take them with me if something was wrong?

Before I could decide what to do, a disembodied hand yanked me into the store and covered my mouth. I tried to scream, but no sound came out. It was muffled by a cloth that smelled like cheap men's cologne.

I knew that whoever was holding me fast was a man, but I was taller than him. I tried to use that to my advantage. I stomped onto the man's instep like Rainwater had taught me. It did little other than make him jerk since he was wearing boots. However, it gave me enough space to elbow him in the stomach and jump away.

My hip connected with Faulkner's perch by the front window and sent it crashing to the floor. I would have thought the crow would protest, but I heard nothing.

I went to the door, but the man jumped in front of it. I ran back to the birch tree and the stairs. Now that my eyes adjusted to the dim light, I gasped. "Hank!"

He glared at me. "This is all your fault. All of it. If you had just bought that stupid book when Roma had come here to sell it to you, all these people would still be alive. You're the reason they had to die. You were too caught up in your own wedding to do the right thing."

"Hank, you're the killer?" I rubbed my forehead. "Why?"

"I needed the money. Money that I never got thanks to *you*," he spat.

"Why, Hank? Why did you need the money that badly that you would steal for it?"

He glared at me, and I was afraid that I might have pushed too far. Then, his shoulders drooped. "Abby's treatments are so expensive. Insurance won't cover everything. I don't want her to miss a treatment because I couldn't pay the bill."

My heart broke for him, but at the same time, I reminded myself that he killed a man with his bare hands.

He balled his fists at his sides. "Don't look at me like that."

I blinked. "Like what?"

"Like you feel sorry for me," he snapped. "I have been doing an excellent job taking care of my daughter."

I raised my hands as if in surrender. "I know that, Hank. I would have never said differently. I know how much you love Abby."

"I love her more than that ridiculous woman loved her book. This all start because of that stupid book. I wish I had never seen it."

"Do you have the book?" I asked.

"It's right there. I left it for you as a present. I was just about to leave, but then you made the mistake of coming in. That's your fault."

I didn't exactly go in. He pulled me into Charming Books, but I wasn't going to squabble with him over that small detail.

"Why did you bring the book here?"

"I knew you wanted it."

Things started to fall into place in my mind. He was here the day Roma had come to try and sell the book to me, and I had seen him speak to Roma outside on the sidewalk. He also knew Heath because he made deliveries to his store. He was in all the right places.

Hank began to pace. "I shouldn't have come here. I could have left. They would never have attached me to the case. Now I have to get rid of you too."

I shivered. "You wouldn't have gotten away with it. Imogene is still alive. She's about to tell the police. She will tell them your name." I didn't know if that last part was true, but I had no qualms about lying to a killer.

All the color drained from his face. "What?"

"She's alive. Your plan didn't work. She's still at the hospital, but the doctors are optimistic that she will make a full recovery."

He rubbed the side of his face so vigorously that his cheeks turned bright red. "No, no, no. I had to do it."

"You had to kill Imogene?" I asked.

"I didn't kill her," he snapped. "The only person I killed was Heath. I didn't mean for it to go that far. I—I lost my head. I was blinded by rage. I thought he had made me kill a person. What else could I have done when I knew he was trying to frame me for murder?"

"I think you should start at the beginning," I said as calmly as I could. I wasn't feeling anything close to calm inside though.

"Heath had asked me to keep an eye out for interesting books. He knows that I deliver to a lot of bookshops, libraries, and antique shops on my route. There have been times when I have helped him acquire a book. He's paid me handsomely for that service."

"When you say acquire, do you mean steal?"

"It doesn't matter how I get them," he said dismissively. "Everyone knows that the kind of books that Heath sells aren't for reading. They are to be placed on a bookshelf and admired from afar. They are signs of status and wealth. I think it's a terrible waste of money, but who am I to judge how rich people do their business, especially when I can profit from their vanity?

"When Roma came to your shop and I overheard what she had to sell, I knew that Heath would want to buy it, no questions asked. When I met her on the sidewalk, I told her about Heath and suggested that she sell her book to him. I knew that if she sold it, Heath would give me a nice finder's fee. She said she would. I thought that would be the end of it, and I would go into Christmas with a little extra money in my pocket."

"It wasn't the end of it?" I guessed.

"No, it was not. She thought Heath hadn't offered her enough money for the book. She said it was invaluable. She refused to sell and walked. Heath was furious and told me that if I could convince Roma to sell the book to him, I would get three times my usually finder's fee."

"So you spoke to her again by the river."

He narrowed his eyes at me. "I know what you're suggesting, and you're wrong. I was there along the river the night Roma died. I'd thought that she might want to speak to you again about the book at your wedding reception. I'd spotted her at the wedding, so I guessed that she would be at the reception too. I was right. What I hadn't guessed right was that there would be another person there trying to get her hands on the book."

"Imogene," I said.

He nodded. "But I didn't know her name at the time. She and Roma were at the river's edge fighting over the book. They were literally yanking it back and forth between them like two cartoon characters playing tug of war. Finally, Imogene pulled it from Roma's grip. Roma scratched the book trying to keep her hands on it. When Imogene had gotten it away from her, Roma fell into the river. She hit her head. Imogene ran away. She didn't even stop to see if Roma was alive. She might have been, but she was unconscious and she drowned in the river," he said with no emotion at all.

I gasped. "You mean that all this time Imogene has been claiming that her book is missing, she actually had it?"

He nodded. "I saw it with my own eyes in her cabin. She told me that she lied about not knowing where the book was because she was afraid the police would take it as evidence related to Roma's death. She made a big fuss over it so that they would look for it and stay away from her."

Imogene was right. Rainwater would have most certainly taken the book.

I glanced around the room. The only light came from skylight above the tree, the porch light through the windows, and the security light by the kitchen door. One thing I knew for sure was that Faulkner wasn't in his favorite spot in the tree. He would have been clearly visible in the skylight. Emerson was MIA too. I took this as good signs. The animals were hiding, which meant they were safe. That also meant I didn't have to worry about them to get away from Hank. Assuming I could do that, of course.

As far as I could tell, Hank had no weapon on him. He hadn't pulled a gun or a knife. But he had killed Heath with his bare hands. It was a terrifying way to die, but he would have to catch me before he could do that to me. I wasn't going to allow that to happen. All I had to do was get out the back door of Charming Books, which meant I had to run through the kitchen and get past the cranky old lock that I hated so much. Sometimes it took me three whole minutes to unlock that door.

He'd surely catch up with me by then. I had to distract him enough to give me more time to escape. I might not get three minutes' worth, but every second counted.

I promised myself I would replace the locks on that door as soon as this was all over.

"I told Heath what I saw down by the river," Hank said. "And that Roma was dead. He asked me to tell Imogene about him. He didn't care much that Roma was dead, but he was still very interested in the book. If he couldn't buy it from Roma, he would buy it from Imogene. I did as he'd asked me."

"Why?" The question practically fell out of my mouth, and I wished that I could grab it and shove it back in.

He narrowed his eyes at me. "Were you not listening to me before? My work for Heath was very profitable in the past. I had no way of knowing that this would be any different."

"But you had to see it was different. A woman was dead."

"Because of an accident caused by a squabble between two old women," he snapped.

I almost argued with him over it, but I could see he was becoming more incensed. Since he'd beaten Heath to death because he'd lost his cool, challenging him on this point didn't seem like the best idea I had ever had.

In a quieter voice, I asked, "What happened when you told her about Heath wanting to buy the book?"

"She said she would never sell it, and that's when I learned her crazy story about being related to the author. I didn't care if she was related to him or not, but it was clear that she wanted someone to believe her. I reported this back to Heath, thinking this would be the end of it."

"But it wasn't," I said.

He scowled. "No, it wasn't. He told me to talk to her again and deliver a message."

"What message? And why didn't Heath just talk to her himself?"

"When she found out that he'd wanted to buy the book, she didn't want to have anything to do with him. She didn't want anything to do with me really, but at least she would talk to me."

"What was the message?" I asked again.

He balled his fists at his sides. "That Heath could help her. He said that he could get a lock of Thoreau's hair that would prove once and for all that she was his descendent. He said that he knew another collector who had a hair wreath that was made of the four Thoreau children's hair that could be used to compare to her DNA. She just needed to take the DNA test. In exchange, she had to give him the book."

"And she agreed to this?" I asked.

"Not at first. It took several days to talk her into it." His eyes darted around the shop. "The woman is insane. All she talks about is this long-dead author. He is her whole life."

"How did she get the test?"

"I was to give it to her, which I did earlier tonight. She gave me the book. That would have been the end of it if Heath had paid me."

"He wouldn't pay you?" I asked. I took two small steps in the direction of the kitchen. Every inch I moved closer to freedom, the less likely I was to get caught.

"When I gave him the book, he said that he wouldn't pay me for it because it wasn't as valuable with the scratches on the cover. I told him that he had to pay me. He refused. I threatened to call the police." He took a shuddered breath. "He told me that

I shouldn't do that because then I would have to answer to killing a woman."

"Heath was the one who put penicillin on the cotton swab?" I asked.

"Yes, and he made me deliver it. He said that he couldn't have Imogene coming back looking for the book when she learned that he didn't have any Thoreau DNA. He'd had to get rid of her, and he framed me for the murder as an insurance policy."

Two more steps toward the door.

"I went into a blind rage then. I don't know what happened after that. When I realized that Heath was dead on the ground, I knew I had the blood of two people on my hands."

One more step.

"What are you doing?" His voice was sharp.

That was my cue. I bolted toward the back of the shop and through the kitchen. I hit that back door with a thud. My hands fumbled with the lock. The dead bolt was stuck. I couldn't get it to move.

I screamed as I was yanked back from the door by my hair. I felt like it was being pulled from my scalp by the roots. He let go of my hair, wrenched my right arm behind my back to a breaking point, and marched me back into the main room of the bookshop.

He tossed me onto one of the sofas like a ragdoll. I was taller than him, but he was strong. I remembered how many heavy boxes of books he could carry at once. He loomed over me, and I kicked at him. I wasn't going to make this easy.

He pulled my feet across the floor, and my head connected painfully with the hardwood boards. I saw stars. I was too dazed to fight him off. Right when I thought he would hit me just like he'd hit Heath, there was an awful screech.

In my dizzied vision it looked like a whole flock of crows were descending on Hank simultaneously.

But it was just one crow. And Faulkner was mad. Hank cried as the crow dug his talons into the top of his head.

It gave me enough time to get to my feet. In my dazed condition, instead of running out the door, I ran up the spiral staircase, planning to lock myself in the apartment and call for help.

Hank managed to knock Faulkner away, and the crow cried in pain. I almost turned around to go back and save him, but at this point, Hank was running up the stairs after me.

I made it to the top, and the apartment door was unlocked. I always left it unlocked after hours.

I just touched my hand to the door when Hank grabbed me by the arm again. Emerson screeched this time, jumping from one of the children's bookshelves. Hank screamed and covered his head. I kicked him toward the staircase. To my amazement, the steps disappeared before my eyes. It just a sheer drop to the floor below. I grabbed Emerson, who was teetering halfway over the edge, and held him fast.

Hank fell and screamed all the way until he hit the floor below. The stairs reappeared. The tree shook as if dusting itself off, and a handful of birch leaves fell to the floor. One landed on Hank's unconscious face.

The front door burst open, and Rainwater, Officer Wheaton, and what appeared to be the entire Cascade Springs police force rushed inside. They all pulled up short when they saw Hank on his back on the floor.

"Violet!" Rainwater yelled.

I leaned over the railing in the children's loft with Emerson clinging to my chest. Our hearts beat in tandem. "I'm here."

"We were rushing here to tell you Imogene woke up and said that Hank gave her the test. The test was from Heath. Since Hank was the only one who wasn't dead or in the hospital, we assumed he was dangerous."

"I sort of figured that out," I said.

He stared at the man at his feet. Hank groaned and rolled to his side. I was glad to see he was still alive even after everything he had done.

"I can see that. Is there anything else you figured out that you haven't told me yet?" He looked up at me. The light from the skylight reflected in his beautiful amber eyes.

"Just that you should have married me sooner," I said with a smile.

Epilogue

It was the first week of February, and Rainwater and I had just returned from a much deserved week-long honeymoon in Vermont. The resort where we'd stayed had been so kind to move our reservation at no charge. I discovered that people were inclined to help you when you tell them that someone had tried to kill you.

It was a wonderful trip, but I was happy to get back to Charming Books, sell books, and teach. While we were gone, Richard covered my classes for the week. He owed me, and I had no trouble cashing in on the favor.

Rainwater wasn't due back to the department until the next day, so he stayed in the shop with me while I walked around and made note of all the impractical changes my grandmother had made since I left.

I held up a volume of poetry. "Why on earth would Grandma Daisy put this in the science fiction section? It makes no sense. I'd never be able to find it if I needed it."

Rainwater looked up from the book he was reading by the fire. "How do you know it was Grandma Daisy? It could just as easily have been the bookshop itself."

"No, it was Grandma Daisy. She did it just to mess with me."

The front door opened, and Imogene came inside. We had asked her to meet us at the shop at four that afternoon. She was a half hour early. Neither Rainwater nor I were surprised.

"I hope I'm not too early," she said.

Rainwater stood up.

Faulkner cawed from his spot in the tree. As of last week, he had just been able to fly again after Hank had sprained his wing. He and Emerson, who was asleep in his cat bed by the hearth, had received a lot of praise and treats since they'd saved my life. Faulkner was particularly basking in it.

Imogene looked at Rainwater. "Do you have my book?"

He nodded. Since Hank pleaded guilty to the murder of Heath and took a plea deal for a shorter stay in prison, there would be no trial. Without a trial, there was no reason to hold Imogene's book as evidence any longer.

Rainwater walked over to the sales counter and pulled a plain brown box from under the counter. He set the box on the counter and lifted the book out of it. He carried the book over to Imogene and placed it in her outstretched hands.

Imogene held the book close to her chest. "I'm so happy to have it back. It felt like I had lost a piece of myself. It was never about how much money it was worth, or what I could do with the money if I sold it. If it had been, I would have sold the book long ago."

Rainwater removed a piece of paper from his jacket. "I have something else for you. This is a researcher in Massachusetts. I spoke with her. She does have access to a lock of Thoreau's hair. It's from a hair wreath that his mother had made of all her children when they were young. Perhaps that's where Heath got the idea to tell you about the wreath in the first place."

Imogene stared at him.

"She is willing to do a real DNA test for you. Free of charge. She seemed eager to delve into the research, and since the academic article that Dr. Richard Bunting wrote about you was so well-received, there is academic interest to see if your family's story proves true." He held the piece of paper out to her. "This is her name and number."

She took the piece of paper in her hand and closed her eyes for a moment as if she was in the process of absorbing its power.

"What are you going to do with it?" I asked breaking the silence.

She lowered her hand, uncurled her fingers, and stared at the paper. "I—I don't know. What can I do?"

"You can call the researcher and have a conversation," I said. "It's a start."

She curled protective fingers around the paper. "How do I know that she really has Thoreau's hair? What she has is just as much of a story as the one I have told."

"You can't know," I said. "You just have to decide what you want to do with it, and if you decide to do the DNA test, you have to decide if you believe it."

"But I *know* that I'm Thoreau's descendent. I *know* I am."

"Then why do the test?" Rainwater asked. "If you know, what more do you need? Is the validation really necessary?"

She blinked at him like she'd never considered this before, and maybe she hadn't.

"What do you want to do with the information if you can prove it to be true?" I asked.

"I—" She looked down on the ground. "I never thought about that before. I have been so intent in proving it true; I've never made it to the next thought." Her voice wavered. "I just want to know and want the world to know. For the acknowledgment."

It was the most honest thing I had heard Imogene say since I'd met her. She wanted the recognition. The problem was, there would always be doubters even if the DNA test came back in her favor.

"Sometimes you don't need to know without a shadow of a doubt," I said. "Sometimes the mystery of the possibility is enough. You need to weigh the possibility of disappointment against the mystery of it all. If you're doing this just for yourself, do you really need to? If you're doing this for others, will it be worth it?"

"I suppose those are the questions I will have to ask myself." She looked at Rainwater and me, and back again. "Thank you for returning my book." She shuffled out of the shop.

Rainwater looked at me. "What do you think she will do?"

"I honestly don't know." I winced as queasiness washed over me for a second time that day. It seemed to come in waves, and later in the day they became tidal waves. I had done my best over the last week to ignore them, but it was impossible to now. Thankfully, Rainwater had his back to me as he went back to the fire and his book. At least that's what he I thought he was doing.

He reached behind the couch cushion and held something behind his back. "I have something for you too."

I blinked at him. "What is it?"

He handed me a long jewelry box.

My hands hovered over the box. "What is it?"

"There is a very easy way to find out what's in the box."

"But what is it for? It's not my birthday, and Valentine's Day is two weeks away."

He grinned. "Does everything need an explanation?"

"Well, yes," I said seriously.

He chuckled. "It's the gift that I wanted to give you our wedding night before everything went crazy with Roma's death. When I finally thought to give it to you, I knew it needed a few changes, so I had those made while we were on the honeymoon."

I stared at him.

"Are you going to open it?" He laughed.

"Okay, okay." I pulled on the blue ribbon and it fell away from the box. Rainwater took the ribbon from my hand. Carefully, I opened the lid. Inside, on a velvet pillow, was a necklace. I recognized it right away. "It's the birch tree."

"That's right. A silversmith in my tribe made it for me. One day, when you weren't paying attention, I took pictures of the tree from every angle, so that she would have something to work from."

"It's beautiful. It looks just like the tree." I peered more closely at it. "Is that Faulkner in the branches?"

He nodded and pointed at the bottom of the charm. "And that is Emerson at the base, taunting the crow. It's just like real life. I decided after the dynamic duo saved your life, they needed to be added in."

"It's such a thoughtful gift. I love it so much." I looked up at him. "And I love you."

"I love you too. Let me put it on you." He took the chain from my hand, stepped behind me, and clasped the necklace around my neck. His fingertips brushed the back of my neck. Just as he did, a wave of dizziness overtook me, and I bent at the waist.

Rainwater rubbed my back. "What's wrong? Violet, are you all right?"

I still felt a bit woozy, but I was able to stand up. I leaned on my husband. It still felt odd to think of Rainwater in this those terms. With all that had happened since the wedding night, it was crazy that we were here, and I had this news to share. "It's not something wrong. It's something right."

"Right?" The Cascade Springs chief of police stared at me. I've stared into those unusually colored amber eyes and lost myself in them so many times, but this time, he was the one who seemed to be lost.

My face broke out into a smile. "Very right. I know it's sooner than we'd planned, but…"

His mouth fell open. "No!"

"Yes," I whispered.

Rainwater's eyes went wide, and he placed a hand on my stomach. "We're having a baby?"

I nodded with tears in my eyes.

He lifted me off of the ground and crushed me in a massive hug. "Oh no." He set me on the ground again. "I shouldn't have done that. Are you all right? Is everything all right?"

I patted his arm. "I'm fine, Chief."

Emerson leaped from his cat bed and rubbed his lithe body against our legs. Faulkner cawed and flapped his wings.

His eyes glowed golden. "I can't believe this."

"You're happy?" I didn't bother to hide the anxiety in my voice. "I know we wanted to wait."

"I've never been happier in my life." He grinned. "Should we find out the gender? I know it's a little early yet. Some people don't want to. We never talked about if we want to find out." He was chattering away faster than I had ever heard him talk.

"It's a little early yet," I said. "But we don't need the test."

"Why not?"

I smiled up at him and then looked at the birch tree in the middle of my shop—a tree that one Waverly woman after another had cared for and protected for over two hundred years. "It's a girl. That much I know."

Author's Note

I read *Walden* for the first time when I was in high school. It was one of the most transformational books of my life. It certainly impacted my view on nature, on frugalness, and on weighing want verses need. Thoreau has been a writer to whom I have returned time and time again for wisdom. He was not a perfect man, and there are even some scholars who say that his roughly two years living in his cabin on Walden Pond was the indulgence of a rich man who knew he had finer things waiting for him on the other side of his self-assigned poverty, but there is no denying the impact that he and the American writers of his time had on the creation of truly American literature. These writings were not the rephrasing of European ideas but new American ideas. As an American author, I'm grateful to those writers for this.

There are characters in this novel who would suggest, some rather strongly like Imogene, that Thoreau had a child out of wedlock, and therefore, there are descendants of the author walking the earth today. There is no evidence of this in real life. In fact, as Violet points out time and time again in the novel, Thoreau never married and had no children. The same was said for his two sisters and one brother. The four Thoreau children were the end of their family line. I can say confidently that the suggestion of Thoreau's indiscretions are purely fiction. I hope that you will allow me to use this fictional idea for the story, which is really more about how far a person like Imogene is willing to go for her truth—no matter how many times she is told she is wrong.

In this series, I have highlighted Violet's interest in transcendentalism and nineteenth-century transcendentalist authors, both those who ascribed to that philosophy and those who were just on the periphery of it. When I was in fifteen, I learned about transcendentalism for the first time, and although I don't accept all transcendentalist tenets, many did strike a chord with me at that young age and remain with me today. It's been an honor to highlight these writers and their great works in a new and magical way. Thank you for that chance. And, as always, thank you for reading.

Acknowledgements

Thank you always to my readers for reading my books. My career as a mystery author would be nothing without you. I especially thank you for loving the Magical Bookshop Mysteries, and I'm so grateful that I'm able to share Violet's and Rainwater's journey with you.

Thanks always to my agent Nicole Resciniti for tirelessly working on my behalf. I do not know what I would do without you. Thanks also to everyone at Crooked Lane Books for supporting this series, especially Matt Martz, Melissa Rechter, and Marla Daniels.

Special thanks to Kimra Bell for reading this manuscript.

And love and gratitude to my husband, David Seymour, for his unwavering support.

As always, thank you to God for allowing me to live this dream come true.